Twilight

by

Jamshid Fanaian

Sunrise Book Promotions

Copyright © 1999 Jamshid Fanaian

ISBN 0 9586345 0 5

Sunrise Book Promotions
P.O.Box 238 Kiama
N.S.W. 2533 Australia

info@jamshidfanaian.com

www.jamshidfanaian.com
reprinted 2009

Printed and bound in Australia

Contents

Chapter One

REVOLUTION

1.

It was a freezing cold night in winter. Like a huge white blanket, snow had covered the tall mountain in the north and the farms and barren land in the south of the capital city.

For some months, people were restless and could not sleep well. Many stayed awake all night, watching television or listening to the radio. They were anxious to know the latest news of a dramatic political change which was sweeping the country. Rumour had it that the two-thousand-year old monarchical system, which ruled over the country, was crumbling. A republican form of government would replace it. Some people were worried and anxious about the change; some were excited about the changes ahead. They were looking forward to seeing the break of a new day, the dawn of a new era.

A political thunder, rumbling in the distance, was fast approaching with a terrifying threat. It could turn into a frightening and destructive storm.

It was a cold winter night, but the whole city fermented with wild emotion.

To ease himself to sleep and put his mind at rest, Cyrus read a fascinating book portraying a spiritual journey through its many stages, from the earth we live on to the mysteries of heaven above. Reading brought him the peace of mind and tranquillity he longed for in those difficult times of political change.

He stopped reading and looked at his watch. It was 10:03.

He looked out of his bedroom window. The moonlight had iced on the snow. He brushed back his dark brown hair with one hand. His black eyes were mysterious, and his face, creased with concern, reflected what was on his mind.

Cyrus felt surprised that many of his neighbours were still awake, leaving their lights on for all to see. He glanced past the roofs, mesmerised by the beauty of the snow on the mountain.

The sky was clear, letting a thousand stars twinkle like snowflakes suspended in the air. Under the moonlight, the mountain shone in full splendour, leaving him in awe. He loved the mountain, which was covered in snow during the summer just as in winter. It gave him much inner peace in times of turmoil.

Many times, day or night, he stood at the window admiring the giant rock, enshrouded in a magical mist. The great mountain was a dormant volcano, huffing and puffing like an old dragon sleeping for a thousand years.

Although it wasn't really late, Cyrus decided to go to bed. His day had been filled with teaching and worries, and he needed a good night's sleep.

He closed his eyes, losing himself in a dream-like state, when suddenly the weather changed swiftly, engulfing the city in a storm. A strong wind blew ferociously, banging doors and windows, causing everyone to panic. The wind sounded like a wolf howling into the dark night.

Cyrus tossed and turned, trying in vain to get some sleep. He blocked his ears with his pillow. He didn't want to hear the wind, which made him think of the cry of a child lost in the dark night. It saddened his heart.

The storm went on for hours; but, exhausted, Cyrus

finally fell asleep.

At around 3:00 a.m., a bullet shattered Cyrus's bedroom window.

Cyrus woke up in a frenzy of horror, standing fully erect on his bed, wondering what in the world was going on. At first he thought it might have been the storm, but more gunshots were fired at the bedroom window, sending him diving under his blanket. He was terrified and unable to comprehend what was happening.

When the gunshots finally eased, he peered from under the blanket. Alerted, he listened to the running footsteps of soldiers and civilians. He knew what was going on. Soldiers still loyal to the monarchy were fighting in vain with the revolutionaries. The army was desperately struggling to save a tottering monarchy. He believed civilians were too blind to see that they would never take part in running the country.

The regime's painful passage toward death was fitful and lingering. The waves of revolution swelled into a well-led and organised attack that was perfectly timed. Those who longed for freedom kept their ears to the ground in hope of hearing the regime's death knell.

Suddenly, once-paralysed human rights' organisations grew active, rising to protest that human rights had been sacrificed. Amnesty International bellowed its protest, appealing for more justice, and the Human Rights Commission condemned violation of universal equality.

Some journalists worried that they had neglected their duty by not investigating the cruelties of a dictatorial regime. Their guilty consciences drove them to interview the King and expose the country's suffocating political atmosphere. Articles in prestigious international newspapers awakened the world to how the regime denied its citizens social and political justice. The global community grew angry at the inequalities that were revealed and demanded action.

The State's intelligence service attempted to demonstrate their usefulness by countering the revolution. They had to justify the large salary, ridiculous bonuses and immense benefits that drained the nation's resource. They believed that using political tactics was the key to saving the collapsing regime.

2.

Alone at home, Cyrus was enjoying the beauty of an unexpectedly mild evening. Suddenly the quiet of the night was interrupted by commotion from the street. The sound could be heard of people's feet pounding the pavement, and cries of confusion forced their way through his window.

Someone pounded urgently on his door.

He anxiously rushed to the front door to let the caller inside. He opened the door slightly when a man burst desperately in, stumbling into Cyrus's arms.

'Fire!' the man panted, horrified. 'The factory is on fire!' Fear had etched itself into his face.

The chattering of people on the street floated in behind the man. Cyrus glanced outside and saw people rushing toward a building engulfed in angry, crimson flames.

Cyrus was curious. Climbing onto the roof of his three-storey house, he was startled to see how close the fire was to his home.

Sheets of fire shot into the air. They were threatening to engulf the sky, curling across the horizon like flying dragons. They breathed spears of heat from their fiery mouths.

The crackling of burning wood and the crash of toppling

roofs rang in Cyrus's ears. The dense, black smoke stung Cyrus's eyes and scorched his throat. Wreaked with coughing and unable to breathe, he covered his mouth with his right hand to prevent further smoke from entering his lungs. The effects of smoke made his eyes stream. Wiping his fingers across his stinging eyes, he fought to clear his eyes of water.

A flash of red to his right caught his attention. He turned to see that another building had caught fire. A thunderous explosion rang out behind him, and he felt the roof beneath him shake. He spun around to discover the whole city alight, the anger of the flames beating back the darkness of the night and creating spectacular silhouettes against the all-engulfing smoke.

The flames of fire whirling and flying in spirals came from every part of the city. Clouds of smoke had shrouded the city and darkened the moon. Cyrus wondered who could have wreaked such devastation. Who would dare destroy the property and possessions of honest people? He climbed down from his roof and went out into the street to see the victims of such an evil act.

Wandering the blackened town, he first believed that the destroyed properties had been randomly selected. But then he realised that most belonged to two or three religious minorities located in different parts of the city.

He could not understand the reason for such horrible havoc. He rationalised that the arson was a tool to make citizens believe the revolutionaries were a deadly threat. The arsonists, whoever they were, had deliberately victimised the minorities. The revolutionaries had struck those who were least able to fight back.

He believed the national security organisation, the

country's intelligence service, would do something. Ideas crossed his mind: 'They will deal with the criminals. Justice will be served, and the culprits will pay dearly for their act of terrorism. Such a waste! All these innocent people will have to be compensated one way or another. Homes and businesses will have to be rebuilt.'

The following day was uneventful. A great sadness hung heavily over the entire city. Many people had lost their homes. A handful of businesses managed to keep their doors open.

Cyrus walked the streets to assess the damage done by the great fire. Many people were walking the city, contemplating in horror the damage done.

The factory close to his house, which provided hundreds of jobs for many citizens, had been completely destroyed.

Opposite the factory was a three-storey residential building which had been partly destroyed by the raging fire. Thank goodness, someone had managed to extinguish the fire before it spread to the upper part of the building. Cyrus puzzled over who had managed to contain the fire.

Other people stood in front of the building, making their own analysis, coming to their own conclusions.

Cyrus overheard a man say, 'Just as well someone managed to put the fire out. All those people living in the upper storeys could have been burnt to death.'

A rage was building up inside Cyrus. He felt anger at those who committed such a crime.

Cyrus walked amongst the crowd, listening to other people's comments.

He stood still when a conversation caught his interest.

'They set many buildings on fire,' an old man said, 'many factories, many houses. They set on fire the whole city.'

The second man was young and curious. 'Who did that?' he asked, getting closer to the older man.

'*They* did it,' whispered the older man.

But the young man was confused. 'Who are *they*?'

'You don't know who *they* are?' The old man seemed amused.

'If I knew, I wouldn't be asking.'

'The security organisation.'

The young man took two steps back. 'Why?' he gulped.

'To blame it on the revolutionists. To discredit and disgrace them in the eyes of the public.'

'But how did they do it? How could they burn so many buildings?'

'They used paid terrorists.'

The young man shook his head in disbelief. 'That can't be true. The security organisation would never do a thing like that.'

The old man laughed at the naivete of the young man. 'My friend,' he giggled, 'politics is like that.'

Cyrus stood breathless for a few seconds. Never would he have thought the security organisation could be responsible for the act of terrorism. He was shocked by the betrayal. His eyes glared at the wreckage and the glowing cinders while his heart was filled with sorrow and anger.

3.

In a city in the south, there were a large number of the followers of a new global faith.

One night, hundreds of angry people, afire with hatred, rushed out of the mosque, weapons in hand, heading toward the followers of the new faith. They roared, swore and shouted, carrying knives, sticks, spades and axes, determined to avenge the death of dozens of killed brothers. They had just mourned over their dead, their faces aglow with anger.

In the streets not yet touched by the charging crowd, the followers of the new faith were sitting close to their hearths, reading books or chatting. Unaware of what was about to happen, children were engrossed in their homework or playing happily.

The followers of the new faith knew their homeland was in the grip of destructive turmoil. Their faith taught them to rise above politics and to avoid involving themselves in it.

The crowd of angry men came down the streets and charged through twisted lanes like a raging bull. The hissing cobra got close to its prey. As the shouts of the advancing mob became audible to the followers, panic grew. The followers listened to the angry gangs uttering the name of their faith and threatening to kill them. Suddenly they knew the dragons of death were surrounding them, puffing flames of anger that would destroy them. At any moment, they would leap upon them.

Bare-footed and scantily clad, the followers rushed from their houses and fled into the icy evening. As they passed the houses of fellow believers, they rapped at the doors and urged them to run. 'Quick, escape,' they called breathlessly, 'a violent mob is coming.'

Some followers managed to find refuge from the armed crowd. Hiding in dense scrub, watching the violence pass by, they whispered amongst themselves.

'Why are we being attacked?' hissed an old woman, wearing only a nightgown.

'I don't know,' answered a teenage boy, clutching his

shoes close to his chest. Tears glistened in his eyes. 'Has one of our people committed some wrong?'

'Oh no,' a young girl cried, covering her eyes with her fists, 'they're destroying the houses!'

The mob had reached the house of a follower who was a successful businessman. A rough-bearded young man, who had been leading the crowd, threw up a hand and commanded them to halt.

The mob jostled around him, trying to hear what he was saying. Straightening his turban, he pointed to the businessman's house and screamed 'Burn the houses of the anti-God sect.'

The crowd cheered.

'Destroy them all. Don't let anyone get away.'

Wild-eyed and fevered, the seething masses raced to the house and broke down the door. They grabbed rocks from the edge of the road and hurled them against the windows, growing even more restless with the sound of shattering glass. As they spilled into the house, some intruders paused and admired the expensive rugs, carpets and decorations. While the house and its contents were set alight, those more intelligent rioters looted the goods, satisfied that they had attracted the pleasure of God.

The house was quickly demolished. Those who did not have fire-lighting tools or picks and shovels used their hands and feet, pushing and kicking anything that remained standing.

A patch of rubble aglow with the embers of toys and household utensils was all that remained of the house. What had taken months to build was destroyed within an hour.

The looters moved on to the next house. As they carried the useful items out into the street and lugged them back to their own homes, the rest of the mob arrived to burn the house to the ground.

Not one of the followers stayed to protect his home. Terror had forced thoughts of possessions from their minds, and they never suspected the crowd would be cruel enough to raze the empty houses.

Within some hours the gang had plundered and demolished the only shelter the followers of the new faith had owned.

Footage of the blazing houses was shown on television two days later in the United States. It was horrible to watch scores of houses on fire. The reports inaccurately portrayed the destruction as civil unrest between two rival religions.

News of the horror spread across the nation.

Cyrus heard that fanatics had plundered and burned houses belonging to the followers of the new faith. His stomach churned when he heard that hundreds of people, many of them children, were now thrown to the mercy of the streets.

His brother lived in that city.

He flew out to see if his brother had been affected.

The southern city was one of the most beautiful areas of the country, known for its roses and nightingales. Whenever Cyrus had visited the city in the past, a great joy had overwhelmed him. He delighted in the azure sky, and grew intoxicated inhaling the fragrant flowers. It was the birthplace of some famous poets. Whenever he entered the city, he would chant as many of their beautiful lyrics as he could remember by heart.

But this time it was different.

The climate was cold, dark clouds hung from the sky, and the roses seemed to have lost their vigour. The warbling of the nightingales sounded sorrowful.

Cyrus was relieved to find his brother safe. The unrest had happened on the other side of the city.

Yet, still, he could not feel at ease. His heart dwelled on the stories he had heard. His mind recreated the scene of children screaming and running away from their burning homes. They had no time to look back to watch how the flames were destroying their lives.

At night, he visited those now barren residential areas. He was surprised at how cold it was compared to the rest of the city. Savage gusts of wind stormed through the new openness, determined to demolish the little shelter that remained. He pulled his thick coat tighter around his chest as he wandered through the ruins.

He glanced down a dark lane and noticed a small group of people sitting amidst the ruins of a scorched house. He could not make out what they were doing until the harsh wind carried their voices to him.

They were praying.

Cyrus's eyes grew moist. He could see they were members of a family. The woman held three children tightly against her body, and her husband cradled the other two. The parents nestled the children close to keep them warm, but Cyrus noticed their small bodies trembling with coldness.

Cyrus listened to their prayers.

'Let the world be purged of hatred,' they pleaded. Occasionally the parents caressed their children's heads to ease the pain.

In spite of the darkness, Cyrus could make out a pile of objects at their feet. These must be their only belongings, he thought. Everything else they owned has been destroyed. He was saddened by the small size of the bundle.

Two small girls raised their heads to look at Cyrus. A sad smile appeared on one of the girl's lips, her wet innocent eyes shining in the dark.

Cyrus's heart melted at the sight of the children's quiet tears.

Cyrus sank to the ground and rested against what used to be the front step of a house. He could go no further. Staring at the scene surrounding him, he pondered how people could deliberately inflict so much hatred and cruelty.

He knew these atrocious actions could not comply with the teachings of any religion. He believed all faiths preached fairness, compassion and love. He could not accept that these crimes had been motivated by religious emotions alone.

Cyrus was too depressed to continue his journey through the ruined houses. He returned to his brother's home on the other side of the city.

They sat together on the front porch and looked out onto the street in silence.

Suddenly Cyrus asked, 'Why do you think they destroyed everything?'

For a moment, his brother stared at him in confusion, then lowered his head. He remained silent.

Cyrus touched his brother's hand. 'I don't think genuine religious feeling is the motive.'

His brother sighed, clasped his hands behind his head, and leaned back in his chair. 'Neither do I.'

'Has anyone claimed responsibility?' Cyrus asked.

'The religious leader of the revolutionaries sent a message from overseas denying any involvement.'

'I believe him,' confirmed Cyrus. 'So who could be the

instigator?'

Thoughtful, his brother gazed at a point on the wall.

Cyrus shifted in his seat and leaned toward his brother, sensing he knew something, but was not willing to discuss it.

A few seconds went by. No one said a word.

Cyrus finally broke the silence. 'Please, tell me what you know about this. I know these kinds of incident are often not as simple as they seem.'

'But the television in the United States said it was religious strife.'

'They often spread lies disguised as news and mislead the public.'

'They portray things as they happen, not as they really are,' added his brother.

'Not knowing enough is sometimes better than being misguided.'

'In the West, the media are free to inform the public, so why don't they tell the truth? They have freedom of speech in a democratic society.'

'Freedom of speech is not always what it implies. They're free as far as they 're allowed to be free.'

At this time the clock started to strike. His brother looked at the clock on the wall, realised it was already 12:00 a.m., the end of another day, and suggested, 'It's late. You look tired. Why don't you go to bed?'

'I don't think I'll be able to sleep until you tell me what's on your mind,' Cyrus said. 'You know more than you 're telling.'

His brother pursed his lips and hesitated for a few seconds. He locked his eyes into Cyrus's and finally confided, 'Some paid terrorists led a group of fanatics to commit the destruction.'

'So there was a hidden political agenda, and religious people were only tokens in the game.'

'Exactly.'

'Extreme emotions, whether religious or racial, are easy to manipulate for political ends.'

'Fanaticism is a dormant dragon. Once woken up, all hell will break lose.'

Both thought over the issue awhile.

'So,' Cyrus said, 'who's been leading this cowardly act?'

His brother whispered into Cyrus's ears, 'The security organisation. The intelligence service.'

A look of surprise crossed Cyrus's face. He opened his mouth, but no words came out. He brought his hands to his face, covered his eyes and released a heavy sigh. He puzzled over the way the country was being run.

He lifted his eyes to his brother and said, 'Why? Why in the world would they do something like that? To their own people? Their own country?'

'You know why, Cyrus? They don't really care about people. They only care about saving a tottering regime. They want to divert the anger of the religious revolutionaries who are against the monarchy, I mean, to divert it against the followers of the new faith. They're using the fanatics' anger and bitterness against the followers of the new faith for their own political end. And wait for it, Cyrus, this is just the beginning. Thousands of new faith followers will be killed in the next few months. Their homes will be destroyed, their children taken away, and they won't even know why.'

'They want to save a falling regime by killing people?' asked Cyrus, but already knowing the answer. He felt bitterness in his heart.

'Does that surprise you?' asked his brother, almost

mocking Cyrus.

'It's a wicked world!'

'Yes, it is. But this is the way it is with politics.'

'But it is so wrong,' protested Cyrus. 'It is so unfair. They're committing a horrendous crime.'

'Politicians don't see crime as crime.'

'Obviously, politicians have a different idea of what crime is.'

'Indeed, they do. Telling lies and cheating is not a crime. It is a needed weapon used for political ends.'

'But surely, if people knew a political party came to power by cheating people, they would lose faith in that party?'

'You're discrediting many regimes and governments,' said his brother, mocking him.

A moment of silence took over.

Then his brother had a sour look on his face. He moved closer to Cyrus and whispered, 'Be careful what you say. You never know who could be listening. One word to the wrong people, and they'll be looking for you. Can you honestly tell me of any government that came into power without resorting to some form of dishonesty?'

'No, I can't,' Cyrus said. 'But it doesn't mean it should be that way. Governments should set the example by being honest and dignified. They have to change their image for the better, teach spirituality and wisdom.'

'Cyrus, be careful who you talk to. I can understand where you come from, but not many people will accept your ideals. If the word is out that you hold anti-government ideals, they'll send you to an asylum. They'll even torture you to make you change your mind. I've seen it before, Cyrus. Be careful what you say and who you say it to.'

'Justice and wisdom is all that's needed for a government to be effective. If they hold those virtues, everything will fall into place.'

They puzzled over the conversation. Cyrus's brother knew Cyrus's ideals were right, but impossible to implement, and yet he respected Cyrus for expressing his viewpoint without fear.

Cyrus broke the silence, 'Could you explain to me how they instigated the attacks?'

'Religious fanatics threatened a man, a follower of the new faith. They told him they would rape his wife and daughters, and kill him if he didn't recant his faith. He rang the army and told them of the threat. The army advised him to call them as soon as something happened. And one night, the religious fanatics went to the man's home to execute the threat. He called the army, which arrived promptly and killed everyone, including the man who called them for help.

'The bodies of the dead were taken to the mosque the following day. The people were angry and swore to take revenge on their dead brothers. They gathered and fired each other up, building up much hatred toward the followers of the new faith. They gave slogans, swore continuously, mourned over the dead bitterly. Paid terrorists masterly instigated a large multitude gathered to express their sympathy or out of curiosity. They succeeded in arousing wild emotion.

'The people's long stored prejudice was an explosive powder only needing a spark to explode. They became wild and savage. Then the paid agents led them, rushing toward the houses of their victims, roaring to take revenge, to burn, to kill, to demolish.'

'And who was leading the operation?' asked Cyrus, now

completely absorbed by his brother's story.

'The security organisation, of course.'

'I guess security organisation personnel are getting paid for something after all. They're not just sitting behind desks all day to idle away their time,' said Cyrus sarcastically.

'They're doing what they've been trained and paid to do.'

Cyrus shook his head. 'Can you believe this? Whatever happened to choosing the wisest person to run the country? Do you remember, long ago, before we were even born, philosophers were advisers to the King.'

'And now it's the army and the security organisation.' His brother laughed at the absurdity of it all.

They talked a while longer, but by 1.00 a.m., they were exhausted and decided to get some sleep.

Cyrus stayed awake for a long time. Thoughts crossed his mind. He found it sad and depressing that so few hypocrites could cause so much damage. His heart was filled with sorrow to see how politics could degenerate into tricks. He prayed for a better world, a peaceful world where governments would be righteous and truthful.

But he knew this day was still far away.

4.

One night, at the lobby of a large cinema in the city centre, the crowd was alive, laughing and joking, enjoying a night of entertainment, forgetting about the political turmoil that had engulfed the entire country in the past few months.

The lights went out, the hall submerged in darkness. Everyone was engrossed in the movie, enjoying his time.

Suddenly someone shouted, 'fire!'

All stopped watching the movie and were shocked to see flames of a horrible fire blazing all around the amphitheatre.

They stood up in terror, and chaos followed. Terrified people screamed, shouted, cried and pushed one another. Everyone tried to make it to the emergency exits and the main doors. Every single door in the cinema was locked. Many people lost control, pushing and stepping on one another, trying to find a way out of the blazing inferno.

The amphitheatre turned into a furnace of hell. Hundreds of young people burned alive. A heap of burnt meat remained. The young people died a horrific death, which sent the city into frenzy.

Forensic investigations later confirmed the worst. Someone had deliberately lit the fire and kept it going with gasoline.

When Cyrus first heard the news, he was completely devastated. He couldn't believe someone could commit such an atrocity.

It didn't take long for rumours to spread that the revolutionaries were responsible for the fire. They, of course, denied any involvement. Some said they were not brave enough to take responsibility for their action. They killed people to show how powerful they were. It seemed that the revolutionaries believed a revolution did not make sense without violence, murder and disaster.

Being of a sensitive nature, Cyrus did not cope well with the news. Although he tried hard to see the event as just another incident, the social injustice was getting to the core of him. He refused to eat, and spent most of his time alone in his room. He knew some of the young people who died in the fire. He couldn't understand how a group of revolutionaries claiming to end social injustice could commit such a horrific crime.

After a few days, a friend came to visit Cyrus because he

hadn't shown himself for a while.

When the friend stepped into Cyrus's room, he was stunned at how sick Cyrus looked.

'What is wrong with you?' asked the friend. 'Do you want me to call for a doctor?'

'No. My soul is sick, not my body.'

The friend was puzzled. 'Why, Cyrus? Have you lost your job?'

Cyrus looked up from his bed. His eyes full of tears, he said, 'Haven't you heard about the fire at the cinema?'

'Of course I have. It's been all over the papers. Is that all that's worrying you?'

'All? Is that all?' Cyrus threw his hands in the air. 'Hundreds of young people died in the fire! Hundreds!'

But his friend remained cool and apathetic. 'And a hundred more will die tomorrow. Really, Cyrus, you're too sensitive. Try to be indifferent for a change. Look at what you're doing to yourself. You look as if you've lost twenty kilos. Why don't you come with me to the restaurant and forget everything?'

Cyrus gave his friend a cold stare.

His friend's face changed colour. He was obviously embarrassed by his own indifference toward the people burnt alive.

Cyrus fell back on the bed, rolled his eyes and sighed.

Realising he'd only made Cyrus feel worse, the friend tried to be more tactful.

'Look, Cyrus, terror is just part of everyday life. Sometimes it's the revolutionaries; sometimes it's the government. Even people, not just organisations, bring terror to each other.'

'What do you mean?' asked Cyrus, puzzling over his

friend's comment.

'Surely you've heard of people running down the street and shooting by-standers just because they're unhappy with their personal lives? Nothing can stop that.'

Cyrus shook his head sadly. 'Terrorism is a disease that seems to breed in some societies.'

His friend shrugged. 'Well, I think no matter what society it is, terrorism in any form should never be encouraged. In fact, it should be unanimously condemned.'

'Of course,' agreed Cyrus, smiling at his friend's change of attitude. 'But just condemning terrorism won't stop it. The society that breeds it must change. After all, disease is spread by the sick.'

5.

The whole country fell into turmoil and agitation. Horrible events were happening every day. Soon the decay spread to the whole country. Not a day would pass without bloodshed.

Growing frustrated by the denial of their rights, people banded together and demanded free speech, political freedom and release of political prisoners.

The King had no choice but to respond to their cries, and the security organisation had to allow people to demonstrate without fear of retribution.

Yet, the King never expected that allowing political freedom would be like lifting the gate of a dam. Suddenly suppressed forces flooded out like destructive waters, giving a horrifying roar as they threatened to wash the King, and all he stood for, to certain death.

The guardians of the dying regime were shocked when they realised so many people supported political freedom. They never expected people with such different political beliefs to join voices in demonstration.

One day the tension between the people and their suppressors grew unbearable. When they realised things were about to explode, a high ranking general in the security organisation rushed to the King. His skin pale with fright, he stammered in fear, 'Over three million people are marching toward the palace!'

The King froze, nails digging into the arms of his chair.

The King felt trapped. He had been cheated. His advisers always praised him as the best king the country ever had. His policies fulfiled people's needs. At times his policies might have stifled the political freedom of some, but it was a necessary cost.

How could his people turn on him and claim they had no freedom?

Realising the extent of the King's fear, the high-ranking general pushed aside his own anxieties and tried to offer some advice.

'If the King of kings agrees, soldiers can surround the palace and shoot trespassers on sight.'

The King breathed deeply and rubbed his forehead wearily. He pondered over the general's idea for a few minutes.

Raising his head, he looked directly into the general's eyes. 'You can't exactly shoot three million people. '

The general cleared his throat and shifted uncomfortably, not quite sure what to say.

'A few soldiers stationed around the palace are enough,' the King said in a shaky voice.

The general was relieved when the King waved a hand to discharge him.

Realising he must act, the King instructed secret police to

give him constant reports on the demonstrators' movements from their helicopter surveillance.

The crowd of three million demonstrators rolled through the streets, leaving no road or pavement free. They moved from street to street, from avenue to avenue, shouting and roaring like tigers.

A shared hatred of the Monarchy dissolved protesters' ideological differences. The religious stood side by side with the anti-religious. Liberals joined forces with left wing fanatics, and young and old marched together. Their once-competing voices now blended to sing the songs of freedom.

Or so it appeared.

While each group did hold the same intention, it was not just to overthrow the Monarchy. They all aimed to seize power for themselves. Factions saw nothing wrong with using the power of their rivals, as trickery was a part of politics. For them politics was politics. Nothing wrong with tricks.

The secret police informed the King that the demonstrators could reach the palace within one-and-a-half hours.

The King restlessly paced the palace hall. Sensing that his life was in danger, he looked at the luxuries surrounding him. The expensive Persian carpets, the gold decorations hanging from the walls and the priceless jewelry were all useless. Not even the millions of dollars in Swiss bank accounts could save him now.

He pondered over his ultimate fate. He felt he was miserable. He was as miserable as many of the crowned heads of the modern age that met tragic fates. He knew he would join them soon; the children of the future would read about him in their history books. It was time to tell his wife of the approaching danger.

The King found his wife in their bedroom, writing a letter.

'The demonstrators are marching toward the palace,' he warned his wife. His voice was husky and emotional.

Her hands flew to her face and she let out a sob. Letting her hands fall to her lap, she tried to take a deep breath. 'How many are there?' she stammered in horror.

'Reports say at least three million.'

He watched her face grow pale and her eyes well with tears. 'What do we do?' she whispered.

The King hesitated. In a quivering voice, he explained the plan. 'We must commit suicide. All of us, even the children.'

The Queen's body began to tremble and the room swam around her. 'Can't the army and police force stop the demonstrators?' she begged.

The King shook his head. 'I can't order the forces to shoot three million people.'

'So what do we do?' she repeated.

'We'll swallow poison tablets. They'll cause no pain, just make us fall asleep and then stop our hearts.'

'But can't we just escape?' she cried. 'Can't we slip out of the palace and drive to the airport? Leave the State and seek refuge in another country?'

He took her hand in his. 'Darling, they will only hunt us down. And until they do, we'll be living like prisoners, too scared to leave the house and trusting no-one.'

The Queen slumped back in her chair and buried her face in her hands. The sound of her sobs made the King's own eyes water.

The King caressed and kissed her hair. He knelt beside

her and tried to comfort her.

'This is better than being captured by our enemies. They'll torture us to death before we even reach trial. Then they'll slander our good name.'

She did not answer, struggling to stop her tears.

The King gently pulled her to her feet. Together they collected the children and climbed to a sitting room on the top floor of the palace. The King asked his family to take a seat and try to relax. His children anxiously perched on the edge of armchairs. The Queen stared out of the window for a moment before settling in a chair as well. A teary-eyed maid entered and placed a glass of water on the coffee table in front of each person. She handed a pair of binoculars to the King.

The King paced the floor, talking on his mobile telephone to each head of his security forces. At the end of every call he explained to his family how far away the demonstrators were.

In the middle of a call, the King suddenly rushed to the window and lifted the binoculars to his eyes, and stared into the distance.

'There're almost here,' he whispered.

The whole family knew it was time to end it all. With trembling hands, they reached for their glasses of water.

Anxious, the King was still looking through his binoculars; his face was white as a corpse and his hands shook.

A few minutes went past. The King put down his binoculars and took his seat with his family. Fear was consuming him little by little.

His wife and children glared at him, waiting for the King's command to swallow the deadly tablets. But the King froze like a statue, exhausted by fear and anxiety. Neither his wife, nor his children dared say a word.

Minutes went by.

And then, without warning, the King gently lifted his head, looked towards his family, and a bitter smile appeared on his lips. 'The danger has now departed,' he said in a tone of voice suggesting relief. 'The demonstrators are moving away from the palace.' A report had just come in, informing the King that the demonstrators were running away from the palace and toward a large city square.

A look of relief was drawn on everyone's face. Still trembling, they drank their water.

Within a few days, the King and his family left the country.

It took sixty aircraft to carry the royal family's belongings, which included jewelery, clothes, gold and antiques. But it took a long time for the royal family to find a permanent home. They were shuffled from one country to another, as no one was willing to give them asylum. The richest king became a homeless refugee. The King died after two years, apparently because of a cancer.

The empire collapsed. Blood and fire ended the two thousand five hundred years' monarchy.

The King, like his colleagues, did not realise what wrong they had done to have such a tragic end. Why had crowns fallen on the ground one after another in the past hundred years? Why had dynasties dissolved and empires crumbled in a catastrophic way? Why were kings and emperors either murdered, or jailed, or banished from their own countries? What responsibilities had they failed to fulfil?

6.

The King and his family left the country; the military curfew ended. The demonstrators decorated the soldiers' guns with flowers. The soldiers marched side by side with the revolutionaries, down the streets of the capital city, chanting and claiming victory over the monarchy. Shooting aimlessly in the air, chanting and hailing the new regime, the military revolutionaries took over the streets, occasionally aiming their rifles at pedestrians to scare them.

The chief commander of the curfew was executed on the roof of a house. While singing the national anthem, he ordered the firing squad to kill him. His executioners could not help admiring his courage until the very end. He remained loyal to his job until his last breath. Four generals, commander-gererals of the navy, air force and army of the old monarchy, were also killed.

By blending religious and political beliefs, religious traditionalists were active in the overthrow of the monarchy.

They drove in the streets giving slogans of liberty and prosperity to the public through loud speakers.

Everyone who participated in the revolution had a tale to tell. They spoke of their efforts and sacrifices with pride and joy. They took great pleasure in detailing their joys and sufferings.

Rich and poor, blue and white collar, men and women, people from every corner of the country felt victorious and excited at gaining what they had fought and longed for-freedom and prosperity!

Believers and non-believers sang hand in hand songs of freedom and hope. They had different views of what the new government would be like, but all aspired toward the same goal. Hope was now near because they thought a better system of government, a new regime of human values was ahead.

They hoped the blinding storm was coming to an end, and that it would be followed by days of endless sunshine, where love and beauty would rule over each and every person.

But all did not share the same dream of true liberty and prosperity. The main religious group, which helped to overthrow the monarchy, took control of the country. It began making its own rules, and to exert its power. To make the public sense the revolution, it started to execute anyone who supported the old regime. With passive confusion and despair, people had to accept this action as an inevitable part of the revolution. They were the unlucky random victims of the revolution.

But the new regime did not limit itself to executing those served the old regime. Soon enthusiastic revolutionaries became targets of the sharp blade of the revolution- those who helped the triumph of the new regime.

One night, Cyrus was sleeping at a relative's home, about half a kilometre from the main university, located in the capital city. In the middle of the night, he woke up in terror at the sound of bullets tearing through the air and entering his room. He froze in bed, pushed aside the blanket, sat at the bed's edge, and rubbed his eyes. He listened attentively, wondering what was going on.

He realised that bribed revolutionary guards were shooting at the university students within the campus from a roof adjacent to the university. Their aim was to confiscate any literature arousing revolutionary feelings.

Being a university lecturer, Cyrus felt a great pain in his soul. He stood up, determined to rush to the university and ascend the roof of the building where the snipers were. He wanted to throw them down from the building with their machine guns. He hesitated. Rubbing his forehead, he paced in the bedroom, thnking how he could achieve his purpose. It was only a fantasy. He would never get the chance to even approach the building before being showered by a hail of bullets.

'I have to do something,' he muttered. 'I have to stop them, even at the risk of my life.' Enraged, he dressed and raced down the front yard of the house. The sound of the machine guns was deafening.

He looked up.

Stagnant clouds hovered over his head, hanging like dead corpses in the air. The air was filled with gunpowder and stifling with the smell of blood. Death was everywhere around him. The wind had stopped blowing, as if life had ceased.

He heaved a deep sigh. 'Freedom died before it was born.'

My God, will it ever end? How many students have to die by the hands of cowards with their political agenda? Can people see what is going on? It takes so long for the world to realise how politics is interwoven with tricks.

Standing still in the front yard, he was uncertain as to what to do next. Anger and confusion paralysed him.

And yet, the love he felt for the students gave him strength. 'I have to shield students against the bullets of snipers. I have to use my body to protect them,' he muttered. He clanged his fists. 'I know what I want to do.' But his mind wouldn't let him. He was torn between his raging emotions and sense of self-preservation.

He had to get to the rooftop. He had to stop the snipers

from shooting any more students. But how could he do it? He didn't have a gun. He had never had a gun or fired one, and he never wanted to touch one. It repulsed him. Guns were nothing but killing machines, their purpose was to destroy humans and cause great misery.

I have to stop them. I can't just stand here and watch them die one by one. I have to do something.

And then, suddenly, he snapped.

He left the front yard and ran toward the snipers, determined to grab the guns from their hands and end the butchery.

'Come on, you cowards!' he shouted, his rage fuelled by grief. 'Show your faces! Don't you know you're selling your soul to the devil? This is a million times worse than selling your body in the streets! God help you all!'

He was now running fast toward the rooftop. His lungs were burning from the gunfire and hot air. Nothing was going to stop him now. He had made up his mind. Even if it would cost him his life, he could no longer stand back and watch so many people die innocently.

The night was dark and merciless. He was running and approaching fast his field of martyrdom. He did not notice there was a rock in the way. And then, without warning, he lost balance and fell flat on the ground. A sharp pain pierced his leg. He looked down at the side of his trousers and saw blood. He had to get up before the snipers shot him. He moved, but the pain was unbearable. He wondered if he broke something.

He wanted to go and stop the snipers, but now, he could barely crawl. He was left with little choice. They will kill me with a single bullet before I even get to one of them. I must get back to the house, he thought.

Bitterness filled his blood as he dragged himself back to the house, an excruciating pain jolting down his leg. He glanced back, wanting to try again, but he realised there'd be no point. There would be other ways to win. *Evil must be destroyed.*

The sounds of the machine guns still hung in the air as he stepped back inside the house, his left leg hanging and leaving a fresh trail of blood behind.

Once in the house, he disinfected his wound, a two-inch wide cut made by a sharp stone on the ground.

After that, he returned to his room, lying in bed, realising there was so little he could do all by himself.

The world has gone crazy. God! Give me the strength to carry on.

The next morning, after bandaging his wound with fresh gauze, Cyrus left for college.

He found the dean of the college and some of his teaching colleagues discussing with anxiety the previous night's events. The dean was a well-built tall man. In his shirt and tie, he had an air of authority.

Too busy with their problems, no one realised the torment Cyrus went through the previous night. As he moved toward them, he could still feel his leg hurting from the wound he received when he fell over.

'We've been told to hand in the keys to their rooms,' one staff member said.

'I know,' answered the dean. 'But it's these booklets on revolution which are the cause of all this. Don't they understand that their lives are in danger?'

Cyrus joined in the conversation, 'Yes, why do they resist? What reason did they give?'

'They want people to know,' the dean explained. 'They want people to come to the college to check those booklets. They want to prove that they're doing nothing wrong.'

'It's too late for that,' Cyrus said. 'The revolution is over. They're too innocent to realise the underlying aim of revolution has already been achieved. All they're doing now is making a nuisance of themselves. They're exposing everyone to danger. We should really talk to them.'

The rest of the staff agreed.

The dean and Cyrus approached the students' quarters to speak to them.

Cyrus glanced over to the nearby hills. He saw some heads peeping now and then. They were the revolutionary guards and paid mobs, hiding behind the nearest hill, waiting for a signal to attack.

Meanwhile, outside the building, a man with a turban seemed to be waiting patiently for the students to hand over the keys to their rooms. The man was a representative of the new regime.

Cyrus tried hard to convince a group of students to give up their keys. 'Let it go. It's better to give them the keys.'

'No,' protested a female student. 'Why should we? We want people to know that we love our homeland. Why should we give in? All we want is justice, peace and joy.'

'You're too good,' Cyrus said, a look of sadness crossing his face. 'But sometimes giving up means winning. If you keep the keys, and they kill you, who will be left to stand for your cause?'

All the students remained speechless.

'Is that what you want?' Cyrus asked, his tone of voice becoming louder. 'Do you really want to die? I don't think you do. I don't think you understand the implication of this political revolution. Give up the keys.'

The students whispered amongst themselves, while Cyrus waited anxiously in one corner of the room, thinking:

If only they could understand that it's not worth it. How many thousands of students die, thinking they can make a difference, thinking they're doing the right thing for the right cause? How many can't see that they've been used for political ends? I do not know how to save them from their innocence.

Finally, the female student who resisted at first, spoke, 'All right, we will give them the keys.'

Cyrus felt a great sense of relief. He went into his room at the college, thinking about the aspirations of the young enthusiasts for a better world. His heart sank, remembering them standing in front of the building, hopeless and disillusioned.

In the early days of the new regime, many people thought freedom would finally come. People shared ideas about how society would function.

Various political parties tried hard to entice youth into their cause. They actively tried to lure enthusiasts aspiring for a better society. Political ideologies preyed upon the emotions of the youth. They made all kinds of promises for a better life and a better future.

But it was all nothing but a trap, a web of deception for the thousands of students who got involved.

A new day of liberty and prosperity did not dawn. In the months that went by, darkness fell upon the whole country. The power of darkness was unleashed upon their land. There was no freedom. Instead, prisons were filled with people from all walks of life.

The establishment of a new democratic form of government proved to be an illusion.

Civilians had built their lives on hope, but only despair remained. Their hands were tied, and there was nothing they could do.

Youths were trapped by promises of freedom and a healthy political and economic system, exactly what they wanted to hear. So they were used when they were needed; then got rid of whenever it suited those with power in the new regime. They should never have trusted those who were trying to seize political power.

It took a little time for people to realise they had been fooled once more. They woke up to the horror of being trapped in nets. It was too late to free themselves. Even the mere thought of freeing themselves was endangering their lives. They paid heavily for their naivety- A pattern experienced by many nations of the world.

If there ever were a name for this Dark Age it would be 'The Age of Frustration'. The frustration of all hopes turning into despair.

7.

On a cold morning, Cyrus met his friend, Bijan, at the park in the City Square.

'What's wrong?' Cyrus asked, as he tapped his friend on the shoulder. 'You seem unhappy.'

Cyrus stared at him, waiting for a response.

But Bijan said nothing, sitting on a bench, looking thoughtful and sad.

'Tell me, my friend, what is bothering you. Maybe I can help.'

Bijan let out a heavy sigh. 'With all the modern

technology we have, we still live like savages.'

Cyrus winced. 'You're not going to give me a lecture on how bad the ruling party is? Are you now?'

'I don't give a damn about who rules the people.' There was anger in his voice. 'I'm just tired of all the hate and violence. I wish it would end.'

'That's the way it is with all governments who use violence as means to an end. Where there is violence, there's something wrong.'

'Then, if we know there's something wrong, why do we let them rule?'

'Easily.'

'How's that?'

'They have the weapons, they control the army and the media, and therefore they control the masses.'

'This is dictatorship, Cyrus. How could we still have dictatorship in this day and age?'

'Dictatorship is the symptom of a disease.'

'What are you talking about?' Bijan shook his head, as if Cyrus had lost his mind. 'You're trying to tell me that the world is sick?'

'Yes, I am. A sick society breeds a sick regime.'

Bijan tilted his head, puzzling over Cyrus's observation. The two friends recalled the horrid events of the past and the present century, wondering where the root of all evil came from.

Cyrus turned to Bijan and said, 'Journalists who report what they see are only scratching the surface. There is much more than meets the eye. They don't try to dig and find the horrible truth.'

They sat in silence, observing people in the park.

Cyrus had a look of sadness etched on his face. His soul

was fading away. Everything around had lost its beauty. The air, the trees, the sky, all appeared lifeless and dull.

Bijan glanced at Cyrus occasionally, but never said a word. He too was lost in his own thoughts.

Eventually, Bijan grew tired of the silence and said, 'There's a story I want to tell you. It happened recently.'

Cyrus glanced sidelong at Bijan and said, 'Go on.'

'Early one morning, a revolutionary guard knocked at the door of a house. The owner opened the door, wondering who the hell it could be so early in the morning. He was surprised to see a revolutionary guard standing right there in front of him, a parcel in his arms. The guard gave him the parcel, and whispered something in his ears.

'Suddenly, the owner's face lost its colour. His teeth started chattering. He began trembling and feeling a weakness in his legs. The words of the guard burned his soul. He felt as if his heart was drilling through his chest and his whole world had collapsed from under his feet. He bent down to pick up the parcel, but he could not. He remained crook-backed. His spinal column seemed broken.'

'Who was this man?'

'Ironically, he was one of the people who financed the new regime. His daughter was actively involved in the revolution. She helped with posters and brochures. She was always good at drawing, even as a child.'

'And what happened?'

'No one really knows for sure, but the ruling party had a clash with a political group she belonged to, and decided to get rid of them. It didn't matter to the new regime that it was still in debt to that party. It didn't matter that the party had helped the new regime to come to power.'

'Surprise, surprise,' said Cyrus. 'With politics, you never

know who your friends are. One day they're friends, the next day enemies.'

Bijan nodded. 'That's right. Doesn't it sound ridiculous to think of a politician as someone selfless? And so, the friendship between that political group and the ruling party ended. They arrested the daughter. She was sentenced to twenty-five years' jail.'

'What did the father do?'

'Everything he could. He bribed guards, government officials, absolutely anyone who he thought would be able to help. His daughter's sentence was shortened to two years. Again he paid a lot of money to remove the two years. And then, they executed her instead.'

'And that's why the guard came to the house?'

'That's right.'

'What was in the parcel?'

'A gift of sweets and cakes for the parents.'

Cyrus was confused. 'Sweets and cakes? For her parents?'

'That was to tell them they had taken her daughter's virginity before they killed her. They claim that they had to. It was their duty.'

'Duty? I don't understand.'

'According to their tradition, a virgin cannot be executed.'

'So, that was their way to not break any religious tradition?'

'That's right. First they raped her and then killed her.'

Cyrus opened his mouth, but no words came out of it.

'And she wasn't the only one,' added Bijan. 'They're hanging and executing young girls everywhere, mostly virgin teenagers-'

'First they rape them and then kill them!' said Cyrus, trying to comprehend what he had just heard.

And then silence took over the next thirty seconds.

Bijan went on, 'They torture them. They hang them upside down for many hours. Then they take them to dark cellars, and torture and rape them in the worst way you can imagine.'

Cyrus was too upset to hear any more. He shouted out loud, spat on the ground and ran down the park.

Bijan wondered what in the world was happening to his friend. Maybe he's gone crazy, he thought. And then he regretted having told the story to Cyrus. He knew how sensitive Cyrus was to injustice and cruelty. He wondered where did Cyrus go? What could he do?

At the other end of the park, Cyrus was running with nowhere to go. He just wanted to get away from all the madness. He had grown tired of living in a mad world. He wished for a world free of politics, injustice and brutality. He dreamt of a new world of love and wisdom.

People watched Cyrus running, tears in his eyes. They stared as they wondered what could have made the young man so sad.

Someone whispered, 'The poor man must have received news of the death of his fiancée or wife. They must have loved each other deeply.'

Cyrus continued to run until he was out of breath. He sat on a bench, panting. His lungs were on fire, and big drops of perspiration were running down his face.

Crazy thoughts were running through his head. What if he went to the prison and freed the young women? He would give his life in return. He would *beg* them to take his life in return.

And then his crazy thoughts turned into a command. He knew it was something he had to do. He knew he could not just sit there like the rest of the world and pretend nothing was happening. Someone had to free those girls. His soul had been touched, turned into a flame of emotion. Restraining reason had no control on him.

He stood on his feet and ran toward the prison.

He knew he was running toward his own death. But that didn't matter. He had to save the girls.

A cold wind slapped his face, drying away his tears and perspiration.

Meanwhile, Bijan was still in the park, feeling guilty at having infuriated Cyrus with his tale. It had been well over an hour since Cyrus had left him. He'd thought Cyrus would be back shortly after his burst of anger. But Cyrus had not returned. Maybe he had gone home.

Bijan stepped into his car and drove around the park, trying to locate Cyrus. But there was no sign of him. He tried to imagine where in the world Cyrus would go. And then, he realised there was only one place he could have gone to. The prison. *Cyrus has gone to the prison to free the girls!* Bijan was certain of that. It was just like Cyrus to go and save other people's lives at the cost of his own.

Bijan drove to the prison, keeping an eye out for Cyrus, just in case he happened to still be around the park. But there was no one.

Bijan drove around the park again, drove into streets he had never driven into, looked in places he never knew existed. But Cyrus was nowhere in sight.

Finally, just when he was about to give up, he saw Cyrus running in a lane off the street he was driving on, and by his own will he was hastening to the gallows. He immediately parked his car and rushed toward Cyrus.

Cyrus was in tears and seemed very distressed.

Bijan hugged him affectionately, and said, 'Everything is going to be all right, Cyrus. Where were you running to?'

'I'm go...go...going,' panted out Cyrus in broken words, 'I'm going to the prison to ask th...them to stop the brutality, to release the young women and teenage girls from prison.'

'How?'

'I'll ask th...th...them to execute me instead,' sobbed Cyrus.

Bijan grabbed Cyrus by the shoulders, shook him and said angrily, 'You are totally out of your mind.'

'Am I now?' asked Cyrus, taken by surprise by his friend's judgement.

'Yes, you are,' Bijan replied, but he could see a celestial innocence in Cyrus's eyes. He knew Cyrus was not mad, but he had to tell him something to stop him going to the prison and getting killed. 'You know they will kill you if you go there.'

'You really think I'm mad,' Cyrus said, regaining his breath. 'You think I'm mad because I feel for other people. You think I'm mad because I hurt like all those girls in prison. You think this makes me mad?'

'But you're a teacher, Cyrus, not a savior.'

'You think I'm going to stay here and watch people being killed without trying to do anything? How can I enjoy my life while I see such brutality? They rape and kill those young women. These women could be your daughter, your sister. Can't you see that? All they ever wanted was love, freedom and justice. But all they got is death in return.'

Bijan stood at awe. He knew Cyrus was right. But surely, there was little they could do. 'I'm taking you home, Cyrus.

You need to rest.'

Cyrus gave him a cold stare and suddenly took off running toward the prison.

Taken by surprise, Bijan didn't know what was happening. It took him a few seconds to realise Cyrus was running away from him.

Bijan ran after Cyrus, trying to catch up with him. But Cyrus was a fast runner. He tried to run faster. He had to stop Cyrus. If he got to the prison, he would be killed. They wouldn't even ask him his name.

Bijan took one deep breath and ran the fastest he ever ran.

At last he managed to catch up with Cyrus. He grabbed the back of his collar and pulled him backwards.

'Let me go!' Cyrus cried. 'Let me go and save those people.' And then he broke down to his knees. 'Please, let me go.'

'Cyrus, please understand the situation. If you go to the prison, no one's going to give a damn about you. If you offer your life in exchange for the prisoners, they'll kill you, but they won't release anyone. Whatever you do won't make any difference. Don't do it, Cyrus. Please, don't do it.'

Cyrus looked up at Bijan, eyes welled with tears. 'So, there's nothing I can do to stop them raping and killing those young women?'

'Nothing,' Bijan confirmed, taken aback by Cyrus's child-like innocence.

He helped Cyrus to his feet. He placed his hands on Cyrus's shoulders, their foreheads touching one another. They both cried in unison.

'Let me take you home,' Bijan said.

When they arrived at Cyrus's home, their faces were

swollen from the tears they had poured forth. It was as if they had just come back from a funeral.

Both stepped into the house, lost in deep thought.

Suddenly, Cyrus broke down. He went down on his knees, and cried out loud.

Bijan could feel the fire burning in Cyrus's soul. He could feel his pain as if it were his own. It was good that Cyrus shed tears, poured out his anguish. Bijan let him be.

Cyrus sat on a chair. He looked sad and gloomy. Disturbing thoughts and images invaded his mind. As if he were hearing the crying of the victims, tortured in dark pits. He was hearing the wailing of fiancées, wives, children and parents of the tortured ones. They were lamenting the deaths of their loved ones, trying to come to terms with all the pain they had suffered. So much torture and death when all they ever had was the inspiration for a better world.

Silently, Cyrus stood up from his chair and walked to a shelf filled with books. He grabbed one of the books, flicked through the pages and said, 'I want to read you something, Bijan. It's very relevant to the world of today. It's a warning to all the evil people in this world.' He stopped at a specific page and began reading, ''Oh, oppressors of the earth! Withdraw your hands from tyranny, for I have pledged myself not to forgive any man's injustice. This is my covenant, which I have irrevocably decreed in the preserved tablets and sealed with my seal.''

He read the entire page. He had strong faith in its content. His voice rose high, turning into thunder, shaking the thrones of the pharoahs of the earth.

Cyrus never mentioned who the author of the text was. But he read the words with a reverence one may only show to divine words.

Cyrus's soul was elevated by reading the sacred text.

Bijan said nothing. He listened to the power and authority of the words. He wanted to know who wrote them. He wanted to know if those words were from God or man. But as he continued to listen, it was obvious that these words were not from the pen of any men on this planet. Those words came from the King of kings, the Almighty, instructing kings, presidents, dictators, army generals, security organisations and everyone else in this world to follow the path of righteousness. And those words warned of the results for those who would walk a crooked path instead.

Cyrus read the sacred text three times, each time putting his heart and soul into what he was reading.

In spite of not knowing who the author was, Bijan was in awe of the depth and authoritative words of the sacred text. He felt it was charged with divine power.

It was close to midnight when Bijan left Cyrus by himself and headed for home.

Walking alone in the dark street, Bijan's thoughts were confused and disturbed. He found it hard to understand men's cruelty toward one another.

He glanced up at the sky and could have sworn it was coloured red. Perhaps it was filled with the blood of martyrs making their way to heaven; those killed by the sword of tyranny.

Up in the sky, written in bold red letters, Bijan read, 'Oh, oppressors of the earth! Withdraw your hands from tyranny, for I have pledged myself not to forgive any man's injustice.'

Bijan could hear the voice of God thundering across the universe, warning tyrants, dictators and the potentates of the earth that justice would be served.

When Bijan left for the night, Cyrus locked the door of his home. He went to his room and meditated. It was late, but he needed some spiritual guidance through those difficult times. The only solace to his ailing soul was to ask God to cleanse the entire planet from tyranny and injustice.

Past generations carried diseases in their blood. Illness dominated the planet in the shape of tyranny, wars and revolutions.

The following day, Bijan was up early, his mind still confused by everything he had experienced the previous night. He remembered the writing he saw in blood letters in the night sky.

As he sat by himself at home, he wondered if Cyrus had a relationship with any of the young girls or women imprisoned. Was there any motive behind his action other than just being of a holy nature?

Curious, he decided to go and ask Cyrus in person.

And so, within the next hour, he found himself at the doorstep of Cyrus's home.

Cyrus was glad to see him. He gave him a welcoming hug.

But Bijan looked sad.

Cyrus offered him a drink of water and a seat.

'What's on your mind?' Cyrus asked, wanting to help his friend.

Bijan sank in his armchair, and, turning to Cyrus without any preamble, said, 'I'd like to ask you a question.'

Cyrus's face creased. 'Go on.'

'Were you in a relationship with any of the girls imprisoned and killed?'

Cyrus smiled. 'No, Bijan. I don't know any of them personally. I'm a lecturer, and they are mostly students. I feel a spiritual link. Nothing more, nothing less.'

Bijan rubbed his chin with his forefinger. 'And what do you think of the political groups they eagerly support? Do you support the political groups, too?'

'Absolutely not.'

'You don't?' Bijan asked, looking surprised. 'But then, why do you defend them? You didn't have a relationship with any of the girls; you don't believe in what they believe; then why in the world did you want to risk your life for them?'

'Because I believe in who they are. Students and young people are usually pure in their motives and aspirations. But the political groups they support are not.'

'But surely, the political groups are only a channel for the students to express their needs?' Bijan said, confused by Cyrus's logic.

'That might be so, but they're the wrong channels.'

'How is that?'

'History has shown that political groups prey on the emotions of young people for selfish political reasons. Political leaders are only interested in getting support, and young people are easier to persuade because they're always looking for a better answer to life. And then one political regime takes over another. But life goes on and nothing changes. Misery is here to stay.'

'What is the alternative?'

'Do you know the saying, "Who seeks, finds"? If young people focused their energy on other channels than political parties, they might just find an answer to their problems.'

Bijan puzzled over Cyrus's comment.

'Would you like some coffee?' Cyrus asked, realising Bijan had finished his glass of water.

'Yes, please.'

Cyrus left for the kitchen.

Bijan walked to the only window in the room. The snow-capped mountain stood tall and proud, beautiful and pure in its natural state of being, in contrast with the turmoil of the civilised world.

Cyrus walked back in the room with two cups of steaming coffee. The aroma filled Bijan's lungs.

Cyrus handed Bijan a cup and took a sip from his. 'I still can't understand people who rape those young women and then kill them.'

'Yes, that's a horrible thing to do. It's unbelievable.' Bijan sipped from his cup.

'So, they cheat God! All they do is betray him.'

'I don't think they're true believers. They go to mosques and churches because of habit, not because of faith.'

Bijan could see that Cyrus was still highly strung by the fate of the young women. He decided it was time for Cyrus to get his mind away from it all. 'Why don't we go for a walk?' he suggested, while empting his cup of coffee. He knew that taking Cyrus outdoors might get him absorbed in the beauty of nature and help him forget the ugliness of political turmoil.

Cyrus agreed, and they both left for the park.

Within ten minutes, Cyrus seemed happy, watching birds play around the lake, filling up the air with songs of joy.

Cyrus noticed a butterfly circling a beautiful red rose. The rose and the butterfly are like two lovers, thought Cyrus. It was as if the butterfly tried to kiss the rose, but the rose resisted. And then, the butterfly managed just one kiss. The furtive kiss inflamed the heart of the butterfly.

Bijan glanced toward a group carrying the corpse of a

young man executed the previous night. His young spouse had collected the body from the revolutionary guards. She was walking behind the coffin. She was not mourning because she could not do so in public. If she shed tears, she would be suspected as a traitor and be arrested.

Only a few people were following the young woman. They all turned into a lane and disappeared from sight.

But it was too late. Cyrus had seen the coffin, and suddenly his mood had changed. His happiness was short-lived.

Bijan was upset that Cyrus didn't remain happy for the rest of the afternoon. He realised turning a blind eye to the darkness of the world was impossible. It was like turning to drinking or drugs to relieve the problem, but instead making it only worse. They had to find a solution.

'Let's go home,' Bijan suggested.

Just as they left the park, they came across another group of people who were carrying two coffins, those of a brother and sister. The mourners were walking in silence, lost in their grief.

The parents of the deceased were crying silently as they walked next to the coffin, although they were afraid to do so.

Bijan and Cyrus returned to Cyrus's home.

They sat in silence for a little while.

'Why can't people mourn the loss of their loved ones?' asked Cyrus.

'They're expected to be happy,' Bijan answered.

'Happy about what?'

'Happy that they are able to collect the bodies of their loved ones. They even have to pay for the bodies.'

'What do you mean?'

'They have to pay the revolutionary guards for the bullets

used to kill their loved ones if they want to take them home.'

'That's not true! Surely, you must be exaggerating.'

'It's true. I swear to God.'

Cyrus thought for a few seconds. 'And what if they don't pay?'

'They can't take the bodies home. And the guards might even decide to arrest them.'

'How many people have been executed?'

'According to figures released by the BBC in London, no less than 40,000. These are only estimates based on reported missing people. There are many more thousands, which haven't been reported.'

Chapter Two

SELF-EXILE

1.

The college where Cyrus taught nestled at the foothills of a great plain, in a suburb not far from the city centre.

There was a valley sloping down to a creek running smoothly with a melodious music. Wild fruit trees were scattered on the face of the slopes.

The college buildings were located over two hundred acres of flat field and swerving hills, east of the city. Like many of the great universities around the world, the college had various departments in the fields of teaching, from physical education to sport science, literature, foreign languages and philosophy. In addition, an amphitheatre with one hundred thousand seating occupied the north side of the campus.

Students loved life on campus. The air was fresh, and there was plenty of room to move around. Dormitories accommodated hundreds of male and female students. They were provided three meals a day at the college restaurants. All earned a decent allowance to help them maintain a reasonable lifestyle. Their future employment was secured as teachers of secondary schools around the country.

Early one afternoon, Cyrus arrived at the college to teach his class of English. He was surprised when he saw hundreds of students in an uproar, surrounding the Dean of the College.

The students wanted revenge. They were willing to

attack, burn and destroy if it took that much to get their point across. The office of a newspaper, the organ of the ruling party, would be their main target. It was terrifying to see a crowd of students prepared to move fast toward an office and set it on fire, to teach the editor a lesson.

The Dean of the College was standing on a stool, trying hard to advise the students against an uproar. He told them that if they wanted to make a point, burning the newspaper office was not a clever way to do it.

Cyrus parked his car and rushed to where the gathering was taking place.

Amongst the students, there were lecturers. Cyrus recognised some from his own department. He approached one of the lecturers and asked, 'What's going on?'

'An article was published in the ruling party newspaper,' explained the lecturer. 'The author criticised the presence of a lecturer in the College. The author believes that the ideals of this lecturer are anti-God, anti-religion and dangerous. The article criticised the Dean for supporting the lecturer instead of dismissing him from the College.'

Cyrus realised that the lecturer in question had to be him. He was not greatly surprised or disturbed by the incident. He smiled to himself and said to the other lecturer with a sense of humour, 'The article doesn't say who this person is. It could be anyone. It could be you.'

The lecturer looked at Cyrus and saw the cynicism in his eyes. He sensed that Cyrus was the subject of the newspaper article. 'I personally respect his beliefs and ideals,' he added, smiling at Cyrus.

Cyrus was now certain that his presence at the College was being felt.

When Cyrus got hold of the controversial article, he

realised why the students had been so angry. The author of the article also attacked the students' sense of morality for having males and females use the same swimming pool on the campus. The students felt deeply insulted. They had done nothing wrong by sharing the swimming pool. They felt that the newspaper article insulted their reputation.

It took a good hour for the Dean of the College to calm the students down. He told them that if they wanted to make a point, they didn't have to destroy anything. He would arrange for five buses to transport a certain number of students to the newspaper office, where they could protest peacefully. And the students did just that. They sat down around the newspaper the whole night to express their anger and protest.

The following day, a retraction appeared in the college newspaper, apologising for the article which had caused so much anger on campus, explaining that the article had been a mistake. Cyrus's life was providentially saved.

2.

Early one morning, Cyrus arrived at the college and parked his dark blue car under the shade of a willow tree in the vast parking area.

It was a cool but pleasant morning, mild sunlight spreading itself like a blanket over the campus and its buildings.

Cyrus killed the engine, grabbed his leather-bound briefcase and stepped out of the car. He locked the door and stood still under the branches of a tree. He closed his eyes and breathed in the fresh air, filling his lungs with nature's sweet aroma. When he next opened his eyes, he glanced toward the serene hills, bathed in morning sunlight. He felt at peace and happy to be back on campus.

When he arrived at his office, he found a letter slipped under the door, lying on the floor. For a few seconds he stared at the letter, as if it were a time bomb. He placed his briefcase on his desk and walked back to the letter. He circled the piece of paper a few times. And finally he bent down and picked it up.

When he read the contents, he felt perspiration dripping down his back. He was stunned by what he'd just read.

He rushed to the office of the Head of the Department.

The Head was a short man, with short hair and rimless glasses. He was dressed in black slacks with matching jacket and a white shirt. His mere presence radiated authority.

When the Head saw Cyrus walk into his office, huffing and puffing, not even bothering to knock on the door, he knew something was wrong. Immediately, his eyes gazed down at the piece of paper Cyrus held in his hands. Cyrus did not have to tell him what the letter was.

'You've received a note. It must be of some import. Would you like to share it with me?' the Head said, a look of concern crossing his face. He recognised the distress on Cyrus's face. 'Show me the letter,' he added encouragingly, moving his hand toward Cyrus.

Cyrus obeyed and handed the letter to him.

The Head read the note, and the colours were drained from his face. He read the note again and handed it back to Cyrus with a trembling hand. He did not know what to say. He had read threatening letters before, but this one seemed lethal.

Finally, Cyrus let his anger out. 'If those jackals plan to assassinate me, why don't they do it now? The sooner the better. Only cowards write letters like this.' He tore the letter and threw it in the bin next to Head's desk.

During the whole time, the Head never said a word.

Cyrus returned to his office, pondering on the contents of the letter. An extremist fanatical gang who threatened to assassinate him had written it. Although Cyrus wanted to dismiss the incident lightly, make himself believe that it was nothing but a joke, he knew deep down it was not a joke at all. He tried to brush his worries aside and laugh out loud to himself. Hell, he wasn't going to be threatened in his own college. *They're nothing but jackals.* It made him angry to realise how people associated with fanaticism were used for political ends.

Sitting behind his desk, overlooking the college campus, he tried hard to get his mind into some work, but the threatening letter had affected him more than he liked to admit. His thoughts drifted to the growing number of gangs who threatened people. He wondered who was the mastermind behind all those gangs? Who'd fuelled those agents of death? The gangs were obviously at the mercy of some higher authority; someone that implemented a secret political plan- a plan aimed at pushing the country down to its knees.

By early afternoon, Cyrus grew tired and weary. He went home early to get some rest. He needed to refocus his thoughts on things other than the damn letter.

After drinking a cool glass of water, he decided to work in the garden, hoping that this would give him something else to think about other than the political turmoil which had enshrouded the whole country.

The garden seemed to welcome him with all its glory. He watered the flowers, shrubs and trees. He knew that every drop of water he sprayed on them brought joy to their existence. He went to the gazebo and stood there, watching the garden. The flowers were smiling in gratitude. Cyrus thought that if people were more like flowers, the world would be a better place to live in.

Time passed quickly in the harmonious tranquillity of the garden.

The day was coming to an end. The sun was drawing back its golden skirt from meadows and hills. It faded into the horizon, painted the sky amber and disappeared behind the mountain. Darkness took its place.

Cyrus read awhile, but his thoughts kept drifting to terrorism. He walked back and forth in the living room as he wondered how his country could accept terrorism as part of every day life. He stood at the window staring out, but saw nothing. Darkness was everywhere around him. His thoughts drifted to the increasing drug problem in the world. He couldn't help associating drug dealing with fanaticism. *Fanaticism paralyses the mind and drugs paralyse the body, two tools to weaken the public so as to rule them. There's a secret support for drug dealing and fanaticism.*

Tired and weary, Cyrus stepped into the study which was plunged in total darkness. He did not bother turning the light on. He sat at his desk leaning his chin on his arms. He wondered why politics were void of spiritual ethics. Hadn't man learnt anything in the past four thousand years? How long would we go on making the same mistakes over and over?

He walked up to the window of his study. His hands deep inside the pockets of his trousers, he stared out at the darkness. The wind, blowing in the trees surrounding his home, sounded more like a cry than a melody. He was tired of the way his world was crumbling. His eyes glanced up to the dark sky. *May a new light chase away the darkness! May a new day break,* echoed in his soul.

3.

A week later, Cyrus was driving his dark blue car to the college. A crowd suddenly blocked the main road, which he was driving on. Soon it became clear to him that the crowd consisted of two political groups, who were marching and shouting slogans in two different side streets, and met each other at the main street. They became engaged in fighting to demonstrate who would be best at ruling the country.

One group consisted of religious fanatics. They were farmers, labourers and young people from religious families. Most were villagers from different parts of the country, attracted to the capital city to fight atheist university students.

The fanatics were well-nourished, accommodated and generously paid for their time. Every one of them was in possession of a brand new dagger imported from Switzerland or another country. They were obsessive about their weapons and loved holding and admiring them. Looking at those well-shaped and glittering daggers gave them pleasure, thinking about using them. They kept them secured under their long coats or overcoats. They were willing to do anything, even kill, in the name of God. They threw stones, sticks and bricks at the other group, which consisted mainly of university students. They screamed in unison, 'Atheist whores!'

Before Cyrus had time to react, people surrounded his car. The street swarmed with people like an anthill that has been disturbed. He ducked under the dashboard every time a stone or brick passed close to his car. He feared one would eventually go through the windscreen. He feared being killed when he was just an innocent by-stander who supported neither of the two groups. He was stuck amidst the fighting groups. He could neither move the car forward nor turn back. Finally, afraid of the danger, he climbed to the car's rear and pulled the front seats down towards him as far as he could, and hid under the seats to protect himself from flying debris. There was no way he would make it to college that day. When the crowd dissipated, he was safe, but the duco of his car had been damaged.

One month later, when he arrived at the college, the leader of the Student Union greeted him. 'Cyrus, it's good to see you.'

'It's good to see you too,' Cyrus said, recognising the Student Union leader as one of his English students the previous year. 'What have you been up to?'

'Well, Cyrus, I'm actually here to tell you that the students of this college like you and respect you. We stand by you all the way.'

Cyrus was taken by surprise; he smiled, filled with gratitude. 'Thank you. That's nice of you,' he said, patting the student gently on the shoulder.

'Some wanted to kill you. But we stopped them.'

'Thank you.'

'You know we're on your side. We will choke them.'

Cyrus realised the students were engaged in hidden battle with the extremists to save his life. He knew they had to be the same people who slipped that threatening letter under his door the previous month. He felt grateful for what the students had done to protect his life. The students became dearer to his heart than ever before.

His country had become a land infested by gangs whose only aim was to kill and destroy.

The same gang that sent the threatening letter to Cyrus had already kidnapped a distinguished university professor, who taught philosophy and mysticism at the main university in the capital city. He was taken in the early hours of the morning during his daily walk in a park not far from his home. At the entrance gate of the park, three masked men jumped on him, put a gag in his mouth, and dragged him inside a car. No one ever found out what happened to the professor. But rumours had it that he was taken to a black pit in a secret location. He was encouraged to recant his faith if he wanted to be set free. But he resisted. Most probably he was tortured and martyred.

More kidnappings occurred. The gang used to drive in a black Mercedes Benz and preferred stalking their targets at night time before kidnapping.

Kidnapping, a method normally used by political groups, was now being favoured by religious gangs. Political criminals had taught the religious fanatics. The blind leading the blind.

Cyrus had never been interested in or involved in any politics, nor had he any attachment to any party, his mind uncorrupted by other people's propaganda. He could still move freely. But he intuited that an invisible shadow was following him. The ghost of terror was getting closer and closer. He knew that one day he would be caught, tortured and hanged. He had been warned many times by his friend to hide and to avoid being seen in public. He felt insulted to hear such admonition.

4.

One night Cyrus came home exhausted. He stood still by the window of his study, overlooking his backyard, which included an old garden at the far end. He stared at the tall trees of the old garden, which looked mysterious. He felt someone was watching him but dismissed the sensation as paranoia.

Soon afterwards he went to bed, but could not sleep. As he tossed and turned, he could not help thinking that someone was hiding in the old garden, waiting for the right moment to break into his home.

Outside, the wind was howling like a battered animal, twisting branches and trees, and shaking shrubs in the old garden.

Unable to settle down, Cyrus got up and moved to the window. He pushed the curtain aside and peered toward the old garden. He was certain he could make out the shadow of a person down at the far end. But with the darkness, his certainty was weakened.

He went to the kitchen and made himself a cup of hot tea. The coldness of the night was chilling him to the bone, so he wrapped himself tighter in his nightgown. Not wanting to return to his bedroom, he fell asleep sitting on the sofa in the living room.

Only a few nights later, he woke up in a frenzy, certain he'd heard footsteps in the hallway of his home. When he looked at the clock by the side table, he realised it was well after midnight. He went downstairs to the living room, drew the curtains slowly and peered outside. But there was no one there.

It took him a while to get back to sleep. He wondered if

he wasn't a prisoner of his own fear. He decided that it was time to stop seeing himself as being in danger. He had to force himself to believe that the world was a beautiful place, where justice and truth ruled, where political corruption, religious fanaticism did not exist; then he could gain peace of mind. If only he could believe he would never be kidnapped and assassinated, then maybe he would be able to get some sleep.

5.

As the months went past, and the threats to his life grew, Cyrus had arrived at a crossroad. He knew he had to decide whether to stay or leave the country. But it was a difficult decision to make. On the one hand, he had a burning desire to stay in his homeland and risk his life for his beliefs. But he also knew that if he stayed, eventually they would arrest or kidnap, torture and kill him. For his own life, he had little concern; but he felt passionately about what he stood for. He did not want to be assassinated in the middle of the night or hanged in the early hours of the morning. He had an ardent desire to dedicate his life to a new world. He believed that terrorism, wars, dictatorship, and poverty were the symptoms of an old system breeding disease. The whole world had to be restructured. He saw good-hearted people, the younger generation, especially the women, as those who would help build a new world whose foundation would be wisdom, justice and global unification, an end to the miseries of a man-made world.

Thinking about the possibility of a new world gave Cyrus a pleasant feeling of hope. He felt as if his life had a purpose. And for that reason, he did not want his life to end sharply at the hands of murderers. A passion was burning in his heart, a desire to witness a great change in the history of the world.

But more months went by, and Cyrus realised that living in his country was now unbearable. He could not make a decision as to whether he should leave or stay. It was a painful dilemma.

One day, Cyrus was sitting alone in his room, lost in his thoughts. He wondered where his life was heading when suddenly he heard a voice. He couldn't tell whether the voice was coming from inside his mind or from above him.

'You must leave the soils of this country immediately; great danger is coming your way,' the voice said.

Cyrus shook his head, wondering if his subconscious fear had turned into an internal voice. It was an unusual experience. He tried to ignore it. But just as he was wondering the voice repeated, 'You must leave the soils of this country immediately.' And then Cyrus knew he couldn't have been thinking two thoughts at once. All the same, it seemed absurd that a voice could be coming out of nowhere. Uncertain as how to handle the situation, he challenged the voice.

'I will not leave my country,' he muttered. 'To do so is a sign of cowardice.'

He waited a few seconds in silence for a reply.

And then the voice grew louder, its tone filled with authority. 'You must leave *now* before it is too late.'

'I cannot do that. I cannot forsake my land and my people. They need me as much as I need them.'

Like an angry thunder from heaven, the voice grew louder, 'Leave immediately!'

And then Cyrus couldn't deny what was happening. It was an unusual and mystical experience. Could it be that this was the voice of God? Cyrus muttered, 'I have to listen to the voice echoing in my innermost being.' He couldn't be certain either way, but he decided to take the voice seriously. Although he felt unable to explain what was happening, he believed mysterious forces were at work. Why reject the voice when it felt right? Why say no to a voice filled with warmth and wisdom? Wouldn't God know better what lay ahead for him?

Still, as the day went by, even though Cyrus had faith in God, he couldn't help wondering if he wasn't losing his mind. He needed to talk to someone else about this strange experience. But not to everyone; they might laugh at him.

When night came, Cyrus approached his mother to disclose his mystical experience. Only she would take him seriously. Only she would know that he was telling the truth.

Over supper, Cyrus told his mother what had happened that morning when he was alone at home. But his mother did not seem surprised at all. She locked her eyes into those of Cyrus, her heart filled with motherly love. She smiled tenderly, her eyes filled with tears.

Cyrus moved forward and kissed his mother on the cheek. 'I do not know what is happening,' he said seriously. 'But I cannot ignore what I've experienced this morning and carry on with life as if nothing ever happened. If God tells me to leave the country immediately, then I must do it.'

Tears were rolling down his mother's face.

'Do not cry, mother. If it isn't God's Will that I should leave home, then he will let me know in due time, and I will come back.'

His mother placed one hand on his face. 'If it is indeed the voice of God that you've heard, then the voice of God you must follow.'

In spite of having decided to follow the instruction of the voice, it was no easy task to obey. Cyrus's mind was still confused as to why he had been instructed to leave the country.

After an agonising dilemma, Cyrus did decide to leave.

As he planned his departure, he knew he would not be able to *fly* overseas. He would have to sneak out with great risk.

When the time came to leave, he did not tell anyone he was going for good, not his friends, nor his brothers and sisters. All believed he was going on a short journey to another city and would be back soon. The news of his intention to escape could spread around. That was perilous. He could be spied on or caught on the way or assassinated at the border. On his last day at home, he shook everyone's hand warmly, hugged and kissed them with great affection. He tried hard to hold back his tears. He did not disclose that it was the last time he was visiting them. He tried hard to appear composed, not to give them the least suspicion that they might never see him again. Only his mother knew, and he trusted that she could keep a secret.

One night, his mother drove him to the railway station, which was only half a kilometre from his home. Cyrus wore sand-coloured clothes and carried a sack filled with some changes of clothing and personal goods.

Lost in silence, they waited for the train to arrive. Now and then, Cyrus glanced at his mother, wondering if he was doing the right thing. But he had to have faith. He had to be strong. Both tried hard to conceal their grief, pretending to be in a good mood. Cyrus smiled at his mother, but the sorrow in his eyes betrayed his true feelings.

His mother could not hold back her tears.

Cyrus looked upward at the sky. The moon was full and mysterious. It peeped and disappeared in the bosom of the floating clouds. The cracking sound of thunder could be heard in the far-off distance.

A few minutes passed. Suddenly, above their heads, the clouds were clashing in thunder as Cyrus wondered if it would rain. But by the time the train arrived, rain had not yet fallen upon the land.

Finally, when Cyrus boarded the train, he knew there would be no turning back now. The train horned and crawled along the railway tracks, moving towards its destination.

Outside the train, on the railway platform, Cyrus's mother kept her eyes on the carriage where Cyrus was standing at the window and waving good-bye to her. She wanted to look at his face for as long as she could. Tears blurred her eyes as the train disappeared on the horizon.

She stood alone on the railway platform, as if her soul had departed a lifeless body.

A railway worker noticed a woman standing by herself, looking lost in her thoughts. He approached her and said, 'Madam, you've missed your train. It left a few minutes ago.'

Cyrus's mother was startled, as if she'd just woken up from a bad dream. She looked around, wondering where she was and what was happening. And then she realised that she was the only one left on the railway platform, apart from the railway worker. Her mind was filled with confusion as she muttered, 'I think it's time to go home.' She walked out of the railway station, looking like a lost child.

When she got home, everyone had already gone to bed. It was dark and terrifying. From her room, she could hear the barking of neighbouring dogs outside and the howling of the wind.

She looked out through the window of her room, her heart filled with great sorrow. The wind was playing with the branches of a willow tree. It felt as if the swinging willow were moaning and shedding tears.

She turned off the light and sat in the only armchair in the room. She knew she wouldn't be able to get to sleep with all that sorrow in her heart. She closed her eyes and prayed for Cyrus's safe journey. It was as if she'd been forced to bury her son alive, and she'd just come back from his funeral.

In the darkness of her room, memories of Cyrus ran past her mind. She remembered him as a new-born child, sweetness in his eyes. Family members and friends wanted to keep him overnight because he was so cute. Often, she'd had to get him back from different houses.

Already at an early age, he was a fearless boy. He wouldn't let anyone push him around. At the high school, he'd won many awards for making the top grade in his class. A well-known magazine ran a story on him, his outstanding achievements at school. He was already giving speeches which impressed anyone who would listen. Cyrus was a born leader, and his mother had been a witness to the fact.

For the next two hours, Cyrus's mother remembered every little detail of her son.

She did not go to bed, but moved from the armchair to the floor, thinking about the past and shedding tears. It was after midnight when she finally became too tired to stay awake. Her head fell backward against the bed's edge as she slipped into a deep sleep.

Morning sunlight filtering itself across her room woke her. As she looked out of the window, the sun covered the entire city.

She walked outside her home, down the curving stone steps and into the garden. Every step she took reminded her of Cyrus, because with his taste for landscaping, he had created the fascinating garden. She entered the gazebo at the far end of the garden, looking up at the various terraces. But everything seemed to be dying now that Cyrus was gone. Many times she had sat contemplating the garden with Cyrus, admiring the flowering shrubs, the maple, the orange, and pomegranate trees on the sloping terraces. They'd watched the sun's rays play with the olive leaves and flowers.

She knelt next to a flowerbed and smelt the flowers. Every plant reminded her of what Cyrus used to say whenever he planted a tree or a flower, 'Ah! A new life comes into being!'

Cyrus was sitting alone in the compartment. The train was moving fast. Cyrus's thoughts drifted to the people he had left behind. He knew he might never see them again, and that realisation weighed heavily on him.

He left the compartment and walked down the corridor of the train. He opened a window and leant forward, wanting to see for the last time his homeland. But outside it was pitch dark, and there was little he could see. Lighting flashed and thunder cracked on the horizon.

Leaning against the window's ledge, he stared blankly into the darkness. The sound of the train was monotonous and repetitive. A great sadness fell upon him.

Suddenly, Cyrus felt drops of rain on his face. He drew back and passed one hand over his face to get rid of the wetness. As soon as he closed the window, he saw lightning in the sky, and rain splashing against the windowpane.

He walked back to his cabin.

Alone in his cabin, he felt terrified by the thunder outside. He wished he had someone to talk to.

A few minutes went by before a ticket inspector entered his cabin unannounced. He wore a thick moustache and must have been about one head taller than Cyrus.

'Ticket please.'

Cyrus stared at him blankly.

'Ticket, sir. What is your destination?'

'I'm going to—' Cyrus couldn't finish his answer. He did not want to tell him the name of the small town he was heading to. And he didn't want to lie. To begin with, he hated lying, and secondly, the inspector would eventually find out.

'Where do you get off, sir?' The ticket inspector repeated, examining Cyrus up and down.

Cyrus felt embarrassed and uncomfortable. 'Sorry,' he muttered. 'I didn't understand your question. Hold on a second. It's on my ticket.' Cyrus removed the train ticket from his bag and showed it to the inspector.

The inspector looked at the ticket, and then at Cyrus. At first he seemed to dislike Cyrus, but suddenly he smiled. 'Have a good trip, sir,' he said as he returned the ticket to Cyrus before leaving the cabin.

Cyrus felt a great sense of relief. He hoped the rest of the trip wasn't going to be so nerve-wracking.

The following day, Cyrus reached the small town where a man was to meet him in the evening to give him instructions and clothes to help him leave the country.

When night came, the man gave Cyrus tribal garb and a turban, the common apparel of tribes on both sides of the border. The stranger also gave him a small map with instructions on how to make it safely across the border.

As soon as the man left, Cyrus put on the garb and turban. He looked at himself in the full-length mirror in the motel room and was surprised how clothes could change a person's appearance.

At 11.00 p.m., Cyrus left the motel. He noticed a man outside glancing toward him. When the man realised he was being watched, he strove down the street.

Cyrus followed him from a distance.

The man stopped at a spot for a few seconds, and then disappeared into a dark alley.

Cyrus pondered on the homeland he was about to leave. A long time ago, Greeks and Romans had described his country as a land of mystery, wisdom and knowledge. But now, it was nothing but a land of terror, crime and fanaticism. The name of his country meant paradise, but somehow it had turned into a living hell. Cyrus felt it painful that a country which once contributed to the advancement of world civilisation had turned into a land of despair. Saddened by what his world had become, he headed for the border.

He walked a long way to the frontier. He stood there, looked around, and hesitated to step out. He breathed in a deep sigh. His eyes welled with tears. Then he turned his back on his homeland and crossed the border.

Cyrus voluntarily took the path of an exile and a homeless one. He chose a destiny filled with uncertainty and all the risks of living on the run. He tramped wearily along a narrow valley, as if he were carrying his own dead body on his back.

Pieces of dark cloud were hovering above his head, and the moon hung like a huge balloon.

Cyrus kept his eyes on the road ahead, wondering what lay before him. He was alert, listening for anything that could be a possible threat. He was looking for a van which would take him and other refugees across the border.

Now and then, he had the creepy sensation that he was being followed. He wanted to turn around and satisfy his curiosity, but he did not dare. If he was being followed, there was little he could do about it. All he could do was move on and have faith that he would reach his destination.

But after a while the nagging feeling of being followed drove him insane. He glanced quickly over his shoulder, and indeed, he saw the dark shape of a man following him in the distance. Cyrus cast his eyes on the road ahead and increased his pace.

Sure enough, when Cyrus checked again to see if the man was following him, the man seemed to be getting closer in spite of Cyrus walking at neck-breaking speed. He had a bad feeling about it all. In his mind's eye, he could see the man grabbing him by the throat or digging a knife in his back. He knew he would have to hit first before he got hit.

Suddenly Cyrus froze on the spot. He counted to three, turned around very quickly and threw his fist at whoever was behind him with full force. He nearly lost balance when his fist cut through the empty air. He laughed at himself for being frightened by his own shadow. His paranoia and fear had made him imagine things which weren't. He also realised that he was tired, having slept badly the previous night, his thoughts preoccupied with his long journey ahead. Maybe it was also the lack of sleep, which made it difficult for him to keep his mind from wandering.

Well over an hour later the whistling of a bullet passed right by him. Frightened, he glanced around, and threw himself on the ground, expecting a bullet to hit him at any moment. He was in panic, his breath short and rapid.

He was huffing, trying to regain his breath. And then he heard the sound of an engine.

He looked up and saw a Landrover speeding on the upper part of the hill. Revolutionary guards were patrolling the frontier, shooting at random in the air to scare off anyone who might try to cross the border in the middle of the night.

Cyrus stayed flat on the ground until the Landrover disappeared into the darkness of the night. He stood on his feet, relieved no one had seen him. Dusting off his clothes, he continued to walk. He wondered how far his luck would stretch.

After about thirty-five minutes, another vehicle came toward him from the upper part of the road. He threw himself to the side of the road and hid behind a large rock. His heart was drilling in his chest. He could clearly see the vehicle from where he was positioned. It was a Jeep with three or four men, throwing a beam of light across the road, obviously looking out for any fugitive who was trying to cross the border illegally. The beam of light passed right above his head and landed in front of the rock behind which he was crouching. He heard the men talk amongst themselves as he wondered if they had seen him.

Suddenly, the Jeep took off fast in the opposite direction.

Cyrus let out a sigh of relief. He sat for a little while to gather his energy.

It took him another three hours to find the spot, indicated on the map he was given at the motel, where the van would be waiting for him.

There were thirteen other refugees there, as well as the driver of the van with the smuggler.

The driver ordered the refugees into the back of the van and began a race on the twisted road, going up the hills and down the valleys. It was a rough road filled with rocks and dirt.

For the first ten minutes, no one in the back said a word. Finally, Cyrus began a conversation with two young boys who were sitting on his right. They were members of a minority group under persecution.

One of the boys said, 'I want to live where I can be free, where I can say and do what I want. Freedom is a great bounty.'

The other boy leaned against Cyrus and whispered, 'I used to be the best student at my school. But when they found out about my belief in the New Faith, they forced me to stop studying. They stopped me from getting a job. They rejected my application to obtain a passport. I wasn't allowed to leave the country. All I want is to find a place where I can continue my studies without having to worry every minute of every day about my safety.'

Cyrus had been told that border patrols were operating around a vast area on both sides of the border.

No one said another word, thinking of the danger ahead. The rattle of the van going up the hill and down the valley disturbed the silence. The driver was going all over the place, driving dangerously on the rocks of the twisted road. He was driving too fast, making it a certain death for all the passengers if the van turned over.

Some revolutionary guards, patrolling the area, saw a van on the road going fast without lights in the dark night. They immediately sensed that the van was smuggling out some fugitives. They chased the van as fast as they could, shooting with a machine gun.

Suddenly, Cyrus saw that they were being followed. Headlights from a Landrover behind them were closing in. Shots whistled past his ears. Everyone in the back of the van began to panic and lie down low. They were sure they were going to die.

It was a terrifying moment for all of them.

Darkness and wind surrounded them as the Landrover moved in close.

Cyrus was lying on the floor of the van, could not see anything. He heard the sound of squirting; some drops splashed on his face. He thought it was raining.

The driver increased speed, driving recklessly like a crazy man. The van was moving and shaking, turning from left to right, when suddenly it veered off the road, and the driver lost control.

The van overturned two hundred metres off the side of the road.

The revolutionary guards drove right past them without noticing a thing, and disappeared.

At first, no one seemed seriously injured.

It took the passengers a good five minutes to figure out what was going on. With instructions from the driver, the passengers tried to turn the van over. But it was too heavy, and soon it became obvious they were wasting time.

'What the hell are we going to do now?' yelled one of the passengers.

'The first thing you have to do is calm down,' the driver said. 'The less we panic, the better our chances of making it across the border.' And then his tone of voice became even more serious. 'I want all of you to stay here,' he ordered. 'I'm going to a village nearby to get some help.'

'No way,' shouted the same man who first complained.

'We're not going to let you go and leave us in this dangerous place. If you don't come back, we've got no way to make it out of here. We've got no food or water to live on if you leave us. And how do we know you're going to come back? You've already got our money, so why should you risk your neck for us?'

'I won't do such a thing.' ·

'Yeah? What about two months ago? I heard a group got lost in the desert and died without food and water?'

'It was a different charter. Nothing to do with us.'

But other passengers refused to stay behind, so the driver had no choice but to give in.

Amid the darkness, they did a head count to make sure everyone was there. But three people were missing. They searched the overturned van and found one boy dead. The other two were bleeding and moaning. They brought them down. One boy trembled and died immediately. Another one was bleeding and looked unconscious.

A four-year old child kept crying, making it even more difficult for everyone to stay levelheaded. Because the child wouldn't stop crying, the mother checked him over, wondering what was wrong with him. At first she'd thought he was crying because of the incident, but soon realised a bullet had hit the child's right leg. The driver of the van took out a first aid kit from the glove box and did the best he could to help the agonising child.

The driver ordered them to leave the dead people behind with the injured. Taking them would slow the group down too much. Only one seemed to be alive.

They heard a voice. 'Please, don't leave me,' the injured boy pleaded desperately. 'Please, take me with you.'

Finally they decided that leaving him behind was too

cruel, so they took turns in carrying him on their shoulders. Mostly Cyrus carried him.

For two hours, they fought harsh winds and uncertainty.

At last they came across a deserted house with no doors or windows, which they used for shelter until dawn.

In the morning, a bordersman suddenly appeared, and came into the ruined house. He saw people standing or lying on the ground with faces, hands, shoes and clothes bloody, and some were moaning and crying. With bloody hands and faces, they looked at him fiercely. He trembled as if he had seen ghosts.

The bordersman stepped back in fear until he went out of the ruins. He was armed, but he became scared and ran away.

While fleeing away, now and then he looked back to make sure that they were not chasing him.

He disappeared and never came back.

At about 11 a.m. the smuggler who had run away at the time of the van wreckage came back. The two smugglers, Cyrus and four of the other male passengers went to the spot where they had left the dead bodies, the damaged van, and the luggage the previous night. The rest stayed behind in the shelter.

When they arrived back at the scene of the accident, one of the men asked if they should take the bodies with them.

'We cannot carry the bodies anywhere,' one smuggler said. 'We have to bury them.'

Cyrus and other passengers stayed behind silent and sorrowful, watching the smugglers carrying the dead bodies on their shoulders. The smugglers went further up the hill and put down the bodies. Then they started to throw them one by one into a deep valley.

From the distance Cyrus's eyes were following them all the way up the hill. Seeing the men threw the dead bodies into a valley brought tears to his eyes as he wondered how the families of the dead people would ever know what had happened to their dear ones.

They gathered the luggage and returned to the deserted home where the other refugees were waiting. The van was damaged. So they left it there.

The smugglers said they could arrange to have only the injured child, his father and mother, the injured boy and a friend of his travel by car. The rest of them would have to travel by means of camel for five days and nights to reach a small town where they would change over to cars.

Waiting for transportation seemed to be taking forever. The injured young man was moaning constantly. The child with the bullet in his leg cried without stopping. Cyrus tried hard to be near the child and his mother, talking to them to ease the pain. Whenever he approached them, he caressed the forehead of the child with sympathy and love. Now and then, he walked out of the shelter and scanned the horizon, impatiently waiting for the arrival of their rescuers.

It took until dusk for the car to arrive to take the injured ones with their relatives.

It would be days before Cyrus could learn that the young child had lost his right leg and the young man an eye. He understood that when they reached the doctor and the hospital, it was too late to treat the child. They had to cut off his leg to save his life. The youth did not die, but he lost one of his eyes because the bullet had struck his left eye.

Two hours after sunset, a caravan of six camels arrived.

By 9.00 p.m., the survivors began their long journey, some on camelback, others on foot. Cyrus, who was still strong in spite of his tiredness, walked beside the camels.

Four hours later they stopped near a small pool of water, where the camels replenished their water supply for the journey.

The camels were then fitted with bells.

When the caravan set out again, tramping on the dusty road, the bells twisted and dangled in rhythm.

After a while, Cyrus changed places with a male passenger. He was now riding on one of the camels.

The harmonious sounds of the bells echoed in the valley, sounding magical and mysterious in the darkness of the night.

Cyrus looked up to the sky where thousands of stars were twinkling in the vast space, and the moon was pacing graciously.

While pressing ahead toward an uncertain future, Cyrus recalled one of the youths who died when the van overturned. He remembered what the young man told him: 'All I want is to find a place where I can continue my studies without having to worry every minute of every day about my safety.' And then he heard the voice of the other young student: 'Freedom is a great bounty.' His heart was heavy at the thought that the young men would never see the freedom they'd dreamt about for so long. He wondered how in the world people could make a living killing other people.

Suddenly, in the quiet of the night, something moved in the bushes by the side of the road and frightened one of the camels, which began running away. In the process, the camel knocked a walker to the ground, injuring his kneecap.

Cyrus commanded the caravan to a halt.

The camel-driver managed to calm down the rest of the camels.

The injured person was a young man. He could no longer walk, and yet no one seemed eager to share a camel, except Cyrus.

The young man protested, claiming that he was all right.

But Cyrus knew it wasn't true, so he gave him his camel and chose to walk instead.

By mid-morning the next day, the temperature had soared high, making it unbearable to travel. Luckily, the caravan found a pool of water. The leader told everyone it was time for a break, and if they wanted to, they could refill their water supply.

Men and women rushed to the pool, cupped their hands and drank the water. But one of the drinkers spat the water back. 'This water is disgusting!' he shouted. 'It smells like death. We're all going to be sick.'

Then the leader stepped forward. 'I'm afraid we don't have much choice. This is the only water available for drinking and cooking until we arrive at the village. Either you drink, or you die of dehydration.'

And so everyone drank the water with a solemn face, hoping it would not make him or her sick.

They rested in the shade behind some large rocks, where many of them fell asleep. It was far too hot to be travelling, and most travellers were tired of being on the camels' backs for so long.

It wasn't until late afternoon, when the scorching temperature settled, that they continued their journey.

Soon the sun set, and darkness enshrouded the whole area.

With heavy heart, Cyrus walked wearily mile after mile toward an unknown destination.

Cyrus's feet were burning with pain. But no one seemed

willing to trade places with him.

It took another three hours before the leader of the caravan offered Cyrus a turn on his camel. When Cyrus climbed on the camel, he felt a great relief. He didn't notice how tired he'd been until then. His eyes were heavy, and he felt like falling into a deep sleep.

In the far distance, he saw the flames of a fire blazing up in the air in the middle of a mountain. The shadows of shepherds were stretching long on the slope. They were resting with their flocks. The dogs were nestling against their masters. One shepherd played a sad melody on a wood pipe, a song expressing the sorrowful tale of people who suffered deprivation and cruelty through the centuries. The wood pipe music blending with the sound of bells echoed in the valley and filled the darkness with melancholy.

As the caravan moved away from the shepherds, a veil was lifted from Cyrus's inner eyes. The melody of the wood pipe music and the rhythmic dangling of the bells in moonlight late at night awakened in him a mystic emotion. Something that he could feel, but he could not explain it. His spiritual potential was opening a door unto a blissful world. Looking around him, even in the darkness, everything seemed beautiful and in harmony. The stars and the moon seemed perfectly happy. He felt a strong bond between himself and the world around him. He wondered why humans have brought upon themselves so many miseries. He knew that miseries were more often man-made than not.

It was a quiet night. The harmonious dangling of the bells and the regular tramping of the camels enhanced the silence.

Cyrus glanced at the vast heaven; innumerable stars were shining brightly and the moon seemed amorous. He wondered if there was no force of attraction and love how the universe could continue its existence in such amazing harmony. As Cyrus contemplated the beauty and the harmony of the universe, he wished that human institutions would reflect the beauty and the glory of celestial love. He wished for when every man would live in harmony like all the stars in the universe.

Because of the hot weather, the caravan took rest during the day and travelled at night.

The caravan was travelling in the middle of an empty desert, where no man or animal chose to live.

A gentle wind turned into a desert storm in less than an hour. The fierce storm blew sand at the faces of the travellers, forcing them to take refuge behind large rocks on the side of the road. The blowing sand clouded the moon.

The travellers stood close to one another, waiting for the storm to end. The cold temperature of night cut through their bones, so they rested against the camels, sharing their warmth.

Two hours passed before the storm eased into quietness. The caravan leader, who knew a great deal about forecasting the weather in the desert, told the group it was time to move on.

As they crossed the desolate area, everyone was getting anxious that something would go wrong.

Cyrus was following the caravan, feeling like a person lost on earth. He'd never been so lonely in his life. He thought about his mother and the warmth of his home and wondered if he had done the right thing.

A chilly wind was howling like a wild beast, lashing at his face mercilessly. In spite of his protecting his face with the turban hanging over his shoulder, sand got in his eyes, making them water. Involuntarily he closed his eyes.

Walking in pitch darkness, he followed the bells of the camels.

Walking in darkness with closed eyes, he could hear terrifying noises- the cry of jackals, the hissing of the snake, and other beasts in the near distance. His loneliness made him even more weary of the road he had chosen, a road to an uncertain destiny.

After a short time, the wind calmed down. He sensed that some of the camels were agitated. He knew animals could sense danger long before humans. He became aware of the danger.

Cyrus opened his burning eyes gently. Alert and watchful, he looked attentively around. Suddenly some eyes shining in the darkness attracted his attention. He stared more closely into the darkness. Wild beasts, sniffing, with widely opened mouths, were approaching the caravan.

And then, in the distance, less than fifty metres from the caravan, he noticed a pack of wolves travelling slowly by its side. He wanted to alert the rest of the group, but suddenly the leader of the caravan shouted, 'Do not be alarmed. There are wolves around us. We're going to step off the camels calmly and chase them away. No one is to wander around by himself.'

The men got off the camels and armed themselves with sticks.

Now that the caravan had stopped, the wolves closed in on them, making the camels even more restless.

Cyrus lashed forward, screaming at the wolves. The leader of the caravan and two other men joined him.

The wolves moved back a few metres.

A few minutes went past; the wolves were heard howling from another side, approaching the caravan with mouths wide open. It was now clear the wolves would not go away until they'd got what they came for.

'Let's give them something to eat,' Cyrus suggested. 'Maybe then they will leave us and fight over the bait.'

The leader of the caravan unpacked a large bait of meat and threw it at the wolves.

One wolf took the bait and ran away fast. The other wolves, not satisfied with the unfairness of their colleague, chased the wolf with the bait, jumped on the unjust companion with full anger and violence. Struggling and fighting, one of the wolves succeeded in taking the bait from the mouth of the other, and ran away to make the bait its own. The other two did not give up, battling fiercely with the combative wolf, one pulling the bait, the other its tail.

Eventually, they left the bait aside and got engaged in a fierce battle with one another to resolve the conflict, to settle between themselves who had the right to possess the booty totally. The wolves were fighting and tearing at each other over the meat. They pulled one another's ears and tails, ripping flesh from their bodies.

The leader of the caravan said, 'Watch them eat one another. An animal does not eat its own kind. Wolves eat their own when wounded.'

The group watched in amazement as their battling sound and screaming faded away. The wolves destroyed one another, until there was only one wolf left with the meat. They had no sense of sharing. Each wanted the whole bait for itself.

As the caravan took off again for its journey, Cyrus was amazed at the similarity between wolves and men.

It took five days for the caravan to reach the small town

where they would continue their journey by car.

As the caravan moved into town, the group came across green pastures where herds of sheep and goats grazed on the mountain slope.

A gentle breeze came down on them, caressing Cyrus's face. He passed his hand across his face, dusting off the excess sand from his brow and eyelashes.

With his loose-fitting trousers, high-collared white shirt, a cashmere shawl around his waist and a turban covering his head, Cyrus looked like a tribesman. He rode on camelback and walked mile afer mile on foot for five days and nights. The caravan ended its long journey. But all the way he wondered what was happening to his world. Traditional values were collapsing, giving room for a new world, but still the traditionalists and fundamentalists were refusing to let new values set in. 'What sort of values will emerge from the chaos of our present-day society?' he wandered.

6.

A 747 took off heading toward Amsterdam, with a changeover to Prague. Cyrus couldn't stay in the country where he took refuge. He decided to move on to Czechoslovakia for two reasons: the cheap cost of living and his belief that there he might be more secure, compared to the United States, England or Germany.

On the plane, he was lost in thought, anxious about his new life in a country he knew little about. He could not speak the language and knew nothing about Czechoslovakia's customs or culture.

When the captain announced their arrival in Prague, Cyrus rubbed his eyes as if he'd woken from a deep sleep, and wondered for a few seconds where he was. He fastened his seat belt and looked through the porthole of the plane at the land below. But all was cloud for the next few minutes. And then, without warning, snow-covered land took his breath away. He was amazed at the scenery's beauty.

At last the plane landed.

On leaving the plane, he was greeted by two slim air stewardesses, who wished him a pleasant stay in Czechoslovakia.

Down the hallway from the airport's terminal, Cyrus eagerly glanced into the outside world. He noticed that snow had painted a beautiful white landscape in the middle of a cold winter. The snow hanging on the bare branches reminded him of home, when it sometimes snowed for days.

He left the warmth of the airport hall for the below-zero temperature of the street.

A cold wind blew, cutting through his bones, burning his eyes and face. He shivered, pulled up the collar of his raincoat, and wiped the tears from his eyes. His breath turned into steam. His nose was burning in freezing cold; he put down the two briefcases he was holding, and rubbed both hands on his nose. Then, once again ready to tackle his unknown destiny, he tried to maintain balance on the frozen pavement.

Taxis were lined up close to the airport terminal. He stepped into the first taxi in the rank.

He gave taxi driver a note with an address given to him by the tourist information bureau at the airport. The driver looked at the note and at Cyrus and drove off.

The taxi drove through narrow lanes and wide roads. Cyrus stared out through the window, coming to terms with the new country he had chosen to live in. Buildings were partly sooty, giving a melancholic impression.

In less than half an hour, the taxi pulled into a narrow, cobbled street, in front of a four-storey building. Cyrus paid the driver, thanked him, and stepped out of the taxi. He checked the number on the piece of paper he was given, walked up to the building and rang the bell.

Within thirty seconds, a middle-aged woman opened the door. Cyrus handed her a letter from the tourist information bureau. She scrutinized Cyrus from head to toe, as if assessing whether he was worthy of stepping inside her home. She talked to him in a foreign language he couldn't understand, and forced a smile, which looked more like a grimace.

Cyrus had arranged to rent a room in a family home. The rent was cheap, and he believed the neighbourhood to be safe.

The woman took him to his room without showing him the rest of the house. She left him alone to unpack his belongings.

Cyrus sat on the edge of the bed and circled the room with his eyes. This was his new home. This was what he had left his country for. A small barren room with an old wardrobe and a smelly mattress. And yet, he felt somehow fortunate that he had made it so far.

Before unpacking, he removed a photograph from the inside pocket of his raincoat. He stared at his family members in the picture, wondering if he would ever see them again. He kissed his mother on the picture, feeling tightness in his throat. Too upset to continue looking, he placed the picture back inside his raincoat.

Then, knowing he was not in a rush to do anything, he lay on the bed with his clothes and shoes on, hands clasped beneath his head, wondering what in the world he was going to do all by himself in a country he didn't know. His eyes remained fixed on the ceiling, thinking of his uncertain future.

He was sleepless during the first night. Anxiety tormented him. His mind was restless as if a shadow was following him. The slightest sound or movement startled him. He could not feel secure in a house he didn't know anything about. He knew it would take a little while for him to feel at home, but still he couldn't help feeling jumpy every time he heard a noise in the house.

Finally, some time after midnight, he turned the light of his room off, but still sleep wouldn't come. The walls around him, the pictures and the door made him feel strange and uncomfortable.

In the darkness, his eyes focused on the door, as if he expected someone to burst into the room at any moment, gun in hand, pointing it at his head, with his finger on the trigger.

At around two in the morning, just when he was about to fall asleep, a shadow crept past his window, sending a jolt throughout his body. The first thing which came to mind was that *they* had found him. How could they have found him so quickly, especially now that he was in another country?

He jumped out of bed and sneaked to the window. The shadow shifted to one side and disappeared. Gently he pulled aside the drapes, and stealthily and cautiously he glanced out of the window to see who it was. The shadow moved away. He looked at it more closely. The shadow was nothing more than a stray dog which disappeared into a dark lane.

He felt relief that it was a dog and not a human being. He laughed at himself for being so paranoid. He still hadn't got used to the idea that there was very little chance anyone would find him.

He stared attentively through the window at the full moon in the dark sky. The city was asleep, drowning in heavy silence. Darkness had taken over every corner of every street. People were sleeping in their tiny houses and flats, snoring, lost in the land of dreams.

In Czechoslovakia, Cyrus led a quiet life, isolated from the outside world. His life was a sort of self-imprisonment. He knew he was a free man then and could do anything he wanted, but somehow he felt more like a prisoner than at any other time. His room was the size of a prison cell and turned out like a solitary prison. He was his own jailor. He enacted the rules and regulations of self-imprisonment, not allowing himself to be out at night, to go to clubs or parties, to stroll in town during the night or establish a meaningful friendship with anyone. He was very strict in following his rules and regulations, which he'd created more out of fear of being found than fear of belonging.

At night, he pulled the curtain of his room over the entire window, fearing someone might be watching him while he was reading. He couldn't help wondering if one day bullets would shatter the small window of his room and aim straight for his heart. He feared dying that way. An unknown man killed by an unknown assassin, the morning newspaper would read.

If he had to die, he would rather to do it in public, in front of a crowd and for a worthwhile reason. Many times he visualised himself standing brave and erect on the gallows to be executed. 'You can shoot me, but you cannot stop the process of global unification,' would be his last words before they'd drag him to the gallows to be executed.

When tired of reading, he'd turn the light of his room off, pull the curtain to one side, and sit in an armchair, staring at the twinkling stars in the dark sky, pondering over the mystery of the universe. A creation with no frontiers and no limits. The idea appealed to him.

At other times, he thought about his homeland, remembering the place where he spent his childhood, where he used to walk, play and run in the mountains, valleys, and along the river banks. He remembered the flowers, especially the scented roses, the mountains and the fountains of his homeland. He remembered only the beautiful things about his country, and chose to forget the horrors of civil unrest. In Europe, his country was known as 'the land of rose and nightingale'. Sometimes, alone in the darkness, engulfed by loneliness and melancholy, he whispered to himself, 'no more red roses bloom, no more nightingales sing love songs to fill the air with hope and joy'.

And he used to remember the college he taught at, and the students, who were dear to his heart, especially those who had risked their lives to save his. The memories of his loved ones brought tears to his eyes.

In his new country, he didn't want anyone to recognise him or know where he came from. He didn't want to be asked why he lived in Czechoslovakia. Since he could not speak the language, no one could bother him with questioning.

One day, he entered a small boutique where someone spoke English.

'Where do you come from?' the shopkeeper asked.

'Me?' replied Cyrus, a look of concern crossing his face. 'I live in Prague. It's a beautiful city. Don't you think so? How long have you lived in Prague?' And he changed the topic rapidly, leading the shopkeeper into a new conversation.

He decided if somebody would ask him where he came from, he would only give them the name of the small town where he was born, hoping it would mean nothing to them.

Cyrus visited a museum in Prague. The museum guide spoke fluent English, but his knowledge of geography was scattered.

When the guide asked Cyrus where he came from, Cyrus gave him the name of his birth town.

The guide believed the town to be a country he had never heard of, so he decided to seize the opportunity to increase his knowledge of geography.

'Could you tell me exactly where is this place you came from?' asked the guide.

Cyrus was confused and embarrassed. He mumbled on purpose, pretending he didn't understand the question.

But that only increased the guide's curiosity. He was now determined to find out where Cyrus came from. He rushed to his office and fetched pen and paper. 'Please, draw me a sketch of where you come from.'

Cyrus didn't know how to get out of the situation. He wanted to tell the guide that it was none of his business, but he couldn't be so rude after the guide had been so polite to him. So instead, he would have to lie, which he was reluctant to do.

He took the piece of paper the guide handed to him and scribbled a bad sketch, with the name of three countries and said, 'my homeland is somewhere close to the borders of those countries.'

The guide looked at the sketch, his brow creasing. And

then, a relaxed look crossed his face. It looked as if he had given up. 'Thanks for giving me those details. I was always weak at geography back at school.'

Cyrus felt a great sense of relief, but was also ashamed that he had lied to the guide. His shame grew even stronger when the guide offered him a drink.

Cyrus sipped his Coke and turned to the guide. 'You know, the names of countries are not all that important.'

'What is that?'

'Well, borders don't really exist. It's a man-made thing. The only thing borders do is promote racism, a bit like religious fanaticism.'

The guide puzzled over Cyrus's comment. 'I guess you're right in a way. Wars are fought over land most of the time.'

Cyrus went on, 'The earth is but one country and mankind its citizens.' The guide's eyes flashed showing interest. Cyrus continued, 'As long as man promotes national prejudice and fights in the name of country, conflict between nations will be never-ending. What we need is a world free of military nationalism, free of prejudice.'

'It's a nice concept,' commented the guide. 'An end to six thousand years of war and violence.'

'I believe it is the future for mankind. Love, peace and harmony.'

Cyrus grew a beard to change his look. He didn't really like beards because in the past he had found people who wore them to be fanatical and violent. But he knew this was not always true, and wearing a beard would prove him wrong.

One beautiful morning, at the city's market, Cyrus noticed a black-bearded man staring into his eyes. Cyrus avoided eye contact with the man, but the man persisted, and Cyrus knew he was trying to provoke him.

Cyrus felt uncomfortable and began to worry. What in the world did this man want from him?

Anxious, Cyrus crossed the market, and raced to the bus stop.

But the man was following him.

Cyrus increased his pace, trying hard to lose the stranger. Who the hell was that man? Was it someone who knew him? Someone who wanted to kill him?

Suddenly, Cyrus turned into a narrow lane, hoping he had lost the stranger in the crowd. But the bearded stranger turned into the same lane. Cyrus felt his heart pounding in his chest. He knew now this had to be a bad thing. Why in the world would a total stranger follow him in a country where he knew no one?

Half way up the lane, Cyrus turned into another street. He had to hide. The black-bearded man followed him in the lane and walked faster. The game of hide-and-seek continued. Cyrus sneaked between a doorframe and the sidewall, and saw the shadow of the black-bearded man approaching. He held his breath, hoping the man hadn't seen him.

The stranger raced past him.

Cyrus stayed against the door for a full minute before moving.

When he stepped out from his hiding spot, the man was no where to be seen. Cyrus rushed to the main street and jumped into a taxi.

When he arrived home, he had to give all the money in his pocket to the taxi driver. It made him bitter to have wasted some of his meagre money on a taxi fare, a luxury he could not afford.

He wondered why he had been so scared of the stranger. Maybe the man just wanted to ask him a question. After all, one shouldn't judge a person merely by the way he looks, and yet Cyrus had just done that. He immediately assumed the man was going to harm him because of the look in his eyes.

Cyrus looked at himself in the mirror and decided that he really didn't like the beard. And now he was also scared that the strange man would recognise him.

He rushed to the barber to have his beard and hair cut. When he got rid of his beard, and looked at himself in the mirror, he was surprised at how young he appeared. He looked like a young boy.

When he arrived home, the landlady didn't recognise him straight away. There was fear in her eyes before he managed to explain who he was. Cyrus felt embarrassed and said in English, 'I'm Cyrus, your tenant.' His gesture and smile, and his glittering eyes made her assured that it was indeed not an intruder but her tenant. When she did recognise him, she laughed and said something in Czech. Cyrus thought that if he had managed to fool the landlady, whom he saw everyday, then he would be able to fool the bearded stranger who followed him from the market.

But the short hair and clean-shaven face didn't last forever. Cyrus changed his appearance every few weeks, by letting his hair and beard grow, and shaving again, by changing his style of clothes, by wearing various kinds of sunglass. Sometimes he wore a cap, sometimes a hat. He got used to his chameleon attitude and became easily bored with the same look for too long.

Self-imprisonment added to the agony of self-exile. It was hard to be alive without being seen, to pretend one didn't exist.

Cyrus remained in Czechoslovakia for nine months, every day worrying what he was doing in this country and where his life was heading. And without a job, the days seemed endless and futile. He had no friends, and his thoughts kept drifting back to his homeland. As a remedy for his loneliness, he spent many hours reading books.

Like many refugees, he knew he was the victim of politics. He was an innocent man, who had to live in exile, every day filled with anxiety and agony.

At times like these, he almost wished he was back home, helping the students he loved so much further their education.

He remembered that when he left the college, he had been voted the students' favourite lecturer. That had meant a lot to him.

Often, when he was alone in his room, he recalled his students' faces and wondered what they were up to now. Had they finished their studies? Did some of them get executed or tortured? Were they in prison? The thought that something horrific had happened to them brought tears to his eyes.

Months went by uneventfully. No one tried to track him down or kill him. But he was not quite sure yet. As time went by, Cyrus gained confidence that he could begin a new life.

7.

The train left Slovakia behind and crossed the border to Budapest. Heading toward another country unknown to him, Cyrus was sitting in the train. An inspector stepped into the carriage and demanded his passport. Cyrus realised that the train had entered the land of Hungary. Night had already fallen. He stood at the window and tried to look out to see his new home. He pressed his nose against the glass and cupped his eyes, but he could not figure out anything. He did not see any difference, but the same darkness. He sank back in his seat, thinking about his future life. He hoped to find a teaching position in Hungary. He arrived at Budapest Central Station at 11.02 p.m.

Cyrus used to walk along the Danube River bank in Budapest. It was his favourite pastime to sit on the terrace of a cafe facing the river and watch the sun play on the water. The river looked so calm, one could believe it was a lake.

One day at sunset, Cyrus was pacing along the banks of the river, absorbed in his thoughts. He was thinking how the world could be a better place to live, how it could be disentangled from various fetters. As he did so, he noticed the golden sun vanishing into the horizon, its rays caressing for the last time that day the surface of the water. In little time, the river changed from gold to amber, and finally to grey and dark blue.

A flight of birds crossed the sky, making their way towards the sunset, their feathers coloured orange from the last rays of the sun. Cyrus stood still, watching the birds on their journey. As the birds made their way to a new day, looking for peace and shelter, Cyrus's mind filled with philosophical thoughts. *Some day, if God may, man will find a new direction in his heart. One day, if God may, the world will be powered by love and not overshadowed by greed. One day, if God may, brutal materialism will change into spiritualism.*

Cyrus stood still, watching the river and its surroundings.

It was darkening. He was thinking how materialism had given man a narrow view of life's meaning. It had simplified everything into profit and loss, inventing hollow theories and a shallow philosophy for man's existence, neglecting God's gift to his children: love.

Staying in Hungary provided Cyrus with inner peace and the confidence that he would find meaning in his life. By looking within, through meditations and prayers, Cyrus found the rays of the Holy Spirit in his heart, the power to carry on and make his life a worthwhile venture.

In Czechoslovakia, Cyrus had isolated himself from the outside world. It took him a long time to overcome his fear of persecution.

But now that he was in Hungary, he decided to live life again, like a flower blossoming in spring.

One night, Cyrus was listening to a section of a radio program from overseas broadcasting the news of his homeland. He heard a report that shook him beyond words. Nine girls, believers in a new emerging faith, had been hanged in a southern town of his homeland. The announcer added, 'The youngest one, who was seventeen, when she stood on the gallows to be hanged, kissed the noose before placing it around her neck. The other eight girls followed her example.'

Immediately, Cyrus felt a jolt in his heart. A dark grief consumed his soul, letting tears stream down his face like a child. He could not believe this kind of atrocity was still going on. He knew in his heart that all the girls ever wanted to do was proclaim peace and equality for all. The tragedy touched the depths of his emotion. He sensed something celestial in their willingness to give their life for their faith. They reminded him of the early martyrs of the Christian faith.

Cyrus turned off the radio, walked up to the window of his bedroom, and watched the rain splash against the window pane. It was grey and wet everywhere. Lightning flashed in the distance, and thunder cracked and clapped, shaking the foundation of Cyrus's home.

'Oh, God!' he screamed to the heavens above, 'When will your wrath burn into ashes the tyrants of the world?' He went down on his knees and cried for hours.

A year would pass before he'd learn that the two men who hanged the girls gave their resignation immediately after the hanging. They'd been deeply moved by the young girls' courage and faith. They went to the girls' funeral, shedding tears profusely. They beat their heads hard with their hands, and hit their heads against the wall, crying, 'we have hanged nine young brides.' The relatives forgot their sorrows and got engaged in solacing the executioners. But they seemed inconsolable.

Every night someone placed flowers on the doorsteps of the homes of where the girls used to live. At first no one knew who had left the flowers. But one night, the brother of one of the girls decided to stay up and find out who that person could be. In a dark room on the second floor, he stood at the window staring out. It was before dawn that he noticed a shadow approached the house. He looked more closely. It was a man creeping slowly and cautiously, looking around to make sure no one could see him. The brother recognised the person. He was one of the two executioners.

The executioners were moved when they witnessed the

young girls giving their lives voluntarily for what they had found; but the world continued to rotate in a spiritual vacuum.

Newspapers around the world paid little attention to the hanging of the nine girls. So, when Cyrus found a newspaper running a story on the execution of the girls, he brought it home to read.

There was a drawing, an artist's impression, with the article, showing nine young girls standing in a line, waiting for their turn to be hanged. The caption read, "Nine young girls sang and prayed on their way to the gallows."

The article read, "The nine young women were followers of what is known as the New Faith. No less than twenty thousand believers have voluntarily given their lives to prove the truth of their faith. Rather than enjoying freedom from persecution, they stood up for their beliefs."

It continued. "The New Faith began in the spring of 1844, but, like the major religions, it faced severe opposition and horrific persecution for its followers. Believers were imprisoned, plundered, executed, hanged and burned alive. In spite of the opposition, the New Faith, heralding the birth of a global and spiritual civilisation, has now spread to over 120,000 localities in 132 countries and territories, from Vancouver in Canada to Tasmania in Australia."

For days, Cyrus couldn't wipe out from his mind the faces of the young girls from the newspaper drawing. His world was engulfed in grief for those young women he never knew but felt so much love toward. He was obsessed with their courage and spiritual ardour. Any horizon he stared at, he saw the young girls standing on the gallows, kissing the noose before putting the rope round their necks to be hanged.

One evening, when Cyrus walked along the bank of the Danube River, he saw something which strengthened his faith.

The sun was setting on the far horizon while Cyrus looked across the river. In the distance he could hear a Hungarian waltz being played from a nearby cafe. As he kept staring blankly at the river, he saw nine young girls dancing to the tune of the waltz. They seemed joyful, smiling and dancing in ecstasy. But they also seemed to be floating on water.

Cyrus rubbed his eyes and tried to focus on what he was seeing, but there was no doubt in his mind. Those were the nine girls whom he'd seen in the newspaper. He became absorbed in the dance of martyrs. A celestial and uplifing dance. He stood still, dumbfounded, too excited to say a word.

The girls were alive, dancing joyfully. They were so real that Cyrus stepped forward to join them. But as he made his way toward the river, they rose in the air and vanished into the darkness of the night.

Cyrus glanced around to see if anyone else had seen the dancing girls. But the people around him seemed only interested in making it home for supper.

Perplexed and stunned, Cyrus stood for a while, staring at the dark river, wondering what was the meaning of this apparition. Before vanishing into the darkness, the girls looked back, smiled and beckoned at him to follow them. And then he felt shame upon his soul. The young women had clearly told him that if he wanted to change the world, he could not hold back in fear of his life. He had to carry his own cross on his shoulders, as they had done.

As darkness took over the city, Cyrus knew he would

have to change. He knew he would have to try harder to change the world instead of just complaining about it.

8.

Still feeling strongly attached to his homeland, Cyrus wished to go back to the country where he grew up, to where his mother, relatives and friends lived.

A letter from his mother had informed him that there was a bounty on his head, and the revolutionary guards were searching for him in any lane where his shadow had once been seen. And if he went home, they'd arrest him at the airport and would take him directly to the gallows.

Living away did not break Cyrus's attachment to his home. Home was always in his heart. There wasn't a day that went past without his thinking about his homeland. He had crossed his homeland's border, but not the boundary of his culture. He breathed in the atmosphere and moved within the walls of his own world.

One day, standing in front of a mirror, he looked into his own eyes. They were sad. His reflection smiled back sadly. He pondered on how lonely he was.

His homeland was still in political unrest with no end of the conflicts in sight. The typhoon blew mercilessly and shook the foundation of his homeland. It was not a short storm to be followed by calmness.

He wished to settle somewhere on this planet. He felt that he needed to move on.

Cyrus preferred to make his new home a third world country, a place where he could help his fellow man, but all his application letters were either rejected or remained unanswered. There was no guarentee of a job for him in those countries.

He knew he would have to settle for a civilised Western culture. But he hesitated to apply for refugee status, although he was aware that Albert Einstein, the great physicist, arrived in the United States as a refugee. Cyrus had to choose between the United States, Canada and Australia. After six months of painful dilemma, Cyrus chose Australia and applied for a permanent visa.

Four weeks after the interview, during a cool morning Cyrus arrived in Sydney. Sitting in a huge black Mercedenz Benz, he was driven to some prearranged accommodation. Staring at the pale sunlight spread on the walls of the buildings, he was surprised to notice that many people lived in villa houses, in contrast to the crowded residential buildings in Europe where the majority lived in block apartments.

Within a few weeks, he found Australia to be a multicultural society where people from every country shared their cultures and knowledge. The various cultures made him think of a garden filled with flowers of hundreds of shades, each different, but all part of the whole.

Cyrus found Australians friendly and helpful. The level of courtesy impressed him in his new and permanent home. When he walked the streets, one could see his shining eyes and a gentle smile of joy on his lips. People smiled and he received back the vibration of love emanating from his soul. They did not possess the look of hatred he had seen in so many people back home. Cyrus had never been so happy in his life. He even told someone that for a long time he believed that angels had dark hair and dark eyes, but now he believed they had blond hair and blue eyes.

One day, while Cyrus was driving to a friend's place, traffic suddenly came to a halt on both sides of the road. He stretched his head from the window to see what was going on. He saw a man, who had no police uniform or cap, standing in the middle of the street, ordering all the vehicles to stop. He wondered what was the reason the cars had to stop in the middle of the street, where there was no crossroad or T-junction. The attitude of the self-assumed traffic officer and the drivers of the vehicles made him guess that a great personage was supposed to cross the road. He thought the Prime Minister; a president or a king from overseas had to cross the street. On the other hand, how they could stop all the vehicles in the middle of a road?

Suddenly there was a hush. He thought the great personage must be approaching the street to cross. Finally, Cyrus got out of his car to find out what was going on. He saw something that he could not believe. He rubbed his eyes and looked more closely. A big snake had decided to go from one side of the road to another. With great self-esteem and self-confidence, the snake crawled slowly, glanced at both sides, thanked the waiting drivers and the passengers for their patience, and smiled for their kindness. The drivers smiled back. He noticed all the drivers were smiling.

Cyrus got back in his car, amazed that people in Australia took the time to protect an animal. He wished those who kill people like flies knew that even a snake had the right to live. He wished that no human could kill another human being, neither for war, nor for revenge, nor for a difference in political views, nor for religious beliefs.

Cyrus placed his hat on his face not to be burnt by the sun. He stretched his hands and feet and took a deep breath. Lying down on the beach on the south coast of New South Wales, he felt himself to be the happiest person on the beach. He was sure no one could realise how pleased he was to be sunbathing. Others were used to a life of freedom, where everything was available just for the asking.

He sat up. Capping his eyes, he stared at the ocean. Many young girls and boys were playing with the waves, surfing and swimming. He wondered if those people knew how lucky they were. He wondered if they were aware of the miseries taking place in other countries right at that very moment. Did they know that their forefathers fighting against terrible odds had gained the freedom they were enjoying?

But within a year, Cyrus realised people were just people, no matter where in the world they came from. Those happy smiling faces which greeted him when he first came to Australia were more of a courtesy. Many people were not as happy as they first seemed. There was a spiritual starvation in many men and women he met. The amount of wealth and freedom in his new country didn't reflect people's level of happiness.

It didn't take long for Cyrus to establish a strong friendship with a young man by the name of Yasha. He found Yasha sensitive, pleasant and open-minded. And Yasha liked Cyrus because of his forwardness, honesty and kindness.

Chapter Three

FLIGHT

It was dark, the darkest hour before dawn. The airliner winged through the air like an eagle, heading for its destination, flashing above a gloomy ocean. It was carrying among its passengers a group of tourists going to East Africa through Singapore. It was a long journey from Sydney to Nairobi. After a short time the muffled chatting of sleepy passengers hushed. And the gentle voices of flight attendants were not heard any more. The lights were turned off. Here and there a few reading lamps were still on.

Some members of the group fell asleep. Yasha and Devi tried to keep themselves awake, but Cyrus and Gloria were fully alert. They were among the tourists going to Africa, continuing on a trip to Europe. They were from different ethnic backgrounds and had the effect of a bunch of flowers of various shades of colour. Gloria was from an Italian background. Cyrus met her at an intercontinental conference in Europe and was impressed by her beauty and bearing, but never had a chance to talk to her.

Gloria sat down in the front row on Cyrus's left. With a sweet smile on her lips, she stretched her head slightly from behind the chair and glanced bashfully at Cyrus. Her beautiful blue eyes were expressive of a tender feeling. Her face was partly covered with long black hair curling slightly at the end.

Cyrus was the most attractive man that Gloria had ever met. He had a charming face and slightly curly dark brown hair. His eyes sparkled like two stars with magnetic effect. His face, especially his eyes, disclosed anything that passed through his mind. His outer facial expression registered his inner feeling. His eyes smiled before his lips with a light of joy.

When Cyrus met Gloria's smiling face, he smiled back. Then, he turned down his head and sank in his seat, absorbed in ecstatic thoughts.

Gloria avoided eye contact with Cyrus's piercing black eyes and dropped her head down with a girlish shyness. Snapshots of Cyrus laughing heartily came to her mind. She wondered what was the source of his upliftment and blissful joy. How he could laugh so frequently while being surrounded by the threats of a troubled age. It seemed he derived his ecstatic delight from a somewhat celestial source, above the turmoil and agony of an ailing age. His ringing voice penetrated her heart when he was talking about human suffering.

Yasha was a tall, slim young man with darkish skin and long black hair reaching his shoulders. He was sitting next to Cyrus, his face showing intermittent flashes of hope, but was mostly wrapped in gloomy thoughts. Yasha knew Cyrus and had heard him expressing his views on some occasions. He did not like darkness and anxiously awaited daybreak. He stared through the window, then suddenly turned to Cyrus and whispered in a depressed tone, 'It's very dark. I can't see anything.'

'Yes, it is. It's the darkest hour before dawn.'

'I hope the day breaks soon.'

Cyrus looked through the window and saw the faint streaks of the daybreak in the far-off horizon. He stretched his head towards Yasha, pulled up his eyebrows and whispered into Yasha's ears with joy as if disclosing a great secret.

'The day is breaking!'

Yasha glanced through the window hoping to find a light chasing away the saddening thick darkness, but he did not see any light to remove his agonising despair.

'No light. Everything is plunged in gloom.'

'You should look at the dawning place.'

'The dawning place? Where's that?'

'The East,' answered Cyrus.

Yasha looked through the window again and tried to locate the dawning place, but failed.

'I can't locate the dawning place. It's too difficult to locate it when one's up in the air. I give up.'

'Don't give up. Do try. To see the first dim light even on the far-off horizon gives you hope and joy. The thick darkness doesn't frighten you any longer.'

'My heart beats at the expectation of the sunrise,' said Yasha. 'But I can't even see the faintest light of the dawn.'

'Be patient. Be alert. You'll see the break of day!'

Yasha sank in his seat, trying to keep himself awake to observe the first glimmer of the sun. He yearned to see the gorgeous scene when the first streaks of sun chase away the retreating darkness.

Most passengers fell asleep. The depressing night had plunged everything into darkness. The effect of the hope-creating conversation with Cyrus did not last long. The death-like silence weighed down in Yasha's heart. The snoring of the passengers was harrowing, not soothing to his painful yearning heart.

Sitting quietly, Cyrus was occupied with his thoughts on

the torpid psychological climate of the human world: yearning and rejecting. A loud voice was echoing in the depths of his soul: 'Why does parading for peace turn into marching for war overnight? Talks for peace sound like the noise of a cistern. All hopes fail to materialise. Good will for peace withers in the bud. After all, is peace a reality or a delusion? The world is rotating like a close-eyed camel used for grinding seeds. The camel has the illusion that it is marching forward, but whenever it opens its eyes, it finds itself on the same spot.'

Then Cyrus opened his eyes and looked around. All the passengers were deeply asleep, except a few. He nestled in his seat and continued pondering over the human situation. Sadness shadowed his face. He thought: 'The youth are pessimistic. They have no plan or enthusiasm for building their future world. The older generation has lost hope and trust. The human world has become vulnerable and impotent as if we are entrapped in a blighted land with no way out.' He took a deep breath, and a strong resisting attitude was aroused in him. He wanted to get up and speak at the highest pitch of his voice to wake up all the snoring, sleeping passengers. He muttered in a protesting mood: 'No, no, we aren't doomed to a frightful fate. How long should we moan and groan within the walls of a collapsing building? Let's move out or prop it up. We shouldn't stay, waiting to be buried under its rubble. If we see a threatening catastrophe approaching, why not to make an effort to avoid it?'

He suddenly turned to Yasha and whispered, 'Yasha! The world is pregnant.'

Yasha was wrapped in his thoughts. He did not hear him well. 'What? Who is pregnant?'

'The world! The world is pregnant.'

'The world! Oh, I see. So, it's pregnant with what?'

'Terrible events, a clash, a big clash between the old and the new.'

'Which one is going to win?' asked Yasha.

'The old is in the throes of death, but still it emits smoke and ashes from its belly.'

'Let's look on the bright side.'

'We have to experience the operation of the dark forces,' said Cyrus. 'But there is a bright side as well. New world order is struggling to be born. But it cannot get out of the clutches of the old one.'

'You mean the new world order that some politicians are talking about?'

'No, not at all. They are trying to clothe the old dying order in a new name.'

Yasha grinned, 'You mean they don't understand what they say. They are not aware of the implications of the new world order?'

Cyrus stared at Yasha and remained thoughtful for a while. 'We can appreciate that they are after something new. At least they use the term "new world order". But, what I have in mind is a new dynamic, organic and challenging world order.'

A flash shone through Yasha's thoughts and his eyes sparkled with excitement. 'I'm not sure what your new world order is about, but what I do know, is that this present world order clothed, as you say, in a new name is what we don't need. I would like to see a new world order which deals with the issues of poverty, injustice in all its forms, human rights and freedom. Yes, I agree that some sort of challenging and dynamic world order is needed. I think we should help with its realisation.'

Cyrus was moved by the statement. He took Yasha's hands into his and pressed them affectionately.

'O, Yasha! O, dear Yasha! The world needs many like you. The more, the better.'

Chapter Four

NAIROBI

1.

It was a long and tiresome journey with a short stopover in Singapore. The airport hall was warm and stuffy. Officials and workers seemed friendly, with shining eyes and broad smiles exposing white teeth against their dark skin. No one was in a rush. The travellers soon took on the same mood, influenced by the warm and inviting atmosphere.

Carrying their suitcases and looking pleasant and happy, Yasha and Cyrus stepped out of the airport shoulder to shoulder as they took their first steps on the soil of the African continent.

Sitting next to Cyrus in the bus, Yasha pulled up the window and a cool, pleasant sea breeze wafted in and caressed their faces. He stared up at the sky. The day was breaking. A few patches of fluffy cloud were floating in the air. The bus passed between some isolated huts and houses, and flowers were hanging over many of the walls on both sides of the street. They were magnificently bright. Gradually the modern, tall buildings of downtown Nairobi came into view.

Yasha turned to Cyrus. 'The city seems to have been well-planned and designed.'

'That's right.'

Yasha stared out of the window, 'Look, the girls and young ladies are quite shapely! They walk gracefully in their colourful dresses.'

'What did you expect to see,' teased Cyrus, 'nude men on the tops of palm trees?'

'Yes, something of that sort.' Yasha dropped his head in deep thought. He felt a sense of shame, for he had believed somewhere in his unconscious psyche that the coloured people were less talented than the white ones.

Cyrus exhaled deeply. 'It's sad to think that God allows discrimination among his creatures. He has given potential talents to all the races with equality and equity.'

The bus driver pulled up sharply and the passengers' heads were thrown back.

'Take all your personal belongings with you and follow me,' said the local guide. 'Leave your luggage and suitcases. The porter will bring them in.'

The hotel was situated in a beautiful valley between two high hills outside Nairobi. It was a quiet spot, away from the clamour of the big cities and was surrounded by bushes.

Before stepping into the hotel, Cyrus held his hand over his eyes and stared down into the bottom of the valley. A stream was running there, making a soothing, musical sound.

In the early morning, Cyrus glanced over the variety of fruits set out in rows, the abundance of fresh natural juices, and an enormous American breakfast. He went around the table filling his plate.

A hospitable Italian middle-aged man ran the hotel. He was going to and fro ordering here, instructing there, to provide the best service he could to make his customers satisfied. His business was his whole life and his character had been moulded by his job.

The meals were included in the package tour. When Cyrus sat at the table for lunch at noon, he realised that the afternoon and evening meals consisted of four courses with a variety of choices at each course. His eyes swept across the table and he saw the customers filling and refilling their plates again and again with a great voracity.

To enjoy such plenitude gave Cyrus a vague feeling of guilt, but he did not know why. He had done nothing wrong. He had paid and he had the right to enjoy his meals. He tried to indulge in eating and drinking as much as he could.

Whenever he looked at the abundance of food and drinks, the skinny faces and dimly lit eyes of starving people appeared in his mind, disturbing his sensual enjoyment. He tried to forget them and indulge himself, but he could not help thinking about the conditions in which they lived. He could not justify such a contrast.

Wearing decorations around their ankles, wrists and necks, the tall, slim, well-built and good-looking Mombasa tribe performers jumped up a few metres in the air in a straight line and came down exactly on the same spot.

It was on the following day that the group was taken to an amphitheatre to watch a performance by Mombasa tribesmen organised to entertain tourists. There were no rows of benches, no entrances and no exits. It was in the open air, surrounded by conical huts of mud and wattle.

Back at the hotel, Cyrus got off the bus and walked through a narrow, twisted path leading to the entrance of the hotel. He stood and glanced over the flowering shrubs and palms on both sides of the path. He stared up at the western horizon. The sun was setting. The faint sunlight reflected in the fountains in the pond was fascinating. The sun plunged into a purple cloud mixed with pale rays. The reddish clouds paled and gradually lost colour, and turned grey, then black.

2.

Devi entered a cosy room to eat her supper. Her eyes swept over the walls decorated with skins of leopards, zebras and gazelles, and the horns of bulls and stags. A stuffed lion, standing alert in the attack position, was in the corner of the room close to the door. Soft music filled the pleasantly warm room. Wearing a dress of African style, she took a seat at the table in the corner of the room near the window so that she could see outside. The sun touched the edge of the horizon and disappeared behind an unknown cliff. The surrounding hills, valleys and bushes gradually plunged into darkness.

Cupping her chin in her right palm, she was absorbed in mystical thoughts. She had broken ties with narrow-minded religious fundamentalists and developed a tendency towards the occult and mystical schools of thought. She was tending to take refuge in the eerie labyrinth of the supernatural. She had acquired an extraordinary outlook, sometimes not in harmony with reason and science.

Devi had heard much about Africa, how the lions and wild animals roam through the jungles at night. She wished she could walk barefooted in the bush at night to feel Africa. She was at peace with all animals. She had a deep sense of sympathy with all creatures in the jungle, but she was not sure that wild animals would have the same sympathy towards her. She smiled with satisfaction. *I'll find a way to visit these places and people,* she thought.

'Excuse me, I would like to visit some places where I can really see the African way of life,' said Devi. 'Can you suggest how I can go about doing this?'

The hotel receptionist raised her head and stared at a slender young lady with brownish skin standing with her elbow on the counter. She had propped up her chin in her hand and looking at the ceiling.

The receptionist frowned in deep thought and suddenly with a burst of joy lifted her eyebrows and said, 'There's a big wedding ceremony of the son of chief in a suburb nearby tomorrow night. You may go and see that one. Are you with other friends?'

'Yes, I am. But how can we get there?'

'No worries. We'll arrange it for you.'

The flames of fire were blazing in the middle of an open field surrounded with scattered huts and houses. A number of black men and women were dancing around the fire. They were leaping through the flames, jumping in the air, lifting their feet in a great primitive burst of mirth. They joined in circles, then one by one jumped and whirled in turn. There was a natural rhythmic grace in their movements.

Devi yearned to experience that genuine primitive mirth. Without being invited, she joined the dancers, laughing loudly, and tried to imitate the African dance. A middle-aged lady approached Devi and started to dance with her and indicated to her how to dance.

Gloria, Cyrus, Julia and Yasha were standing with other Africans laughing and clapping. Victor and Peter had not shown any interest in seeing an African wedding ceremony and had decided to stay in the hotel.

Gradually the ice melted and the distance between Africans and the strangers in their midst narrowed. The Africans felt comfortable and happy with a sense of pride that these white people had joined their wedding ceremony.

A beautiful and shapely African girl with smiling eyes and lips approached Cyrus and pulled him into the dance. He did not refuse. He laughed and started to dance with her.

Julia and Yasha decided to dance too. They whirled and whirled with great joy and mirth. Yasha leaped over the fire. Julia attempted to jump but her skirt got in the way. She hesitated and burst out laughing.

Gloria was watching, laughing and clapping. The girl who was dancing with Cyrus approached Gloria and suggested she dance with Cyrus. Gloria hesitated and tried to excuse herself but the girl pulled her forward. With girlish shyness Gloria started to dance while avoiding eye contact with Cyrus. She was looking at the ground as if she was dancing by herself.

The Africans treated them as though they were their close and long-term friends, and did their best to keep them happy and make them feel at home. They demonstrated the spirit of togetherness, hospitality and sharing of African culture.

They left the matrimonial ceremony to go back to the hotel. When they reached the Land Rover parked on the side of the dusty road they turned back and stared at the ceremony. The rising and falling of the feet of black men and women in the dim light of the fire resembled the dance of ghosts in the bush. Their flickering shadows danced with the flame of the fire blazing in the background.

3.

Cyrus left the hotel and walked around observing the lifestyle of the African people. He passed by many conical huts of mud and wattle. Wherever he met people they nodded, smiled and gestured to show their respect for him in response to his smile.

A young couple sitting on the doorstep of their hut invited him into their home. He accepted their invitation and sat down on a mat covering a part of the floor. When they smiled their faces were illuminated. There was simplicity and innocence in their shining eyes.

Two children came in and timidly approached Cyrus and sat down close to him. They studied Cyrus a long time without saying a word. To them, he appeared an interesting creature. They had never seen such a creature, a white man. They examined him curiously, trying to guess from which jungle he might have run away. Because of his attitude and loving smile, they felt he was not as savage and wild as they expected him to be.

The hostess offered him two boiled eggs, which was all she could provide. Cyrus ate one to make them happy and gave the children well-decorated pens as gifts to use later when they grew up. It pained him to see people living in such primitive conditions. It was agonising to see such a wide gap. In one part of the planet some people didn't have enough bread to eat while in another part they threw away half of their daily meal. How could it be accepted that one part of humanity lived in humiliating poverty, and another part lived in sickening opulence?

He left the hut and continued to walk. All the way he was thinking: those who contributed to technological and scientific advances had no intention of making the rich richer, rather they wanted to make life better for every human being living on this planet. They did not dedicate their lives to science so that the fruits of their hard work would give more power to the already powerful and enslave the poor nations and impoverish them.

He stepped into a small shop selling soft drinks. Five

beautiful young women sitting lazily in the rear casually glanced at him and smiled. Their faces registered innocence, simplicity and naivety.

He asked the owner of the shop, 'Where are these ladies from?'

'They're of different nationalities.'

'Who are they?'

'They're my wives,' smiled the shopkeeper.

'Oh! I see. That's interesting.'

Cyrus could not understand how a man with such meagre resources could manage to support five young women. He realised that in certain African countries the husband was not obliged to support his wives financially. The women supported themselves and the children.

He bought a bottle of Coke and left the shop. The exploitative attitude of the male and submissive attitude of females in underdeveloped countries saddened his heart. On the way he was talking to himself, almost outloud: 'How long are females, such delicate creatures, to be exploited, humiliated, subjected to man's injustice and dominance?'

The sun was burning and he walked, sweating profusely, until he reached a big tree where he took refuge in the cool shade. He inhaled a deep breath, enjoying the pleasant coolness. The sea breeze wafted, caressing his face and drying the beads of sweat on his forehead.

A few boys playing around noticed a white man sitting under the tree. Smiling broadly, they approached him and circled around him. He was not embarrassed but rather curious to study their manner and behaviour. They did not look on him as an unknown, dangerous stranger. They did not suspect him of being an exploiter in the guise of an explorer. He believed Africans and indigenous people in many parts of the world paid a heavy price for their genuinely welcoming and friendly attitude. Often the primitive simplicity turned out to be naivety.

When he lifted his bottle to sip, all the boys stared at him with an obvious eagerness to have a share, but no sign of aggressiveness to possess it. When Cyrus noticed those eager eyes staring at him, he could no longer enjoy his drink. He did not know how to divide a bottle of Coke among the boys, so he gave the bottle to a boy without telling him what to do. To his surprise the boy took one sip and passed it on to another boy. One by one all the boys drank in turn, with an amazing sense of sharing, no evil greed, no insatiable thirst for exclusive possession. The sense of sharing in African culture aroused his admiration.

He stood up and walked away. On the way he met a group of children who were standing in a row under the shade of a thatched roof that extended over the wall of a house. They greeted him by uttering some words with the effect and rhythm of a song. He could not understand what they were saying. He asked a passer-by to interpret the words for him.

'It is not a song,' the interpreter said, 'but they are uttering it with the tone of a rhythmic song: "O white man, O white man, greetings to you, greetings to you."'

Their warm, welcoming attitude, politeness, and smiling eyes affected Cyrus so much that he approached them to show his tender gratitude. The passer-by became interested too, and joined Cyrus.

One small girl, slender and beautiful, about eight years of age, approached Cyrus. She put her hand gently beside his and said something in her native dialect that he could not understand. He asked the passer-by to interpret what she was saying. The interpreter explained, 'She's comparing the colour of her hand to yours. This is the first time she has seen a white man. She thinks the colour of your skin is very beautiful.'

Cyrus's heart was touched and aroused in him a feeling of tenderness. He lifted her up and hugged her affectionately and with a voice touched with emotion said, 'You are beautiful, your face, your body, your soul all are beautiful. No colour is more beautiful than any other colour. Every colour has its own beauty. The garden of humankind is fascinating and beautiful because of the variety of so many shades and colours. You are a pearl, a black pearl.'

She did not understand his words, but she felt the vibration of a tender love. No words were needed to convey the feeling. The pure heart of the small girl responded with a loving gratitude. She put her little arms around his neck and pressed her head on his chest. Her face was shining with a deep joy.

This genuine love touched his heart. He felt a burning sensation in his nose, and tears welled in his eyes. He tried to choke them back but one spilled over the rim and rolled down. The small girl put a gentle kiss on his cheek, catching the tear on its path.

Cyrus walked away, his head bowed with a sense of shame. He could not help carrying the crushing burden of crimes against coloured races. He could hear the cries and lamentations of downtrodden people and races in bearing the injustice. Many pictures of cruelties passed through his mind: the ships carrying stolen black Africans to the United States to be sold as slave labourers in the fields; the hunting parties arranged to shoot Kooris for fun; the brave North American Indians who were mown down; other people's cultures and values belittled and suppressed. The evils of racism and exploitation. He suddenly cried out, uttering words out of anger, 'How can they justify their mistreatment? How can they blot out those records? How can they avoid the wrath of God?' Wrapped in his thoughts, he walked and walked but didn't know where he was going. No direction, no destination. Breathing rapidly out of tiredness and anger, he reached a big rock. He looked like a lonely ghost standing in a remote place.

He stared at the sky. The day was drawing to an end. The clouds were rolling one over another, taking the shape of a terrifying wolf snarling on the western horizon. Slowly the sun dropped and disappeared. The reddish clouds paled, then thickened and blackened. At the same time the burning clouds of anger were rolling over one another inside of him. Lightning and thunder were shaking his whole being. A force, a tremendous force, was being released in him. He felt he was holding a great power in his grasp, connected to an unknown source. He didn't know if it was a magical force or a spiritual power. He had an amazing emotion that he could invoke the wrath of God, bring into operation mysterious forces capable of turning the oppressors into crippled, creeping creatures wandering perpetually on this planet, utter a spell and curse them to roam forever in a blighted land.

Strangely, he was not able to utter even a word. His throat was choked, as if an invisible hand was grasping it. He could not even breathe properly.

Gradually new rays of light shone through his inner colliding clouds. The new waves of love linking him to the white people began to billow from the unconscious part of his being. Blue-eyed and blond-haired people with beautiful faces shining with the love of humanity paraded in front of his inner eyes. He could see a new enlightened generation purged from the evils of racism with affectionate hearts, willing to wipe out the tears of the downtrodden people and races with their gentle kisses. His feeble body was being pulled between two passions: anger and love. The contrary emotions were crushing him, dragging him in opposite directions. He could not bear it. The waves of opposing emotions collided and clashed. The rising and falling tides of anger and love submerged him in the depth of an unbearable feeling. He felt he would collapse.

Suddenly he burst into tears and wept. The colliding positive and negative clouds produced cleansing rain. The agonising anger vaporised. The crystal-like tears washed and cleansed his heart and mind from the taint of anger. The roaring storm calmed down, and the gentle light of compassion and love shone through. He felt inclined to pray. His heart was in a supplicating mood. The gentle breeze strengthened slightly and could carry the fragrance of prayer to the hills, valleys, meadows, villages and cities. With clasped hands and closed eyes he began praying:

'O Lord, thou possessor of infinite mercy! O Lord of forgiveness and pardon! Forgive our sins, pardon our shortcomings, and cause us to turn to the kingdom of thy clemency.

O Lord God! Make us as waves of the sea, as flowers of the garden, united, agreed through the bounties of thy love. O Lord! Dilate the breasts through the signs of thy oneness, and make all mankind as stars shining from the same height of glory, as perfect fruits growing upon thy tree of life.'

His eyes remained closed as he fell into a meditative mood. Suddenly, a gust of wind slapped his face and

disturbed his meditation. He opened his eyes and glared at
the lightning flashing on the far off horizon. The wind blew
carrying the smell of rain. The darkness had already
shrouded the bush and the huts and houses. He realised that
he was far away from the hotel. He had walked for hours. He
would soon be trapped in a terrible thunderstorm.

He walked towards the hotel as fast as he could, fearing
the rising tempest. The howling thunderstorm was following
him like a snarling wolf. The first drops of rain sparkled on
his face. He began to jog and walk alternately. After a few
minutes the thunderstorm reached him and he heard the echo
of a cracking and ripping sound. A clap of thunder exploded
over his head. He instinctively crouched until his chin
almost touched the wet ground. He realised he could not run
away from the thunderstorm. He was trapped and
surrounded. The torrential rain splashed, the thunder roared
and the lightning flashed from every side. If he took refuge
under the big tree he could be struck by lightning. He had to
battle on in the thunderstorm.

While jogging, he glanced at the trees convulsing and
swinging in the turbulent wind. Strong gusts howled and
shook the rainforest, plunged in pitch darkness. The storm
swirled with dazzling light and deafening sound
reverberating throughout the forest. The torrential rain
poured down. The lightning and thunder, with bomb-like
explosions, terrified every moving creature. The wild
animals and birds were running and flying hurriedly to and
fro to find a shelter to shield themselves from the angry sky.
Water splashed and lightning flashed everywhere. He still
had a long way to go.

Julia, Devi and Yasha were sitting in the lounge of the hotel drinking coffee and chatting. Suddenly a strong gale shook the building. The light blinked. Lightning and thunder followed it. They turned to the window watching the splashing of the rain.

Gloria was in her room listening to music and writing postcards. When the thunderstorm shook the building, she stood at the window and stared out watching the rain splash and the lightning flash everywhere. Afrer a while she sat down again and continued to write postcards to her numerous friends. An hour and a half later, it suddenly occurred to her that Cyrus had left the hotel for an excursion among the Africans in the surrounding suburbs. She approached the window. The rain was still pouring down in torrents and the strong gale was twisting and crying among the trees. She looked at her watch. Two hours had already passed since sunset. She became worried and wondered whether Cyrus had come back from the excursion.

She hurriedly climbed down the stairs and stepped into the lounge where she met Devi, Julia and Yasha. Without any preamble she inquired, 'Has Cyrus come back from the excursion to the surrounding suburbs?' She tried to hide her deep anxiety but her tone and face betrayed she was deeply worried.

'You're right,' said Devi. 'We have to find out what has happened to Cyrus. We haven't seen him. Let's ask the receptionist whether he has returned to his room or not.' Devi went to the reception desk and inquired.

'No, madam,' said the receptionist. 'He has not come back yet. The key to his room is still here.'

Gloria's face showed her deep anxiety. They looked at one another silently for a few seconds, worried. 'We can do nothing,' said Devi. She lifted her eyebrows and held out her palms upwards. 'We don't know where he has gone. Hopefully he's okay.'

Gloria rushed back to her room. She was restless and did not know what to do. Pressing her nose, eyes and palms on the window, she stared out at the pathway of the hotel, looking closely in the hope that Cyrus might walk in at any moment. The torrential rain blurred her view.

She climbed down the stairs and went out of the main door and stood under the balcony staring at the pathway. The sound of water was heard from every side splashing and running. She became disappointed that there was no sign of Cyrus. She went back to her room and sank in the armchair. She covered her eyes with the heel of her palm and pushed her fingers in her hair thinking of Cyrus. In her heart she prayed for his safety.

She stepped to the window, brushed her hair back and stared out of the window at the sky. The storm eased and the shower turned into mild rain. The growling thunder gradually abated and its angry grumbling faded away. Now that the storm was easing Gloria felt less anxious.

Cyrus was struggling with the thunderstorm. The howling wind, turning and twisting through the thick trees, brought to his mind images of bereaved mothers. They were wailing, lamenting, crying, screaming, beating their breasts, pulling their hair at the deaths of their loved ones, either killed as victims of the crime of war in a Godless world, or executed as victims of the merciless communist or fascist regimes. He could see through his mind's eyes the skeletons of the dead rising from their graves carrying corpses. They were busy killing or carrying the corpses or burying the dead. Wailing and lamenting rose from every side.

The torrential rain poured down his face and body as he jogged and struggled with the horrifying thunderstorm. The crying wind twisting through the swaying trees now brought to his mind the lamenting of the bereaved fiancees at the deaths of their dear ones at the hands of dictators or in evil wars. His inner and outer worlds were both in thick darkness.

The thunderstorm started to ease. The grumbling clouds flew away. He stood gasping for breath. The hotel building came into view. He stood under the porch of the hotel to squeeze the water out of his shirt and trousers. Gloria was standing inside at the door in the hope that Cyrus would come back. She stretched her head out of the door and saw Cyrus's back as he stood under the porch. She startled in surprise and withdrew inside immediately. Her heart beat faster. She stood in the lobby close to the door. Cyrus came in, his hair clinging to his neck and forehead and his clothes stuck to his body. He was surprised to see Gloria standing alone in the lobby. He smiled. 'You are still awake.'

Her head down, avoiding eye contact, she shyly whispered, 'I was worried.' She spoke so softly that he did not hear what she said. He was embarrassed to be seen in that condition. Without asking her to repeat what she had said, he waved goodnight, rushed up the stairs and disappeared.

4.

There was a rumour that a maneating lion had appeared in an area not far from Nairobi. It had already killed two boys and one man and the lives of the villagers were under threat. It was rumoured that some men in the nearby villages, skilled in hunting lion, were planning to kill the maneater.

Devi and Yasha were interested in seeing how a dangerous maneating lion would be hunted. Yasha talked to the receptionist. A Land Rover took Victor, Yasha, Julia, Cyrus, Gloria and Devi to the area. Peter did not want to go. He stayed at the hotel.

They were driving across a vast field. A cloud of dust and smoke rolled in the air behind the vehicle darkening the view. 'We're approaching the area where the lion has been seen,' said the driver. 'We don't know where the lion is. It may appear at any time.'

'Will it attack us?' asked Julia with a sense of fear.

'If it sees us; probably.'

Julia became scared and wondered why they had come to the field of their death. With a voice trembling slightly, she said, 'can't we go back to the hotel?'

They frowned deeply. They realised what they had come to watch was not a movie. It was real. They stopped chatting and became silent. The driver felt their fear. He smiled, exposing his white teeth against his black skin, 'I don't think the maneater can kill us.' They became a little relaxed, but the anxiety was still there.

They were passing through an open, flat field with scattered tall trees. It was the middle of the day and terribly hot. Holding the steering wheel with his right hand, the driver cupped his left hand over his eyes and stared at a reedy spot in the distance. He noticed some movement in the reeds. He looked more intently, then turned to his passenger and said hurriedly, 'Please, close the windows.'

Julia paled and started trembling. Cyrus bit his lips. Yasha clenched his fists and tightened his mouth. All seemed worried, expecting something terrible to happen at any moment.

Suddenly a huge lion jumped out of the reeds. Bouncing and jumping, it came fast towards the Land Rover. Within two minutes it reached the car.

It jumped up onto the bonnet. The driver lowered his head over the steering wheel. All of them instinctively threw their heads back and held their arms up to ward off the lion attack, as if it was already over their heads.

Julia turned her head back and screamed. Covering her eyes with her hands, Devi could not help trembling. Cyrus tried to comfort Gloria, sitting close to him. Victor's face was as white as a corpse.

The lion scratched the windscreen with its paws and pressed its open mouth on the glass. It almost covered the whole windscreen with its terrifying open mouth, spread paws and head. It roared, exposing its front teeth menacingly. It stared at them fiercely, determined to tear them into pieces at any moment. It was a horrifying scene.

'Don't get scared,' said the driver. 'The lion cannot break in. The glass is hard and thick enough to keep it out.'

The driver turned the car fast. The lion climbed on the top of the car, roaring and scratching the roof. Suddenly it jumped down and came to the side of the car, jumping up at the window, threatening to break in. Then it moved to the other side of the car, jumped up and scratched its paws on the window. All instinctively turned their heads to the other side.

Yasha stared out of the back window and saw the shadows of some people. 'The lion hunters are there,' he whispered hoarsely.

The hunters saw the lion around the Land Rover and immediately fell into position. They knew the lion would attack them. They were nine Mombassa tribesmen, tall and well-built. Each one was holding a long sharp spear. One stood about two metres ahead, four men behind him, two on either side. The man standing in front, who was supposed to shout and provoke the lion to attack, was the hero of the team. He shouted and waved the spear in the air, threatening the lion.

The lion ran towards them. Jumping and bouncing, it soon reached them. The lion crouched and leapt onto the front man. He fell to the ground. The lion was still in the air when the four men standing behind him speared the lion on both sides with one harmonised, quick move. The other four rushed and thrust their spears on the back, head and tail. The maneater died instantly. The hunters quickly skinned the lion to stuff as a memento of their heroic achievement.

'They were skilled and nimble,' said Yasha.

'If they were not, they could have been killed within a few minutes,' said Victor.

'It was a daring deed.'

5.

The friends stepped out of the Land Rover and breathed the fresh clean air, very different from the smog that seemed to be part of everyone's life in the big cities.

They entered the hall and glanced at a crowd of worshippers, people of all ages. Men and women, dressed either casually and formally, occupied the hall of a small church to its full capacity.

Their faces aglow with enthusiasm, they were laughing. For them religion was the spirit of life, a mystic link to an unlimited spiritual reservoir beyond the material world. It inspired in them strength, courage, tolerance, compassion and love.

The pastor came in, his face illumined with a big smile. A churchman approached him to inform him that some white and brown tourists had come to the church. While looking from the corner of his eyes at the tourists, he whispered into the pastor's ears that two or three of them were not Christian.

The pastor laughed loudly. 'All paths lead to one destination. Welcome them with genuine love.'

They sang a hymn, their joyous cries of hallelujah, hallelujah filling the hall with rising waves of emotion that seemed to touch the edge of the heavens. They were immersed in an ocean of emotion at the threshold of rapture.

'It is as if the whole building is rocking and dancing on the waves of emotion,' whispered Yasha to Cyrus.

'If one's spiritual being is not touched during worship,' said Cyrus, 'worship, in its true sense, has not been fulfilled.'

When the service was over the worshippers did not leave the hall immediately. They stayed on, chatting, laughing, hugging and kissing one another in a genuine show of love.

Peter, Yasha, Devi and Cyrus strolled around the hall greeting the worshippers. They nodded and smiled, and in return received warm and welcoming smiles. At the altar there was a life-sized statue of Jesus Christ carved out of ebony. Peter had never seen a black statue of Christ. He had never imagined that Christ could be portrayed as a black man. He was shocked and expressed his anger. 'It's disgusting. How could they be allowed to make a black statue of Jesus Christ!'

'Christ is Christ in any colour,' said Cyrus.

Peter tightened his mouth in contempt. 'No,' he cried, 'Christ cannot be black.'

'The soul has no colour,' smiled Cyrus. 'What makes Christ a saviour is not the colour of his skin. It is his soul, the divine essence of him.'

But Peter protested: 'Most portraits of Jesus show that he had Western features with blue eyes and blond or red hair.'

'One thing we know,' said Yasha, 'is that Christ's mother belonged to a tribe in Palestine who had black hair and black eyes with a dark complexion. It is quite likely that Jesus had black hair and dark skin.'

Devi smiled, 'So they coloured Jesus' hair to Westernise him.'

'I think each artist portrayed him in his own image,' said Cyrus.

'They changed the colour of his hair and his features to such an extent that he was no longer recognisable,' commented Yasha.

Devi grinned, 'If Jesus looked at himself in the mirror he'd be shocked. He would see that there is little resemblance between his real image and the portraits produced over the centuries.'

Yasha led Peter out of the hall to get some fresh air so as to distract him from the black statue of Jesus. They stood under the shade of a tree in the churchyard.

Peter looked at Yasha and said thoughtfully, 'It appears to me that Cyrus might be the follower of an emerging global religion originating from the East.'

'I have no idea,' said Yasha.

'The East cannot give birth to a religion to guide the West,' said Peter in a complaining tone. 'Christianity is enough for Westerners.'

Yasha laughed, 'You speak as if Christ was born either in London or Washington.'

They returned to the hotel, the singing of the worshippers still ringing in their ears. Devi sipped her orange juice and turned to Cyrus. 'Those black people we saw seemed to be sincere in their faith and worship.'

Cyrus nodded.

'And joyful too,' added Devi.

'Spirituality brings a genuine sense of joy,' commented Gloria.

'I'm a religious person,' said Peter, 'but I can't say I'm deeply happy.'

'To go to church or the mosque doesn't necessarily mean one's a spiritual person.'

'I think being religious and spiritual is the same.'

'There are people who are not religious, but they are spiritual, and vice versa,' said Gloria.

'There are people,' said Cyrus, 'who call themselves materialists because of their outlook, yet their lifestyle is quite spiritual. They work for social, economic and political justice. I think if someone works for the good of others that's spirituality.'

'The heart should be the home of God,' said Devi. 'It doesn't matter if one enters a place of worship or not.'

'If one's heart beats for the love of humankind regardless of race, nationality or creed, that person is spiritual,' commented Cyrus.

'Well said!' exclaimed Gloria.

'God does not reside in a heart where hatred has made a home,' said Cyrus.

'God is love,' said Peter, quoting Jesus.

'It's a bounty to experience love,' said Cyrus.

6.

Clenching the strap of the handbag hanging on her shoulder, and with her hair swinging, Gloria strolled with Devi in Nairobi at night. Cyrus and Yasha were a few metres behind followed by Victor and Julia engaged in conversation.

Cyrus occasionally glanced at Gloria, strolling in front. Her shadowy figure evoked in him the sense of an angel walking on the air. Suddenly his eyes sharpened as something stirred in the shadows of the side lane. His heart beat faster when the shadow turned into a menacing figure who headed straight for Gloria.

'Gloria!' His shout mingled with her scream. Before Cyrus could figure out what was happening, a black man loomed out of the darkness and grabbed Gloria's handbag. Gloria resisted, holding the bag firmly. The man hit her cheek with a brutal fist, pulled the handbag with one hand and pushed her in the chest roughly with the other. Gloria fell to the ground groaning. Within a few seconds the man had snatched the handbag and run away.

Barely aware how dangerous it was to follow a mugger in a dark street in an African country, Cyrus chased the man as fast as he could.

Wrapped in his thoughts, Yasha had not seen the incident. Startled to hear a scream, he noticed Cyrus rushing towards a man. Victor and Julia, absorbed in their conversation, could not figure out what had happened.

Everyone rushed to Gloria who was lying on the ground. Devi and Julia took Gloria by the hand, pulled her to her feet and dusted off the dirt from her dress. Her legs trembled badly and she gasped silently.

'Are you all right?' asked Devi.

Gloria nodded in response, her hair tumbling untidily

around her face and the fear apparent in her blue eyes.

'What happened?' asked Julia.

'A man snatched her handbag and ran off,' explained Devi.

Trembling and gasping for breath, Gloria pleaded, 'Go and help Cyrus, please. He ran after the man. People like that are capable of everything.'

'Which way did he go?' asked Yasha, worried.

'That way.' Devi pointed to a dark lane on the left a little way down the street.

Yasha rushed down as fast as he could. He turned into the lane until he reached a T-junction. Uncertained which way to go, he ran one way but did not see any sign of Cyrus so turned and ran the other way. He did this several times until he was exhausted and gasping for breath. He became more and more concerned about what could had happened to Cyrus.

Cyrus rushed after the mugger who ran through several different dark lanes, changing his direction. Cyrus finally grabbed the man in a deserted dark corner of a side lane and forced him to stop. The man threw the handbag at Cyrus, the buckle scratching the side of his face near his ear. He felt a burning sensation. They continued to struggle and the man finally gave up and disappeared into an empty field.

Yasha met Cyrus on the way back. 'You could have lost your life trying to save a handbag,' he said.

'When I heard Gloria screaming and saw her stretched on the ground,' said Cyrus, 'I just ran after the mugger to grab him. I don't know what happened to me. I just wanted to catch the man. I wasn't thinking of whether it was a wise thing or not.'

Yasha grinned. 'The man could have easily killed you.

Black people can be rough.'

'Yes, you're right. All races have the potential to be rough and violent. Africans can be as savage and violent as Europeans and Americans.'

When they approached the others, Devi was demonstrating in detail to Julia and Victor how the man had attacked Gloria and snatched her handbag. But Gloria was staring down the street, impatiently waiting for Cyrus to return safely.

When Cyrus and Yasha came into view, Gloria breathed a sigh of relief, her lips curved in a faint smile. She forgot the pain of her bruise.

'Are you okay, Gloria?' enquired Cyrus as soon as he got close to them.

'What about you?' asked Gloria.

'I'm safe and sound,' smiled Cyrus. 'This is your handbag.' He handed it to her.

Gloria gazed at Cyrus inquiringly, examining him under the light.

'O, my God!' she said covering her mouth with her hands. 'What happened?' She stared at Cyrus in horror. 'There's blood on your jaw and on your shirt.'

They all turned and looked at Cyrus and the semi-dried blood on his face and the red stain on his white shirt.

Cyrus touched his face and then stared at four red tips of his fingers. 'Nothing serious, just a slight scratch. Don't worry.'

Gloria hurriedly delved into her bag and pulled out a handkerchief, which she held out to Cyrus to clean off the blood. With some hesitation, Cyrus took the handkerchief and cleaned his jaw. He clenched his fist, holding the handkerchief, not knowing what to do with it. He put it into his trousers pocket.

'Please, give it back to me. I'll wash the blood off,' Gloria insisted.

'I'll wash the handkerchief.'

7.

A well-dressed elderly black man with white curly hair was sitting in the corner of the hotel lounge, his smiling eyes and glowing complexion making his face luminous. Wearing a white shirt, red tie and black suit, he sipped a glass of juice and put it back on a coffee table in front of him. The clock struck 9:00 p.m. when Cyrus entered the lounge to have a drink. His eyes swept across the lounge and he saw the man. He was intrigued by him and said, 'May I join you?'

'Please do, it's a great pleasure,' the old man replied promptly with a smile that illuminated his whole face. He made a move to rise up and welcome him but Cyrus hurriedly sat down, so as not to make him stand up.

Cyrus ordered a soft drink. 'By the way, my name is Cyrus. I'm on a tour from Australia.'

'My name is Olinga,' replied the old man. 'Australia has a small population, but it has the potential to play a valuable role towards world peace.'

Silence took over. Cyrus wanted to find a topic they could discuss. He asked, 'How do you see the materialistic civilisation?'

The old man smiled, his face lighting up and his white teeth glittering, 'The materialistic civilisation has contributed a lot to the world in the field of science, technology and knowledge, but...' the old man hesitated, swallowed his words, and then smiled.

Cyrus, hearing chatting, turned towards the door and saw

Yasha, Victor and Peter coming into the lounge. He invited them to join the old man and himself.

Cyrus was eager to know how a wise man from another culture viewed modern civilisation, which had originated in Europe and had made the United States the centre of its operation, dominating the world.

Leaning forward, Cyrus stared at the old man and smiled. 'Please be frank.'

The old man looked at Cyrus's eyes to see whether Cyrus was sincere in seeking an answer. His eyes flashed against his dark skin. 'Western civilisation is like a beautiful body, but it has lost its soul.'

There was a pause. Gazing at the ceiling, the old man muttered, 'When the soul departs, the body starts decaying.'

'Many people in the West,' said Yasha, 'don't feel the urge to search for an alternative pattern for society. They enjoy comfort and pleasure.'

'But what about the bliss of spiritual joy and the sweetness of mystical exaltation?'

'What?' Victor's face registered confusion. 'I don't understand what you are talking about.'

'Man has a spiritual potential,' argued Cyrus. 'Don't you agree?'

'If somebody doesn't care about it, what will happen?' asked Victor, teasing.

Cyrus hunched his shoulders and stretched his hands with his palms upward. 'It will become atrophied.'

Victor forced himself to laugh. 'Pleasure, pleasure, sensual enjoyment; this is something tangible. Everything else is mystical, mythical and unreal.'

The old man cleared his throat. 'Modern man is half-dead. He's like a man with half his body paralysed.'

Silence took over. In a pleasantly warm, cosy lounge, their shadows were reflected on the wall in the dim light. Outside, the sky was cloudy and threatening. Now and then there was a flash of lightning followed by the grumbling of thunder in the distance.

Yasha looked thoughtful, then suddenly blurted out what was on his mind. 'Europe experienced pain, turmoil and horror at an advanced period of industrial development.'

'A spiritual void was exposed,' commented the old man. 'It shocked men of thought. The spiritual vacuum bred disease and misery.'

'The very validity of materialistic civilisation,' said Cyrus, 'came under inquiry and question.'

The old man rubbed the back of his neck and turned to Cyrus, confirming his statement. 'Yes, you're right. I've read *Decline of the West* by Spingler.'

Victor forced himself to laugh but his tone betrayed a sense of despair. 'Ha! Ha! Don't take the views of an author too seriously.'

Cyrus looked sad. 'I'm afraid he's not the only one. An increasing number of thinking people are deploring the spiritual destitution of the modern age.'

'What do you mean by "spiritual destitution"?' asked Victor contemptuously. 'The wonders of technology and science in recent times cannot be denied.'

The old man leaned forward, 'Technology and science give you the tools, not the values.'

A dazzling flash of lightning interrupted their conversation. They leaned back, staring at the window. A thunderstorm was fast approaching.

They remained silent. No sound was heard save the grumbling of an angry sky. Cyrus and Yasha felt that it was not fair to keep the old man engaged in conversation. They turned to him and suggested that he should go home, 'We're afraid you might be caught in the storm.'

The old man smiled. 'Don't worry,' he said.

Cyrus wanted to continue the conversation so he turned to the old man and asked, 'What do you think of atomic power and its horrible capacity for devastation?'

The old man did not answer. He remained silent and thoughtful, but his face registered worries and despair. Cyrus added with a warning tone, 'The world has got access to atomic power. I believe if the world is not spiritually mature-

Victor interrupted. 'So what!'

'Great danger is in store for the future. The very existence of the human race is under threat. That's it.'

'The devil has got a sword,' smiled the old man.

'We have conquered the moon, travelled in outer space. Man is the master of the earth and now he is going to conquer the stars,' said Victor excitedly, as if he had achieved all these wonders himself.

'What's the use of all these wonderful achievements if he's going to commit suicide?' questioned the old man.

'Modern civilisation has lost its balance,' said Cyrus. 'It has passed the limit of moderation. Its beneficial influence has turned out to be pernicious.'

'When the human body,' said the old man, 'loses the balance of its elements, it gets sick. The same rule is true about civilisation.'

'The knowledge that has been accumulated in this age,' said Victor, 'is more than that in the whole of recorded history. That's a great achievement.'

'Secular knowledge,' said Cyrus, 'with no root in the deepest sources of being, is mechanical knowledge. It has no warmth of life.'

'The hypocrisy of some nations arouses in me contempt and suspicion,' the old man said bitterly. His heart ached at the thought of the hypocrisy.

His palms upward, Yasha put his hand on the table. 'An increasing number of people are trying to bring back human values to society.'

Cyrus shook his head. In a tone betraying despair, he said, 'I'm afraid nothing can stop the deteriorating process.'

The old man was thoughtful. He said in a serious tone, 'Modern civilisation has lost its life-blood; the tinkering reforms cannot bring back the vital energy.'

'We may have a total collapse, a universal convulsion,' asserted Cyrus.

Lightning flashed outside, and the grumbling of thunder was heard in the distance.

Peter and Victor stared at the window, worried and restless.

The old man made a move to stand, but noticed that Cyrus wanted to say something. He sank back in the sofa out of politeness to listen to Cyrus.

'Some people have just diagnosed the symptoms of the illness, not the main causes,' Cyrus continued, 'no medicine has been prescribed to cure the ailments.'

'Many books have been written,' said Yasha, 'to diagnose the ailments.'

'I've read their books,' said Cyrus. 'I doubt if they can regenerate humankind.'

'Why not?' asked Yasha.

'It's simply beyond their power.'

'Do you think their books are useless?' asked Yasha.

'Certainly their books are useful, but the world is in need

of a quickening force- a force capable of regenerating the human race.'

'What's that force?'

Cyrus knitted his eyebrows in deep thought, staring at the ground. He hesitated to reply. They looked at him, waiting for an answer. He was rubbing his chin, thinking. Then he dragged his gaze up at the ceiling and remained silent.

Silence took over.

'I don't know what to say, how to explain,' he stammered.

Patting his cheek and staring at Cyrus in deep thought, Yasha said, 'Just tell us what you think.'

Cyrus drew his fingers of his left hand through his thick hair, rubbed his neck, and gestured with his other hand. 'I don't know,' he said, 'but we certainly need something different from what we have. Completely different. Something above human folly. Something divine. Some sort of divine wisdom.' Cyrus drew in a deep breath, dropped his head and remained silent. He could not convey what he wanted to say. None of them grasped what he really meant.

'Nietzsche wrote,' said the old man, 'that there will be a "breakdown, destruction, annihilation, revolution, a spreading darkness and total eclipse." This indicates that he had no hope that the philosophers and reformers could turn back the rising tide.'

Suddenly, the thunder cracked loudly, shook the building and interrupted the debate. The sound was terrifying. The voice of the old man was muffled, and his last words were inaudible.

When the noise had abated, the old man returned to his thought. 'Nietzsche writes,' he said, 'about a spreading darkness and total eclipse, the like of which has never before occurred on this earth.'

'They are very ominous words,' Peter muttered, becoming apprehensive, terrified, 'they give the impression of the end of the world.'

'I'd like to quote Nietzsche again,' said the old man, with a touch of emotion, 'Nietzsche, in the words of a madman, says, "God is dead. We have killed Him." '

The lights flickered. All rose to their feet, terrified. A strong gust of wind shook the very foundations of the hotel.
 They found themselves surrounded by a terrible storm. Everyone stared at the windows, horrified. The continuous sound of thunder was deafening and the flashes of lightning blinding. The old man hurried out to go home. At the lounge door he turned back and said good night while holding his hand on his chest as a sign of humility and respect to the others. They left the lounge.

Cyrus switched off the light in his room and stood at the window staring out. The raging storm was so strong and tempestuous that it could uproot the trees and throw the islanders into the sea.

The last words of the old man thundered in Cyrus's mind: God is dead. We have killed Him. God is dead... We have killed Him. God is dead... these words echoed in the bush, in the valley, in the mountains, in the sea, in the whole universe: God is dead, dead, dead, dead, we have killed, killed, killed Him. God is dead, dead.... It appeared to him as if demons abounded and the angels had departed. As if the whole universe was echoing: God is dead. We have killed Him. He felt that the whole world had been plunged in darkness with such an awful sin. God, the generator of spiritual values, was dead. The lamp of truth, the light of divinity had been put out. The sun of faith had set. It was as if darkness had enveloped the world and dark forces were released. The waves of calamity surged above the heads and below the feet of human beings, and made them taste what their hands had committed. Gigantic and formidable evils, horrible wars, incredible crimes, political corruption and cruelties became acceptable. Murder, terror and crime became a part of life. Shocking events became the norm. As if the world had fallen into degradation and vulgarity, enshrouded in profanity, desensitised to its heinous existence.

Sitting at the edge of the bed, his feet apart and leaning his elbows on his knees, with his chin propped in his palm, he pondered over the plight of humankind. In a praying attitude, he wished a sun would break through the enshrouding clouds to chase away the gloom and illumine the world.

8.

The five minibuses followed each other like iron horses galloping towards their destination, the hired buses that carried tourists to the heart of the Serengeti wildlife park in Tanzania. The world famous national park teeming with wildlife encompassed an area as large as Northern Ireland. It was the home of more than two million wild beasts, including 500,000 Thomson gazelles and 250,000 zebras, as well as numerous lions, rhinos, giraffes, elephants and many other wild animals and birds.

The minibus that carried Gloria, Devi, Julia, Victor, Yasha, Peter and Cyrus led the caravan as it travelled on dusty roads. A cloud of dust curled in the air behind, obstructing the view from the rear window.

At the heart of the jungle, with no huts or houses around, at the border of Kenya and Tanzania, a hotel came into view where accommodation had been reserved for their stay.

Wearing light clothing, sweating, grumbling about the hot weather, they stepped out onto the hot sands burning under their feet like a hot sheet of copper. The women started fanning their faces with their hands and large leaves. The men had unbuttoned the upper part of their shirts and were trying to cool themselves by blowing and fanning their chests with their hands. It was early afternoon.

When Julia saw a swimming pool with crystal-clear water in a covered spot, she could not resist the temptation. Without bothering to change into a swimming costume, she glanced at Gloria, smiled, waved, then suddenly jumped into the pool and splashed around. Victor and Yasha, who were standing close to the pool, got splashed and began laughing.

They, too, were tempted to swim in that hot weather so they rushed to their rooms and changed and came back.

The blue-eyed Julia was fairly tall and fit. She was a good swimmer. She swam one lap and stood at the other edge of the pool, droplets of water dripping from her blonde hair and a sweet smile lingering on her lips. She waved to Devi, encouraging her to join her.

Devi was not tall, but being petite she did not appear short. Devi shyly entered and stood with her hands on the edge of the pool staring at the blue sky. Julia swam under the water and emerged a few centimetres from where Devi was standing. Devi startled and screamed. Both laughed.

Victor, a good swimmer and athletic, well groomed with red hair glistening with oil, approached the pool and dived in. His head broke the churning surface of the water, revealing his enjoyment. Yasha jumped in the pool and splashed water over Peter who was standing at the edge of the pool.

Peter, with a pale face and gloomy eyes, stepped towards the pool and looked around and smiled. He was tall and slim. He entered the water slowly and cautiously.

Peter, Victor and Yasha all swam, laughing and chatting at one end of the pool. Peter and Victor had white skin; Yasha was darker. After a while they came out of the pool and sat under the pleasant, cool shade of a tree. A gentle freshening breeze wafted over them. Sipping soft drinks, they started telling jokes and laughing.

That night, a Nairobi TV channel was showing an African dance that could be viewed in some parts of Tanzania. The dancers, glowing with genuine happiness, made the whole lounge vibrate with the rhythm and beat of their dance. Absorbed in the dancers' natural movements and genuine joy, Yasha leant forward and said, 'Africans seem to be born dancers.'

'Yeah, they dance away their troubles,' said Cyrus. 'Dancing is a balm for all their pains and deprivations.'

A shadow could be seen behind the window. Her dress oozing elegance, her long hair hanging over her shoulders, Gloria appeared from the lounge door. Her bluish eyes shone with enthusiasm like two bright stars, and, combined with her jet-black hair, gave her an air of distinction. She was from an Italian background, she might have been of mixed race.

With a Mona Lisa-like smile on her lips, she walked towards a seat with dignity and self-confidence. Her beauty and bearing impressed Cyrus. To him she was representative of a woman of the New Age. In her, gracious tenderness was combined with refined courage.

Cyrus made a gesture to rise, but Gloria found a seat next to Devi and sat down. Cyrus nodded, greeted her with a faint smile and dropped his head thinking: Plato and others have portrayed woman as a tie binding man to the earth. How strange! Everything is changing! Today's woman is proving that she is helping man to break his fetters from an outworn pattern of six thousand years of history. A history plagued with strife, war, violence and passion for power.

Staring at the dancers, Yasha murmured, 'How wonderful to be joyful in poverty!'

Cyrus turned to Yasha. 'A rich person might have a nightmare and wake up in horror.'

Victor snickered. 'More wealth, more joy. Why are you trying to deny the fact?'

'If that's the formula, I don't understand why the children of some very rich people commit suicide,' said Julia.

'No excitement of achievement,' explained Gloria. 'Life becomes boring with no purpose.'

Devi smiled, 'I have no wish to be rich or have a high position. I want to be happy and joyful.'

Lifting her eyebrows in surprise, Julia stared at Devi. 'I can't believe you. Haven't you ever wished you were a princess?'

'Never,' Devi chuckled.

'You're kidding!'

'Believe me, I'm serious.'

'Every woman wants to be a queen or a princess.'

Devi's eyes shone and she smiled, 'I don't want to be a queen. I'd like to experience ecstatic upliftment. It is not easy for a queen or a princess to have that experience.'

'Why not?'

'Their life is burdened with formalities. To experience ecstasy you have to have spontaneity.'

Devi leant forward to express her sympathy for the deprivation of the ruling class. She muttered, as if disclosing a secret, 'Oh! The poor people. They're the disadvantaged class!'

Yasha stared at Devi and a cynical smile appeared on his lips, 'They cannot be spontaneous. Even if they know something is false, they have to accept it for political expediency.'

'They wear,' said Cyrus, 'a mask in public. They appear as they are expected to be, not as they really are.'

Resting her elbow on the table and cupping her chin in her palm, Devi murmured as if talking to herself, 'In a sense they're slaves. The glamour that one sees from a distance is an illusion.'

'So, they're in a cage,' said Gloria.

'Yeah, but in a gold cage.'

'When you experience ecstatic joy,' said Cyrus, 'when you find God in your heart, that gives you an inner satisfaction and tranquillity. No more would you yearn for high worldly position.'

'Even kingship!' said Julia, surprising everyone.

'No, one wouldn't yearn to be a king.'

'That sort of experience is very rare,' said Julia.

'A time will come,' said Cyrus, 'when no one will be willing to be a king, or even to have it offered to them.'

'What!' Julia's mouth remained open in astonishment for a few seconds. 'Not to accept to be crowned, even if it's offered to them. That's ridiculous. They would have to be crazy.'

A broad smile lit Cyrus's face. 'On the contrary, it's a

sign of wisdom. A sign that humankind has reached maturity.'

Devi's face shone with joy. 'When do you think that will happen? That needs a change of human mentality and outlook.'

'Exactly.'

Julia looked confused. 'I can't understand all this. When I see a princess, I gape at her beautiful dress and jewellery.'

Victor snickered, 'I wish I was a prince.'

'I wish you were,' said Cyrus, 'then you would realise you were cherishing an illusion.'

'Let me tell you,' said Devi, 'my impression of a program on television reporting the daily activities of an heir to the throne.'

'Oh! It must be exciting!' exclaimed Julia.

'No, it was boring,' Devi laughed. 'He was dragged here and there, mostly unwillingly, according to a pre-scheduled program. But as a prince he had to perform. He was instructed how to walk, how to talk, where to sit and where not to stand. Even his mind and thoughts were under control. He was not even free to read what he wanted. I tell you the poor guy was a slave to the system.'

'I think he should have some free time to enjoy himself.'

'Yes, he had,' continued Devi. 'He was travelling in a country close to the beach. He had some free time to enjoy painting, his favourite hobby. The police were stationed all around the area to guard him. Everybody had to keep away, as if he was a leper. Even the birds flew away. The police popped their heads up now and then behind the trees to make sure the prince was still alive and hadn't been assassinated.'

'To me, to be royal means being a prisoner,' said Cyrus. 'A prisoner is one who isn't free to move about. For a prince or a king there isn't freedom to even go to the seaside, to sit alone to watch the rising moon.'

'I felt a deep sympathy for that prince. I said to myself: poor guy! What sort of a life does he have to lead,' added Devi.

'To be born into a poor family is bound to lead to misery,' said Victor.

'Someone born into a royal family may be bound to misery in another way,' said Gloria.

'A dictated way of life,' said Cyrus, 'is a bondage which is not easy for them to break.'

'They are not free to be free,' said Gloria.

By now the television dance performance was almost coming to an end.

Eight bush tents had been set up as part of the accommodation. For a slightly higher rate those wishing to experience the jungle could rent a tent. This option was generally taken up by newly weds looking to heighten their romance, or adventurous nature lovers wanting to bond with their beloved.

'I'll sleep in the tent,' said Cyrus. 'I'm the only person who stays in those tents tonight. In case something happens to me and the wild animals kill me, let me say my last farewell to you.'

A shadow of anxiety passed over Gloria's face. She turned to Devi, who was sitting next to her, and whispered into her ear. They both left the lounge and returned after a few minutes.

'Devi and I have arranged to sleep in Julia's room tonight,' said Gloria, with a slightly trembling voice. 'You can use our room for tonight.'

'You are very kind,' smiled Cyrus. 'I appreciate your

concern, but I'm not scared of anything, even lions. No worries at all.' He laughed and his attitude eased Gloria's concern.

They left the lounge except for Gloria and Cyrus. Gloria and Cyrus sat silently for a while in the dimly lit cosy lounge. It was late in the night. No voice, no noise was heard from anywhere. It was discomforting to Gloria to sit there speechless. She thought it would be better to leave the room and go to bed, but an invisible chain bound her to the chair. So she didn't leave the lounge but sat coyly looking down at the floor.

Cyrus, normally very expressive, remained speechless. He tried to break the silence but found it difficult to think of anything to say. All the words dried up before they could be uttered.

Cyrus breathed in the fragrant air perfumed by the presence of Gloria. His eyes swept across the lounge, glanced quickly at Gloria's face, soft as the petals of a flower, partly covered by her long black hair and adorned with light cosmetics and a light blue shadow on the eyelids. Small shiny crystal earrings blended with her shoes. Her blue eyes, black hair and beaming face in the dim light of the cosy lounge made her charming and attractive. She was like a rose at full bloom.

He dragged his gaze away from Gloria quickly, unable to meet her eye. He looked down like a shy boy. His heart started to beat rapidly. A gentle current of emotion was being discharged from both sides.

Gloria's heart throbbed. The gentle and pleasant streaks of a rising sun of love warmed her heart. She tried to be reserved.

Cyrus tried to bring his emotion under control, not to let

waves of passion electrify his whole being. It seemed his self-discipline and self-control were being melted away like wax before a burning fire.

For Cyrus, love was something celestial and sacred. He believed love was an uplifting and purifying force. True and genuine physical love was spiritual in its essence. Moreover, it could become a bridge leading to divine love.

He had a feeling, a sort of respect mixed with tender love for Gloria, a respect for her emotion, her career, her life, a sense of caring for her. He believed the heart of a well brought up young woman was a sacred spot, and dirty feet should not tread on it. It should not be abused. Cyrus felt responsibility towards Gloria. He decided not to give any sign until he was prepared for such a commitment.

A heavy silence hung in the air. Cyrus tried to find a topic of conversation to break the heavy silence. He remembered that he had seen Gloria at an intercontinental conference in Europe. He turned to Gloria and said: 'Do you remember the intercontinental conference in Europe?'

'Yes, I do,' replied Gloria, looking down.

'I wanted to talk to you, but I didn't get the chance.'

'It's always like that.' She raised her head slightly and stealthily looked at Cyrus. 'At that sort of conference one hasn't enough time to talk to everyone.'

Devi appeared at the lounge door, glanced at Cyrus and Gloria engaged in conversation, and not wanting to intrude on their private talk, she turned back to go to her room. Gloria called her in.

Brushing her hair with her left hand, she said, 'I waited for you in the room, but you didn't turn up.'

Gloria drew in a sigh of relief. 'I didn't feel like going to bed.'

Cyrus smiled at Devi, then continued his interrupted chat with Gloria. 'Did you attend any other conference after that?'

'Yes, I did,' replied Gloria. 'I attended an international youth conference in Switzerland.'

'What was that conference about?'

'To encourage the youth to cultivate their spiritual potential.'

'That's interesting,' said Devi, 'but I don't think if a number of youth cultivate their spiritual potential they can change the world.'

'Every human being is a world with its own orb and orbit,' said Gloria.

'Self-purification,' said Devi, 'is normally for elderly people preparing themselves for the next world.'

'In the next world one reaps what one has sown here.'

'If innate spiritual potential in human beings,' said Gloria, 'is nurtured and developed, it gives warmth, meaning and beauty to their lives.'

'What will happen if it's not developed?' asked Devi.

'They atrophy. A void will appear in their lives,' replied Cyrus.

'My heart aches when I see so many dissatisfied young people,' said Gloria.

Cyrus took a deep breath. 'Their hearts cry out for something, but they don't know what for.'

Devi got up, said she was tired, and asked to be excused. Gloria joined her. They both said good night to Cyrus and left the lounge.

Standing side by side at the window, Gloria and Devi stared at the rising moon. With a pleasant tone, Gloria asked, 'Do you mind if I play some music?'

'Not at all,' smiled Devi. 'It's a sweet night and romance is in the air.'

At the far edge of the hotel yard the isolated tents could be seen.

Gloria pointed at the tents, 'They're almost in the bush. Beyond it is a rainforest. Cyrus is going to sleep in one of those tents tonight. They say wild animals roam around at night.'

'Don't worry,' smiled Devi, naughtily.

Standing under the shower with the lukewarm water running over her body, Gloria felt relaxed and pleased in the warm climate of Africa. She remained motionless, her eyes closed, breathing deeply and slowly. Her long, dripping hair had almost covered her breasts.

She dried her hair, then switched off the light and sat on the edge of the bed. Every night before going to bed, she used to take a shower and say a prayer to cleanse her body as well as her heart and mind from the grime of daily life. The prayer released an innate energy and gave her a sense of relaxation and exaltation in a world of tension and vulgarity. She knew a prayer from her childhood. In the dark room Gloria prayed silently: O God, guide me, protect me, illumine the lamp of my heart, and make me a brilliant star.

Lying on the bed, Gloria pulled the blanket over herself but could not fall asleep. Her eyes were wide open and shining like the eyes of a female leopard in the darkness. Through the window she could see the stars twinkling and smiling and she felt joy mixed with a hint of sadness. Happy and unearthly, she wanted to fly to the sky, hug the stars and kiss them. Everything seemed beautiful and attractive. Her soul was budding and flourishing.

She remembered when she was a child how her Grandma used to point to the stars and tell her the name of each one and its function. When she captured the psychological mood of her childhood, the whole universe appeared a mystery, the surrounding earth and heaven an alluring magical world full of secrets and wonders. She used to cherish a desire to find the secret passage leading to the unknown world.

When she was a child, every moment of her life was full of astonishment. The whole universe was covered in a halo of mystery and beauty. She wished she could recapture the pure heart of a child, and to flower in full spiritual beauty. She hoped that the vulgar world would not tarnish the mirror of her soul, and make it stick in the mud of egoism and materialism.

Gloria tried to sleep but could not. She stared at a vague point in the darkness. Cyrus's eyes sparkling with enthusiasm appeared as if on a screen. Seldom had she seen anyone's eyes shine with such lustre, each ray of that light like a dart penetrating her heart. Gloria tossed and turned in bed trying to sleep, but she could not. The penetrating eyes of Cyrus would not leave her mind. Various images of Cyrus's face, smiling, arguing, laughing, came into her mind and kept her awake. She tried to avoid the images but could not. She couldn't stop thinking of Cyrus. The moon had risen high, and the mild moonlight had shed its glow on the edge of Devi's bed. Something was being activated in her soul. It was about two hours after midnight that her eyelids drooped down and she fell asleep.

Cyrus left the lounge to go to bed. He was going out of the main door when the assistant manager stopped him on the way to his tent and warned him, 'It's dangerous to go alone to your tent.'

'Why?'

'At night the wild animals roam in the jungle and probably around the tent. They could tear you to pieces.'

Cyrus stared at the assistant manager, shocked. 'What kind of animals?'

'Any sort of animal. It may be a lion, or a leopard.'

'So, what can I do?' asked Cyrus, afraid and surprised.

'A watchman will go with you.'

'The wild animals will not attack the watchman?'

'No.'

'Why?'

'The watchman has a torch with him. The strong light of the torch makes the wild animals run away.'

'Why?'

'The torchlight appears to the wild animals like a large shining eye of a very dangerous and mysterious animal. They are scared and run away.'

Cyrus was relieved to hear this and he and the watchman walked together to the tent. When they got close to the tent, some zebras galloped away.

Cyrus opened the front zip and entered the tent. The watchman returned to the hotel and closed the main door. There was a lantern, a bed, but no electricity or phone inside the tent.

Cyrus found himself alone in the bush.

Slowly and cautiously, he opened the back zip door to go out to the toilet, which was located at the back of the tent in the bush. He opened the zip a little and hesitated. He knelt down to see if there were any wild animals around. He saw a shadow moving away rapidly. He quickly zipped up the back door. Breathing rapidly and irregularly, he held the zip firmly, so that it could not be pushed open by an animal. He waited and listened attentively then decided to try again. Cautiously and bravely he unzipped the back door and glanced stealthily around. It was too dark to see clearly but he could hear the chirps of grasshoppers, the hooting of the owls and all sorts of animal and bird sounds. At night the jungle was more awake and alive than in the daytime. He stood there for some moments, no longer afraid. He stared at the sky and could hardly see the twinkling stars through the dense trees and branches. The moon was gracefully pacing the sky, but the dense tall trees did not let the moonlight pass through. He remembered when he was a child he had listened to and read many stories about the jungle being the home of magicians, witches and wizards. The jungle was a world of its own -a mysterious world.

He went back inside the tent, zipped open the window facing the yard of the hotel and stared out at the hotel building. It was in complete darkness. All the residents were sound asleep. He gazed at the sky. The air was clean and the stars were very bright, as if they had come down close to the earth.

He zipped up the window and sat down, thinking. A deep feeling of loneliness possessed him. As if all his relationships with other people and objects had been cut off, and as if he had been stripped of all labels describing him or ascribed to him. He thought this would be how he would feel when his soul departed this world. It was frightening to think that suddenly all ties forming his identity would break, that the illusive foundation upon which he was standing confident would be removed. His identity: his name, his birthplace, his language, his nationality, what property he owned, what skills and schooling he had received, all had been added to who he was. So who was he? He was well aware that when he left this world he could not carry with him social position, material possessions, name or fame. What appeared to him substantial had no permanency. He felt that he lived in a world of illusion. One day all these things would vanish in the twinkling of an eye. Then what would he carry with him? What would be his real identity, then? He realised that everything a person built up as his social status, his identity was unreliable. They might melt away like ice on a hot day. It was difficult for him to accept that he was a tiny mortal, a fragile being. He was but a shadow that could disappear in a moment.

He got up, zipped open the window facing the jungle and stared out at the sky. A gentle breeze was singing through the trees. The branches were dancing in the moonlight. He could clearly hear all sorts of bird and animal sounds. It aroused in him a sense of mystery, the mystery of a creation that had never been unveiled. He felt an amazing harmony in the universe, an ocean of wisdom hidden in every tiny atom of creation baffling the greatest mind.

A new consciousness started to develop. He was linked to the universe. If creation was a mystery, he was the mystery of the mysteries. He was the mystery of God in the universe. He was the apex of the physical world, and the potential spiritual worlds were wrapped in him. If his inner sun rose, it would shed light on his physical senses and illumine his mind. He was no longer a lonely, feeble, mortal and cowardly creature but an immortal and never-dying being. The wrapped-up spiritual worlds in him would unfold gradually when he passed through realms and levels of existence. His consciousness expanded and it gave him a blissful joy.

It was hours after midnight. Cyrus lay in bed and pulled the blanket over him and closed his eyes but did not fall asleep. The image of Gloria came into his mind. She was walking among the stars and turned to him and smiled. The rays of light emanating from her beautiful eyes warmed his soul. He saw a halo around her face. A shining invisible crown made her worthy of being adored and worshipped. She looked heavenward as if staring at an unknown and mysterious realm beyond the universe. To him she seemed not to be a creature of blood and flesh, but an immaterial being, a celestial creature. She slowly moved away into the distanced and gradually disappeared.

9.

The engines roared; the mini-buses moved towards a new destination, taking the tourists to another National Park in Tanzania.

They reached the Serengeti Plains, where wildlife could be observed in a natural environment. Gloria stared out of the window watching thousands of gazelles scattered here and there grazing. Sometimes they raised their heads and glanced at the tourists with gentle and lovely eyes, while the birds on their back enjoyed a free ride. It was a breathtaking view.

Absorbed in watching the gazelles, Yasha turned to Cyrus and remarked: 'Wildlife all over the world is under threat.'

'Not only wild animals, but also plants, trees, the water, the air, all are under threat,' said Cyrus in anger, shaking his head.

'Do you think the air may be poisoned in the future?'

'Many countries have chemical bombs in store. If some

explode in a certain way, they can poison the climate of a region of the earth.'

'If there were world peace, what would they do with these bombs? They cannot use them. They cannot destroy them. Even to store them is dangerous.'

Cyrus grinned. 'The only solution is that they swallow them one by one.' They both laughed.

Yasha opened the small window of the car to get some fresh air. The air was pure and pollution-free. Wild animals could be seen everywhere. Close to the road, a rhino was shaking its head as if in greeting. A little further, another rhino with a baby were standing and watching.

A group of giraffes was crossing the road; when they saw the approaching mini-buses they galloped away, disappearing in the thick jungle.

'That's gorgeous!' exclaimed Gloria in excitement, staring at a spot.

They stretched their heads and stared at two lions sitting majestically in the shade of a big tree with hundreds of gazelles grazing close by without the slightest sense of fear of being hunted. Devi and Gloria asked the driver to slow down so that they could watch more closely.

'It's amazing that the gazelles are not scared of the lions,' remarked Julia.

'They're sure that the lions won't attack them,' replied Cyrus.

'How?'

'Animals can sense danger. They know that the lions won't jump them.'

'Why?'

'Lions only attack for food.'

'A lion doesn't kill another animal to demonstrate its

strength and to prove that it is a superanimal,' said Yasha.

'Human beings can kill thousands of people within a few days and bury them half-alive,' said Cyrus.

'It's a shame, a terrible shame,' said Devi; her voice was trembling.

'You believe it's a shame,' Yasha snickered, 'but those who commit these crimes receive medals of honour with spectacular ceremony and homage.'

'It's a shame,' repeated Devi.

The drivers slowed down occasionally to give the tourists a chance to have a better look at the wildlife or to take photos. They stopped close to a group of trees where eight sleepy young lions were lying. They opened their eyes lazily and then closed them without paying any attention to the intruders. Some older lions lying on the ground nearby raised their eyebrows, opened their eyes a little, looked contemptuously at the tourists, then yawned and fell asleep.

'The young lions seem as gentle as lambs. I'd like to go out and hug them,' said Devi.

'Please don't do that,' smiled Julia, 'they may hug you back, and like you so much that they never let you go.'

After miles of travelling they reached a spot where a motel, a wooden building, the ground floor an open space, had been constructed in the bush for tourists visiting the national parks. They had to stay one night there, and the following day start driving back to Nairobi. They went to bed earlier than usual so as to get up early the next day.

It was about two hours after midnight when Cyrus woke, trembling with anxiety. He heard loud noises all around. Sitting up in bed, he listened attentively. He realised that the lions were strolling and roaring around the building. Many worrying thoughts passed through his mind: perhaps they had attacked a tourist and were tearing him into pieces. Would they come up the steps to break the doors and windows? Had anyone gone outside for fresh air and fallen prey to the lions?   He jumped out of bed, drew the curtain slightly, and stealthily looked through the window. He was shocked to see a number of lions in the motel yard, roaming and roaring around the building. He heard they could come up the steps and break the doors and windows to kill his fellow tourists. He comforted himself with the thought that such a thing could not happen. Surely the proprietors would not run a motel in such a remote place if such events occurred.

The lions in high spirits after hunting, like drunken men, raised their heads and roared. He heard them several times roaming around the building, roaring and roaring, their voices echoing through the jungle.

Chapter Five

ROME

1.

Standing at the entrance of the hotel, Cyrus stared at the darkening horizon of Africa for the last time. The sun was plunging into the horizon, seemingly reluctantly. He became sad; a vague tie was dragging him back to Africa.

On the way to the airport, Cyrus was pensive, thinking of Africa and its future. The faces of downtrodden people passed through his mind frequently. He wished them a good future.

He knew that the centre of civilisation shifted from continent to continent. Once, Asia held the torch of civilisation and, in comparison to Asia, Europe was a land of barbarism. Later on it shifted to Europe and extended to the United States. But now both were on the downward path. Africa might have a turn some day. The coloured races might have a valuable input in building the future world order. He hoped Africa would rise up. It might become the centre of civilisation some day.

The sun had already set and it was getting dark when they started to board the plane heading for Rome, the passengers standing in a queue in the open air. It was a pleasantly warm night. The breeze wafted a warm breath over their faces. A drum hanging from his neck, one of the tour members began to beat the drum gently. Another man, wearing a leopard skin around his waist like a skirt, started dancing. It was unusual to sing and dance when boarding a plane but not this one. All were laughing and joyful.

It was still dark when the sleepy passengers woke up in fear. They became alert and sat up, frightened. The hostess announced: 'Please remain seated and fasten your seatbelts.'

The plane dropped as if falling from a roof to the ground floor. It jerked and dropped repeatedly.

Some were holding firmly onto their relatives or friends. Some were crying, horrified that they might lose their lives at any moment. Devi and Gloria were pale but calm. Victor looked restless. Julia tried to smile, but a faint panic showed on her lips, distorting her face. Yasha stared at Cyrus and saw that he was at peace, his eyes closed. It seemed that he was praying.

When Cyrus opened his eyes, Yasha asked him, 'You were praying to save your life?'

'Praying for us all.'

'What's the use of prayer at a time like this? There's the formula of cause and effect. This happened either because of a fault in the plane or because of natural forces.'

'Don't you believe that there may be metaphysical forces that can influence the physical world?'

'I don't understand how something immaterial can influence the material world.' Yasha replied, expressing his doubt about the effect of prayer.

'Have you ever noticed,' asked Cyrus, 'that if you talk or sing to show love to an indoor plant, it grows faster and becomes more healthy?'

'Yes, yes. That's right. It's very strange.'

'It seems there's another formula of cause and effect. Love and affection, which are immaterial, may influence something physical.'

'Many people pray, but they don't see any result or effect. How about that?' persisted Yasha.

'They don't bring into operation the mysterious forces on high.'

'Why can't they?'

'Simply, they cannot connect to that source.   Prayer is like a plug.'

'How can the plug be inserted into the socket?' smiled Yasha.

The plane landed. Yasha clapped and laughed. 'Bravo! Cyrus, you proved your prayer was effective.'

Everyone was greatly relieved to have landed safely.

Devi and Gloria hugged and kissed each other. Gloria looked back and saw that Cyrus was composed and tranquil. Tears sparkled in the rays of happiness beaming from her eyes. The deadly silence broke. Laughter and chatting were heard everywhere. Some were still nervous, not completely relieved of their agonising fear.

Rome, the city of Caesars and Popes, of Michelangelo and Mussolini, came into view. They felt the lure of Rome. There was a lot that they could see.   One week was not enough to study the architectural and artistic splendour of St Peter's Cathedral.

In the bus from the airport to the hotel, Cyrus thought of Rome's past and was eager to see once more the ruins of the Colosseum, the Forums, and the Pantheon. For him they were not just cold stones put in place by one past despot or another. For him the ruins of the past were the mirrors of the future.

2.

Cyrus gazed with astonishment at the majesty and beauty of St Peter's Cathedral. It was more than just beautiful. He wondered how religion inspired architecture. He was amazed that many wonders of architectural art had been built under the influence of religion. Once, art and religion were considered to be as two channels expressing the human search for absolute beauty. In those days art was looked on as something sacred.

A young slim lady, the guide, followed by tourists, stood close to the Basilica to explain how it was built. She told the story of how Peter came to Rome to carry the message of the new gospel. He was beaten many times, and each time his half-dead body was thrown outside the city. But as soon as he could walk, he came back stealthily and continued his underground preaching. Eventually, they crucified him and buried his body at that spot. Later on, on his grave the Basilica was erected, and gradually the cathedral was built. The tour guide was trained to tell the story as a part of her job-hundreds of times- regardless of whether the tourists were interested in hearing it or not.

Cyrus listened attentively to the stories of the martyrs of early Christian history. Tears welled in his eyes. They brought to mind the martyrs of his time, the modern age that he was living in. He was thinking that people were never ready to tolerate the saints. The prophets and the saints were always ridiculed, rejected, imprisoned, exiled and even martyred.

Peter's heart was touched. He looked around to see the reaction of the tourists to the story of the early martyrs in Christian faith. He was astonished to see that Cyrus's eyes were wet with tears. He approached Cyrus and in a friendly voice said, 'I see tears in your eyes. You're not a Christian. Why the tears?'

'I love Christ no less than a Christian.'

'How is it possible? A non-Christian loves Christ no less than a Christian!' exclaimed Peter, amazed.

'I love Christ because he gave his life so that the others might live.'

'Then why aren't you a Christian?' asked Peter.

'I love Krishna, Buddha, Zoroaster as well.'

'No, no,' protested Peter, 'only Christ is the redeemer and saviour.'

Cyrus smiled and his tearful eyes gleamed. He tapped Peter on the shoulder. 'Now perhaps you can understand why I can't be like you.'

The guide walked towards a room in the Vatican to show the tourists some paintings. They stared at the ceiling covered with a masterpiece of art. Holding her head back, pointing at the ceiling, the guide explained, 'The artist had to lie back on a scaffold to paint on the ceiling. It was a hard job lying on his back all day for many years.' Then, as an exciting part of the story, she added, 'When the artist finished the painting, he committed suicide.'

Victor smiled, 'That's interesting.'

Devi sighed, 'Oh, the poor man!'

Gloria's eyes remained fixed on the painting, her face gloomy.

Cyrus was stunned and his jaw tightened. 'Why would they show us the result of such cruelty?'

'They have to show us eveything. This is their heritage,' said Peter.

'It's a tourist attraction,' said Victor. 'Every nation is proud of its national heritage. All governments try to restore and maintain tourist attractions. Sightseeing is a means of income for them. The Egyptians are proud of their pyramids, the Chinese are proud of their Great Wall, and so on.'

'If they knew,' said Cyrus, 'how many labourers died under the lash to build the pyramids or the Great Wall of China, they could never be proud of such a heritage of cruelty.'

When they left the Cathedral the sun was shining bright overhead, immersing the statues of the saints on the walls surrounding St Peter's Square in a flood of brilliant sunshine. They strolled to the other end of the immense square. Standing in the shade of a wall, they stared at the entrance facade of the Cathedral. Doves were flying around the statues and the dome of the huge building.

They bought ice cream and started licking the cones and chatting to one another.

Yasha stretched out his tongue to lick the drops of melted ice cream from his lips, and said, 'What a magnificent museum St Peter's is!'

Cupping her hand over her eyes and staring at the building, Julia said, 'It's a wonderful piece of architecture, and a great tourist attraction.'

'From that window,' said Peter, pointing to a window at the upper part of the building on the right-hand side, 'the Pope gives a sermon every Sunday and thousands of people listen to him.'

Pointing at the same window and fixing his eyes on Cyrus, Yasha asked, 'How many more popes do you think will speak from that window?'

'Less than the number of fingers on my right hand,' replied Cyrus, holding up his hand.

Peter was shocked. He stared at Cyrus as if he wanted to choke him. Trembling with resentment, Peter said, 'That's blasphemy. The popes will continue to speak from that window forever and ever.'

'This is not my view,' said Cyrus. 'The famous French astrologer and seer, Nostradamus, prophesied that there would be about twenty two popes.'

'How many popes have there been so far?' interrupted Yasha, with great interest.

'About nineteen,' replied Cyrus, doubtful of the exact number.

'The damned man must have been anti-Catholicism,' said Peter, angrily. 'Nowadays, there are many people like that.'

'He was a religious person,' explained Cyrus. 'He prophesied this over four hundred years ago.'

Peter was puzzled, paused for a while, then asked, 'Why did he say such a thing?'

'He foresaw it,' said Cyrus. 'The prediction doesn't determine the event. The seer sees the future. He cannot shape the course of history.'

'He made a big mistake,' said Peter, furious. Gesticulating angrily, he said in a loud voice, 'I'm not obliged to accept everything Nostradamus has prophesied.'

Rubbing his neck, Cyrus stared at him. 'Why don't you just ignore it?'

Nastradamus's prediction deeply disturbed Peter. On the way back to the hotel, and when he was back in his room, Peter was obsessed with the conversation about the last Pope.

He stretched out on his bed, and resting his forearm on his eyes, muttered, 'No more popes! That's impossible. It's unthinkable. Only ungodly people could think like that.' He tried to ignore it, but felt annoyed beyond control. He tossed and tossed in bed. A storm was shaking his whole being.

He sat up in bed thinking: those ideals, which sound new and dynamic, are a threat. I have to shield the church against the rising tide. I hate new ideals. I don't understand why Cyrus is so liberal and supports them. I have to argue with him, to repudiate his views and thoughts. I cannot tolerate them.

Peter stared at a small ivory statue of Christ standing on the table in front of the mirror. He carried it with him whenever he travelled. He felt a great attachment to that lifeless statue. He gazed at the statue remembering the sufferings of Christ. It puzzled him that Christ had so much difficulty getting his message across. Those who were waiting for his coming rejected and persecuted him, and demanded his death. Peter sighed, rubbed his forehead and rested the heel of his hand on his eyes and muttered, 'When Christ comes back I'll give my wealth and life for him. I wouldn't treat him the way his countrymen did.'

He walked to and fro in his room battling with the image of Cyrus. He raised his fist several times and punched the air as if to knock Cyrus out. One time he swung his arm so hard that his hand struck the statue. It fell on his feet and hurt him. He tittered. His face looked grotesque in the wall mirror.

It was late in the afternoon when he decided to go to the lounge to confront Cyrus. He wanted to repudiate strongly the prophecy that the papacy was destined to end. He felt that if he could convince Cyrus that the prediction had no value, then the popes could continue to speak from the Vatican window till the end of time.

Enraged, he entered the lounge and sat there impatiently

waiting for Cyrus. He repeatedly stared at the door to see if Cyrus would enter. Twice he went to the door and stretched his head out to see if Cyrus was in the corridor. After a while Cyrus came in, greeted Peter and sat down. Peter turned to him, and, with no preamble, said in anger: 'You're a hypocrite. You claim that you love Christ no less than a Christian does. But you believe that the papacy will soon end.'

Cyrus was surprised to see Peter pale, furious and insulting but tried not to take offence. After a short pause he asked in a gentle tone: 'Peter! Why are you so furious? You're almost trembling.'

'You said the remaining number of popes is less than the number of fingers on your right hand.'

Cyrus felt guilty for making Peter so upset and felt an unconscious compassion for him. He smiled. 'I just quoted a prediction by Nostradamus.'

'But you said it quite seriously.'

'It seems that you've taken it more seriously than I have.'

Peter banged on the table in anger. 'It's impossible that the papal institution will be dissolved.'

'I told you to just ignore it.'

'I can't. I want you to agree that it's impossible that the papacy will end.'

'Everything is possible,' said Cyrus. 'The caliphate institution in the Islamic world was dissolved.'

'Caliphate? What's that?' asked Peter, bewilderd.

'Caliphs assumed to be the successors of the Prophet Mohammed, just as the popes believe they're the successors of Christ.'

Peter's anger subsided a little, and he felt that he had been rude to Cyrus. After all, it was not Cyrus who wanted to overthrow the papal institution.

'I'm sorry; as a matter of fact I did feel hurt,' Peter apologised.

'No worries. It's normal to be emotionally attached to our beliefs and ideology. That's why we don't verify them objectively.'

'To tell you the truth,' said Peter, 'my religion is my soul, my heart, my very being. I don't allow myself to use my intellect to verify something, which I believe to be the absolute truth.'

'Blind love-attachment and fanaticism walk hand in hand,' commented Cyrus.

'I'm glad that I'm not a fanatic,' said Peter. 'I hate fanaticism. Jesus Christ suffered at the hands of the fanatics of his time.' His face became gloomy when he thought the sufferings of Christ, and anger filled his heart. 'I wish those fanatical people were alive now. I would choke them and throw their corpses one by one into the sea.'

Cyrus stared at him and said nothing. There was a pause for a while.

Yasha entered the lounge, followed by Devi, Julia, Victor and Gloria. They ordered coffee, tea, and soft drink and then started chatting as usual. Everyone had something to say about their impressions of their visit to St Peter's that day.

Peter was gloomy and thoughtful. As soon as he saw the other members of the tour join Cyrus, he got up and left the room without saying anything.

Yasha felt that something must have passed between Peter and Cyrus. 'What's the matter?' he asked.

'Peter's not happy about the prophecy of Nostradamus,' replied Cyrus.

'Oh! Nostradamus, he's a very mysterious person,' said Devi. 'He predicted many events of modern history, even the names and life stories of some famous people.'

'Such as?' Julia asked, interested to know.

'As I understand it, he said that there would be only twenty two popes, and the last one would not live in the Vatican,' said Yasha.

Julia shrugged her shoulders. 'To be or not to be, it doesn't make any difference for me.'

'I think all the traditional religions are on a downward path,' said Devi.

'It seems that the Christian Church is bewildered and is on defensive,' said Yasha.

'I think that every religion has a rise and a fall,' said Devi. 'The Christian Church at its early stages was able to roll up the "ism" schools and mystical cults.'

'Cyrus, I'd like to know what you think of Nostradamus's prediction about the papacy?' asked Yasha.

'I think he was right.'

'How is the papacy going to be eclipsed?' asked Yasha.

'When a Pope mobilises all his resources to battle against those who hold the banner of the new era.'

'There is already a covert battle going on,' said Gloria.

'Eventually an overt war will be declared.'

'So, when we hear the sound of the trumpet of war blown by the Pope against the rising sun ' said Gloria.

'Then the star of the papacy will set forever,' interrupted Cyrus, completing the broken sentence.

3.

They got off a public bus and walked to the Trevi Fountain. The footpath was occupied by parked cars so they had to walk on the hard, narrow cobbled streets and lanes. Now and then they had to give way to the small cars passing through lanes so narrow a horse could barely walk through them.

It was a pleasant and bright morning with fresh air and no dark clouds to make the sky look gloomy. All the way they told jokes and laughed.

When the fountain, well known as a rendezvous for lovers, came into view, Gloria's heart started to beat fast. She stared at the water falling over the statues with a pleasing sound.

Devi shared some coins with Victor and Yasha. A sweet smile on her lips, Gloria approached Cyrus and fished out some coins from her bag and offered them to him.

Teasing each other and laughing, they stood side by side with their backs to the fountain. Yasha said: 'One, two, three!' They all threw their coins over their heads.

Standing next to Cyrus, a big smile on her face, Gloria looked up at the sky, closed her eyes and threw her coin. When she opened her eyes a dove was flying over her head in the sky. She felt she would like to be a bird soaring in the sky. She made a wish to come back to Rome hand in hand with Cyrus and threw in another coin.

Gloria turned to Cyrus and gave him a shy smile. 'Did you wish that you would come back to Rome?'

'Yes, I did.'

She blushed and dropped her head. She wanted to know whether he would like to come back with his life partner.

They teased one another about their wishes.

Devi approached Gloria and asked, 'Did you wish that you would come back to Rome?'

'Yes, I did.'

'With whom?'

Gloria smiled and tapped Devi's shoulder. 'Don't be naughty, Devi.'

4.

The sun set and gold light filled the city. The dusk was enchanting and alive when they reached the Spanish Steps. The tourists as well as the Italian boys and girls were moving up and down or sitting on the steps chatting or playing musical instruments, enjoying themselves.

Victor, Yasha and Julia strolled away to a nearby cafe to have a drink. Peter walked up the steps to see the church at the top. Sitting on the steps, Devi and Gloria chatted and watched the passers by.

Cyrus strode away. He met a group of people standing in a circle around a fountain. A man was playing a guitar and a Gipsy girl was dancing, Barefooted and wearing a colourful dress with jewellery around her neck, wrists and ankles, glistening under the light, she was performing a Spanish dance. Her movements were quick, brisk and energetic. She danced on her tiptoes, sometimes moved fast to and fro like a bird. Her looks were wild and her gestures natural and simple. Her unpretentious air contrasted with the sophisticated people around her. She was like a wildflower growing on the top of the hills, smiling in the sunshine. Cyrus enjoyed her performance and put a note instead of a coin in the box and walked away.

It was a pleasant, cool night. The soft music of a flute, heard from afar, penetrated and touched the depths of his soul. It awakened in him a sense of mystery, opening up doors to unknown worlds. The melody uplifted and detached him, as if the cells of his body were scattered throughout the universe. He looked up at the twinkling stars in the sky and wanted to soar beyond them. In an ecstatic mood, he stared up at the Milky Way and muttered, 'We are walled up in a limited world. I wish we could soar in the celestial atmosphere to see the dazzling lights, to experience the breathtaking beauty and to inhale the sweet fragrance wafting from the holy rose-garden on high.'

His mind switched to Rome, the cradle of the ancient Roman civilisation. He thought: Europe has fallen into the mire of materialism. Can it rise up? Can the warmth of the rising spiritual orb vaporise the dampness of excessive materialism? Is it possible for Europe to disentangle itself from intellectualism, to gain access to the unlimited source of divine knowledge, and to become spiritual some day?

5.

Sitting on a bench, Devi, Julia and Gloria were enjoying the gentle breeze wafting over their faces. The sea breeze licked their soft cheeks with a moistened tongue in the pleasing sunshine. From Naples, the group was travelling by boat to the isle of Capri.

Gloria was wearing white cotton trousers and a short-sleeved blue blouse. Her eyes closed, she took several deep breaths. It was exhilarating and uplifting. A wind blew through her long hair. She opened her eyes, stared at the dark blue sea, and breathed in the clean air.

With his chin on his palm, Yasha was absorbed in the beauty of the Mediterranean Sea.

Holding a bottle of Coke in one hand, Victor drummed the bench with his fingers, in tune with the rhythm of a favourite song.

Devi turned to Gloria. 'Did you know that I can read

palms and tell the future?'

'Really! I didn't know.' Gloria smiled broadly and showed a great interest.

'Do you want me to read your palm?'

'Please do,' Gloria brushed away a strand of raven hair blown across her face by the freshening breeze and held out her hand.

Devi took Gloria's hand in hers, examined it carefully, searching for something, and suddenly exclaimed, 'Oh! You'll marry someone you really love.'

'Really! You're a good fortune-teller, dear Devi.' A heartfelt smile lit up Gloria's face. She hugged Devi affectionately.

The boat was ploughing through the sea. The seagulls followed the boat, preying on the fish coming up to the surface. Sitting on a bench at the rear of the boat, Peter and Cyrus were absorbed in watching the furrows and foams and staring at the seagulls flying over the waves.

Yasha, Victor, Julia, Gloria and Cyrus descended the steps cut into the rocks. The Blue Grotto cave behind the seashore rocks was a great tourist attraction. Peter was standing on the rock watching the tourists. He did not want to risk riding in a boat to visit the cave with its potential danger.

Canoes were floating in a queue waiting to carry the passengers into the cave through a narrow entrance. The sea was rough and the waves were splashing on the rocks. The canoeists were well skilled at paddling, but entering the narrow cave could be dangerous. It was the scariest part of the grotto tour. Victor, who was a keen sportsman and adventurer, was the first one to descend into the canoe. Yasha joined him. The canoeist shouted, 'Lower your heads.'

Yasha and Victor lowered their heads and passed through the cave entrance. They burst out laughting as they entered the cave.

Cyrus went down and sat in the canoe.

The canoeist was waiting for one more to fill the canoe. Gloria, after a moment's hesitation, entered the canoe. Cyrus sat at one end, the paddler at the other end and Gloria on the bottom of the canoe.

The canoeist shouted, 'The sea is rough. Mind you don't hit your heads on the rocks.'

As they entered the cave, Gloria became afraid. She closed her eyes and instinctively held on to Cyrus's feet.

Gloria breathed a deep sigh of relief when they entered the grotto. She opened her eyes. It was another world- one of breathtaking serenity and beauty, calm and quiet. She could hear the sound of her breathing. Stretching her head down, she stared at the water. It was clean and as clear as crystal. The water, splashed by the soft strokes of the paddle, produced a tranquillising, musical sound. The canoeists paddled away deep into the sea cave. The entrance became smaller and smaller until from afar it appeared like a tiny opening letting in the light. It was a romantic and dream-like world. Sitting quietly, the passengers were enjoying the atmosphere. Whenever the canoes passed one another, the passengers exchanged smiles without saying a word.

Sitting at the bottom of the boat close to Cyrus, Gloria felt the warmth of his breath blowing over her hair. She could not see him, but she could feel his presence. An electric wave was emanating from his being, charging the air around, passing through her veins, and electrifying her delicate body. She was breathing faster than normal. She tried to look at Cyrus, but was not able to see him.

Cyrus immediately bent down to hear what she was going to say. Their faces close to one another, they stared at each other and smiled without saying a word.

Gloria settled back in her previous position, a faint smile still lingering on her lips.

6.

They walked through a half-lit and eerie underground passage where there were many old tombs. There were graves at every dark corner with the repugnant smell of death hanging over them.

Julia entered a low-ceiling underground corridor and got lost in the labyrinth of the various twisting passages of the Catacombs. She remained alone and terrified feeling that the dead had arisen from their graves, stretching their bony hands to catch her. The ghosts had broken free of the tombs, making faces and horrible noises. Trembling with panic, she ran away but could not find her way out. She felt the ghosts were following her, stretching their bony hands to grip her, to take her into the graves. She let out a desperate cry, but no voice was heard, as if her throat was choked. She hit the wall. With closed eyes she stood gasping, struggling to breathe. When she opened her eyes a tomb in a dark corner in the narrow passage attracted her attention. She stared at it, terrified. A bony head emerged from the grave snarling and stretching its hands to grasp her. She screamed and fled.

Suddenly she found Devi and the others. Pale and in a panic she embraced Devi, put her head on Devi's shoulder and gasped, 'Oh Devi, it was horrible.' Then she cried.

The tour guide stopped at one spot, a small room where St Peter used to preach the gospel. The guide explained that, two thousand years ago, St Peter, under difficult and hazardous conditions, used to come to that underground room to tell people about Christ and his message.

'I can visualise,' said Cyrus to Yasha, 'Peter's face aglow with enthusiasm as he sat there talking about Christ. His heart, beating with the love of God, would have captivated the hearts of his listeners by his enchanting words.'

'I can't feel anything of that sorts,' said Yasha. 'The place has the chill of a dungeon.'

'Peter could transform his listeners,' said Cyrus. 'Later on, they gave their lives to spread the life-giving words of Christ.'

'But now the dead cannot quicken the dead,' smiled Yasha. Cyrus tried to visualise the vigour, dedication and selflessness of the early Christians who could bring the Roman Empire under the feet of Christ.

But Yasha smelt only the deadly chill of graves. It was sickening.   After a while, Yasha emerged from the labrinynth of the Catacombs. 'Oooch! It was disgusting. I could not breathe properly.' He took a deep breath and was glad to be out in open once again, breathing in the fresh air and enjoying the pleasant rising sun.

'One could get used to that fetid air,' said Cyrus, 'and not want to leave that atmosphere.'

On the way back to the hotel, the bus passed by many churches. Victor turned to Yasha, 'There are so many churches in Rome. Are the people really so religious?'

Yasha rubbed his chin in thought. 'What's the use of so many church buildings? I don't see that the church can play a practical role in saving our troubled world.'

Sitting in the same row across the isle, Devi stretched her

head towards Yasha and whispered, 'The church suffers the same anxiety, confusion and despair as the other institutions.'

Peter was sitting behind Yasha. He heard their conversation and anger filled his soul. He could not tolerate unfair judgement.

The day was drawing to an end when they stepped into the lounge. Devi sipped the steaming coffee and put it back on the saucer on the small table. She leant forward and said to Yasha, 'I think the church has lost its soul and its body is split.'

Yasha stared at Devi. Holding his chin with his thumb and tapping it with his index finger, he thought for a few moments, then said, 'The church is a part of an afflicted world.'

Peter sank back in his chair. He gulped and let the air out with a sound. His jaw tightened in anger. He dropped his glass of soft drink on the table. The glass toppled over and the remaining drink spilled on to the table. He struck a defensive attitude. Almost trembling with emotion, he said: 'The church can solve all the problems of the world.'

Cyrus smiled to ease the tension. 'I wish it could.'

'The church is lagging behind the times,' said Julia. 'It is still battling not to accept the equality of men and women.'

Peter swung his hand. 'God made women inferior to men.'

The ladies felt deeply offended. No one spoke.

Gloria broke the silence and said, 'That might have been the views gone by, but today people believe that men and women are equal.'

'The church was once the channel of the will of God,' said Cyrus. 'I hope it doesn't turn out to be a stumbling block in the path of God.'

'I think,' said Gloria, 'the church has to make an effort to attune itself to the will of God for this day. If it doesn't, it will decline more and more. It will lose its influence altogether.'

'Religious truth,' said Cyrus, 'is relative, not absolute. Divine revelations are continuous and progressive.'

Peter protested, 'God doesn't change and the religion of God doesn't change.'

'God doesn't change, but the human world changes.'

Yasha was surprised. He narrowed his eyes and stared at Cyrus, 'If I understand you correctly, you are saying that religious law can change!'

'The world changes and the law changes to satisfy its needs.'

'Who determines this change?' asked Julia.

'God does,' answered Cyrus.

'I believe,' said Peter, 'the Bible has answers for all the problems of the world today. That's enough.'

Yasha stared at Peter. 'Then why are the problems of the world not solved?'

'Christian charitable services carry the compassion of our Lord to the poor, to the refugees, to the victims of war around the world,' said Peter.

'Charity is needed when there's no economic justice. People become refugees when political tyranny dominates a country. People become homeless when there's a war. What can be done to uproot the cause of all the misery, injustice and problems? That's my point,' explained Cyrus.

'So charity is,' said Devi, 'given medication, not a healing treatment for the sick world.'

'If one doesn't get sick, one doesn't need medication,'

said Yasha.

'The religions whose time is over still have supporters within the political systems in many countries. That puzzles me,' said Julia.

'Those religions can function within the structure of a dying order,' said Cyrus. 'The effete systems can continue their existence around the religions that have less relevance today.'

'So let the dead carry the dead,' smiled Yasha.

It was late in the night by now and they felt the conversation had gone far enough for one night. They left the lounge.

Victor, Yasha, Devi and Julia went to the ballroom to dance. But Peter was so gloomy that no one dared to invite him to dance.

Cyrus shut the door behind him and sank into the armchair in his hotel room. Peter's face as he sat sulking came into his mind frequently and it pained him to think that he might have hurt Peter's feelings. That was not his intention and he wished he had not spoken out, but it seemed there was someone else in his innermost being prompting him to speak out. He tried to convince himself that there was nothing wrong in his argument, but, strangely, his heart did not agree with his mind. He thought of some of his Christian friends and he knew they were sincere in their faith.

He visualised the early disciples who had scattered far and wide with detachment, devotion and enthusiasm to carry the word of God. They forsook their earthly pleasures and comforts and endured great hardship. To his surprise, he did not feel that the early apostles would blame him for exposing a static religion. He knew that there were many prophecies in the Bible, and in nearly all Holy Scriptures, predicting that a great Divine Revelation would occur on the earth with a tremendous outpouring of celestial grace and potential energy. It would revolutionise the whole world. He could even quote the gospels and the other scriptures to affirm it.

It was late and the night was growing cold. Cyrus shivered. He plucked a blanket from the cupboard and sank back into the armchair. He wrapped it around his shoulders and snuggled into the warm folds. Holding the end of the blanket to his chin, he pulled it tighter feeling the warmth of his breath on the back of his hands. He thought about the life story of Jesus Christ. In his earthly life, the Saviour used to smile and laugh a lot. The most agonising moment of Christ's life, like a vivid picture, appeared in Cyrus's mind. Jesus cried from the depth of his heart and died on the cross. This mental picture of the suffering of Jesus struck Cyrus with great force.

He dropped to his knees trembling with emotion. The blanket slipped to the floor. He burst into tears and prayed, 'O Lord! Forgive me. I had no intention of denying that you breathed new life into the body of humankind when you were crucified. You offered the chalice of eternal life to those who were thirsty to drink, and you shed the light of perfection on the path of those who were willing to tread.'

7.

It was a chilly morning. A biting wind was blowing at Cyrus's face. He walked through the ruins of the Forum and glanced at the broken columns and walls, a reminder of the once bombastic empire and civilisation. He sensed that a frightening tragedy had occurred. He shuddered. The sunlight on the broken walls and fallen stones appeared pale and melancholy. No more did the senators sit there to listen to reports from the commanders of legions who brought glory and honour to the Roman Empire. What glory! They used to report, with a sense of pride and victory, that they had burnt and plundered the cities of other countries, and massacred the population of other nations. They had razed to the ground all the buildings as if no towns had ever existed or moving creatures had ever lived in those areas. He wondered about the history of humankind, a record of violence and animalism.

The wind howled and wailed over the ruins of the Capitol. Cyrus closed his eyes and covered his face with his hands to shield it against the sharp wind.

He squatted on a stone seat and turned up the collar of his coat, feeling the chill of the grave. He stared at the ruins thinking that some day the owl would hoot and the jackal would cry in the ruins of the capitols of the super powers. He pondered over the decline of Rome and the underlying causes that had brought about the gradual collapse of the Empire. He remembered Gibbon's *Decline and Fall of the Roman Empire* and murmured, 'Gibbon was too optimistic to believe that Europe would be secure from such a tragedy in the future. Maybe it was too early for Gibbon, who was proud of European civilisation in the eighteenth century, to realise that similar internal corruption would cause the decline and collapse of present-day civilisation as well.' Cyrus could draw parallels between the Roman and contemporary civilisation.

Cyrus heard the chatting and laughter of people approaching. He gazed at the entrance and saw Yasha and Victor followed by Gloria, Devi, Julia and Peter coming to the Capitol.

They found Cyrus squatting and pensive. Victor teased Cyrus: 'Don't shed tears on the ruins of a past empire.'

'I shed tears for the future.'

'Do you think modern civilisation may fall as the Roman civilisation did?' asked Julia.

'If one can see,' replied Cyrus, 'a similar internal decay and similar underlying forces one can expect a similar fate.'

'I've read Gibbon's *Decline and Fall of the Roman Empire*,' said Yasha. 'He mentions four principal causes for the ruin of Rome.'

'For Gibbon,' said Cyrus, 'the reasons for the decline of Rome and its ultimate fall were more material than spiritual, more external than internal.'

'It's hard to accept,' said Yasha, 'that Gibbon did not discover the main reason for the collapse of the Roman civilisation. He worked many years on the history of Roman civilisation and its course of decline.'

'Gibbon was too appreciative of the Roman Empire,' explained Cyrus. 'He was very unhappy about its fall. He wanted to study why it collapsed.'

'I think his book is valuable in giving us a clear picture of the Roman world,' said Yasha.

'Certainly it is,' said Cyrus. 'He had a narrow view of Roman civilisation. He believed the fall of Roman civilisation was an unexpected tragedy. I think its fall was inevitable. It was the result of an internal decline.'

'It seems,' said Gloria, 'he was wrong to believe that such a tragedy would not be repeated in Europe.'

Cyrus nodded, becoming thoughtful and sad.

Chapter Six

VENICE

1.

They landed in a city situated on 120 islands: the Queen of the Adriatic.

The boat carrying passengers headed towards their hotel situated on the bank of the Grand Canal, which winds through the city and passes under bridges. Gloria glanced at the classical buildings, famous palaces and churches lining its banks. She admired the city as one of the most beautiful in the world. She muttered, 'Venice, rising from the sea like Venus.' Staring at the gondolas fastened at the door of almost every house, she turned to Devi and said, 'Look, isn't it fascinating!'

Devi smiled. 'Private cars.'

Gloria sensed that she was entering a city of romance, where the bud of love, growing secretly in her heart, would flourish into a scented flower.

She gazed at various boats of different size and shape, travelling to and fro in the canal. One small boat passed by fast, its siren wailing. It was an ambulance. A larger boat stopped at a spot where the passengers embarked and disembarked: bus No. 3. It was amusing to enter a city where the canals were the streets, the avenues and the freeways, and the boats were the main means of transport.

2.

It was a pleasant, cool night. No wind was blowing and no

sound was heard except the gentle splashes of the oars in the canal. The two gondolas carrying Yasha, Victor, Devi, Julia, Peter, Gloria and Cyrus, were going gently and slowly through the winding canals. The moon was rising and the moonlight touched the tops of the buildings and palaces along the canal. A musician played the mandolin while another sang an Italian song. All members of the group remained silent, listening. It carried Gloria away. It was an old love song that seemed to echo her own emotions. It awakened in her the spirit of lovers, their tears and smiles. When the gondolas drew close together, side by side, Gloria was too shy to look at Cyrus sitting in the other boat. The stars were smiling and the moon bathed in the water.

Absorbed in her thoughts of love, the image of Cyrus flashed through Gloria's mind. She wanted to put her head on his shoulder and murmur love songs. It was a tender and pleasant feeling. It had the gentle warmth of the early morning sunrise.

The gondolas stopped at the main door of their hotel. Everyone went straight to their rooms to sleep.

Cyrus entered his room, but he could not go to bed. A feeling was being awakened in him, a feeling of joy and melancholy. He leaned back in the armchair and sucked in a deep breath and closed his eyes. He saw Gloria standing there staring at him with a sweet smile. His whole being yearned to be with Gloria. He felt that he was falling in love.

He stepped onto the patio. The air was fresh and cool. He stared down at the Grand Canal. The full moon was bathing in it like a young girl in the full bloom of her beauty. The atmosphere was charged with romance, arousing in him a feeling of romantic love.

He plunged into an armchair and closed his eyes thinking: may Gloria become my permanent partner. Oh! How lucky I will be to live with someone whom I can love dearly and respectfully. That sort of love reflects divine love. How joyful, sweet and uplifting it will be.

He stared up at the stars twinkling in the sky. His gaze swept to the candle crying on the coffee table. Its soft light was adding to the charm of the moonlight. The image of the beauty and sweetness of the nights of lovers came to his mind, kissing and hugging each other under the veil of darkness. The touch of their burning lips would make their souls fuse into one. He looked up at the sky and stared at the Milky Way consisting of billions of stars. He pondered over the grandeur of an unfathomable universe, something incomprehensible. His soul and heart conveyed to him that there was something more than the elements and particles. He thought that the impression of the poet, the mystic and the prophet of the cosmos was more beautiful, more mysterious, and more profound than the approach of the scientist. Scientific analysis was soulless and mechanical, stripping the universe of its beauty and mystery.

He felt that he was melting away drop by drop. A stream of love flew from the depth of his being connecting him to the universe. He wanted to hug and kiss the stars.

His soul was emitting its innate capacity for love. When the potential seeds of his soul started to germinate he felt that he was breaking the chains fettering him to the physical elements. Unburdened, light-winged and detached, he soared high.

He wished to get close to the Most Great Spirit to acquire spirituality. Like a piece of cold rough black metal, to be heated by fire and acquire the warmth, softness and the light of fire.

Clasping his hands at the back of his head, Cyrus gazed up at the limitless space. He drew a deep breath and muttered, 'The universe is a mystery. If only the mystery of creation could be disclosed.' He shook his head in despair. 'No, it's impossible.'

The serenity, romance and beauty of the night evoked in Cyrus such emotions and thoughts. His heart yearned to get in touch with that source of all beauty, all mystery and all knowledge. He wished he could burn away the veils hindering him from seeing the beautiful Countenance hiding behind the physical forms. He wished he could come face to face with the object of all adoration, to gaze upon the Ancient Beauty. 'Oh! That breathtaking ecstasy!' he whispered, 'At that moment I'll swoon. I can't stand that dazzling light!'

Cyrus was immersed in his mystical thoughts. His palms cupped his chin, he leaned forward, stared at the candle still burning and muttered, 'I wish I could experience that moment of illumination, that moment when the Ancient Beauty unveils his resplendent countenance. Oh! That's the most precious experience! All the mines of gold, the leadership of the whole planet are nothing before that most uplifting, most blissful, most sacred experience.'

Cyrus was sitting alone immersed in his meditative and emotive thoughts. He knew that the inner part of his being was much more celestial, unlimited, spiritual and finer than the earthly, limited, sensory and rough part of his nature.

The candle on the coffee table was glimmering at its last breath of life. Absorbed in his mystical thoughts, he suddenly sensed the presence of somebody on the patio, like a ghost in the darkness. Before seeing anything, he felt somebody was there. He was like a person who is asleep and is suddenly awakened by the movement of an intruder in the bedroom, though he is not able to distinguish anything clearly for some moments. He felt the electric waves of the presence of a mysterious being passing through the air. His gaze swept around. His eyes met a shadowy figure in the dim moonlight. He was startled to see the profile of a young lady, standing there motionless staring up at the twinkling stars. She was elegant, well shaped and with long jet-black hair hanging over her shoulders. Her presence added to the poetic beauty of the atmosphere and animated the romantic surroundings. A gentle breeze blew, kissed her hair and then with perfumed lips wafted over Cyrus's face. The fragrance of the perfume was intoxicating. He breathed it in deeply. Suddenly, he realised who she was. It was as if an electric current had passed through his body and made him tremble. His breathing became irregular. He felt he was too excited and too shy to look at her.

She glanced at Cyrus with a sweet smile on her lips. Her eyes were beaming a great light. Now her face was quite visible in the moonlight.

It was Gloria.

She was standing there, looking more beautiful than ever, wearing a purple dress, her long earrings sparkling in the moonlight. In the dim light, she appeared as an angelic creature that had come down from heaven. Bewitched and speechless, he gazed at her.

She walked to a chair. There was a dignity and grace in her movement. Sitting dumbfounded, he welcomed her with a timid smile. She sank into a chair and returned his smile. 'I hope I haven't disturbed you.' Her voice was sweet.

'Not at all,' said Cyrus, his voice trembling. His heart was beating rapidly. He could hear it pumping. He wished he could kneel down before his adorable queen and take her delicate hands to kiss.

The air was fresh and fragrant. A heavy silence hung in the air. He wanted to break the silence but could not. He was too overwhelmed with emotion to find words to say something.

The bartender came to the patio, brought a new candle and asked for their order. Both ordered coffee. Again both became silent and too shy to say anything.

The continuous silence was becoming embarrassing.

Gloria glanced shyly at him, turned her face away and stared upwards at the sky, musing over the harmonious movement of the stars. She decided she had better say something. 'It's pleasant weather, not cold, not hot.'

'The air is fresh and the moon is full.'

They became silent again.

Gloria leaned forward and sipped her coffee. She tried to say something. 'The roses on the walls of the patio are in bloom.'

'The roses and lavender make the air smell wonderful.'

Their conversation dried up and both became silent again.

Gloria looked up at the stars. As if talking to herself, she muttered, 'I feel the stars are singing.'

Cyrus became philosophical. 'That reminds me of a Greek philosopher who believed he could hear the voice of a singing universe.'

'I wish I could fly to the stars,' said Gloria.

'If you fly beyond the Milky Way and reach the other galaxies, you will still be in the physical realm. I wish I could fly beyond the physical world, to find that secret passage leading to the realms on high. I wish I could soar through creation after creation and world after world beyond the physical world.'

'Who has discovered there are realms beyond the physical world?' asked Gloria. 'The philosophers and the scientists have not fully understood this physical world. How could they discover the higher realms?'

'Those who are the source of knowledge and wisdom,' replied Cyrus.

'Who are they?'

'The prophets.'

'The followers of the major religions believe there's a next world; but you say world after world.'

'Bahá'u'lláh - the Glory of God - who introduced himself as the spokesman of God for the new era, presented a new understanding of the world of being. He says there are limitless spiritual realms.'

Gloria became thoughtful. 'I should know that. I always thought there was only one next world.'

'Another point is that the world of being is one. There are levels and realms.'

Tapping her lips with her finger, Gloria asked with great curiosity, 'Is it possible to see the higher realms?'

Rubbing his neck in deep thought, after some hesitation, Cyrus replied, 'It seems it's possible to catch a glimpse of the higher realms.'

'Oh! That's fantastic!' exclaimed Gloria. She stood up with excitement. Looking at the moon, she murmured in a state of ecstasy, 'Oh! After all, there's a secret passage to those realms of mysteries and wonders!'

Gloria sank in the chair and became silent and closed her eyes. Listening to the soft music being played, she felt as if, on the wings of an angel, she was entering the worlds of joy, bliss and light. She went into rapture at the mere thought of higher realms, of the possibility of experiencing those spiritual worlds.

Devi entered the patio and was startled to find Gloria with closed eyes and Cyrus in deep thoughts. Her presence was noticed neither by Gloria nor by Cyrus. Devi stood there motionless and surprised.

Gloria opened her eyes and stared at Devi for a few seconds without saying a word. She looked dreamy. As if waking up, she suddenly cried out, 'Devi, come. We are having a very interesting conversation. We're venturing beyond the universe.'

'That's interesting,' said Devi, but she was confused at what could have been said on such a topic to make Gloria so excited.

A broad smile illuminated Gloria's face. 'Devi, Cyrus says it's possible to catch a glimpse of higher realms.'

'There are many mysteries not yet disclosed,' said Devi. 'Human intellect has no access to some of the mysteries. There's a border that the human mind cannot go beyond.'

Cyrus stared at Devi in deep thought, and after a pause he said, 'But the universal mind can cross that border and bring us back a report of those realms.'

'I prefer to experience it myself,' said Devi. 'Since I cannot see those realms I give up.'

'You may try to see the higher worlds through the eyes of those who have seen them.' A smile lit up Cyrus's face.

'Who are those who have seen the higher realms beyond the physical world?'

'I mean those who had the greatest influence on human history, the great beings like Krishna, Buddha, Christ and

Bahá'u'lláh.'

Gloria became curious and asked, 'How can one see the higher realms through their eyes?'

'One has to borrow their eyes.'

Devi raised her eyebrows. 'Can everybody borrow their eyes?'

Victor and Yasha came onto the patio. They heard Devi's question.

Victor interrupted the conversation and teased Devi, 'To borrow someone's eyes! That's funny. We can borrow a pen, a book, a tie, but not eyes. Whose eyes are you going to borrow, Devi?' Victor and Yasha laughed.

'Don't be crazy, Victor. It's a very serious and significant subject we're talking about.'

'Could I know what significant topic you are talking about which requires borrowing eyes?' asked Victor.

'We're trying to find out if it is possible to experience at least a glimpse of the worlds beyond this physical creation,' explained Devi in a serious tone.

'The very existence of a higher world or worlds is in question. How can we experience them?'

'Who has rejected the existence of the higher realms? Who dares to deny the worlds of God?' said Gloria in a challenging tone.

'Some philosophers argue that they haven't seen or experienced any realm beyond the material world,' said Victor.

'Leave them in their closed world,' said Cyrus.

'If they cannot experience anything beyond the material world, that's their problem,' said Gloria.

'There was a time,' said Cyrus, 'when the philosophers of the world believed that the whole universe was just the earth, the sun and certain stars. They believed the earth was the centre of the universe. That was all they could understand.'

'It's now an established fact,' said Devi, 'that there are unnumbered galaxies. Each galaxy consists of millions, if not billions of stars and suns. Some of the stars are a million times bigger than our earth and even our sun.'

'To give you a rough idea of the distance between the stars,' said Yasha, 'let's measure them by the speed of light. You know that light travels a distance of ten thousand million kilometres in one year. It takes more than several hundred thousand million years for light to reach the earth from some of these stars. Can you figure out the distance?'

Victor opened his mouth in surprise.

'You're talking about the stars that have been observed. There are stars and galaxies so remote that they haven't been discovered yet,' said Cyrus.

'It's incredible,' Gloria shook her head in astonishment.

All became silent for some moments, overwhelmed by the awe-inspiring vastness and grandeur of physical creation.

Victor, bewildered and perplexed, asked, 'Where's the border of the universe? Where does it end?'

'It has no end. It has no border. It's limitless,' replied Yasha.

'Also, it has no beginning and no end from the perspective of time,' added Cyrus.

'I don't understand why some people insist on limiting the incredible cosmos to just physical creation,' said Gloria.

'Some philosophers and scientists limit the cosmos to what is perceptible by the senses,' said Cyrus.

'The limited mind sees the cosmos limited,' said Devi.

Victor did not reject Gloria and Cyrus' beliefs, but sat

puzzled.

Yasha was amazed, thinking of the grandeur and vastness of creation. He felt that Cyrus and Gloria might be right in their argument. But he did not have Cyrus's faith or Gloria's enthusiasm that the worlds of God were unlimited.

Gloria became more confident in her hope that one day she might find a loophole and catch a glimpse of the higher realms.

Everybody remained silent and thoughtful. They stared up, examining the twinkling stars in the sky. Each of them tried to work out which star's light took millions and millions of years to reach the earth.

3.

Gloria entered her room. She stared out at the soft and mystery-evoking moonlight spreading a mantle of silver. She gazed at the ferns in the corner of the hotel yard where moonlight was reflected through the foliage. But her mind was on Cyrus. His image was being etched in her heart and mind deeper and deeper. Does Cyrus really love me? Does he love me to an extent to marry me? No, it might be just affection, she thought. Tears came to her eyes. She groaned, I am writing a love story on the sands.

She knew that Cyrus had a noble character. He was the type of person who could feel a tender affection towards a member of the opposite sex that was pure and free of sexual desire. He could establish a profound friendship with a young woman based on genuine moral discipline. This sort of relation was normal and natural for him.

His self-esteem and nobility fascinated Gloria. Even though he might not be thinking of marriage, he would show his respect and affection for any girl who might signal a covert message of love, she thought. She knew that he would make anyone who loved him realise that he could not go beyond a certain limit. She could feel that he was attracted to her but she could not understand why Cyrus concealed and controlled his emotion. Then a thought passed through her mind that made her eyes fill with tears: there might be somebody in his life.

Gloria closed her eyes, tried to imagine the girl who could capture Cyrus's heart and muttered, 'Who could be that lucky girl? Is she very beautiful? Is she more attractive than I am? I wish I could find out who she is.'

She stared at her reflection in the full-sized mirror, examining her features and stature to see how beautiful and attractive she was. Her beautiful blue eyes were sad and emitting a light of love. A teardrop rolled down and stopped on her cheek like a dewdrop on a flower. She wiped her face with the fingers of her right hand. She dropped down into the armchair and sighed, 'What's happening to me! I am falling more and more deeply in love with Cyrus. I don't know where it will end. I hope I will not be left with a broken heart and tearful eyes. Oh Cyrus! I wish you knew how I do love you. For me, you're like a diamond shining in the vulgar world. You're precious. When you're absorbed in your lofty thoughts, your eyes sparkle with a great light. Your eyes have a magnetic quality that is irresistible. I can barely look at you during those moments. Your eyes transmit an electrifying power that makes my heart throb. I try to hide my feelings. Oh! Those magnetic eyes! I don't know what's the mystery in them that captivates my heart, making it melt. Now I realise what is it meant by the words "the eyes are the windows of the soul." Your soul is attracted to the celestial realm and attracts anything that comes in its way. If my love were not returned, I would wish that I had never seen you. I wish I were blind, so as not to look at those eyes that could ruin my heart.'

The stars were twinkling in the distant sky. Moonlight covered part of the corner of the room. Plunged in an armchair, Gloria fantasised about Cyrus. She imagined him riding on horseback, galloping toward noble aims. He might face difficulty and danger but nothing could change his will, nothing could terrify him. She could see a halo of glory and power around him. But there was no roughness in this power. It was sanctified by a sacred motive.

It was late in the night when she went to bed.

4.

Gloria's eyes swept across the famous St Mark Square, the centre and the most frequented part of the city. The pigeons were flying, now and then stopping to take titbits from tourists. Julia and Devi, too, held out their hands, trying to feed the pigeons. Gloria was inclined to stay away from her companions. Once Cyrus got close enough to say hello to her, but she pretended she had not noticed his approach. She avoided having any eye contact with him. She wanted to be cool and distant. She deliberately went further and further away until she was quite separated from the group. Holding her palms upward to feed the pigeons, one flew towards her and landed on her hand and began to eat. With the other hand, Gloria gently caught the pigeon, kissed its head and pressed it on her chest. The pigeon, like a well trained pet, did not resist at all; rather it pressed itself against Gloria's chest, enjoying the warmth of her breast. She amused herself by feeding and chasing the pigeons to and fro.

Cyrus and Yasha strolled away to visit the famous Bridge

of Sighs at the rear of the Doge's Palace. It connected the palace to the public prison. It was built by the Doge of Venice, an oligarchic ruler, as part of his plan to destroy those disloyal to the ruler. It was the route taken by those of his subjects who were sentenced to prison. Some never returned to freedom.

Cyrus and Yasha bent down to enter the solitary prison cells. They were small, measuring one metre by two metres. The ceiling was so low that they could not stand upright. There was not even a peephole to look out to view the birds flying across the sky and the children laughing and running in a playground.

Cyrus could not bear it, so he covered his face with his hands and became silent for a while. Then he turned to Yasha. 'This is a grave. It's very painful and agonising to rot in the grave while you're still alive.'

'They were not even criminals. Their crime was that they had brains to think and the courage to express their thoughts.'

'To destroy a human being for his advanced thoughts is the blackest crime,' said Cyrus.

'In the past they thought they could torture and destroy anyone not willing to pay homage to a tyrannical dictator.'

'It's the same today. Political records of many countries are plagued with cruelty, corruption, tricks, hypocrisy and lies.'

'It seems virtue cannot go along with politics,' said Yasha.

'Politics should be the embodiment of virtue, truth and human values.'

'That has never been and it seems will never be,' said Yasha.

'Until a system based on spiritual values is established in the world,' said Cyrus.

'You mean the reign of philosophers that Plato suggested?'

'I mean the reign of saints that John, the author of the Book of Revelations, prophesied,' replied Cyrus.

Yasha and Cyrus stood up, both filled with great enthusiasm at the expectation of a day when politics would be purified from ego, passion for power and crime. They swung their arms in the air and with one voice they cried aloud, 'The world will be ruled by saints.'

Chapter Seven

NICE

1.

Hooking her fingers around the railing of a small balcony on the third floor of the hotel, Gloria stared down at the Mediterranean Sea, exploring the vista of Nice in the south of France. It was built around a bay, situated at the foot of the Maritime Alps, a city of romance and beauty. Her eyes swept across the boulevard extending along the bay shore.

She felt like a bath after the flight from Venice. She stepped into the spa, murmuring love songs. She relaxed in the warm water, her head held back and her legs stretched out. Rubbing her cheeks and forehead, she closed her eyes. The patio in Venice, the candle, the fragrance of the lavender, the twinkling stars and glittering eyes of Cyrus came to her mind. She sucked in a deep breath and murmured, 'Oh! Cyrus.'

She stared at her reflection in the mirror, listening to a love song being played. She moved her body gently with the rhythm of the music, repeating the song while brushing her long hair.

Drawing aside the curtain, she stared out at the waves of the sea in the soft moonlight. The sea was rough, a contrast to the calm water in the canals of Venice. The moon was not full, but its pale light had a mild beauty, mixing with the foam of the rising and falling waves.

She was still haunted by the thought that there might be somebody in Cyrus's life. The thought of losing him tormented her. She had already developed an infatuation for him and it was painful to imagine that one day she might have to erase the loving picture of Cyrus that she had tenderly painted on her heart with the brush of love. She dropped into the armchair and sighed audibly. Her throat became choked with a sob. 'I can't bear to think that I may never have him.' Her heart sank with the agony of heartbreak. She burst into tears and sobbed like a child, murmuring, 'I wish I had never met you, I wish I had never seen you.'

Her face was soaked with tears but she felt relieved, the clouds of agony having turned into tears and poured down. She tried to convince herself that, after all, her grief was the result of her imagination. And she had no proof that Cyrus's heart was in the bondage of someone else's love. Her heart was still heavy, but a spark of hope flashed through her and lightened her mood.

It was pleasant to bask in the warmth of love. She played a love song: 'I Can't Stop Loving You,' over a cassette player repeatedly. She wished that she could hide her feelings. But how could she? She was pulled by a magnetic power too strong to resist. Cyrus's dignity, his nobility, his magnetism, his charming face and flashing eyes hallowed by his courageous dedication to humanity had made him adorable to her. She wished she could kneel down before him and voice her feelings. She muttered, 'Oh Cyrus, I do love you. I adore you. I worship you. You're precious. But I'm worried about you. You're brave and detached. You express your ideas and feelings with sincerity and courage. You speak directly and to the point.'

Listening to the song with closed eyes, she dreamt of being with Cyrus. Her head on his shoulder and his arm around her waist, they strolled barefooted on the white sands of the beach. She left his side and ran to the sea and plunged into the water. Afer a few laps, she stood up in the water up to her waist. Her long loose dress spread on the gentle waves of the sea. Cyrus reached her and hugged her. Both burst into laughter. Their eyes met and their amorous gaze held one another and their souls mingled. The cassette reached the end and stopped.

Gloria woke up from her dream. She rubbed her eyes, brushed her fingers through her long hair and pushed it forward while it hung over her breast. She stepped to the window and gazed out at the billowing, thundering sea, now very rough. The waves rose up and up with a frightening approach to the seashore, then suddenly fell and thumped down onto tall rocks with an amazing submissiveness. Still Cyrus was in her mind. Wherever she looked she saw him. Her imagination developed to such an extent that she saw him standing on a rock looking at the distant horizon. Whenever the waves splashed on the seashore she had a strange feeling. She wanted to wash Cyrus's feet with her hands and dry them with her long fragrant hair.

Gloria stepped back and dropped into her armchair, wondering how she should approach Cyrus. She remembered that at St Mark square in Venice she had tried to be indifferent to him. When he greeted her, she had ignored him and let him go away. Remembering how he had recoiled, disappointed, burnt her heart. But what was she to do? She still doubted that Cyrus really loved her. He was so conservative that she did not know his true feelings. It could be just spiritual affection and respect, his normal attitude. Gloria decided to continue her respectful attitude towards Cyrus.

2.

It was late at night. Wearing her favourite spotted purple dress and velvet slippers, Gloria slowly climbed down the stairs. In the dimly lit corridor, she walked towards the lounge to have a cool drink. She peeped into the lounge and was startled to see Cyrus sitting there alone, his back to the door, writing a postcard. Her heart pounded. She hesitated to enter and thought: 'Maybe he is writing a postcard to his loved one.' She held back her tears and decided to hurry back to her room.

Cyrus turned to the door and looked surprised and delighted to see Gloria standing at the threshold. He waved his hand and invited her in. His lips curved in a smile. 'You're still awake. I thought you would have gone to bed already.'

'You thought I was in bed?'

Cyrus blushed. 'I think the other members of the tour are already in bed at this time of night.'

'I came down to have a cool drink.' She sank into an armchair and ordered a soft drink. She leaned forward and sipped her drink and remained silent. After a few seconds, as if talking to herself, she murmured, 'It's a beautiful night. I watched the rising and falling waves. It's fantastic.'

'Yes, it is. The waves seem to be dancing in the moonlight.'

'Some time, when the sea is not rough, I'd like to swim at night, but I'm too afraid to go in alone.'

'I wish I could accompany you, but I cannot.'

The constant sound of the waves splashing on the rocks could be heard. Gloria felt it was a good opportunity to tell Cyrus to be more conservative and cautious. She opened her mouth but no words came out; she swallowed. She leaned forward and sipped her drink instead. She struggled with herself as whether she should confide in him or not. Staring down at the floor, she ventured to express her concern. In a low voice, she said, 'By the way, I wanted to tell you something which worries me a lot.'

'Something worries you! What's that? Please, tell me.' Cyrus's tone betrayed his concern.

Gloria tried to express her feelings but she was shy and it was difficult for her to express her deep concern about his life. She mumbled, 'You know, you're a very special person. You speak with courage and faith. Your words open up a new vision of a glorious age.' With a trembling voice she added, 'When you speak your voice vibrates through my soul.' She blushed with a girlish shyness and became silent.

Cyrus blushed. 'Please, don't speak about me. To be honest, it is very embarrassing.'

'Sorry. I just wanted to explain why I'm worried.'

'What's wrong if I advocate building a new world?'

'You speak openly. That may put your life in danger.'

'You're dramatising. I just say what I believe. For me, they're simple truths.'

'People of truth become trapped. They overlook the presence of the devil, who tries to silence the voice of truth.'

'Forget the devil and think of angels,' smiled Cyrus.

'I wish I could. The devil stays around lurking, watching.'

'What I express doesn't harm any individual or any group. It's just for the good of humanity. Why would anyone be alarmed? I don't hate anyone on this planet. Even if I criticise someone, it's only because I want them to do something for their own good, before it's too late.'

'You're too pure to suspect evil in anyone,' Gloria shook her head in despair. 'Even the prophets suffered at the hands of the people they tried to save. They accepted all the hardships for the people. What did they receive in reward? Persecution, jail and death!'

Cyrus raised his arm in the air as if uttering a slogan, 'It's better to follow the steps of those great beings. We have to hold the torch of divine guidance in front of us to shed light on our path. That light can shield us from the evil spirits. They cannot get close to the light. Let them hide in dark pits.' Cyrus's face glowed with intense emotion.

'The world is too degraded to tolerate saints.'

'Would you prefer crooks to dominate over a false world?'

'No, I wouldn't. I would like a world cleansed of all the dirty plots and plans.'

'So, you have to do something.'

Gloria sucked in a deep sigh and leaned back and closed her eyes for a few seconds. She realised with despair that her words would not change the course of his life. With an appealing tone, she suggested, 'At least you veil your meanings in allusive and symbolic language. Entangle the devil in literary techniques- that's what most writers do.'

'To wrap up the meaning of words in a symbolic language so that one has to decipher them like a puzzle. I don't like that.'

'When a work requires interpretation, it gains greater dimension.'

'To gratify everyone's prejudice.' Cyrus grinned. 'The symbols should convey the message, not veil it.'

'To tell the truth openly may endanger your life!' said Gloria, her voice trembling with emotion.

Cyrus stared up at the ceiling. Using poetic language, as if talking to himself, he muttered. 'The goddess of truth is sure of her irresistible beauty and charm. She demands sacrifice from her devotees. Anyone wishing to enter the temple of this goddess has to put on the garb of a pilgrim. He has to purify his soul from all earthly defilement.'

'Falsehood has polluted the atmosphere of politics,' said Gloria, taking on the emotional tone of a speaker at a large meeting. 'A few people dedicated to truth cannot purify the polluted atmosphere. They will be crushed ruthlessly. The wheel of reactionary forces is terrible.'

'The people of truth have to purify the face of the earth from falsehood,' Cyrus continued in an emotional tone. 'Anyone committed to truth has to carry his cross upon his shoulder.'

Gloria let out a deep breath. 'I hope you're not going to be a martyr.'

'This is the path I've chosen to tread. I cannot be apathetic to millions of people groaning under the lashes of tyranny and poverty.' His face was aglow with an intense emotion.

Gloria stared at him and met his eyes glittering with a great light. They were too sparkling to gaze at. She turned her head away and remained speechless.

A silence took over.

She closed her eyes, meditating. It flashed in her mind that Cyrus was standing on a scaffold waiting to be hanged. Her eyes welled with tears. She turned her face away to hide her tears, walked to the window and disappeared behind the curtain, pretending to watch the sea in the moonlight. She wiped away her tears with the back of her hand and tried to bring her emotions under control. She glanced at the billowing waves under the silver moonlight.

Not to give Cyrus the impression that she had deserted him, Gloria popped out her head from behind the curtain and called to him, 'Come and see how the moonlight dances in the rising and falling waves.' She pretended that was the reason she had disappeared behind the curtain.

Cyrus responded immediately and crossed to the window. They stood side by side, leaning out of the window, watching the roaring waves. Both were silent for some moments. Their breathing sounded loud. They were absorbed in the beauty of sea, rocks, waves and moonlight with its sense of mystery in the night.

After a while Cyrus turned to Gloria. She looked up and their gaze met. The pale moonlight was highlighted on her long black hair dropping on her shoulders. Her full lips were slightly parted, seemingly waiting to receive a warm and passionate kiss. Cyrus's heart throbbed and he was tempted to hug her most affectionately and press her lovingly to his chest, but he restrained himself.

She glanced up, sensing that beyond those glittering eyes Cyrus's soul treasured a precious mystery that he could not share. She dropped her head, blushing and shy, feeling the warmth of his breath. Her heart was beating fast.

Cyrus stared at her innocent face. In his mind's eye he could see a crown shining on her head. She was a pearl.

A faint smile hovered on his lips and he stared up at the sky, musing over the twinkling stars. Thus, the emotional atmosphere became a little relaxed.

She glanced up to see what Cyrus was watching. The sky was fresh and clean, as if the stars had come down close to the earth, smiling. Gloria had vague and mixed feelings but was uplifted. 'I wish I could soar in the limitless space. I don't like the earth polluted by falsehood and exploitation. I would like to live in heaven, not on the earth.'

'We're labouring to make the earth an all-glorious paradise,' said Cyrus.

Gloria shook her head in disbelif. 'How can this earth be a heaven?'

'When the earth reflects divine justice, glory and beauty. When everybody has a fair share of the wealth of this planet. When universal peace makes the earth a blessed homeland. When all nations live as members of one family. Then, the earth will mirror heaven. That's the meaning of the Kingdom of God on earth promised by the prophets.'

3.

Gloria was in her room, reading a novel. It was a love story. She was very curious to know the end, but could not concentrate. Her mind was distracted by the thought of Cyrus. She wished she could share with him some parts of the novel expressing emotions similar to hers. She wished Cyrus would knock at the door and come in. But she knew that he would not do such a thing. Gloria closed the novel, dreaming of how she had met Cyrus in the lounge the previous night. She had tried to persuade him to be cautious and conservative in expressing his views but had not succeeded. She felt an admiration for his courage and sincerity. She stepped to the window and stared out at the beach. The sun had already set and it was growing darker. In contrast with the previous night, the sea was calm and looked endless. No wind was blowing, no wave was roaring. The moonlight had spread a silver cloth on the wrinkled face of the sea. Patches of cloud were floating in the sky.

Her eyes fastened on a shadow on the beach and she could make out that it was the figure of a man. Someone was strolling alone by the seaside rocks. He walked light-winged as if his feet did not touch the ground. Curious, she followed the movement of the figure closely. He climbed onto the top of a rock and sat down staring at the sea in a meditative mood. He seemed very thoughtful. The movements of his limbs, his light tread and his meditative attitude told her that the figure could not be anyone but Cyrus. She gazed at him for some moments. In the pale moonlight, he was sitting alone on a seashore rock, meditating. He had the aura of a saint. But not a saint who would turn away from society in disgust, to take refuge in a cave to meditate for personal salvation, to unburden himself from the cares and anxieties of life. Rather, a saint involved in activities to contribute his share to bring about changes for the betterment of society. One who could spiritually develop through social intereaction and burnish his heart by passing through tests. Gloria wondered why Cyrus had gone there to sit alone, and what he was pondering over.

The moon appeared from behind a floating patch of cloud and lit the whole seashore. Now she could clearly see Cyrus sitting on a rock, not far from the hotel. She wished she could sit beside him on that romantic night, to stare at the gentle short waves on the wrinkled face of the sea. But she hesitated, not wanting to start the rumour-mongers talking. She knew that she would be safe with Cyrus in a room or on the seashore, alone, in the daytime or at night. She knew that Cyrus had self-esteem and dignity and would not debase or degrade himself by misleading a girl. Her intellect told her not to go out to the seashore and be seen with Cyrus at that time of night. But her heart was driving her to be close to Cyrus. A battle was still going on between her reason and her emotion when she realised that she was walking on the beach towards Cyrus.

When she got close to him, she walked on tiptoes so as not to be noticed. He was sitting there, deep in thought, as if bearing the burden of a wayward generation.

Cyrus felt the presence of somebody before he saw Gloria. He looked around and stared down at Gloria. But, wrapped in his thoughts, he did not recognise her for a few seconds. Suddenly his eyes met Gloria's, as she stood at the foot of the rock, smiling and silent. Delight flashed in his eyes. A wave of electricity passed through his veins and his heart beat faster. Cyrus smiled back and did not know what to do. Both were silent for a few seconds. It was quite unexpected. Gloria broke the silence. 'When I was watching the seashore from the window of my room, I saw you strolling on the beach. And when you came onto this rock and started meditating, I wanted to join you in your meditation.'

'Sometimes I like to walk on the beach at night to meditate, especially in the moonlight.'

'Meditating on what?'

'I'm wondering if the human race is going to perish or be reborn.'

'Isn't there a third choice?' asked Gloria.

'No.'

'Why?'

'If we are not guided by spiritual wisdom, we will self-destruct.'

Gloria wanted to change the course of the conversation. It was a romantic night. She moved closer to Cyrus and sat beside him, hoping he might disclose his heart to her. Both were silent, staring at the gentle waves of the sea. The air was fresh and pleasant. Gloria was breathing deeply and could hear within herself angels singing a love song. She turned to Cyrus. 'I've learned to read palms. Devi taught me.'

'Really.'

'If you don't believe me, I'll prove to you that I can tell you how long you will live.'

Cyrus smiled. 'I will live long.'

'Let me see your hands.'

Cyrus stretched out both hands. Gloria put them on hers to examine them. To her surprise, in that cool night his hands were very warm. They were extraordinary, with many deep lines. She looked at the lifeline and saw that his life would not be short. She was delighted about that discovery. She examined the lines of marriage without telling him what she was looking at and murmured, 'Your wife will love you very much.'

'You think so?'

'Your palm lines show it.' With a slightly trembling voice she whispered shyly, 'You deserve it. She will be very lucky.'

She looked at his hands more closely and suddenly, with the joy of a discovery, she said, 'Look, in both your hands there are stars. It's strange. That cannot be seen in everybody's hands.'

Cyrus glanced at Gloria and with an appealing tone said, 'Gloria, Gloria, please, forgive me. I cannot switch off my mind from the news that I've received today. One hundred thousand people have been killed within two days. Some were buried half-alive. These people have children, wives, fiancees, brothers, sisters, mothers and fathers. It seems nobody cares. These atrocious happenings have become normal. It's unbelievable that the world has become so degraded, so debased and apathetic. I wonder why the cries of the victims, the lamentation of bereaved mothers, sisters, fiancées and spouses of those who are killed in war or executed by the hand of tyranny are not heard. It seems God has turned his back on a degenerate race. No one is secure and happy or has peace of mind. Everywhere, people are threatened with instability, turmoil and agitation. Is this really a natural and healthy life? Or is something wrong somewhere? Please, forgive me, please forgive me.'

He kissed Gloria's soft hands, then freed them. He closed his eyes and became silent.

Gloria was disappointed. But she knew that Cyrus was spiritually linked to the people of the world and could not help feeling their suffering. He looked upward and stared at the moon floating in a patch of cloud. With a gentle and sad voice he suggested, 'Let's pray.'

Gloria became silent and her head drooped sadly. After a while she raised her head and glanced at Cyrus. His eyes were closed and his lips were moving, muttering something. She realised that he was praying. The tears rolling down his face had an angelic beauty in the reflection of the moonlight. His genuine love for humanity touched her heart. She joined him in prayer.

4.

Wearing an embroidered African shirt, Yasha waved his hand to the others to join him around the table under the pleasant cool shade of a willow tree. Julia had taken a shower. With uncombed and wet hair, drying in soft little curls, she rushed to the shade of the willow and sat on a bench fixed in the ground. Wearing an Indian-style dress with a turban on her head, a broad smile on her face, Devi stepped towards the spot.

Newspapers, national and international, were scattered on the table. Captions caught the eye reporting war, mass killings, murder, rape, corruption, explosions on the ground and in the air. Hundreds of people killed on purpose or by mistake added to natural disasters such as flood, earthquake and cyclone.

Julia glanced at the reports. 'No good news, all disaster.'

Peter leaned forward, reached for a newspaper, stared at some captions and tossed the paper onto the table. 'I hate these newspapers. All they report is violence, tragedy, disaster, murder, and war. Is there nothing else to report?'

Yasha grasped a newspaper, glanced at some pages and tumbled it onto the table. 'Most of the news is depressing.' Then he stared at the creek running through the hotel's extensive grounds to distract his mind from the distressing situation.

Rubbing his jaw in frustration, Peter said, 'Sometimes I feel like tearing up the newspapers and throwing them into a rubbish bin.'

Yasha stared at Peter and smiled. 'Don't tear up the newspapers. They're just a mirror reflecting the society.'

'Our society and our planet are both sick. Both have lost their balance,' said Cyrus.

Devi let out a sigh. 'The unusual natural disasters portend a horrible catastrophe.'

'Sick blood suppurates,' said Cyrus. 'If you treat pus in one spot, it appears in another spot. No healthy blood runs in its veins.'

Tapping his lips with his index finger, Victor protested,

'Don't philosophise about bad news. The public likes shocking news. If the news doesn't shock them, it's not real news.'

'That's a bad habit,' said Devi, 'to get used to being-shocked all the time.'

'The most shocking news is the news most in demand,' said Victor.

'Top news belongs to the terrorists, not to the scientists and artists,' said Devi.

'I repeat,' Victor tapped on the coffee table angrily, 'people like shocking news and the mass media feed them with what they like.'

Yasha stood up and stared at the soft-murmuring creek. It was late afternoon, calm and pleasant, growing cool. The birds filled the air with their sweet songs. A gentle breeze was blowing.

Yasha glanced at an international newspaper and picked it up. His face grew gloomier and gloomier with every line he read. 'Terrible!'

'What is?' asked Victor.

Absorbed in the news, Yasha did not hear the question. He shook his head in disappointment and murmured, 'Moving from right to left, and from left to right, left right, right left doesn't make much difference. Restlessness, problems and poverty are still there.'

His palms resting upward on his knees, Victor leaned forward and teased Yasha. 'Right, left, left, right! You sound like a military commander! Please tell us what you're reading.

Yasha dropped the newspaper onto the table. 'Look at Russia. They trumpeted out that they would build a paradise for their people and a model for the rest of the world.'

Victor laughed mockingly. 'They believed they could force the other nations to follow their ideals.'

Waving his hand in the air, Cyrus said, 'They have come to a standstill. They're trying to find a way out but don't know which road to take as an alternative.'

Devi sipped from the soft-drink bottle. 'It's incredible! Their political and economic assumptions suddenly appear to be empty and shaky.'

Victor swung his hand in the air, as if uttering a political slogan. 'The star of socialism is setting.'

Yasha stared at Victor for a few seconds, then leant forward. 'My friend! That doesn't mean the star of capitalism is rising.'

'The failure of the communist ideology means the *victory* of the capitalist system,' said Victor, with emphasis on the word victory.

'One concept doesn't necessarily follow the other,' argued Cyrus.

Silence took over. They wondered which ideal was without defect. Cyrus turned to Victor and expressed his view. 'In my opinion capitalism and communism are two sides of one coin.'

'What's that coin?'

'A collapsing materialistic civilisation.'

Victor was startled and stared at Cyrus in anger. The statement was quite unexpected and too difficult for him to digest. He wanted to repel and repudiate it promptly.

Victor hated and feared the Left movement, and he had done so from childhood. He thought the enthusiastic advocates of Communism were mistaken in believing that Marxism was the ultimate salvation for the whole world. Then their built-up propaganda had unexpectedly toppled down. After the collapse of the USSR, he gained more confidence in the validity of capitalism as a secure and solid system.

A thought suddenly flashed in Victor's mind: how can one be absolutely sure of the stability of the Capitalistic system? It was a vague feeling but it disturbed him to think of it. He tried to convince himself that this was impossible. He simply said to himself that Marxism was a mistake from the beginning. The mistake was now exposed. Let it end.

With a tone disclosing anger as well as despair, he asked Cyrus, 'Do you think the Western Bloc will have a similar fate to the Eastern Communist countries?'

Cyrus stared up at the sky as if trying to discern something flashing on the distant horizon. With a voice betraying sadness, he muttered reluctantly, 'It certainly looks like it.'

This answer made Victor's head spin. His face paled. He felt as if the foundations upon which he stood so proudly might crack at any time just as an earthquake might come without warning to shake an apparently solid building, making it crumble. He remained speechless with his head down for a few seconds. Then he raised his head and tried to retrieve his confidence so as to repudiate Cyrus's statement; but there was an unconscious despair. There was neither hope nor faith in his voice.

'The Communist countries are beginning to realise that the capitalistic system works better.'

'You think so!' said Cyrus. 'They are passing through a period of frustration. They are desperately looking for an alternative.'

'If they don't find that alternative, what then?'

'They may fall back into capitalism.'

Devi shook her head in despair. 'Futility, futility of human effort, a waste of energy and lives for an illusion.'

'It's pitiful and frustrating to slip back to the first rung of the ladder,' said Yasha.

'We live in an age of frustration,' said Cyrus. 'Man has broken his ties with the old ways but hasn't found the new path. He's floundering with no direction, hope or vision.'

'Look at our youth,' said Yasha. 'They are a disillusioned generation with no hope or plan for the future.'

Julia smiled. 'I'm not a youth, but I belong to the younger generation. We can't do anything. We have no role in building our world. The world has been made for us. We have to fit in willy-nilly.'

Cyrus stared at Julia, thoughtful. 'Pessimism is no good. It paralyses the younger generation. It can destroy their will to build a better world. They are like the passive inhabitants of a collapsing building.'

'Politicians are expected to solve political and economic problems,' said Victor.

'I wish they could,' said Cyrus. 'I think it's a mistake when people focus all their hopes on politicians.'

'Politicians try to find solutions for economic, social or political problems.'

'But they feel they can't. They are frustrated. They don't know why.'

'So what! They do their best,' Victor repudiated the criticism.

'They're skilful performers.'

'But the script is wrong,' interrupted Devi. 'Something's wrong somewhere.'

'Some of them sense,' said Yasha, 'that the present world

order is defective. But they are enmeshed in the system. They can't disentangle themselves from it.'

'Politicians are as bewildered, confused, and impotent as the rest of the people,' said Cyrus. 'The forces that will change society seem to be beyond their control.'

'We are in the same boat,' said Devi. 'I'm afraid they are no less miserable than we are.'

'I wonder what social pattern the younger generation will use to build their future world on.'

'It's better to search for a new source of inspiration,' suggested Cyrus, 'and find a new social pattern which hasn't been tried yet.'

Yasha leant back and rested his head on his clasped palms, gazing at the birds twittering on the boughs. 'I sense a great light is breaking through. But I have neither the vision nor the faith of Cyrus.'

Julia reached for her coffee cup, took a sip, put it back on the table and stared at the running creek. After a short pause, she muttered, 'It's dark, it's dark. I don't see any light.'

Chapter Eight

PARIS

1.

Yasha took a quick shower and rushed out to see Paris. For him Paris was the bride of Europe and the world's most romantic city. He wanted to stroll in the Rue de la Paix, Avenue de l'Opera, and so on, the streets and avenues where once Victor Hugo, Lamartine and his other favourite writers and poets had walked. It was dusk when he got off the train and emerged from the metro at the Arc de Triomphe. He shoved his hands in the pockets of his jeans, and, a smile on his lips, strolled briskly along the broad Boulevard du Champs- Elysees.

He reached Place de la Concorde and his eyes swept across the vast square and he stared at the place where the guillotine once stood. The outburst of emotion which gave rise to the French Revolution swept through his mind. He struggled to avoid the image of Queen Marie Antoinette, who was beheaded in that square. He entered Paris with great joy, eager to see the city where music, art, literature and sculpture flourished.

Absorbed in her dreams, Gloria walked in front of the queue along the banks of the Seine; she occasionally stared at the river flowing through Paris, a city roughly circular in shape, which sat in a low-lying basin.

It was a pleasant, cool morning. The sun was rising in the blue sky, warming up the weather.

Cyrus walked behind Gloria, admiring her shapely body and the gentle curve of her waist. Her dangling earrings sometimes tapped her dress. As she walked she fluffed her softly waving hair so that it tumbled around her shoulders. He breathed in the fragrance that nestled in her hair and wafted over his face. Cyrus wanted to hold the soft hair, to smell it and press it against his cheeks.

Unexpectedly Gloria glanced back and smiled. Cyrus's cheeks coloured and he dropped his eyes.

They reached the Tuileries Gardens where the tall trees formed an arbour around a pool.

Sitting on a bench under the pleasing shady trees, Gloria stared at the white swans gliding on the water and occasionally plunging their heads beneath the surface. She watched the reflection of the sunlight dancing on the gentle waves of the water and looked up at the sun twinkling through the boughs and twigs. The twittering of the songbirds brought gladness to her heart.

A group of young girls and men, carrying musical instruments, their faces aglow with enthusiasm, approached the pool. They were in high spirits, almost as if they were intoxicated, though it was obvious that they were not. Something set them apart. It was as if they drew inner energy from a source above the turmoil of the world around them. Cyrus recognised one of the group members and applauded them as welcoming gesture.

A broad smile on his face, the conductor of the group asked permission to play and sing. The spectators nodded and smiled to show their approval. The group comprised young people of various ethnic backgrounds. The opening chords of their music imitated the warbling of birds at dawn to awaken the sleepy. Melodious singing, accompanied by

music, echoed through the park:
> Behold, behold the sky is cleaving,
> The thick cloud is rapidly leaving.
> The sunlight is breaking through,
> It is not a lie, it's a fact, it's true.

> Lo, lo, a new glorious age is dawning,
> Rejoice; rejoice a new era is coming.

> A new spirit has been breathed,
> Devils and ghosts have retreated.
> Divine words have been revealed,
> Creative energies are concealed.

> Lo, lo, a new glorious age is dawning,
> Rejoice; rejoice a new era is coming.

> No man will be tortured for his ideas,
> No one will be executed for his ideals.
> The dignity of man will be protected,
> Freedom of thoughts will be respected.

> Lo, lo a new glorious age is dawning,
> Rejoice; rejoice a new era is coming.

> Religions no longer be confusing,
> Spiritual paths will be fusing.
> Outworn theories are discredited,
> New values will be merited.

> Lo, lo a new glorious age is dawning,
> Rejoice; rejoice a new era is coming.

Hark, hark a celestial melody is heard on high,
Look, look a brilliant destiny is shining afar.
The long prophetic cycle has already gone,
The day of fulfillment has assuredly come.

Lo, lo a new glorious age is dawning,
Rejoice; rejoice a new era is coming.

To fulfil the vision, there is a clue,
The sweet dream is coming true.
War, tyranny are superstitions,
Peace, justice is man's conviction.

Lo, lo a new glorious age is dawning,
Rejoice; rejoice a new era is coming.

The spectators joined in the chorus - 'Lo, lo a new glorious age is dawning; rejoice, rejoice a new era is coming.' Carried away, some started dancing with the rhythm of the music, as if the song was expressing their aspirations and cherished desires. The song touched their hearts and brought a thirst for unity, peace and love. A new horizon was being opened; a glimpse of a new world was sparkling in the distance. The birds were warbling and twittering, filling the air with their sweet singing. They took flight and flew high towards the horizon where the sun had risen.

2.

Wearing white trousers and blouse, and a blue ribbon around her head matching her blue boots and belt, Gloria was sitting erect on a black mare ready to lead the group for a horse ride. The seven horses stood in a row, snorting impatiently.

It was early morning. The air was fresh and cool. The sun was peeping over the hills, kissing the open mouth of the blossoms waking up in the bosom of the sunlight. The shadows of the riders on horseback stretched long on the meadows.

Wearing blue safari clothes and black boots, sitting on a chestnut stallion, Cyrus was second in line inhaling the fragrant breeze caressing Gloria's pony-tailed hair.

'Why does a woman lead the group?' teased Victor.

Gloria turned back, glanced at him and laughed loudly. 'Why not?'

'Among the tribes of the world, horsemanship has been the male's domain.'

Gloria laughed. 'The tribal system is ending.'

'Man is a man, always and forever.'

'Prove your ability in horse racing.' Gloria urged the mare into a gallop and rode away fast.

Gloria's mare raced into the field, leaving the rest behind. They realised that Gloria was a good rider. Victor did his best to win but failed. He was upset, cursing the horse and losing his temper. Julia and Devi teased him. Cyrus was skilful but had no training. He galloped and thundered after Gloria. They raced in a flowing rhythm. The sun glinted on the brass ornaments on the saddle and bridle of Gloria's horse. Her long black hair was streaming behind. Cyrus tried his best to gallop fast enough to keep up with Gloria. They galloped away, outpaced the others and disappeared. Their companions did not know which direction the two had taken, so they rode at a more relaxed pace, teasing, laughing and chatting.

Gloria did not even glance behind to see if the others could keep up with her. Cyrus wondered why she was racing so fast towards an unknown destination, without considering that the others had lagged behind.

Gloria's horse galloped as if its feet barely touched the ground. It seemed to be flying in the air like a fairy-tale steed, with a princess riding on its back, followed by a devoted lover. The mare moved gracefully, like the waves of the sea rising and falling.

Cyrus could see an aura around Gloria's head, representing woman in the coming age. He foresaw a world of the future where women would lead in most areas of human activity.

Gloria knew that she had outpaced the other members of the group but she could hear the hoofs of one horse pounding behind her. She sensed it was Cyrus's stallion. They approached a dale at the foot of the hill where a cluster of trees formed a shelter. The gentle murmuring of a stream caressed her soul. Gloria reduced the speed of the mare, allowing it to cool down before stopping.

Cyrus forced the stallion to a halt, quickly dismounted and rushed to Gloria to help her down.

Cyrus held out his arms to Gloria. She gently and willingly came down into his arms and clasped his neck to support herself. Her soft breast pressed against his chest. When her body touched his, he was irresistibly drawn to her. He tenderly hugged her, affectionately kissed her petal-like cheeks and lovingly pressed her to his chest. In a waking dream, like an intoxicated man, he was not aware of what he did.

Gloria stared at him in surprise, not disclosing her true feelings. There was no rebuke or blame in her look.

Cyrus's face was pale; he trembled as if an electric current had passed through his body. His breathing was short and fast, and his heart pounded audibly. He felt a sense of shame, as if he had woken up from a dream. He dropped his head shyly, feeling guilty, and avoided Gloria's gaze. He wanted to kneel down before her to apologise, to ask forgiveness if he had hurt her. To him, her feelings and her wishes were paramount. But he found he could not utter a word.

Gloria, speechless, turned away and walked up the creek bank to where a spring was gushing out beneath an old tree. As she walked she picked flowers from the shrubs along the way. Staring at the spring, she threw the flower petals into the stream and watched them dance up and down on the running water. Tides of emotion rose and fell within her and she murmured a love song.

For Cyrus, a new door of emotion had opened. The power of an irresistible love overcame all the other feelings and possessed his being. Gloria was dear to him, but now she was the spice of life, she was life itself. Every strand of her hair, everything about her was precious to him. He knew she respected him, but now he was worried that she might not respond to his love. What then? That meant the end of the world for him. Anxiety overtook him and made him weak. He wanted to go to her and express his love. But he could not walk. His feet were so weak that he felt he might fall. He sat down wondering what he should do. A flame was blazing in his heart and soul that could burn him to cinders. He had that capacity for love that made him willing to die for his beloved. He muttered, 'O dear Gloria! O dearest Gloria! I love you more than my heart. To me, you are more precious than my eyes! Please don't wound my feelings. I love you, I love you more than you can imagine. You're a pearl, a diamond. No, you're more than that. You're priceless. My heart is tender and delicate. Please, don't break it. If you do, you may hurt yourself, because you're enshrined there. Your image is engraved in my heart and your love is cherished.' His eyes filled with tears.

Cyrus sat and thought for a while. He wanted to express his love but he did not know how to propose marriage to his beloved. He was worried Gloria might reject his proposal, which would mean the end of the world for him - a death sentence. A fiery emotion kindled his whole being and made him yearn for Gloria. He tried to gather his strength to be able to approach her to express his love. He tried to regain his self-confidence by convincing himself that he had the qualities Gloria could admire. But he was not sure whether Gloria had already promised to marry someone else.

He walked along the creek and after a few minutes saw Gloria sitting under the trees close to a spring, her face reflected in the crystal-like water. As soon as he saw her he trembled as if an electric current had hit him. He felt weak again and was not able to walk properly.

Gloria seemed absorbed in her thoughts, observing the dance of the flower petals on the running water. The birds filled the air with their pleasant singing.

Cyrus made a great effort and got close to her.

Gloria felt Cyrus's presence, but did not raise her head, pretending not to have seen him.

He stood mute, spellbound by her beauty, possessed of an emotion too powerful to bear.

She raised her head, stared at a patch of cloud in the sky taking various shapes-- a lamb, an eagle, a bear. She felt she had grown wings and was flying in the air.

The atmosphere was charged with an intense emotion. Both were too shy to look at each other. Their hearts were beating with great expectation. It looked as if Gloria's most cherished desire, her sweetest dream, was going to be fulfilled.

Still trembling slightly, Cyrus opened his mouth to say something but the words dried up. He could not utter a word. He was a good speaker, but to his surprise it was difficult for him to arrange a proper sentence. With much difficulty he stammered out with a quivering voice, 'Gloria, dear Gloria, I would like to tell you that I love you. Believe me, I love you. I honestly love you. I love you with all my heart and soul. I hope you know how much I do love you. Everything about you has become dear to me. The dress you wear, even the shoes you wear are dear to me. The horse that you ride is not the same horse any more; it is a lucky horse, a dear one to me. The ground you sit on, the house you live in are dear to me. The city that you live in is the most beautiful city in the whole world.' Cyrus sweated, but crooned his love song. Gloria listened; her head down, she looked at the spring.

Both remained silent. It was a sensitive moment.

Cyrus continued, 'Gloria! I dearly love you. You're very precious to me. I love your very being. I love *you*, that *you* that I can feel but cannot describe.' His words were charged with emotion.

Cyrus wondered if Gloria could feel the depth of his emotion. He knew words alone could not convey his feelings. Words were just the shadows and symbols of the emotion. His throat choked and his last words were muffled. His mouth was dry as if he had run a long race. He stopped speaking, his lips trembling with emotion. He felt a burning sensation in his nostrils and his eyes dampened.

There was a silence.

Still with her head down, amusing herself by throwing flower petals into the creek, she asked in a whisper, 'That was all you wanted to tell me?'

For her, love and life were not separated. If she responded to his love, it meant she wanted to live with him.

Cyrus was encouraged to express his wish, the significant decision, and the most determining event in his life. 'Dear Gloria! It is my cherished desire to live with you. It is an honour for me to be your partner for life. I think we are made for each other. I feel we are like two polar stars balancing and matching one another. We are the perfect match.' He uttered these words with a voice charged with emotion.

Gloria sprang up and gazed at Cyrus. Her eyes glittered with a dazzling light, emitting electro-waves of love too strong for him to bear. He had never seen eyes emitting such an electric power of love. Trembling with emotion, he immediately turned his head away and stared at the ground.

She gracefully stepped towards him, gently kissed his cheek and walked down the curved creek bank without saying a word. She stepped away gracefully carrying his heart with her. She disappeared and his eyes remained fixed on the path where she walked.

Stunned and bewitched, he stood there trembling with emotion. It was a sweet and burning kiss. He never forgot the moment when the soft lips of Gloria touched his cheek for the first time. It was electrifying. A current passed through his veins and bones. He remained motionless, puzzled and bemused as if his mind numbed. A fire flared in his heart, melting his self away. Gloria entered into his heart and became a part of him. She resided in him.

Bewitched and infatuated, he stood there a while. He did not know what to do. His whole being desired Gloria. She was the very breath of life for him. Without her the world was dull and dead. At the same time he felt that he could not get close to her. It was as if the electric current she emitted was too strong for him to approach. He could not resist the invisible magnetism that attracted him to her.

He walked down the path, alongside the stream, in the direction Gloria had taken, hoping to find her. His greatest desire, his ultimate hope soon became that of seeing her. Nothing was more important for him than to find her safe. He prayed in his heart for her safety. He was ready to accept any pain to relieve her. He would rather something happen to him than to her. He searched for her and was worried beyond words at what might happen to her. He felt that she could not have returned to the hotel on foot. It was too far to walk. He knew that her hired horse was still fastened to the tree. Worried, exhausted and baffled, he turned to heaven and prayed, 'O God! Give me back my dearest Gloria safe and sound.' In the grip of an intense emotion, his eyes were wet.

When he lost hope of finding her, he turned back towards the horses with a heavy heart. On his way, he continued to scan the area in despair. In the gloom of desperation, suddenly a light flashed. He saw somebody standing behind a thick tree near the road. He looked more closely.

It was Gloria!

A bunch of wild flowers in her hand, her back leaning against the trunk of the tree, she was staring at the sky absorbed in her thoughts. The agonising despair vanished.

He felt a pleasant relief. A great joy filled his heart and it throbbed with excitement. She was sweet and attractive. He approached her. Gloria glanced at him with a dazzling smile. He took her hands, drew them to his lips and kissed them with great affection. Rays of love were emanating from her shining blue eyes. He embraced her soft body most lovingly. She responded, put her arms around his neck and hugged him, nestling against him. She leant her head against his chest, listened to the regular thump of his heartbeat, breathed his male scent. She stared up at him with her sensual blue eyes and kissed him. Then she rested her cheeks against his chest. The warmth of her soft breast pressing against his chest was too electrifying. He released her. Both stood pale, trembling slightly, breathing fast. Their emotion abated and they sat on the stones silent and thoughtful.

After a while Gloria said, 'We should go back to the hotel. They may become worried.'

They galloped away without saying a word. They found the other members of the group picnicking in a spot off the road. Devi and Julia stared at them inquiringly and smiled. They immediately realised that something had passed between them.

3.

That night, Cyrus tossed and twisted in bed and could not sleep. He sat up and stared at the silver moonlight dimly lighting the room. He pushed aside the blanket, swung his legs out of the bed, went over to the window and stared up at the sky. The moon was gracefully floating amidst the scattered clouds. The moonlit night gave to Cyrus a sense of mystic harmony with creation, which the glaring sun never did. He felt the world of being was covered in a veil of fathomless mysteries. Staring at the twinkling stars, his heart yearned for Gloria. She was to him a heavenly being.

Cyrus's love for Gloria opened a new door to understanding. He saw woman as a delicate creature whose qualities had long been ignored and even despised. For him, Gloria was the herald of the new era-- an era enriched and blessed with female qualities. She was the harbinger of the dawn of an age permeated with the female qualities of love, compassion, mercy, caring and motherhood. He thought: when women reach their potential, human society will be purged from the curse of war, violence and the struggle for power that has plagued the whole recorded history of humankind. Women will no more be sex objects created to gratify man's passion, no more a part of man's household.

He wished that he and Gloria could be two polar stars shining from two horizons, their lights mingling as one-- two distinct entities, but each one matching and completing the other half to become one perfect being. He had no intention of possessing her, or of moulding her to his design. He hoped that their marriage would not turn out to be a cage where they would be doomed to flutter their wings against the bars. He believed marriage was not just the sexual attraction of two bodies, but rather the union of two souls, the most perfect unity that could be imagined between two human beings. To him, marriage was not the enslavement of two people to one another, but rather a union providing healthy and energising conditions for mutual protection and spiritual growth. Marriage could make their lives fuller. Cyrus was certain that Gloria had the potential to contribute much to make their lives richer and more perfect.

He got up and played a cassette. Every word had a meaning for him, expressing his emotion. But still it could not fully express his love for her. His whole being was in the grasp of an intense feeling. For him, love had degrees and stages. No one could reach the last stage. The highest stage of love was the love of God for human beings that could never be measured by human standards. He believed that a true and genuine love between man and woman was a reflection of divine love-- a ray of that celestial sun.

He wished in a dim light he could gaze at Gloria's innocent face, the face of a potential mother, a creature responsible for the continuity of the human race. He knew, in the past, the female qualities had never been appreciated by male standards. He thought: no female quality has been fully understood and appreciated yet. An appreciation has started budding, but is not yet flourishing. It will take time to reach the apex of flowering. He believed the application and influence of female qualities would bring about a great and blessed change in the world. Violence and bloodshed would no longer be glorified as valour and honour.

Cyrus wondered what Gloria might be doing at that moment. Was she awake or asleep? He was experiencing another realm of consciousness-- flying, floating beyond the boundaries of his physical existence. He was dying of himself and living in his beloved. The self-effacement was very sweet. He wished he could perpetuate the sweet moments.

He was curious to know the nature of Gloria's love. He believed that in the past, women had had very limited and restricted chance to express love. Although they had a great potential for love, in almost all cultures the female had no right to fall in love. The pent-up emotion was being released, being expressed. He was of the opinion that a new dimension of love would be introduced into society-- a finer and more spiritual one. It would enrich literature and art. He knew that female love was more enduring and deeper.

He could not accept that a woman like Gloria could be looked down upon. Anger filled him. It was disgusting to think that for thousands of years it was believed that women had been created to satisfy man's sexual desire. The female mental and spiritual potential remained dormant and concealed. He believed that in the past the human world was defective and incomplete because the potential of women had been ignored, neglected and consequently atrophied-- the same potential that ultimately would create a balanced and healthy civilisation. Women had been depicted as cowardly, the weaker sex, unable to go into the battlefield to kill and be killed. It was not understood and appreciated that women had a greater moral courage in time of danger and crisis. Women were not allowed to occupy a responsible position or even participate in religious orders. It was thought that women had not the same ability for spiritual and religious experience as men. On the contrary, it is being demonstrated more and more that women's spirituality is very intense and fiery.

It was a mystery to Cyrus how female qualities had gone unrecognised and unappreciated for so long among the nations and cultures throughout the world. He thought: who is responsible for that? Who can be blamed? The whole structure of society and the way of thinking was such that there had been no opportunity for female qualities to be made active. So, they remained like a buried treasure, as if they did not exist at all. The coming of women onto the stage is an integral part of the spiritual evolution of human society on this planet. A glorious age is dawning. Some compelling spiritual force has set this process in motion and propels it forward. The world is under the effect of a new spirit. The whole structure of the human world is undergoing a great change. One of the factors responsible for this change is the fact that the potential of women is being awakened and made active.

Cyrus thought the participation of women in building the future world would transform the very nature of society. Society would no longer be governed by force. He became excited and punched his fist in the air. 'A glorious age is dawning with dazzling brightness.'

That night, the smouldering fire of love in Cyrus's heart turned into an incandescent blaze. Gloria occupied his mind. He walked down to the lounge for a chat so as to distract his mind. His love and admiration for Gloria extended to the whole female gender. He wanted to roar like a lion to defend the rights of women, to prove that they were not the inferior sex, but rather in respect of spiritual qualities and alertness the superior one. But, at the same time, he was aware that if he uttered such a notion he would be laughed at and be looked on as a sentimentalist, not a real man. In a world where female potential was only now budding, how could he convey a picture of the beauty of the bloom that he could see through his visionary eyes? In a world where, in many lands, women were still belittled and deprived of their basic rights, how could he demonstrate that women would take the lead in many human activities? Those qualities were still not recognisable. No one would believe him, not even most women! He was determined to talk about his ideas, and to prove that women had been the victims of injustice for thousands of years.

Cyrus stepped into the lounge and ordered a soft drink. He did not touch the glass of Coke for a long time. Staring out of the window, he was absorbed in his thoughts about the injustice imposed on women. He did not notice that Victor, Peter and Yasha had entered the lounge. Cyrus was startled when he heard Yasha say, 'You seem very thoughtful, Cyrus. Anything wrong?' Cyrus swept his gaze from the window and glared at the three friends. They were looking at him, smiling.

Cyrus shook his head, 'No, no, nothing. I'm just thinking about a particular issue.'

'Thinking of a particular person or an issue?' Victor giggled. There was a devilish edge to his question.

'Not of one person. I'm thinking of half the population of the world.'

'Half the population of the world!' repeated Victor. He looked confused. Stretching his hand out, palm upwards, Victor continued, 'Come on! How can you think about over three thousand million people?'

'The qualities of women, half of the population, were ignored and despised for a long time.' There was pain in Cyrus's remark.

There was a pause.

Yasha stretched out his hand and took the cup of drink, sipped it and muttered, 'Love opens up the door to understanding.'

As if diverting the subject, Cyrus said, 'Yes, that's right. To love God and to understand God are interrelated.'

Victor bent over the coffee table and stared into Cyrus's eyes. 'Tell us about women, not about God. Why are you so obsessed with women's issues? Let women worry about their own problems.'

There was a bullying note in Victor's voice. Victor and Peter knew that Cyrus was on the side of women and they considered it a sign of weakness.

Peter straightened his back and turned to Cyrus. 'In the past, women have had no significant role in religion, and they should not have any important position in the future.'

Cyrus's eyes flared. Trembling, he said, 'You, as a Christian, should know that Mary Magdalene played a significant role in Christian history.'

'What did she do that was so significant?' asked Victor.

'She gathered together the confused, terrified and bereaved disciples three days after the crucifixion of Christ. She inspired in them courage and confidence to carry the Gospel around the world.'

Yasha became interested. Cupping his chin in his right palm, he asked, 'Did Mary do anything else that was significant?'

'Yes, she did,' replied Cyrus promptly.

'What was that?'

'She met the Emperor in Rome,' explained Cyrus, 'on behalf of the Christian community in Palestine and asked him to order the Governor of Judeah to stop persecuting Jews-- those involved in causing the crucifixion of Jesus Christ.'

Peter pinned his eyes on Cyrus. 'I've never heard that before.'

Yasha tapped the coffee table. 'How about so-called civilised people who persecuted the Jews just because they were Jews? The people who were not involved in the crucifixion of Christ?'

'That's a shame!' replied Cyrus.

Peter made the sign of the cross on his chest.

Victor argued, 'Men can do tough jobs, and women cannot.'

Tightening his jaw, Cyrus stared at Victor.

Victor felt uneasy. 'What do you say about this?'

'In a tough world tough people are the heroes, but not in a gentle world.'

'We still live in a tough world. Men are still the heroes,' stated Victor.

'Your tough world, a male-dominated world stained with blood, violence and aggressiveness, is being rolled up. And a new gentle one is being spread out instead.'

Yasha smiled and clapped with excitement, 'Bravo! Cyrus! Well said.'

Just then, Devi and Julia entered the lounge and heard what Yasha had said. They, too, clapped without knowing what was going on, then sat down, laughing.

Victor was not worried about the arrival of the women. He believed Cyrus exaggerated the potentiality of women to such an extent that even women wouldn't side with him.

Victor tried to preserve his self-confidence and challenged Cyrus, 'Where is this gentle world you're talking about? It's in your imagination; it's a delusion. The world is still armed to the teeth. The arms factories still manufacture ammunition. The members of the decision-making bodies, the parliaments, are men. All over the world.'

'There are women, in parliaments all over the world,' protested Julia.

'Yes, very few,' said Victor. He continued in a teasing tone. 'And these women have been appointed just not to break women's hearts.'

Peter laughed loudly. A bitter smile appeared on the corner of Yasha's mouth. Julia and Devi felt humiliated and vexed. Victor glanced proudly across the tables, a satisfied grin on his face.

The silence that followed was charged with emotion.

Suddenly Cyrus's eyes flashed with rage. He thundered in anger: 'The world is writhing in bloodshed, poverty, war, terrorism and misery. This is not something for the men who run the world to brag about or feel puffed up about.'

There was a pause. They had never heard Cyrus roar in such a way.

'It is disgusting,' said Julia, 'to see parliamentary sessions in which men shout at each other. Sometimes they throw rotten eggs at one another.'

'They do not consult,' said Cyrus. 'They debate, and very often they fight.'

Victor, Yasha, Cyrus, Julia, Devi and Peter left the lounge.

4.

Julia entered the lounge and found Devi absorbed in reading a book. 'What are you reading? It has to be something interesting.'

'Yes, it is,' replied Devi. 'It says that we're entering the Aquarian Age, the age of the universality of humankind, a millennium of peace.'

Holding a book, *Astrology: evolution and revolution*, by Alan Oken, Devi continued reading. Julia ordered a coffee and sat sipping silently, not wishing to disturb Devi. After a while, Devi raised her head and said enthusiastically, 'The ideal of the New Age is global unification.'

She read some more and then her eyes remained fixed on a paragraph. Looking perplexed, she said, 'There's something in this book that I don't understand.'

'What is it that puzzles you?' asked Julia.

'There's something here that I haven't heard before.

Under the heading "Bahá'í Leader", it reads, "One of the main tenets of this relatively recently established religion concerns the inherent unity of all humanity.... As such, within its framework of humanitarian efforts and concerns, the Bahá'í Faith is representative of the ideals inherent in the cusp of the Aquarian Age."

'Is it a religious book?'

'No, it isn't. It's a book on astrology,' replied Devi. 'I'm surprised to see that the author uses many astrological terms and techniques, with a diagram, to indicate that the Bahá'í teaching will be the ideal of the Aquarian Age. And it will be the source of guidance for the millennium of world unity.'

'The author may be a Bahá'í,' said Julia.

'No, he isn't. He writes from an astrological point of view.'

'Could you read a little more?' Julia became curious.

'Certainly. It reads, "Neptune rises in Aquarius in Bahá'í chart, sextiles Pluto, and widely squares the Sun. Neptune's position certainly indicates the doctrine discussed in the previous paragraph as well as the bestowal of the vision needed for the mystical experiences and revelations in this Great One's life..."

'I have never heard about the Bahá'í teachings,' interrupted Julia.

Devi continued to read the book with mixed surprise and interest. 'It reads, "Uranus is closely sextile the Sun and widely trine the Moon, indicating that Bahá'í teachings could become very widespread and that his ideas (Sun in Gemini in the 3rd House) could cover a great cross section of humanity.... As well as the ability of the essence of Bahái teachings to unite people of all generations and beliefs."

'I'm not familiar with astrology so I don't understand how he could predict, from an astrological point of view, that the Bahá'í teachings will ultimately unite the world,' commented Julia. 'But I'm not prejudiced. Any religion or school of thought that believes that the teachings of a great being will be able to unite all the nations, religions and races is worth examining and studying.'

Yasha entered the lounge and saw Devi and Julia sitting face to face at a table engaged in conversation. As soon as Yasha approached their table, Julia turned to him and exclaimed as if she had made a discovery, 'Devi is reading a book on astrology that predicts we are entering a millennium of global unification!'

Yasha's eyes flashed with enthusiasm at her words. He became excited at the thought that world unity was inevitable. Humanity stood at the threshold of a great transformation, ready to reach a glorious destiny.

Yasha stood up and raised his fist in the air, proclaiming, 'Humankind is entering a new era, an era in which world peace and world unity is no more a delusion or a theory.' His voice rose high, 'Global unification is a reality! A reality that even the sun, the moon and the stars have forecast.'

Yasha uttered it loudly. The other guests in the lounge turned and looked at him in surprise.

5.

Cyrus was alone in his room reading love stories and poetry. Some poems expressed the same emotions that he felt. His soul had been walled in and needed a crack. Love was opening it up to new dimensions of emotional experience. Love was the flower of the soul. His soul was flowering.

He believed that what he felt in his heart was more direct

understanding than what he might formulate in his mind. That day he did not go out to join the others. He was inclined to be alone, to communicate with the soul of his beloved. He did not dare approach Gloria. His emotion was too intense. He did not want to reveal his emotions to anyone else. He felt as if his emotions might be stripped naked before prying eyes.

The sun set; night fell. He stood at the window staring out at the pale moon rising and kissing the tips of the leaves and twigs. He glanced at a path leading to a pond surrounded by overhanging willows and palms. Lights were on in various spots among the shrubs, trees and plants. The dim light was colouring the grounds, giving it a sense of romance. He wanted to be alone in that poetic setting to muse on his love. Suddenly a shadow passed through the arboured passage but he could not figure out what it was.

He climbed down the stairs and stepped out of the lobby. He walked through the narrow cobbled passage lined with shrubs and palms, and reached the pond.

It was a quiet night. No sound was heard. In the dim light he stared at the sky through the branches and leaves, as if the stars were singing love songs.

He heard the footsteps of somebody approaching the pond. His heart beat more rapidly. He wondered why such an emotion had been aroused in him, as if he were catching an electric wave passing through the air.

A few moments passed.

Suddenly Gloria appeared on the other side of the pond and was startled when she saw Cyrus sitting there. She began to breathe like a terrified bird.

She looked up at the twinkling stars pretending not to have seen him.

He stared at the ground as if he had not noticed her arrival.   They remained motionless, too shy to let their eyes meet.

Gloria was standing in the dark shadow of the willow trees, the stripes of light falling on her, making her slightly visible. In the dappled light she appeared to be a heavenly creature.

Cyrus slowly raised his head and stealthily looked at her. She was elegant and beautiful with the dignity of a young attractive princess.

She turned and their eyes met. A sweet smile appeared on her beautiful, full lips. Cyrus's eyes flashed and smiled before his lips. The exchange of smiles broke the tense silence.

Cyrus gestured for her to sit down. To his surprise she sat beside him on the bench. The willow trees had created an arch over the pond, forming a cosy room, as it were.

Without saying a word she glanced at him inquiringly. The light in her eyes burned like a fire. He turned away and kept his eyes down like a shy boy. Cyrus could hear the sound of the throbs of his heart.

Her face shone with the purity of her soul and heart. Cyrus had a strong desire to kneel down before her and say, 'Let me love you; let me worship you.' The atmosphere was charged with tense emotion beyond his endurance. He wanted to say something to break the intensity but the words dried up before they could be expressed.

After much effort, with a trembling voice, he said, 'It's a quiet night. It's lovely, isn't it?'

'Yes, it's beautiful.'

'I like the mystic night more than the glaring day.'

'So do I,' whispered Gloria, 'but I don't know why.'

'There's a sense of mystery at night. It's unfathomable. I like that.'

'If one can see the end, and be able to measure the depth, then it loses its mystic attraction.'

'God has ever been an unfathomable mystery. Sages, philosophers and prophets are baffled if they try to unravel this mystery.'

'I think if God could be comprehended, he would no longer be God. He is incomprehensible.'

There was silence. Both seemed to be pondering over the mystery of mysteries behind the creation.

Gloria stared up at the rising moon and whispered, 'I like the mystic beauty of the moonlight.'

'Man has put his foot on the moon.'

'It is an achievement of technology and science.'

'It's a great achievement,' said Cyrus, 'but I'm not too excited about it. What did they find? A pile of rocks. It demystifies the tranquil beauty of the moon.'

'Science tries to discover the universe.'

'Science touches the surface of things. I mean, it tells you about the quality, not the reality of things.'

'Science has helped human beings to build up their new world,' said Gloria.

'But, unfortunately, it is a "brave new world".'

'This is the age of the wonders of science. It's the time of the flourishing of science,' commented Gloria with enthusiasm.

'It's the time of the death of religion, poetry, spiritual emotions, and the decline of art and literature.'

'Yes, I agree,' said Gloria. 'Something's wrong. The balance is disturbed.'

'The intellectual aspect of human reality has been

nurtured but the emotional aspect linking man to the roots of his existence has been neglected, has even atrophied.'

'Yes, that's right,' sang Gloria. Blowing and dishevelling her long hair, the breeze caught a strand of it and snagged it on Cyrus's chin. After a thoughtful pause, she commented, 'Poetry, art, literature and religion are the flower of the soul, the cream of the flux of life.'

'Without them life has no beauty. It's a soulless machine,' confirmed Cyrus.

'I think,' suggested Gloria, 'the emotional aspect should not be neglected. It should be cultivated as well.'

'The trend is,' said Cyrus, 'towards spirituality, mysticism, genuine art and literature. Before long art and literature will flourish. Spiritual forces will erupt.'

'You mean there will be a religious revival?' asked Gloria.

'Materialism will reach the end of the line. Its deadening effects will paralyse human societies. Then, there will be an eruption of spiritual forces which will eclipse the splendours of the past,' lectured Cyrus, in a poetic tone.

'You think the traditional religions will be revived?'

'A new global religion will emerge with the potential to satisfy the needs of the time.'

'Some people think that science can take the place of religion.'

'Science cannot replace religion,' commented Cyrus. 'Because they have different functions. They have different fields of operation.'

'Sometimes religious theologies contradict scientific facts. How about that?'

'Religious truth is relative and it has to be re-revealed and renewed to keep the harmony and the balance.'

'So, religion and science walk hand in hand towards the Infinite,' sang Gloria, relieved and enthusiastic.

There was a long silence. The stars were twinkling up above. The moon was gracefully pacing upwards in the sky.

It became chilly. Gloria wanted to be hugged by Cyrus, to nestle against his warm body, to feel the heat of his love. She crept closer to Cyrus. Cyrus stretched his hand towards her. She put her hand on his. He pressed her delicate hand affectionately. His hand was very warm. The pleasant and sweet warmth heated her in the chilly air.

She glanced at Cyrus. His eyes were luminous, loving. She wished with all her heart that their love would be permanent and lasting and that they could continue their close partnership in the higher realms. She believed that those spouses who love each other truly and genuinely continue their loving partnership in the next world.

For a few seconds they stared into each other's eyes without exchanging a word. Words could not convey the love and emotion they felt for one another. Though they were attracted to one other, they were trying to control their emotions. Cyrus saw a girlish innocence in Gloria's look. He put a gentle kiss on her cheek and whispered, 'I do love you, I adore you, Gloria!'

'I worship you,' whispered Gloria. 'I am trusting my heart to you. I've given it to you. Please, don't break my heart. My heart is very tender. Please take care of it.'

Cyrus was touched and moved. He put his hands on hers, and then held them to his mouth, closed his eyes and kissed them most lovingly, like a devotee kissing a revered and sacred object.

'Could I borrow your shoulders?' requested Gloria.

'Certainly.'

Gloria put her head on Cyrus's shoulder and he put his hand around her waist. There was a sweet silence.

Gloria wished in her heart that the wheel of time could stop and that those sweet moments could last forever.

The wind blew stronger and rippled the pond. Gloria felt cold.

She nestled gently against Cyrus, feeling the pleasant heat of his body. The fingers of wind played a gentle music on the palms and willow trees. To the loving couple, the stars, the moon and the trees were singing love songs in unison.

6.

Gloria and Cyrus strolled hand in hand through the streets at night. It was pleasant to walk in Paris at night. They reached a spot where couples, singles, and groups of boys and girls were sitting, whispering words of love, playing the guitar or mandolin, and occasionally kissing and hugging each other. There was a pool surrounded by large steps and statues. Sitting on a step, a little away from the others, they stared at the silvery water of the fountain spouting down in the moonlight.

They noticed shadows stretching in the moonlight, some leaving the area, going out of sight, disappearing like ghosts.

After about two hours, the moonlight suddenly disappeared and the whole place was plunged in darkness. They looked up at the sky where the clouds were rolling over one another, gradually getting darker. The smiling stars and the amorous moon could no longer be seen. Galaxies and unnumbered suns, planets and stars went out of sight. The limitless space narrowed to a closed cage. The clouds capped the city and turned it into a tomb. The breeze stopped wafting over the grass. The shrubs and trees drooped their heads, looked sleepy. The city was like a patient lying on a stretcher after an operation. A terrifying silence dominated the whole area.

There was a contrast between Gloria's inner sphere and the outer world, and no similarity between her inner universe where she could warm herself in the sunshine of her own sun and the outside world that was growing darker and colder. She wished she could take refuge in her internal space and totally forsake the external world as if it did not exist. But the pressure of the outside atmosphere was too strong and too crushing, making her feeble and unable to avoid it. She had the feeling of being chained to the surrounding environment and stuck to the ground, not being able to get up and move away. The outer atmosphere penetrated her heart, made her sad, sick and heavy. Her joy vanished.

The silence was terrifying. The slightest sound horrified Gloria. The weather became unpleasantly chilly. She was not prepared for that as her clothes were not suitable for the cold. She was terrified, but did not know why, as if ghosts were around.

Paris had turned into a tomb, an unreal city.

She was puzzled at her impression but could not help sensing it. She shivered, crouched, nestled against Cyrus, and whispered, 'Don't speak, please. Listen. I hear hooting. It is horrifying.'

'Hooting!' exclaimed Cyrus. 'Hooting is the sound of an owl. I don't think we have any owls around here.'

'I can see one sitting on the top of the column there, hooting.' Gloria pointed to a far column, hardly visible in the darkness. 'I don't like it. It's terrifying.' She crouched and grasped Cyrus, desperately taking refuge. It was apparent that the mournful cry of an owl penetrated her soul.

Cyrus stared at the column that Gloria had pointed to but could not discern an owl sitting there. To his surprise, Gloria seemed quite serious. He put his arm around her waist and pressed her to him, 'Honey, I don't think there is an owl here. Owls usually live in ruins, not in Paris--the bride of Europe, the cradle of modernism.'

'Owls often appear as an omen of bad news,' said Gloria, pressing herself against Cyrus, terrified.

The silence had become quite frightening. Paris was like a dead city, a city of ghosts. The slightest sound, even the movement of an insect, scared Gloria to death. Time hung heavy. Unconsciously she was waiting for some sort of catastrophe to happen. The silence dragged on. Suddenly she opened her mouth in terror and grasped Cyrus's forearm. She had heard a terrifying sound from far off, like the sound of something falling and breaking. Startled and scared, she pressed herself against Cyrus to feel more secure. He put an arm around her and moved his hand over her hair comfortingly. As if throwing a protective quilt around her, he took her under his arm and asked, 'Do you feel better?'

With a trembling voice she whispered, 'Something is cracking. Something is crumbling.'

There was a pause. Gloria closed her eyes and put her head on Cyrus's shoulder. She suddenly opened her eyes, stared into the distance, scared. 'Hush, hush! The owl is hooting again! Oh! It's terrible. I can't bear it any more. It's as if the world is ending.'

Cupping his ears in his hands Cyrus listened attentively but could not hear an owl hooting nearby. Gloria saw and heard something that did not exist. In a voice betraying his irritation, he said, 'Honey! You're hallucinating. It's only your imagination.'

He took off his coat and offered it to Gloria, 'Here, take this. Cover your ears and eyes so that you won't see and hear anything that you feel is predicting terrifying events.'

'Sorry,' muttered Gloria. She dropped her head, feeling guilty.

There was an unpleasant silence.

Cyrus became remorseful for having rebuked Gloria and of accusing her of hallucinating. He wondered how he could be so sure that Gloria's observation was just her imagination. It might well have been a vision. She could sense something that he was not aware of. Her woman's intuition might have enabled her to sense something that he could not. Maybe she was a visionary whose power had materialised. Maybe what she saw and heard was a warning, a prophecy.

Then the prophecies and warnings of the prophets came to his mind. They had mostly fallen on deaf ears. The exact words of Moses, recorded in Deuteronomy, chapter 31, came to his mind. How the Israelites were warned to follow the teachings of Moses strictly, otherwise they would suffer: 'For I know that after my death you are sure to become utterly corrupt and to turn from the way I have commanded you. In days to come, disaster will fall upon you because you will do evil in the sight of the Lord and provoke him to anger by what your hands have made.' It was amazing how this warning had come to pass. The sufferings of Jews over a long period made his heart sad.

Then the words of persecuted Christ came to his mind: 'if thou hadst known...the things which belong to thy peace! But now they are hid from thine eyes. For the days shall come upon thee, that thine enemies shall cast a trench about thee, and compass thee round, and keep thee on every side, and shall lay thee even with the ground, and thy children within thee; and they shall not leave in thee one stone upon another; because thou knewest not the time of thy visitation.'

Christ uttered these ominous words and wept over the city, but the inhabitants of the city did not take his words seriously. Before long the Roman soldiers surrounded Jerusalem. They destroyed the Temple, ruined the city, massacred the Jews and made the remaining inhabitants scatter throughout the world. Cyrus thought: how dreadful! Why did the voices of the prophets always remain unheard?

The prophetic voice of Bahá'u'lláh's warning, uttered over one hundred and thirty years ago, echoed in his soul: 'O ye people of the world! Know, verily, that an unseen calamity followeth you, and grievous retribution awaiteth you.... The signs of impending convulsion and chaos can now be discerned, inasmuch as the prevailing order appears lamentably defective.' Cyrus was amazed how that warning threw a light upon the fortunes of sorrowing humanity. The world had been experiencing the rolling up of the old order in a furnace of fire and a bath of blood.

Cyrus thought that the prophets saw something hidden from the eyes of others. That was the reason their warnings and prophecies remained unheeded, ridiculed, until the calamity occurred with attendant agonies and tragedies.

Cyrus stared at the sky and saw the black clouds gathering. Suddenly a nasty wind blew. He crouched and shivered, covered his face with his hands to protect it against the angry gust. At this time another dire warning of Bahá'u'lláh, a prophet who appeared in recent times, passed through his mind and made him tremble: 'And when the appointed hour is come, there shall suddenly appear that which shall cause the limbs of mankind to quake.'

The wind howled and beat at the buildings around there. All of a sudden the calm and quiet atmosphere changed into a violent storm. The sudden change was totally unexpected. It seemed they would be caught unprepared. He sensed a thunderstorm rapidly approaching. In the distance lightning flashed violently, first vertical, then horizontal. After a few moments the terrifying sound of thunder was heard. The explosive sound shook the trees and the buildings.

Gloria was scared and clasped Cyrus, trembling.

Cyrus knew that the damp gust would soon turn to rain. He realised he had to save Gloria from the approaching thunderstorm. He sprang up quickly and hurriedly helped Gloria to her feet and they ran away from the approaching storm as fast as they could. While holding Gloria firmly, he rushed to a cafe, not far away. The nasty wind followed them, snarling and howling like a wolf. The lightning blinded their eyes. Cyrus released Gloria and both started running. Gloria lost her balance and slipped. Cyrus's heart sank and he rushed to help her to her feet.

She felt pain and could run no more. They walked slowly. Before they reached the cafe, a drop of rain splashed on her cheek, then another and another. The rain sprinkled on their faces and heads. Her hair clung wetly to her neck. She pushed back her wet and tangled hair and they hurried to a nearby veranda to take refuge. They stood side by side under the porch, the rain rolling down their faces.

Cyrus held Gloria gently, kissed her, sucking the rain from her soft cheek.

The torrential rain reached them and mixed water and fire poured down on them. Water started running in the street and the thunder was roaring and shaking the trees violently.

The sound of successive explosions was deafening.

Gloria and Cyrus entered the café. It was cosy, pleasantly warm, and soft music was being played. Gloria felt warmed and relieved. The terrifying sound of the storm had been left behind, but she worried about those caught in the storm without shelter.

Gloria and Cyrus stepped towards a corner of the café and were surprised to see the other members of the group playing cards, looking like lifeless ghosts risen from their graves in the haze of smoke. It was difficult for Gloria and Cyrus to breathe in that smoky air but the others were used to it.

They stood close, watching, without saying a word. Absorbed in their competition, the players did not notice the presence of Gloria and Cyrus.

Julia looked up. Her eyes met Gloria's. 'How come your hair is wet?'

'Didn't you notice the big thunderstorm?' replied Gloria, surprised. 'We were lucky not to be caught in it.'

Holding the pack of cards in his hands, Victor stared at them and teased: 'You were lucky not to be carried away in a roaring flood.'

'And you were too absorbed in playing cards not to notice that a storm shook heaven and earth.' There was accusation in Cyrus's voice.

Victor put aside the cards and turned to Cyrus. 'I'm concerned about my self, my life and my interest. I don't see anything wrong with that!'

Cyrus stared at him in silence.

Gloria's throat burned and she started coughing continuously. She could not bear the smoke any longer.

Yasha got up and suggested moving to another room, so

they moved to a smaller room at the other end of the café where the walls were covered with dark red velvet. There were black sofas set against the walls, and two candles burned on the table giving a dim light to the place. No one else was in the room. Lightning flashed and dazzled the eyes; thunder cracked and reverberated against the window. All turned and fixed their eyes on the window, worried at the anger of the sky. They wondered how they had been so distracted that they had not noticed the approach of the storm. They were concerned that they might suddenly be caught in a terrible situation.

Yasha said, 'It's no good to be suddenly caught in a storm and not be prepared for it.'

'It's no good,' said Devi, 'to get so distracted that you don't realise the actual situation you're in.'

Victor protested. 'So long as I'm secure in a cosy room, I don't worry whether a threatening storm is approaching or the sky is roaring.'

They dropped their heads, thinking.

Cyrus turned to Victor. 'It's better not to feel so secure in a cosy place. You may suddenly find yourself struggling for life in a lake of water.'

'I think dykes should be made to prevent flooding,' suggested Devi.

Gloria and Cyrus were thinking how horrifying it would be to get caught in an unexpected flood. Gloria closed her eyes and thought about the terrifying hooting of the owl in the darkness followed by lightning, thunder and the torrential rain which had the potential to wash away villages and towns.

'Yes, dykes should be built to prevent the flooding before it is too late,' proposed Cyrus.

'I believe everybody is responsible for the whole world,' muttered Gloria, looking at the ceiling.

They remained thoughtful, wondering if they were responsible for war crimes, for political crimes, for economic injustice. It was horrible to think that their apathy helped injustice to be considered normal.

'Certain things are beyond our control,' said Julia. 'For example, we know war is horrible. War demoralises individuals and society. It causes misery and tragedy. War destroys the economy of a country. It leaves cities burnt and its inhabitants buried. But we can do nothing to stop war and establish world peace.'

'If politicians decide to go to war, they go ahead,' said Julia. 'The public are taxed heavily to finance war and are dragged to the battlefield to be killed.'

Yasha shook his head in contempt. 'Those who plan war indulge in parties, drinking and dancing in their mansions.'

'The people have no role in establishing world peace,' said Julia. 'Everything is out of our control. We are the victims of politicians' schemes.'

'I believe,' said Cyrus, 'pessimism poisons and paralyses the public.'

'This is our world,' said Gloria, 'We should have a say in the sort of world we want to live in. We should not be used for the benefit of a few.'

'I strongly support world peace,' said Yasha. 'But we have no control over world affairs. I think world peace is impossible because it is against the interest of big business and some countries.'

'World peace is not only possible. It's inevitable,' said Cyrus with faith.

'World peace is not only possible. It's inevitable!' Julia

repeated Cyrus's words, surprised. 'You're very optimistic and visionary, Cyrus. Don't you watch the news? There are wars and conflicts everywhere. The world is threatened with an international convulsion.'

'Visionaries close their eyes to the facts and to reality. They live in their imaginary world.' Victor seized the opportunity to repudiate Cyrus's views.

'This imaginary world is beautiful, but your realistic world is ugly,' Devi sympathised with Cyrus.

Yasha heaved a sigh. 'The history of the world is a history of war, conflict and struggle. The world has never been at peace at any time. I wish the old era of war and conflict would end and a new era of peace would begin.'

'World peace is an academic subject for some intellectual people,' Peter joined the discussion, 'not the concern of the public.'

'That's not true,' protested Yasha. 'If you conduct an opinion poll, I'm sure you would find that at least ninety-five per cent of the people in the world would prefer peace and hate war.'

'If that's correct, why is peace still a utopian ideal?' questioned Peter.

'The people have the wish but not the will to work for peace,' commented Gloria.

'The world is entangled,' said Cyrus, 'in an economic system breeding disease. It is beset by complicated political problems. The hope for world peace withers in the bud.'

Devi sighed and looked sad. 'So there's no hope for world peace!'

'World peace cannot be dealt with as an isolated issue. It is related to other issues,' said Cyrus.

'So, we're faced with a giant,' said Devi.

'The world has to change,' commented Cyrus. 'Systems based on self-interest, racism and exploitation are not in harmony with the ideals of world peace and justice.'

'There is a need for a fundamental change,' added Gloria.

'The economy of some countries,' said Yasha, 'is partly based on the manufacture and sale of weapons. They are not serious about world peace. They will lose their financial interest.'

'The great powers pay lip service to peace,' said Devi. 'They do not commit themselves to establishing peace.'

'All nations will be forced to make peace,' commented Cyrus. 'The driving force will not be a spiritual motive. It will be the fear of human annihilation.'

'How?' asked Devi, surprised.

'There will be no other choice. They have to make peace. Moreover, people will not be willing to finance war any longer. They will not be able to endure the burden of high taxation for the purpose of war.'

'Still, I have no hope that world peace is possible,' said Devi.

'It's happening,' said Cyrus. 'It's a gradual process, step by step and stage by stage.'

'The world is threatened with international convulsion,' said Yasha, expressing his doubt.

'War accelerates the process of world peace,' said Cyrus. 'It is a painful period. But it is a transforming stage. I mean, it helps a new political structure to develop.'

Yasha leant back in his chair, breathed in a mouthful of air and forced it out audibly. 'Some countries try to kindle the fire of war in other parts of the world. They want to make money by selling weapons.'

'It's awful, it's disgusting,' screamed Julia, banging the

table, shaking with emotion. 'What sort of world do we have? Death, massacre, burning and destruction are the means whereby some make money. Billions of dollars are wasted, thousands of lives lost, tens of thousands of hearts broken so that a few companies can make money.'

Devi became emotional. She burst into tears, put her head on the table and cried bitterly. 'What kind of wise people run the world. We are the victims, victims of their machination. People carry the burden and endure the suffering.'

Silence took over the conversation. They sat thoughtful. Gloria glanced at the window where the slanting rain sent rivulets streaming down the glass.

Yasha thought: 'It's dreadful. People are manipulated! Are human beings lifeless objects with no value or dignity?'

The howling of the wind outside was heard. Its terrible sound was like the crying of orphans weeping over the dead bodies of their fathers killed in war.

Cyrus was thinking seriously about peace. For him, peace was not just a good idea. He believed world peace was a divine principle, a law of God.

Suddenly he tapped the table and said in a manly voice, 'Let's work hand in hand to establish world peace.'

They were startled and baffled and stared at Cyrus with eyes lifeless as empty holes. His heart ached to see that people had the wish but not the will to fulfil their cherished desire. He became disappointed. He wondered how he could enthuse them to do what was best for them and everybody on this planet.

Gloria noticed Cyrus's despair. She took his hand in hers and pressed it affectionately. A new energy ran through his veins.

Gloria whispered into his ear, 'Honey, you have told me several times, "Never get disappointed." Don't look at the inertia of people. Fix your eyes on the bright horizon ahead. A new day is breaking. It doesn't matter if most people are not aware.'

Cyrus smiled. He warmed himself in the sunshine that shone within his inner world. He knew that so long as the orb shone inside his soul, he would be able to withstand the dark forces outside. He regained his dynamism. 'If we had world peace and a healthy economic and political system, we could work twenty hours instead of forty hours a week to earn our living.'

'I don't understand the connection between world peace and the hours of work,' said Peter, confused.

'We pay indirectly for the purchase of weapons and the maintenance of the army.'

'Oh, that's great!' exclaimed Devi. 'Then, we won't have to work so many hours. We'll have enough time to enjoy life, to develop our artistic talent and spiritual potential.'

Julia, Gloria and Cyrus nodded their heads in agreement.

Yasha's eyes flashed with enthusiasm. 'Then, we work to live, not live to work.'

Julia stepped towards the window and looked out. 'It's not raining, but the wind is blowing. The sky is very overcast and terribly threatening.'

'Let's continue our talk tomorrow night,' suggested Yasha.

'Yes, I'd be interested,' said Devi, 'in continuing our conversation. Cyrus's faith in peace warms my heart. But it's better to go back to the hotel now. It may start raining again.'

On the way to the hotel Cyrus told Gloria he was not

inclined to follow up the discussion on the following night. 'It was alarming. I was depressed. My enthusiasm ebbed away. I need to be alone to meditate and draw energy from the celestial source so that I'll be able to battle against the dark forces.'

'Those marching towards a glorious goal have to polish their souls from time to time,' agreed Gloria.

'The inertia of the public can bring us down.'

'High aspiration stimulates us to put our efforts into something ahead of our time.'

'We have to walk on a thorny path to reach the golden age,' said Cyrus.

7.

The following night Gloria informed the other members of the group that Cyrus would not join them. She went back to her room. Sitting on the balcony alone, she thought of Cyrus. 'Oh Cyrus! I love you so much that your mood can change my mood. When you're sad, I'm sad.'

When Gloria left the lounge, silence took over for a while. Victor turned to Yasha, 'I think Cyrus realises that he is too much of a visionary. His views don't comply with the realities of the present-day world.'

'Those people,' said Yasha, 'who have no vision will get lost and perish.'

'I think your mind has been contaminated by Cyrus's visionary world,' said Peter. 'To tell you the truth, I'm alarmed by Cyrus's vision of an ideal world.'

'Why are you worried?' asked Devi.

'It disturbs the stability of the church. We should do something to stop these dangerous ideas.'

'I agree that visionaries are dangerous,' affirmed Victor.

Anger flared in Yasha's eyes. 'The great men of the world were always accused of stirring society and misleading the people. I mean the prophets, the advanced social thinkers. Those who shaped the course of history.'

'Those who want to introduce new social or political patterns,' said Victor, 'are looking for trouble. And they'll get into trouble.'

'Let's have fun. Let's not think about building the future world,' suggested Julia.

'Let's drink. Forget the world,' said Victor. 'I'll pay.'

'That's more like it!' exclaimed Julia, excited.

'I'll have something,' said Devi, 'but only a little.'

'I'll only drink on special occasions,' smiled Peter. 'but I'll join you tonight, but not too much.'

Yasha smiled bitterly. Devi and Yasha lost their vigour, looked gloomy and confused. They cherished advanced ideas, but they were fleeting and had no solid foundation. They were not connected to any celestial source from which to draw their energy.

That night Victor got drunk. Julia took him to his room. Julia got off Victor's bed and left him. He lay exhausted and immediately fell into a deep sleep, snoring.

Cyrus closed his door to spend time in prayer and meditation. For him prayer was not just murmuring words as a religious duty or ceremony. It was a communion with God. It could purify him from the defilement of earthly life and uplift him spiritually. It made him soar into an atmosphere of spotless purity.

He took a shower and put on some clean, soft clothes. He switched off his mind from the petty thoughts of daily life and focused on the eternal and celestial. He knelt down, raised his hands in supplication to be filled up with divine energy. He turned to the Dayspring of revelation and the Fountainhead of divine energy who had uttered these mighty words of assurance: "I am the royal Falcon on the arm of the Almighty. I unfold the drooping wings of every broken bird and start it on its flight." He was a broken bird. He needed a divine hand to be stretched towards him to unfold his drooping wings. "And start it on its flight."

His physical reality melted away drop by drop. He became detached, as if he was all soul flying in an atmosphere full of light. In an intense emotional mood, he prayed, hot tears running down his face profusely. He was no longer earthbound, but floating in the air, moving towards a dazzling sun shining in the far-off horizon. Those were sweet moments, very sweet, close to the experience of ecstasy. How sweet, how joyful, how uplifting it was to be close to God. He was filled with great courage, riding on the crest of a wave in a stormy ocean, battling against the rising waves. All fear disappeared. Nothing could frighten him. Even death could not scare him. He felt that he was an immortal being. Even to die for the good of humanity would make him eternal in the memories and hearts of people. He was getting closer and closer to the level of total reliance on the will of God where nothing could disturb him. Energy was released in him. Regaining his confidence and zest, he walked to and fro in the room while his arms swung forward and backward. Emotional and excited, he murmured with poetical rhythm, 'The road is thorny and the night long, but I shall never lose my hope in this misty way. This is the path I have taken.'

He sank into the armchair, pondering over the miseries that people had become used to, accepting them as their lot. He thought: hypocrisy has plagued the world. People are not even true to themselves. They belong to a religion without really believing in it, or practising it. They go to the polls to vote for a party without trusting it. They have no will to examine and study an alternative way of life. They work like slaves to survive. They groan under the heavy taxes to maintain the army and to buy weapons to make the rich richer, as if it is their predestined fortune. They seem to be paralysed and condemned to perpetual suffering in a blighted land. To find themselves languishing and vulnerable in a prefabricated structure. But they are able to be the masters of their fortune. They have the right to think, to search for an alternative, to choose. They have the right to build their world.   He   was aware that the world was enmeshed in a structure that seemed difficult, almost impossible to break through. Moreover, the crafty had utilised ignorance against the ignorant. Greed, perversion, superstition had assisted the crafty to have their way. So the people of various lands were partly responsible for the predicament, ailments and the miseries that afflicted them.

He stared at a point on the wall with a heart heavy with sadness. In his dream-like state, an apparition appeared to him. It looked like a terrifying hairy giant with scary sharp claws beating on the ground, shaking its arm, threatening and roaring with laughter, sneering and snarling. He was scared. He realised he could not run away. He had to fight with the giant with all his strength. He gathered his energy to face the horrible sneering apparition. Feeling a great strength in his arm, he threw his fist at the giant with all his power. The giant seemed invincible. He became aware that physically he could not defeat the giant, but spiritually he could, because the terrifying giant was soulless. That was the only hope he had to conquer it.

Suddenly he remembered that when he was a child, his Grandma told him a story about a boy lost in a valley. It was night. The boy saw a terrifying ghoul coming towards him. But the boy uttered the Greatest Name of God, and the ghoul disappeared.

He repeated the Greatest Name several times and approached the giant with great daring. There was fear at the back of his mind that the giant might jump on him at any moment to swallow him. He had full trust that a power would be released by uttering the Greatest Name that no ghoul could withstand. He rushed towards the giant repeating rapidly and loudly the magic Name of God. He felt an amazing spiritual strength in himself. Suddenly the giant cracked with a harrowing sound, crumbled, then vaporised. Cyrus laughed loudly. His fear and anger had both vanished.

The giant that had seemed terrifying suddenly disappeared as if it did not exist at all. He wondered why it had appeared to him so substantially? He muttered, 'The Greatest Name is a magic key to open any locked door, and a spell possessing the power to make all the evil spirits run away.'

He heaved a sigh of relief, stepped towards the window and gazed at the twinkling stars. It seemed the stars were smiling and dancing. The moon was singing an eternal song. Every part of the universe was animated and exuberant with a great energy flowing from an unknown source. A new light started shining within his inner universe, filling his heart with love. There was a change in him. Like a holy man, he felt a deep sympathy for the people of the world. In a prayerful mood, he thought: may we disentangle ourselves from the fetters in which we have been enmeshed. May we experience a life more meaningful, more beautiful and more rewarding than what we have. We have chosen a petty and sometimes deceitful way of life as the ultimate goal of creation.

He felt a great love for the people of the world. Their struggles, their sufferings came to his mind. Man-made miseries made his heart ache. He believed people had chained themselves with their own hands. But their inner soul was yearning to break the fetters. They were weak but innocent. His heart brimmed with compassion for those moaning and groaning to be liberated and emancipated. He saw their tears and heard their cries. He burst into tears and prayed that the human world would be freed from the chains that bound them.

8.

The tour was coming to an end. The group members had developed a sort of liking for one another. An imperceptible friendship tied them together.

They had begun to realise that truth was one, but it was relative. Truth was not static or dogmatic, but rather growing, developing and gradually manifesting itself. The goddess of truth would not unveil her luminous face without conditions. She would demand humility. One could not enter the temple where she lived until one removed their shoes, hat and cloak. One had to leave behind the load of preconceived ideas, beliefs and structured views. One had to be willing to burn all the veils covering their eyes and obstructing their views.   To gaze on that beauteous countenance was so enjoyable and uplifting that it was worth sacrificing what one had inherited. One had to toil and search for truth. One had to yearn for truth, to investigate and explore it.   One could not enter her temple without purifying the heart and mind from all the narrowing and poisoning prejudices. Then one could embrace the goddess of truth. Then she would pour her light upon the seeker's mind and heart and energise his soul.

The sun was peeping when Cyrus climbed down the stairs. He stared at the soft rays of the sun reflected on the corridor walls. After stepping into the lounge, he sank into a chair thinking that it was the last day of the tour. The faces of his co-tourists came to his mind.

Gloria sat up in bed and brushed back her hair with her fingers, dreaming of her future life. A scene flashed in her mind-- her wedding day, with hundreds of people attending the ceremony. Her friends would envy her walking side by side with Cyrus, her husband. A joyful smile illumined her whole face.

She pushed aside the blanket, swung her legs over the bed and stood up with great excitement. She stepped towards the wall mirror and stared at the reflection of her body in the nightgown-- slender, shapely and attractive, a beautiful bride. She smiled with self-satisfaction,

After taking a shower, she put on some light make-up and a satin dress. Too excited to stay quietly in her room, she flew down the stairs.

Gloria entered the lounge and saw Cyrus sitting there deep in thought. She briskly walked towards him and sat in a chair opposite him.

Her lips parted with a sweet smile and her eyes glittered with a deep sense of joy; she stared into the eyes of Cyrus to explore his feelings.

Cyrus reached for his cup of coffee. Holding the cup in his right hand, he glanced at Gloria and said, 'The tour is ending.'

'I'll be happy to go back home. Many happy days are ahead.' Gloria blushed.

'Each person,' said Cyrus, 'develops a different sort of worldview. It depends on the social and psychological climate of one's upbringing.'

'Some members of the group were not indifferent to the glory of a new age. All engaged in dialogues often.'

'Their inner heart,' said Cyrus, 'is yearning and searching for something, something more novel, more universal and more spiritual.'

'Why did some of them try to reject the ideals for a new era?' asked Gloria.

'But in the depth of their soul they had a vague inclination-'

'What inclination?' interrupted Gloria.

'To welcome the dawn of a new day.'

'I didn't see any such a welcoming attitude in some.'

'Don't worry. A new spirit is sweeping across the planet. A new vibrance has been released.'

'A new vibrance?' asked Gloria, surprised.

'An increasing number of people are in favour of global unification. They're aspiring to spiritual values. They're searching for new economic and political systems.'

'Yes, that's right,' confirmed Gloria. 'It's strange that sometimes thinking people in different parts of the world express ideas and ideals similar to one another, even though they don't know anything about each other's views and thoughts.'

'When there is vibrance in the air,' said Cyrus, 'receptive souls will catch it without knowing its source. We are like a radio that will catch electromagnetic waves when it is tuned.'

Devi came into the lounge. She found Cyrus and Gloria engaged in conversation. The sunlight had lightened a part of the room, reflecting on Gloria's hair. Devi sank into an armchair, winked and smiled at Gloria and then turned to Cyrus. 'I heard you say a vibrance is in the air. I sense the world is moving towards a new era. It's driven by a mysterious force.'

'In which direction is it moving?' asked Gloria.

'In a direction at variance with present-day materialistic civilisation,' said Devi. 'There is an inclination towards a spiritual civilisation.'

'A new consciousness is being born,' confirmed Cyrus.

Cyrus excused himself and left the lounge. Devi and Gloria stayed.

Peter got up and paced to and fro in his room, thinking of the tour that was ending. He felt a mild sadness. He was wondering why he was always repudiating Cyrus's ideas about new ideals. 'I had to defend my beliefs and creed,' he thought. 'It seemed Cyrus was introducing a new global faith. That's a blasphemy. I had to oppose him, anyhow.'

He stood at the window glaring at the sky. The sunlight was too strong, blinding him. He instinctively turned his head away and stared at the corner of the room, but his eyes blurred and he could not see clearly.

Groping in the room, he sat on a stool, closed his eyes and rubbed his face with his hands to relax the frontal and chin muscles. He remembered his fellow-tourists. Moments of argument with Cyrus flashed in his mind. He recollected that once Cyrus had said that he loved Christ no less than a Christian does. This touched Peter's heart and his negative attitude melted. He muttered, 'After all, Cyrus is not anti-religion.' He felt that his hatred had gone. He did not understand why his attitude was changing.

He stepped towards an armchair in the corner of the room and sank into it. He felt pleasantly comfortable. He could not deny that some of the ideals expressed by Cyrus and Gloria fascinated him. He admitted to himself that his heart sometimes did not agree with his mind. The dichotomy between his feeling and reasoning puzzled him. A shadow of doubt passed through his mind about his beliefs. He tried to ignore it because it could disturb the whole framework of his built-up psychological structure. He trembled at the thought of questioning the validity of what he had been born and brought up to believe. 'No,' he muttered, 'Cyrus's ideals are dangerous. They could influence the way I believe.'

He stood up, opened the fridge and poured Coke into a glass, reviewing the many dialogues they had had. He admitted that the idea of the dawn of a new day held a fascination for him-- a day when the world would be spiritualised, and there would be no more wars, no armies, poverty, terror and cruelty. He muttered, 'These ideals are not in conflict with my basic beliefs as a Christian. Christ preached love.'

In the depths of his soul a tendency was developing, a yearning was growing in expectation of the rise of a new

sun. He felt a conflict between his inner inclination and a set
of inherited views. It was the first time he had examined his
beliefs objectively. He thought: I can't ignore my inner
inclination any longer. I shoudn't repudiate Cyrus's views
and ideals without examining them. *I'll communicate with
him.* He stepped out of the door onto the porch of the hotel.
The air was fresh. He stared at a group of birds flying
towards the rising sun.

Peter went to the lounge and found Devi and Gloria there,
chatting and laughing. Devi seemed to be teasing Gloria.
When Gloria saw Peter she held her hand over her mouth to
suppress her laughter, but she could not help herself. She
burst out laughing loudly. She greeted Peter with a nod and
apologised, 'Sorry. Today Devi is very naughty.'

Peter cleared his throat. 'That's okay. This is the last day
of our tour. It's bettter to laugh than to cry.' They were
surprised to see Peter's face bore no antagonism or tension.

Victor, Yasha and Julia popped in. They had heard what
Peter had said. 'Yes, I agree with that,' said Yasha.

Cyrus's voice was heard, saying loudly, 'That's right.
God loves laughter.'

They turned to the door and saw Cyrus entering the
lounge, chuckling, though his smile betrayed a hint of
sadness.

They sat sipping their drinks, chatting and laughing,
enjoying themselves. There was a sense of togetherness, a
feeling of fellowship and closeness. Their hearts were much
closer than their minds. Their souls had a spiritual quality
that could bring about unity.

A broad smile appeared on Yasha's face. 'For forty-five
days we have been travelling through various countries--

actually three continents. This is the last day of our tour.
Let's be together tonight, go somewhere to dance.'

'That's a good idea,' exclaimed Julia and Devi
delightedly. Victor clapped. They all showed their approval.

'I know a great place,' said Julia. 'They serve the best
icecream, cocktails, crab meat, shrimps, and fruit salads.'

'Oh! That sounds delicious,' said Devi. 'They're my
favourites. But what about dancing?'

'There's a ballroom where you can dance until two
o'clock in the morning,' said Julia.

Victor was ecstatic. 'I would like to dance the whole
night.'

'I have to tell you it's expensive.'

Gesticulating wildly, Victor laughed loudly. 'It doesn't
matter. Let's spend our francs before we leave France.'

They emerged from the Metro. Their shadows stretched in
the twilight. They enjoyed walking, laughing, telling jokes
and teasing each other on the way to the restaurant.

They entered a restaurant that was architecturally unique.
It was famous as rendezvous for lovers and featured a
winding and twisting corridor with corners that formed as
semi-private cosy rooms accommodating a few people,
mostly two. They were taken to a corner that seated eight.
The candles on the tables cast a soft light on the walls. Their
faces looked more attractive in the semi-shady and dim light.
 It gave one a sense of romance and mystery.

Peter seemed relaxed. Victor was joyful, telling jokes.
Gloria was sitting next to Cyrus, holding his hand. Her face
was occasionally lit up with a sweet smile. Devi and Julia
were mostly engaged in conversation, giggling frequently.
Julia appeared to be in the mood to dance the whole night.

Cyrus cast his eyes on his fellow-tourists, his eyes glittering with a loving smile.

The restaurant was full to capacity. They had to wait patiently before giving their orders.

Peter took the opportunity to ask Cyrus a question. He wanted to express his doubt about the dawn of a new age of world unification, but his question betrayed his interest in the topic. He said, 'I think your ideas about the global unification are a utopian ideal. But you speak with optimism. What makes you so sure?'

'World unification,' said Cyrus, 'is the consciousness of the new age that we are entering. There is a tendency towards world unity, universal peace and global solidarity.'

'The talk of new ideals may be just passing phase without actually materialising,' said Peter.

'After colonialism, people demand that their ethnic and national identity be recognised. Global unification is an illusion,' said Victor.

'The border lines of some countries have to be re-drawn,' said Cyrus. 'Unity of the world doesn't mean unity in unity. It's unity in diversity.'

'Sometimes the fire of war is kindled purposely. What about that?' complained Yasha.

'A mysterious force,' said Gloria, 'is propelling the world towards a new goal. Those governing the world are puzzled. They're confused by these sudden and unexpected forces.'

'I wish the tree of world peace would come to fruit!' exclaimed Devi with emotion.

'So, you'd better water it to accelerate its growth,' suggested Cyrus.

'I think,' said Peter, 'that you believe that the new ideals are the Will of God for the New Age.'

'We can say,' said Cyrus, 'that this is the spirit of the new age and the consciousness of a new era. Each divine revelation is the expression of the consciousness of its times.'

'I think religions are losing their vigour and fading away,' said Victor.

'This is a time when old religions are dying and a new one is being born,' said Gloria.

'It reminds me,' said Devi, 'of the Danish mystic, Kierkegaard, who believed the old gods are fleeing and a new God is being born.'

They remained silent for a few seconds.

Rubbing his chin, Yasha said, 'We live in a crucial time. The time of death and birth.'

'A global religion,' said Gloria, 'is gradually emerging from the chaos of the present-day society.'

'I see only cultural and religious confusion,' said Peter.

'I'm not a religious-minded person, but I support the new ideals for the new age,' said Yasha.

Cyrus straightened his back. With his grand gestures and facial expression, he sounded as if he were giving a speech at a big conference. 'Our deepest emotional attitude towards life, towards creation, has a sort of religious nature. Religion in its broadest and deepest sense is not a dogma, or a set of beliefs, nor is it a mosque or a church. It's something mystical beyond the calculating mind, something spiritual or divine beyond ceremonies. It's a mystical tie that connects us to the Creator. It relates to the most profound part of man's emotional nature, to the essence of his very being. Religion in its mystical sense is born with every human being. It can be atrophied, it can be distorted, it can be misled, but it cannot be destroyed. The historical religions are the outer expression of the inner mystical inclination.'

Everyone remained thoughtful for a while.

'The quest for God is innate in human beings,' said Devi.

'We will have,' said Cyrus, 'no deep sense of joy, no inner contentment, until we discover God in the depths of our soul. He is the soul of our soul.'

'I sense,' said Yasha, 'a new civilisation being born. But I doubt that a new religion is being born.'

'Throughout the world,' said Cyrus, 'an increasing number of people are advocating a new global faith, which is unfolding.'

'I cannot believe it. We live at the peak of materialism.' Julia said in surprise.

'Exactly. When materialism reaches a climax, it is followed by a spiritual phenomenon. It will be the progenitor and harbinger of a new civilisation.'

The waitress brought them cocktails and ice creams. They started eating, telling jokes, teasing and laughing.

They moved into the small ballroom to dance. No one was there. The choice of music was theirs. Standing around the stage, they listened to the music and chatted. A love song, Cyrus's favourite one, was played. Whenever that song was played, he could not help dancing. He stepped onto the stage, closed his eyes and whirled and whirled as if floating in the air. The song uplifted him.

They stepped onto the stage to dance. At first they danced briskly as a group, then they formed a circle and each one took turns to dance inside the circle.

Cyrus and Yasha danced an energetic Russian, male dance. Devi, Gloria and Julia danced with every member of the group, quickly changing partners. They danced and danced to various rhythms and beats of music.

They were in high spirits, absorbed in the music. The realm of music removed walls and barriers and unified their souls and hearts. Music awakened their emotions, making them feel very close. In the dim light, their shadows mingled and their souls fused.

An uplifting song, telling of a golden age, was played:

Imagine a world, not dark, but bright,
No sorrow, no grief, no tears, but delight,
Abundant with love, filled with spirit, not dead,
Everyone happy, every face shining with light.

Imagine a world, no poverty, no one sad,
Rich share their wealth, no force, they're glad,
Joy comes from the heart, not from matter or gold,
The needs of all satisfied, no miserable or mad.

Imagine a world, the birds sing the songs of peace,
The breeze blows and gives to every rose a kiss,
No war, no killing, no hatred, no fight, no conflict,
All one family: brother, sister, nephew or niece.

Imagine a world, spiritual, no profanity,
Self-realisation is a sense of joy and spirituality,
The religions are in harmony, one and fused,
They're not for hatred, but for love and unity.

Imagine a world, no more weapons for sales,
No army, all dance in peace in meadows or dales,
The guns turned into tools, the swords into ploughshares,
The mercy of female permeates no more a world of males.

A new era is coming; a great light is breaking through,
The golden age is a reality, not a dream; it's true,
Nations war, racial disunity, creed conflict are false,
World unity is dawning, the youth cheer, the babies coo.

The song portrayed a beautiful world, opened up a new vista. The old world with its animosity, racism, exploitation and disunity would fade. A new world full of life, creativity and togetherness flashed in the distance. They were carried away on the waves of uplifting emotion, soared towards a new horizon. A new sun rose and warmed their souls. They were immersed in an ocean of unison by music, united in their aspirations for a world free from the bondage of man-made theories and ideologies. They yearned for a world unfettered by old political and economic systems. No more would human energy be wasted in conflict and war. A glimpse of the new world flashed in which human talents would be channelled into individual creativity. The concept of the new world excited them at the edge of ecstasy.

They felt they were leaving behind the lingering period of darkness, and entering a new age of light. The period of twilight was ending. Their faces were alight with the enthusiasm of the break of a new day. They whirled and danced with excitement and ecstasy until one hour after midnight. Various records were played continuously. The song of the 'Golden Age' was played repeatedly. The vision of a unified world encouraged them to work for its realisation. It inspired them to march hand in hand towards a world peace that was within their reach. Intoxicated by the vision of the birth of global spiritual civilisation, they danced and whirled with great enthusiasm.

9.

The following day Gloria woke up at 9:00 a.m., jumped out of bed, and rushed to the bathroom and took a shower. She put on a Chinese style dress, embroidered in gold thread. It was blue silk with pale red flowers, slit open on one side to the upper part of the knee, partly exposing her shapely leg. Joyful and excited, she moved briskly to and fro.

Crooning love songs, she combed her thick long hair. Standing in front of the wall mirror, she examined her body, smiling broadly.

She played a cassette and started to dance to the rhythm of the music.

There was a knock at the door.

She welcame Devi in, hugged her affectionately, kissed her cheeks and asked, 'Would you like a cup of coffee?'

'Yes, please.'

Devi examined Gloria from top to toe. 'You look attractive.'   'Thank you, dear Devi.' She bent down and kissed Devi again. She made her a cup of steaming coffee, moving gracefully to the rhythm of the music still playing.

'Do you remember the day we visited Capri in Italy--'

'Yes, I do.' Gloria said, listening attentively.

'We were sitting in the boat and I read your palm and told you that you would marry somebody that you really love.'

Gloria giggled. 'I never forget. You're a great palm reader, dear.'

'Were you dancing when I knocked at the door? I hope I haven't disturbed you.'

'Not at all. I want to dance. I want to fly in the air as if

I'm riding on a magic carpet. I'm impatient to go back to Sydney and tell my parents and friends that I have found my man, a man that I dearly love.'

'Cyrus deserves it. He's a good man.'

'I'm lucky. The tour was a turning point in my life. It was good.'

'If you want to dance, please dance. You have to be happy. You have to dance. Why not!'

'Let's dance together.' Gloria suggested. She played some dance music, approached Devi and pulled her to her feet.

They danced to the rhythm of music, first face to face moving in perfect harmony. They threw back their heads and shook their bodies, their long hair touching the ground. When the tempo changed they danced separately, whirling and moving their bodies to the beat of the music.

'Do you have a cassette of Indian religious dance music?' asked Devi and explained which one she wanted.

'Yes, I have that one. But I don't know how to dance. I have never practised it. That sort of dance is an art, it has meaning. Nowadays dancing is often just a form of exercise.'

'A friend of mine taught me. I'll show you. You imitate me.'

'Okay, fine.'

The cassette was played and Devi danced with skill while Gloria tried to imitate her movements.

When the music stopped they kissed and hugged each other, both laughing out loud.

'I would like to play some very special music.' said Gloria. 'It is called the glory of the universe.'

'It reminds me,' said Devi, 'of a Greek philosopher who

believed he could hear the music of a singing universe.'

'Exactly,' smiled Gloria. 'It conveys the mystical sense of the grandeur of God's creation.'

The music was very uplifting, as if it was echoing in the seven levels of heaven. Devi and Gloria were silent, listening attentively to the music. It filled them with rapture and ecstasy. The music came to an end, but their eyes remained closed. It was as if they were swimming in an ocean of light.

In that ecstatic mood, Devi had a strange feeling of something mysterious and unusual, as if a new door was opening to her soul. She felt vibrations coming to her as waves of light. She sensed something had occurred on the earth. Something affecting the minds and hearts of those who were willing to receive it. It was as if the waves of a revelation had been released in the world. She wondered if the sudden flourishing of science, knowledge and technology could be related to a divine revelation in recent times.

Devi remained in a reverie and then suddenly remembered a conversation between Cyrus and Gloria in Venice.

She straightened her back in the armchair. 'We are scheduled to fly late this afternoon. I may not see you again...'

'We'll be in touch in Sydney,' interrupted Gloria. 'You are a good friend to me now. I'm happy to meet you in the tour.'

'I'd like to keep in touch with you as well,' said Devi. 'You have dignity and self-esteem. I like that. But I wanted to ask you something. When we were in Venice I overheard a conversation you had with Cyrus about somebody who introduced himself as the spokesman of God for this age. I wanted to ask you what you knew about this. But I hadn't had a chance before now.'

'Was it the first time you heard that somebody had declared he was the bearer of a new revelation during the latter part of the nineteenth century?'

'I had never heard of it before,' said Devi. 'But I'm curious to know. I mean, if he declared he was the spokesman of God for this age, he must have something to say. What did he say?'

'He said the time of the old systems was over. He did not devalue them. He just said their time had passed.'

'The time of old systems is over,' repeated Devi. 'That's very challenging. What did he mean?'

'He demonstrated in his writings that the old systems: economic, social, political, moral and religious could not function properly within the context of the new era.'

'New era!' repeated Devi, surprised, 'ninety-nine per cent of the population of the world have no idea that we are entering a new era.'

'It takes decades, sometimes centuries, before the public realises it.'

'If the public don't know a new era requires a new pattern in society, how are they managing their affairs?'

'They are tackling enormous problems within the old systems. And if they are very advanced thinkers, they are tinkering with the collapsing old order.'

'Did he present something new to replace the old ones?'

'Yes, he did. He wrote over one hundred books, expounding how a new world could be built.'

'Oh! Over one hundred volumes!' repeated Devi, surprised. 'He had to be a highly educated person.'

'Not at all. He had no schooling and no private teacher.'

'Then, how could he write so many books?' asked Devi, astonished.

'He said that everything he wrote was an inspiration, not his words. He claimed his knowledge was an innate knowledge, not acquired in schools or through reading.'

'Did he try to get his message across?' asked Devi, interested.

'Yes, he did. He sent letters to the Emperor of France, the Queen of the British Empire, the Caliph and Sultan of the Ottoman Empire, the Czar of Russia, the King of Persia, and the Pope, the Head of the Catholic Church. He also addressed the Emperor of the German Federation, the presidents of the Americas, the wise men and philosophers of the world, and the religious leaders of all faiths.'

'What was their response?' inquired Devi.

'They ignored his message. They threw aside his letter in anger. In one case the bearer of the letter was tortured to death.'

'Oh!' sympathised Devi, 'why?'

'His words did not make sense to them. He was telling them there should be universal disarmament, that all the people should be literate. The students should learn one international language in addition to their mother tongues. Men and women should enjoy equal opportunity for education and social position. No country would have the right to maintain an army and make weapons. There should be a world assemblage where the kings and presidents would deliberate on peace issues. There should be no poor and no very rich class. There would be no clergy. There were many teachings and ideals similar to these. I cannot summarise over one hundred volumes in a few words,' Gloria smiled.

'They make sense,' said Devi. 'Today many people think along the same lines. There are some movements promoting some of those ideals.'

'Yes, you are right,' confirmed Gloria. 'The world is getting closer and closer to the ideals he set as the goals for humankind. But bear in mind that he proclaimed his message over one hundred and thirty years ago. Then, the world was far removed from those ideals. The kings and religious leaders felt threatened.'

'Why?' inquired Devi, 'These ideals don't seem dangerous.'

'They sensed that their authority was challenged. He was an exile and a prisoner, but he wrote with amazing power and authority. So, they united secretly to destroy him and quench the blazing fire.'

'Was he scared when the emperors and the kings united against him?'

'No, he wasn't. He prophesied that the ecclesiastics and the kings would lose their glory and power and would fall, because they did not respond to the needs of the times.'

Devi became curious. 'Didn't he say what might happen if the world didn't take his message seriously?'

'He warned that the world would fall into a great turmoil. The old systems would collapse with agony and tragedy.'

'Did this warning have any effect on the world leaders?'

'No, they shrugged their shoulders.'

They remained silent and thoughtful for a while. Then Devi leant forwards and stared at Gloria. 'If he talked as a prophet it's not easy to ignore him. I mean, nothing happened? For example, people turn into stone; a fire or a thunderbolt from heaven; or an earthquake that shook the earth!'

'No, nothing like that. But the world remained stuck in the mud of the old systems. Now it's trying to disentangle itself from the ties of the old systems. The more it tries to free itself the more it becomes tightened in the coils of the net. The world's trapped in a net like a mouse. The grip of the trap is too strong.'

'It's frustrating. He did not change the world. His efforts and sacrifices were useless.'

'Not really,' smiled Gloria. 'He prophesied a new race would be raised. They would change the world and end the miseries. They would be the champion builders of a New World Order.'

10.

Her face shining with a light of great joy, Gloria stepped into the hall at Sydney airport. Her mother, Maria, hugged and kissed her. Holding her head back, Maria stared at Gloria's shining face inquiringly, 'My love! You look bright and joyful. You look more beautiful than ever!'

A broad smile on his face, Cyrus nodded to Maria. Gloria said, 'By the way, Mum, this is Cyrus, one of my co-tourists.' Her mother immediately sensed that their relationship was more than just casual. She sensed nobility in Cyrus's bearing. It flashed in her mind that he could be an ideal partner for Gloria.

A few days later, Maria and Gloria sat at the window, occasionally glancing at the shrubs and flowers in the backyard garden. Maria was working on a piece of embroidery, and Gloria was reading a novel. They were mostly silent, but spoke as thoughts strayed through their minds.

'Gloria, I feel Cyrus loves you.'

Gloria raised her head from her book, stared at her mother and smiled. She continued reading and did not give comment.

'He has dignity. I think he's a noble person.'

'Yes, he is,' muttered Gloria without raising her head from the book.

There was a pause. Gloria was absorbed in her book, and Maria stitched silently.

Maria put aside her work and stared at Gloria. 'You've rejected several offers. Would you accept if Cyrus proposes?'

Gloria stared at her mother and did not say anything.

'What's Cyrus's job?'

'He's a lecturer. He's also a writer.'

'That's something special.' A broad smile illuminated Maria's face. 'How about inviting him for a cup of coffee.'

'Yes, one day.'

Suddenly Maria's face darkened with concern. 'How on earth can you be sure that he will propose marriage? Nowadays, men prefer to be friends. They don't like to commit themselves.'

'Don't worry, Mum. You just said he is a noble person.'

Maria stared at her daughter with motherly love. 'He would be lucky to have you as his wife.'

11.

The hall was flooded with scented flowers brought by friends. The variety in the colours of the flowers complemented the variety in the differing shades of skin and the colourful dresses displaying the beauty of unity in the diversity, the muticulturalism of Australia. The guests were from various backgrounds: British, Italian, Persian, Russian, Indian and Chinese, and so on. They were all Australian citizens wearing different costumes. Yasha and Devi were among the guests at the engagement ceremony of Cyrus and Gloria.

The music reverbrated around the hall and the guests whirled and danced, full of spirit and joy. The selection of music was also multicultural. The best had been chosen from different countries. The variety of music and songs brought the spirit of the various cultures to the ceremony.

No liquor was served, but everyone was in high spirits. They seemed intoxicated. Their faces were aglow with joy and they had beads of sweat on their foreheads from the continuous dancing. Maria was smiling and laughing, hovering around Gloria like a moth around a candle. Some girls, in the bloom of their beauty, circled Gloria. Like a red rose in full bloom, Gloria was surrounded by flowers of various shades and colours. They danced together with graceful rhythm.

Yasha and Cyrus danced a Russian dance, performing as they had in Paris. The others were standing in a circle around them laughing and clapping. They moved fast, full of life and energy. The music, the laughter, the clapping, the energetic movements of the dancers vibrated in the hall and made the walls seem to move forward and backward in time to the rhythm of the dance.

'Hey, Gloria - ' Gloria turned in respose to the call and saw Devi smiling. 'How about posing behind the flowers for my album. No need to ask you to smile. You're radiant. No wonder you walk on clouds.' Gloria stood behind the pile of flowers and waved to Cyrus to join her. The flashing of cameras continued for more than two hours.

After posing for photos for some time, Gloria and Cyrus came out of the hall, hand in hand for some fresh air. The music was still flooding the hall and echoing in the open air outside. The shadows of the dancers were reflected on the large glass doors of the hall. It was a cool night. Gloria stared up at the Milky Way. It seemed to her that the stars were dancing in the sky celebrating her engagement to Cyrus.

Gloria could hear a song she liked very much. It seemed to express her own feelings: I want to walk with you on the same path with all its ups and downs. I want to be with you in storm and sunshine. I want to be a solace to your pains and a partner in your joys. I want to wake up with you in a hut or a palace.

When the song finished, Gloria instinctively pressed her face to Cyrus's chest and murmured, 'I do love you, my lord.' He hugged her most affectionately. 'You're dear and precious, my beloved.'

The ceremony was still going on when Gloria and Cyrus drove away heading towards a spot on the coast. Maria and some relatives' eyes remained glued to the street as the car vanished into the darkness.

Gloria and Cyrus stood on the rocks and gazed at the silver cloth of moonlight on the sea. It was cool and fresh. No sound was heard save the gentle splash of waves on the rocks. They swept their gaze from the sea and stared into each other's eyes. Standing face to face, holding hands affectioately, they gazed into each other's eyes, transferring the waves of love to the soul. Gloria's face was charming and her hair was beautiful in the dim moonlight.

She pressed her face to his chest, inhaling the pleasant smell of his body mixed with cologne. Gloria squeezed her eyes closed and breathed deeply of his scent, needing to absorb some part of him into herself, to believe in the reality of the moment and that she was engaged to her most loved one. His lips pressing on her fragrant hair and holding her in his arms, Cyrus hugged her affectionately. She raised her head and stared into his glittering eyes. Her eyes welled with tears, and she whispered, 'You don't know how much I do love you. My heart is tender. Please take care of it.' Then, she pressed her face against his chest and cried tears of joy. He tightened his arms round her shoulders and embraced her with intense love. She kissed his chest, his chin and his shoulders. In his arms she felt the warmth of his love and the heat of his body. Their burning lips touched and pressed.

12.

Gloria and Cyrus's love flowered with beauty and purity. They enjoyed the pleasant warmth of love. But Cyrus received news that his mother was not well. Whenever he talked to her on the phone, he sensed that his mother's voice was not as vigorous as it used to be; it was gradually ebbing away. She was not the same fearless lioness whom he knew from childhood. He rang her one Saturday evening.

'Cyrus! O my son! My love!' replied his mother. 'It's kind of you to ring me. You don't know how happy I am to hear your dear voice.'

Cyrus laughed loudly. 'Mum! I'm also very glad to hear your dear voice. How do you feel?' There was no answer. He repeated, 'Mum, Mum,' and listened attentively, but there was no reply. He became worried. He thought his mother might have fainted during the telephone conversation. He could not rush to help her. She was on the other side of the planet. He did not know what to do. He continued, 'Mum, Mum, can you hear me?' But there was no reply. Cyrus pressed the phone to his ear and listened. 'Mum, Mum,' he continued. He could hear a muffled voice but could not figure out what it was. When he listened more attentively he sensed that his mother was sobbing on the other end of the phone. Cyrus's eyes welled with tears but he tried to bring his emotion under control, pretending he was happy to talk to her. 'Mum! Do you hear me?' He forced himself to laugh to mitigate her grief.

Then he heard his mother's voice. She muttered with a throat choked with tears, 'Yes, my love. Your dear voice gives me life.' Then, she burst into tears. While sobbing, she said, 'I will not see you again before I die. I don't think I can see you again.' She stopped talking and continued sobbing. When the telephone conversation ended, Cyrus dropped into the sofa and heaved a sigh of pain; his eyes welled with tears. Cupping his face in his palms, he brooded over his separation from his mother for so many years. 'I have not visited my homeland for more than a decade,' he thought. Wiping his tears with his hand, he muttered, 'Her dear voice was low and sad, as if she was saying her last farewell.'

It pained him to think that his devoted mother would not see her son before she died. He knew well that his mother loved him dearly. It was her last and most cherished wish to see him. He wanted to go somewhere, to a valley, to the top of a mountain, to a cave, to cry out as loudly as he could; to blame, to condemn those who were responsible for the situation he and his people were in. The question came to his mind repeatedly: if certain countries want to plunder other people's wealth with their Machiavellian plans, why did his innocent mother, like many other innocent people, have to become the victim of their schemes? But he did not know to whom to take his complaints.

Many images of his loving mother came to his mind: how she used to struggle with the hardships of life. She did everything to give him comfort and provide him with the opportunity to study. He remembered when he was a six-year- old child, and a snake in the garden had bitten him. His mother used to sit at his bedside to give him the prescribed medicine. With tearful eyes she caressed his curly hair and mopped up beads of sweat from his broad forehead. He also remembered vividly that when he was a child, a stallion kicked his legs hard, fracturing the bones badly. For three months she used to sit at his bedside the whole night. With sleepy eyes she looked at him while praying in her heart for his health. After long hours of keeping herself awake, exhausted, she used to put her head on the edge of the bed and fall asleep. Several times during the night he woke her up because of the sharp pain. He couldn't help crying. She always woke up immediately to see what she could do for him. She tried to solace him with gentle and loving words, never complaining or resenting that she had been woken up repeatedly. He thought also of the happy times when she laughed and played with him and read stories to him. This happened years ago, but memories of her sacrifice and love never left him.

One day, lying on his back on the sofa, clasping his hands beneath his head, he was thinking of his mother. He heaved a sigh and muttered, 'I have to fulfil my mother's wish.' He closed his eyes, thinking. Different scenes started to invade his mind. He imagined that he was at the airport in his homeland. The passport controls officer looked at the black list, noticed his name and immediately informed the revolutionary guards to take him to the jail to be interrogated. They will torture me, they will hang me, he thought. He opened his eyes as if he had been awakened from a nightmare. He stared at the ceiling and let out a sigh. 'What's happening to me?'

To go or not to go occupied his mind constantly. It was very painful. Another day, sitting on the chair, leaning forward, resting his chin on his palms, he thought about Gloria. 'I love Gloria, I worship Gloria. How can I leave her? We are engaged. She is impatiently waithing to get married. If I do not return, Gloria's heart will be broken, and it may never heal.' His eyes filled with tears. He heaved a big sigh. 'O God! Tell me; tell me what I should do. If I postpone my travel, my mother may die, and I will not fulfil her last wish. O! That will bring pain and remorse for the rest of my life.'

He passed through the torture of the agonising dilemma for several weeks. He thought if he was to visit his sick mother, he should visit her before he got married. If something happened to him, he would prefer that it happened before he got married, so as not to make Gloria a widow.

13.

Gloria sprang to her feet and rushed to Cyrus, She embraced him with great joy, snuggling into his arms, inhaling his manly scent. She looked up and stared into his eyes expecting to hear some good news. A broad smile illuminated her face when she felt his hand drift across her forehead lovingly, while with the other hand he caressed and smoothed her hair away.

She closed her eyes and pressed her cheeks against his

chest; his lips buried in her hair. She felt the heat of his body and the warmth of his love. He held her face in his hands and stared into her eyes. 'I came here to tell you something.'

A great joy flashed in her eyes. She wrapped her arms around his shoulders and kissed his cheeks. She pursed her lips and blew against his neck. 'You came to tell me when we'll get married.' Smiling pleasantly, she waited for his reply.

He smiled faintly and murmured, 'That's my most cherished desire, my love. No, it's not about the marriage arrangements this time.'

'So, what did you want to tell me?'

His eyes darkened. He shifted his gaze away from her, looked down at the floor and muttered, 'I wanted to tell you something else. You know how much I care about you...' He became silent and took her hand into his and pulled it to his lips and put a kiss on it. He rubbed her cheek gently with his thumb in deep thought.

'What were going to tell me?' she asked. A faint smile curving the corners of her mouth.

'Gloria.' He whispered her name. She raised her head and met his gaze. She saw a flicker of pain in his black eyes.

Her finger traced a line down his cheek and stopped at the edge of his lips. 'I hope you have no bad news for me.' She ran her finger along his bottom lip.

He sighed. 'I have to travel to--' He swallowed his words and did not finish the sentence.

She stared up into his eyes. With a voice trembling, she asked, 'Where are you going, Cyrus?' She saw a growing pain in his eyes.

He went over to an armchair and sat down. Moving his hand over his neck, he said, 'My love, I have to travel to--'

'Where?'

'To see my mother.'

Gloria was shocked. Her jaw dropped. She tried to say something but no words came out of her mouth. Tears ran down her cheeks. Her tears soaked into his soul. Resting his elbows on the arms of the chair, he covered his face with his palms, a burning pain in his soul.

Cyrus walked over to her and stood behind the chair and put his arms around her shoulders. He bent down and kissed her fragrant hair. 'Please, don't cry.'

He tightened his arms around her. Gloria absorbed the heat of his body. She took his hands into hers and pressed them against her cheek and kissed them. In a pleading tone, she asked, 'Why do you want to go? You know that they're after you. Your name is on the black list. Can't you change your mind?'

The answer was a kiss on her hair. Then Cyrus returned to his chair and sank into it, thinking. 'I must see my mother before she dies. Her greatest desire is to see me before departing to the next world.'

'They may kill you.'

'That black list was prepared more than a decade ago. It may not be valid any more. Hopefully nothing will happen.'

'Can't you at least postpone it until after our wedding?' pleaded Gloria.

'No, honey. It is wiser that I go before our marriage.'

A thought passed through Gloria's mind that Cyrus might know that he would not come back. She felt a burning knife passing through her heart. She shivered. Sobbing, she said, 'Why are you in such a hurry?'

Cyrus heaved a deep sigh and did not answer. He forced himself to smile. A cold smile iced on his lips.

'I think you sense that you may never come back.'

'No, my love. That's not the reason. If I delay the trip she may die. I'll be remorseful for the rest of my life.'

'Your name is on the black list. How can I be sure they will not execute you?' She burst into tears and wept.

Cyrus tried hard to hold back his tears. He covered his face with his palms, his elbows rested on his knees. He closed his eyes and prayed that he might solace her.

'If it is the will of God that I live longer, no one can harm me.'

Gloria raised her head and stared at him, but her eyes were blurred with tears. She heaved a sigh. 'You're just trying to comfort me.'

Suddenly Cyrus remembered that Gloria had once read his palm and told him that he would live long. With the joy of discovery, he smiled broadly. 'Now I have a solid reason to believe that I'll come back. I can quote your words to confirm my belief that no one will end my life so soon.'

'My words…? Said Gloria in surprise. 'I don't remember saying any such thing.'

''Yes, you did. You have to respect your own promise.' Cyrus forced himself to laugh.

Gloria looked confused. She could not remember promising Cyrus that if he went back to his homeland he would come back safe and sound.

'Do you remember when you read my palm?'

'Yes, I do. What does that have to do with it?'

'You told me that I'll live long. I don't think you should discredit your own skill.'

Gloria smiled, a light shone through her eyes. Her tears sparkled.

Cyrus stood up and approached Gloria while holding out

his hand. 'Read my palm if you are in doubt.'

Gloria took his hand in hers and pressed his palm against her cheek. Cyrus put his arm around her neck and kissed her hair. He rubbed her cheeks and chin gently and lovingly. Whenever his hand passed close to her lips she put a kiss on it. She rested her head against his chest and closed her eyes.

She opened her eyes and stared up at him. 'My love, you don't know how much I love you. To be away from you one day is an eternity for me.'

'I'll be back as soon as possible. Only two or three weeks at the most.'

14.

The plane carrying Cyrus soared high. Gloria's eyes followed it as it flew further and further until it turned into a dot and disappeared. Standing motionless, she stared at the spot where the plane had vanished over the horizon. She tried to fight her anxiety but could not help worrying. Love had tied two hearts in such a way that they were no longer conscious of their different cultural and national backgrounds. In the realm of love there was no Eastern and Western, no black and white, no Buddhist and Christian. It was above artificial national borders, false racial animosity, and man-made religious dogma.

Gloria looked sad and pale. Maria approached her, hugged and kissed her. 'Let's go home, my love. Don't worry. He'll come back soon.'

When they got into the car, Gloria looked at her watch to see how much of the three weeks had already passed. Cyrus had told her that he would be away for only three weeks.

Chapter Nine

HOMELAND

1.

Cyrus did not want the news of his visit to his birthplace spread around. It was about 10:30 at night when he rang the doorbell of the house. His sister, Feri, opened the door. She stared at him, silent and stunned, not believing her eyes. She thought it was a ghost. She rubbed her eyes to awaken herself, as if she had been dreaming. But it seemed that she was staring at her dearly loved brother. When she was certain it was Cyrus who was standing there, looking at her with a big smile, her whole face lit up. She opened her mouth in surprise. It seemed she was going to shout out in joy.

Cyrus immediately put his forefinger on her lips and whispered, 'Hush.'

She realised that she had to control her excitement and not to express her joy loudly. It could alert the attention of the next-door neighbours and make them suspicious that Cyrus might have returned to his homeland. Without uttering a word she embraced Cyrus affectionately and kissed his cheeks. He gave her a big hug, and kissed her hair and eyes. Chuckling with delight, she carried his suitcase into the hall.

His mother's health had recovered slightly. She could walk. She came into the hall to inquire, 'Who was ringing the doorbell at this time of night?'

Feri did not reply and waited to see her mother's response. A few seconds passed in silence. His mother looked more closely and realised that somebody was standing in the dim light of the hall.

'Who is that, do we have a visitor?'

Feri did not answer. His mother stared at Cyrus, inspecting him from top to toe. She did not expect to see her most loved son even in a dream after so many years of painful separation. At first, she saw an apparition of Cyrus in a maze of clouds, then in a muffled voice she cried 'Cyrus'. The clouds gradually cleared and the face of Cyrus became real and visible. His mother stared at him but could not believe her eyes. She did not breathe for a few seconds. Then, with a loud and joyful voice, she said 'Oh! Cyrus! Oh, my son! My love.' She flew towards him like a bird. Cyrus rushed to her. They hugged each other for a long time. She kissed his cheeks, eyes, and smelt his hair.

Feri was standing absorbed in watching the scene. Motherly love touched her heart and brought tears to her eyes. It was beautiful, uplifting and spiritual.

Cyrus's mother stared into his eyes. 'Oh! A new life has come to my body. I thought I might not see you again before I die.' Smiling and scrutinising Cyrus from head to foot, she asked, 'What brought you here, my love?'

'You were worried that you might not see me again, so I came to see you.'

'Thank you, my love; thank you for being so thoughtful.' She hugged and kissed him again to express her gratitude.

'Why didn't you let us know you were coming?'

'I'll explain to you later.'

'I would have covered the road with Persian rugs.' A broad smile lit his mother's face.

Cyrus laughed. 'Spread Persian carpets all the way from the airport to home?'

'Why not? You deserve it.' A light flashed in her eyes.

'Mum,' said Feri, 'Cyrus is tired. I think it's better we give him something to eat and drink.'

'Yes, yes. You're right, my sweetheart. Please go to the kitchen and prepare something for my love.'

His father, sleeping in the bedroom, woke up at this time and came out wearing his night attire. He hugged Cyrus affectionately and kissed him tenderly. All sat down drinking tea, eating dried nuts and fruits, chatting, telling jokes and sharing various memories until three o'clock in the morning.

2.

For Gloria, time dragged painfully, and she felt Cyrus's absence deeply. Her friends tried to visit her and invite her to their homes to keep her busy and happy.

Ten days after the departure of Cyrus, a close friend invited Gloria to her birthday party. Young men and women, joyful and merry, were dancing and laughing. Several people approached Gloria in turn to invite her to dance, but she refused. Gloria's friend, the hostess of the party, also invited her to dance.

Gloria smiled. 'I don't feel dancing. Please excuse me.'

'Come on. This is my birthday party. You have to dance with me.' She grasped Gloria's hand and pulled her up.

Gloria stood up and started dancing with her. But after a short while, she kissed and hugged her friend and went back to her seat.

In the dim light, the music was thundering down and sweeping across the hall. Most guests were on the floor, shaking their bodies, jerking their hips, swinging their arms and moving their heads forwards and backwards.

Gloria slipped easily through the dancers and made her way outside. Standing alone on the veranda, she gazed at the water of a fountain shooting up and falling down into a pond. There were garden lights reflected in the water and shedding light on the foliage of the nearby shrubs and flowers.

She remembered Cyrus, as if he were staring at her with an enchanting smile. She recollected the time she had spent with him visiting art galleries and sightseeing. Those moments were filled with joy, glimpses of eternity. She wished those moments were permanent and that she could stop the wheel of time and live in that atmosphere forever.

She stared up at the sky, with its unnumbered stars twinkling. She thought: Cyrus is on the other side of the globe. When he looks at the sky, he sees the same heaven and the same twinkling stars. The distance vanishes. She remembered vividly the moment when the plane carrying Cyrus flew high and disappeared in the distant horizon. When he hugged and kissed her at the airport to board the plane, his smile was sweet but sad.

Sofia, a close friend of Gloria, noticed Gloria's absence. She went out and found Gloria standing on the veranda, absorbed in her dreams.

'Why are you standing here alone?' she said. 'Come in. Dance. Have fun.'

Gloria turned to her, bright tears in her eyes. 'My man is not here to dance with.'

'Try to distract your mind. There are many other men here. Be happy.'

'Dear Sofia! Nothing can fill the absence of Cyrus.'

A few days after the party, it was raining. Gloria sat alone in her room watching the sharp drops of rain hitting the window. The plants and flowers were smiling and bathing in the lukewarm water. Sometimes a wind blew and made the rain splash on the window. The dancing shrubs, trees and plants in the haze of the shower gave her a sad pleasure. Many thoughts passed through her mind: 'Where might Cyrus be now? Is he asleep or awake? Is he talking to his mother or someone else? Is he thinking of me?'

The rain stopped. Gloria opened the window and breathed in the clean, fresh air. It gave her delight. She stared at the plants and flowers given a new life by the rain. She muttered, I wish celestial rain would come down from heaven to cleanse our hearts.

A gorgeous, vibrant rainbow appeared in the sky, bridging the east and the west. The day was drawing to a close, and the horizon had the colour of a blazing fire. The trees on the top of the opposite hill were silhouetted against the sky. They were standing mute and mysterious, looked like ghosts. Gloria stared at the changing colours and suddenly a small cloud attracted her attention. It was in the shape of a horserider rapidly moving across the far-off horizon. It brought to her mind an image of Cyrus sitting on horseback, galloping. She recollected the oft-repeated statement of Cyrus, expressing his wish, even as a single horseman, to invade the troops of darkness and push them back. She could remember him; whenever he spoke of his wish, his face would become serious and glow with enthusiasm, his head erect, his eyebrows like a drawn bow, his voice resonant and vibrating with valour. He used to raise his fist in the air, moving it forwards as if giving the signal to attack. He would give her confidence that it was possible to chase away the lingering darkness shrouding the face of the earth.

Everything plunged into darkness. Gloria went into the kitchen and made a cup of coffee. While drinking, she stared at the telephone and was tempted to call Cyrus. But Cyrus had told her it was better not to phone him. The telephone at his parents' house might be tapped. Still, it was hard to resist the temptation. She got up and went to the telephone. Hesitantly, she picked up the receiver and slowly dialled the code. Before completing the number she hung up and went back to the table to drink her coffee. She sipped it, looking at the telephone. She knew that by simply dialling a few numbers she could hear Cyrus's voice. But something told her not to telephone Cyrus, not to put him in danger. In spite of her better judgement, however, she dialled the number. The telephone started to ring on the other side. She reluctantly hung it up before it was answered and sat down heavy hearted. She so wanted to hear Cyrus's voice. She tried to convince herself that there was no evidence that his parents' telephone was tapped. She muttered, 'it's just a guess, mere speculation.' She plucked up courage and with determined steps went to the telephone and dialled.

Feri, Cyrus's sister picked up the phone at the other end and called Cyrus. Gloria's heart started throbbing expectantly. Then she heard his voice: 'O! Gloria I am delighted to hear you, to hear your dear voice. I always think of you. I hope to see you soon. Please, forgive me. I can't talk long. I have to rush out for something urgent. I will be in touch with you.' Gloria kissed the receiver, gently hung it up, and then started to pace to and fro with quick steps as if flying in the air. Cyrus's voice was still ringing in her ears; it seemed to her that he had shortened the conversation deliberately. She did not understand why.

3.

In his homeland, Cyrus was sitting in the study reading a book. It was about 11:30 p.m. His mother was awake and came into the study frequently. She sat pensively staring at Cyrus in the dim light of the reading lamp. Each time she left without saying a word. She seemed restless, as if she sensed impending danger, though she did not want to disclose to him the terrible intuition she had.

Absorbed in his reading, Cyrus did not notice that his mother frequently stepped in and out. This time his mother came into the study and sat on the sofa for a long time staring at Cyrus, whom she loved more than anyone in the world. His face looked hallowed with purity and the aspirations of his high ideals. She felt a tender love for him in her heart.

Cyrus sensed the presence of somebody in the room. He raised his head and looked around. In the dim light he could see his mother sitting on the sofa silent and pensive, looking sad.

'Mum, why don't you go to bed and rest? It's already late.'

'I can't sleep. I sense a danger that discomforts me.'

'Don't worry. Just go to bed and have a rest.'

'I wish I could. I'm obsessed with a terrible intuition.'

There was a pause.

With a muffled voice, in agony, she muttered, 'I wish you were not here.'

Cyrus was shocked. He closed the book and swivelled his chair around, looking puzzled and confused. 'Please, don't torment yourself with unnecessary worries.' He smiled to make everything seem normal. 'I heard you weren't well and that you were sad and disappointed. That's why I came to see you.' He dropped his head in deep thought. Biting his lower lip, he turned to her, narrowed his eyes and said, 'You really didn't want to see me?'

His mother stared at him and did not reply. Her eyes were sad but full of love. Tears started running down her innocent face. Choked with tears, she murmured, 'Surely, it was my cherished wish to see you. I prayed. I cried. I gave money to charity that I may see you once more before I die.'

'Now I'm here. Look at me.' Cyrus's face lit up with a broad smile. 'This is what you wished for.'

'I don't want you to be here. I wish you weren't here.' She turned aside, sobbing.

Cyrus wondered why his mother was taking her intuition seriously; why she was so deeply worried. She had prayed for his coming, but now she wished he were not here. He stood up and walked slowly towards his mother to solace her. He bent down to kiss her hair, when suddenly, she put her head on his chest and grasped his hands in hers and held them with tender affection, tears running down her face. 'I don't want to lose you. I don't want my blooming flower to be destroyed.'

'What are you talking about? Please, pull yourself together. Nothing will happen. That's just your imagination.'

'They may come and arrest you.'

Cyrus knelt down and looked up directly into her eyes and whispered. 'Mum, I'm under God's protection. No one can harm me.'

'These people can harm even the holiest ones.'

'Mum, the vanguard of the new era will never die, even if they are executed. They're the shining stars in the horizon of history. Even their memory is inspiring.'

His mother stared at him anxiouusly and asked, 'I hope you're not going to be a martyr, are you?'

Cyrus smiled. 'What if I am? What then?'

She was taken aback and sat straight up as if a dagger had been thrust into her back. 'You don't mean it,' she entreated. 'Please, tell me you don't mean it.'

Cyrus felt that he was tormenting his mother. He pitied her. He kissed her cheeks and said reassuringly, 'Mum, I don't mean it. Believe me, I don't mean it.'

She heaved a deep sigh of relief. 'I've much hope for you. I don't want them to end your life with a few bullets.'

'I assure you that no one will be able to end my life so easily.'

She stared at him with a serious look. 'How do you know that? How are you so sure?'

'I know by intuition. The same way that you trust your intuition, I trust my intuition too.'

'What's your intuition?' asked his mother, interested to know.

'My intuition tells me that I won't be martyred.'

'Really!' Her face lit up with a spark of hope that her beloved son might survive while a dark storm was crushing everything in its path. Feeling comforted and relieved, she rose up to bring him refreshment.

Cyrus went back to his desk to continue reading. He was reading a book in Persian entitled *Repository of Mysteries*. It was a book in verse narrating the spiritual journey of a wayfarer who passes through stages and travels from valley to valley to reach the abode of peace and wisdom, the ultimate goal of one's soul, to come into unison with one's innate divine essence. Reading the book uplifted him to a level above the turmoil of a troubled age.

Cyrus went to the kitchen for a glass of water. To his surprise, his mother was still sitting awake in the dark family room.

'Mum! You're still awake! Please, go to bed and rest.'

She pleaded, 'It's late, but we can phone one of our relatives so that you can go there to hide.'

'I'll never hide myself. I'll never run away,' replied Cyrus with emphasis. 'If they're going to execute me for my belief in a glorious age, for my efforts for the unity of humankind, let them do it.' His face glowed with the warmth of his faith.

Both remained silent.

He was standing at the door of the family room. His figure, silhouetted against the dim light of the hall, seemed to his mother to be hallowed with a mystery, like a hero proclaiming the dawn of a new age.

'Mum, I think you should try to be brave. Detachment gives you strength and courage.'

She heaved a deep sigh. 'I'm too attached to you, my love. That's my weakness. No one can understand the nature of the love of a mother.'

'When I was a child, I heard you many times: "let us, we women, arise and build a world of peace, compassion, caring and cooperation. End the man-made world based on power struggle, exploitation, war and slavery." Your words still echo in my mind.'

His mother's face lit up with a smile. 'I wish you were a child. Then I could nurse you on my lap, caress your face gently and sing a lullaby. I could move my hands through your thick hair. When you were a child your hair was so thick that the barber had difficulty combing it.'

'Do you remember my childhood?'

'Yes, yes, as if it was yesterday. Time flies so fast.' She fell back into her previous mood and became gloomy. She stared at him. 'I wish you were not here. I can't help sensing an approaching danger.'

'If anything is going to happen, let it happen. I want you to be like a lioness. Nothing can frighten you. If the agents of dark forces are able to intimidate us, how can we change the darkness into light?'

'You're right. I don't know why I'm in such a mood. Something is bothering me.'

'Please, don't show weakness.'

'It might seem like weakness to you, but it's because of my love for you.' Her eyes became moist. Her face looked innocent.

Cyrus kissed his mother and asked her to be strong should any test come.

Silence took over the conversation.

'Mum, I think I'll go to bed. I feel you won't sleep while I'm awake.'

'That's a good idea. You should be in bed at this time of night. You're tired. It's two o'clock in the morning.'

Suddenly his mother recoiled as if she had heard the hissing of a cobra. She whispered, 'Hush! Be quiet.'

Cyrus was surprised. He bent down and asked in a low voice. 'Mum! What's happened?'

'Shush! I hear footsteps around the house.'

'I think you're imagining.'

She whispered to him: 'I think the guards have come to arrest you.'

Cyrus and his mother became quiet, listening attentively. They heard whispering.

The mother's face turned pale. She began trembling slightly.

Cyrus's heart started beating faster. Then he was certain that something was going to happen. He said to himself that the expected moment had come. He prepared himself for trouble. He slid his hand over his face and pushed his fingers through his hair. He covered his eyes with the heel of his hands. 'O God! Give me strength.' He prayed in his heart that God might give him the strength to pass the tests and bear the suffering of his probable martyrdom. He realised the time of words had passed. The time had come to prove by his deeds how far he was ready to accept suffering and deprivation for the good of his fellow men.

He looked at his mother sitting there as one whose soul had already departed her body. He forced himself to smile, but the dim smile betrayed his sadness and anxiety. He approached his mother and kissed her. She startled as if she was not aware of his presence.

'Oh! My dear, you're here. Many things passed through my mind.'

'I'm still here, standing close to you. Mum, the test has come. Please, show strength and courage.'

She sighed and did not reply.

'Mum, I'm prepared for anything that may happen to me.'

She stared at him as if her mind was blank.

There was a knock at the door. Cyrus and his mother looked at each other and did not answer. There was another knock at the door. They did not reply. Suddenly his mother stood up, alert and defensive. Blood started to pound in her veins. Energy came back to her. A flame of anger flared in her eyes.

'You go inside,' instructed his mother. 'I'll go and open the door, but I won't let them into my house. I'll tell them they can take me to jail, or even to the scaffold for execution, but they cannot come into my house.'

'Mum, please be patient and calm. I'm not going to hide myself.'

There were more knocks at the door.

'Please, you stay in,' pleaded Cyrus. 'They're after me. There's no need for them to come into the house and search around. I'll go and open the door and introduce myself.'

'No, no, my dear, you shouldn't do that,' entreated his mother. Her voice rose to the pitch of a shout. 'How long are we to be persecuted? It's more than one hundred years that we have continuously been harassed, plundered, fired from jobs, jailed and martyred. Is it a sin to have faith in the dawning of a new day? Is it an offence to be infatuated with the glory of a rising sun?'

There were louder knocks.

His mother went to the door and asked, 'Who's knocking at my house at this time of night?'

'When you open the door you will know who we are,' answered an unknown person with a harsh voice.

'I will not open the door until I know who's knocking at the door of my house.'

'Open the door, or we will break it down.'

She opened the door, grumbling. 'You think you have the right to break down the door of someone's home in the middle of the night.'

As soon as she unlocked the door, three men carrying rifles flung themselves in and took up positions immediately. Two other gunmen stayed outside.

'Where's Cyrus?' One of the gunmen asked.

'Why do you ask for Cyrus? Who has given you the authority to come into my house and ask for my son?'

A tall man with a black beard, wearing a revolutionary guard's uniform, seemed to be the team leader. His black moustache lifted and he sneered, showing yellow fangs. He ordered the gunmen to find Cyrus. He shouted, 'Search the house. Don't leave a nook or corner unexplored.'

Cyrus came out of the hall into the front yard, and approached the guards. 'I'm Cyrus. What do you want?'

'We have an order to arrest you,' said the team leader.

'Could you please show me the order?'

The gang leader slapped Cyrus hard on the face. 'Is that enough to convince you that we have an order to arrest you?'

Cyrus stared at him and did not say a word. The other two gunmen who were outside the house came in carrying rifles. One of the gunmen pointed the rifle at Cyrus, warning him that if he resisted, or reacted, or protested he would be killed on the spot. All five guards had short black beards and wore the uniform of the revolutionary guards. Except for one guard, they all looked like drug addicts, with pale, wax-like faces, the colour of the dead. They were not able to smile. Whenever they tried to smile they looked as if they were snarling, exposing their canine teeth. Their eyes were two dark holes fixed in gloomy faces expressing hatred. Cyrus wondered whether they had ever experienced the bliss of true love.

Cyrus's mother felt a tremendous strength, enough to battle against the five gunmen. She approached them like a lioness. 'Who you are to slap my son?' she shouted, reproachfully.

'Mum,' pleaded Cyrus, 'please be calm. Please be

patient.'

Then Cyrus turned to the guards and with a clear voice said: 'Let me tell you something. I'm not the only one who cherishes the new ideals. Men and women of thought in every land aspire to new ideals to create a new civilisation. They believe in spiritual values, something dynamic and global in scope. A new era is dawning. I live in that sphere. I breathe in that atmosphere. No force can stop this process by hanging me or anyone like me.'

None of the gunmen could grasp the meaning of what Cyrus was saying. None of them appreciated his ardent enthusiasm for a new world order. His words fell on deaf ears. For them he was a dangerous person disturbing their torpor and repose.

The gunmen's leader became impatient with Cyrus's speech and snarled violently. 'Don't waste our time with your illusory world. You are up in the air. When you are jailed in the black dungeon, then you will realise what reality is.'

He took Cyrus by the arm and dragged him violently to the Land Rover waiting outside. His mother rushed to Cyrus, and held his arm firmly. Choking back tears, she cried, 'Don't take my son away. I won't let you.'

One of the gunmen hit her hard on her leg with the butt of his rifle. She fell to the ground, her body reeling with pain. They pulled Cyrus into the Land Rover.

In spite of pain she stood up and ran after them. When she came out she heard the roar of the Land Rover speeding away. She ran about one hundred metres after the Land Rover, but it disappeared in the darkness. It was a cloudy, pitch-black night. She could not see the direction in which the Land Rover headed. She stared into the darkness but could see nothing. The cold wind was howling and wailing, knocking at the windows of the rooms where people were fast asleep. There was a thick, heavy silence. Nothing could be heard except the barking of dogs from neighbouring houses.

Cyrus's mother stood breathless and motionless staring into the darkness. She found herself barefoot and dishevelled and felt the sharp pain of the bruise on her leg. It was a chilly night. Reluctantly, she limped back home, locked the door and went into the study. The reading lamp was still on; the book Cyrus had been reading lay open on the desk. She closed the book, turned off the reading lamp, dropped into the armchair and wept bitterly.

When the armed guards had dragged Cyrus into the Land Rover, two guards had roughly held his hands, while the third one handcuffed him and put a gag in his mouth.

Cyrus put his hands together to be handcuffed with no resistance.

They blindfolded him with some thick black cloth. He felt as if he had been dropped into a horrifying dark pit. The outside world plunged into an intense darkness.

A guard sitting in the front turned around, snarled at him and gimaced to show his hatred, regardless of the fact that Cyrus could not see his face.

A guard sitting beside Cyrus hit his ribs hard with his elbow and cursed him. 'You damned people! You misguided anti-God!'

Cyrus paid no attention to their insults. Calm and detached, he sat among the armed guards, ignoring them.

He renounced the outside world and turned his mind inwards. He tried to draw energy from the hidden reserves in the inner chamber of his soul.

The outside world was dark, intensely depressing. But there was a light, an unearthly light illuminating his inner world. It gave him strength, hope and vision to resist and fight against the waves of dark forces battering at his soul.

His mother appeared in his mind writhing on the ground in pain, after a guard had hit her leg hard with the butt of his rifle. He recollected how his mother, choked with tears, pleaded, 'Don't take my son away.' He could still feel the loving hand of his mother holding firm on his arm.

His heart sank. He sighed deeply and prayed in his heart for his mother to be able to bear the cruelties of this troubled time.

It was after midnight. The deadly silence was broken by the sound of the tyres turning on the ground. He did not know where they were taking him: to a solitary prison, to an underground dungeon to be tortured to death, or directly to the gallows to be hanged.

He thought about the day he had spent with Gloria on a beach on the south coast of New South Wales. The beach was covered with white sand, extending as far as the eye could see. The scenery was breathtaking. The pebbles shone brightly with various colours at the bottom of the clean water. A gentle breeze was wafting from the sea, ruffling the surface of the water and caressing their faces. The waves were sparkling in the sunlight.

Gloria was wearing a blue skirt and a white blouse. The skirt was a simple piece of cloth, wrapped round her waist. Gloria looked very attractive.

Happy and joyful, they played, ran, joked and laughed. They swam in the sea, sat under the shade of a tree and watched the pretty scenery of the beach extending endlessly.

It was a clean and innocent world, not defiled.

Completely absorbed in his memory, Cyrus had forgotten that he was on his way to a black pit or to the gallows. The sweet laughter of Gloria was still ringing in his ears when the guard, sitting beside him, hit him hard with his elbow and ordered him to get down from the vehicle.

He became conscious of his situation, like a person waking from a sweet dream to see a scene of horror. The sweet memory vanished. The beautiful and innocent world faded away.

Cyrus stepped out of the Land Rover.

A guard gave him a piece of rope to hold and told Cyrus to follow him. Like a blind person groping in the dark, Cyrus followed the guard. Handcuffed and blindfolded, he tried hard to keep up with the guard who was walking fast.

The guard dragged him forcefully and did not tell him there was a big rough stone in their way.

Cyrus fell over and felt a sharp pain in his chest, as if one of his ribs had been fractured. His legs, arms and chest were hurt badly.

He clawed the ground, struggling to stand on his feet.

Another guard hit Cyrus's back hard with the butt of his rifle and said, 'Get up. Be quick'.

Cyrus stood up, grimacing at the intense pain in his chest, and continued groping with injured hands and face. The guards paid no attention to Cyrus's pain and injuries.

After ten minutes, he climbed down some stairs. He sensed that they had entered a corridor leading to the basement of a building. He was led through dark and intricate passages. He sensed an atmosphere of sorrow and deep gloom.

He heard the moaning, the groaning, the crying and the sobbing of the prisoners being lashed or tortured in various ways in different cells. He sensed hell with all its horrifying agony and torment.

They dragged him to a black pit and threw him into a solitary cell. He hit his head against the ceiling and felt a sharp pain through his whole body. Being blindfolded, he could not see that the ceiling of the cell was so low he could not stand up.   A guard took off his handcuffs and left him blindfolded in the solitary cell. The key twisted and the iron door of the cell was locked.

Blindfolded, he sat on the floor and leant his back against the wall, thinking of the dark world he had to face. He rubbed the floor to explore it. The floor was barely covered with a ragged rough blanket.

He heaved a sigh and thought: 'Why am I in prison?'

But he could not find an answer. He believed freedom of thought, vision and belief was his birthright. 'Is it a crime,' he thought, 'to vindicate the ideals for a better world? What's wrong with believing poverty has to be eradicated from the face of the earth? Is it an offence believing that the material resources in store on the land and in the sea are more than enough for everyone to live in prosperity, and that the spiritual gems treasured in every soul are more than enough for everyone to live a life of blissful joy?

He struggled for breath. The intensity of the darkness seemed to stifle him; the blackness of eternal night had encompassed him. He recollected rumours of how the damned people in those dungeons were tortured, executed and mutilated. 'Will I be tortured to death in this subterreanean world of darkness?' he thought.

He removed the blindfold, rubbed his eyes and looked

around. He could see nothing. In the intense darkness, there was not much difference between having eyesight or being blind. He thought if he stayed long in the dark he might become used to it.

He sat, thinking: 'People have become used to miseries. If a new pattern for a better world is presented to them, they will remain indifferent. They'll reject it as something utopian. They don't trust themselves. Pessimism has made them feeble and crippled.'

The severe pain in his arms, legs and chest interrupted the trend of his thoughts. He tenderly touched the sore spots and felt a sharp pain.

Moans and groans were heard all the time. They were torturing the prisoners. 'They can harm my body, but they cannot subjugate my inner reality,' he muttered.

He heard footsteps and the harsh words of the guards passing by his cell. Whenever he heard the footsteps of the guards approaching his cell, instinctively he looked at the iron door, expecting the key to turn in the lock and the guards to take him out to be lashed with an iron cord. But each time, he heard them walk away, and their voices faded. They were taking prisoners to be tried, or tortured, or executed.

He tried hard to keep his mind under control. He sought the assistance of God. He believed he could draw energy from that mystical source.

He did not know how prayer could perform miracles. But experience had proven to him that this was indeed possible.

In the dark cell, with tearful eyes, he turned to the source of limitless light, prayed and meditated. Gradually spiritual energy was released within him and his soul was charged with a new power. He became less concerned with his physical condition. His injuries became less painful. A space of delight was slowly opening within him.

He wondered why prophets were persecuted whenever they appeared. Suddenly a light flashed in his mind. The secret was revealed: *they were a threat to a declining age.* This thought solaced him and he felt he shared their suffering.

Cyrus was sitting on the floor, leaning his back against the wall, meditating. It was well after midnight. He was exhausted. Involuntarily his head dropped on his shoulder and he fell into a deep sleep. When he opened his eyes the objects around were visible. He was able to see the size and aspect of his cell. He found beside him some food and water. Gradually his eyes got used to the darkness. He estimated that the cell was about two metres by one metre and a half, with a toilet. He smelled dampness in the room, a room that had never seen sunlight.

Because of the pain in his arms, legs and chest, Cyrus could not sleep on the rough cell floor for many nights. Whenever he did manage to sleep it was not a normal sleep. Long after midnight, dropping on the floor, or his head leaning against the wall, he fell asleep-- a sleep like a death.

One night, about three hours after midnight, he suddenly woke up in terror, hearing the terrible sound of a shower of bullets. He sat up, leant his head against the wall, and listened to the horrific sound. He looked around. The prison was very dark. It was horrible. The firing squad was executing some prisoners.

Many nights after that, Cyrus was wakened in terror by the sound of bullets when some prisoners were being executed. By counting the shots he could work out how many were executed each night.

He was left in that dark black cell for two months without having contact with anyone. For him day and night were no different.

Each morning an armed guard opened the door, put some food in his room, then locked the door and walked away hurriedly without saying a word, as if running away from a leper. Sometimes, Cyrus did not notice what time they put food in his room. Even a stray dog would refuse to eat that sort of food.

They treated him as a dangerous prisoner. He was under strict confinement. His whereabouts were not disclosed to anyone. Any outside inquiry about his imprisonment was denied. The armed guards who brought him food were strongly warned not to talk to him.

He could neither stand nor walk in a room of that size. He crawled on the floor like an animal for his daily exercise.

After two months, two gunmen came to his cell early one morning. They informed him that he would be taken to the courtroom for trial. It was strange that the news did not terrify him. He felt relieved instead.

The gunmen blindfolded him and Cyrus stepped out of the cell and stood erect. He could not walk properly after two months crawling on the floor. But the gunmen dragged him mercilessly. He was holding firmly to the end of a rope, following the gunmen blindly.

The guards lashed him with the end of the same rope twice on the way, instructing him to walk faster. He tried hard to keep up with the pace of the gunmen.

They walked downstairs and entered a corridor underground. It was a horrible dark world.

After ten minutes they reached the courtroom. It was nine

o'clock in the morning.

They instructed him to stand at the threshold of the courtroom to wait for his turn. Blindfolded, he stood until three o'clock in the afternoon.

Whenever the guards took him for questioning he had to stand five hours or more, blindfolded, at the threshold of the courtroom, until he was called in.

During the interrogation he had to stand blindfolded so that he could not see the faces of those interrogating him. In the initial stages, the method of trial was lenient and the tone of the interrogation was not rough.

4.

After Cyrus was taken away, his relatives - especially Feri - did everything they could to gain information on his whereabouts. Feri did not leave any stone unturned to find out where her brother had been taken, but she could not gather any information. Was he tortured? Was he taken to a normal prison or to a black pit? Was he still alive or had he been hanged? These were the questions that worried Feri, and she had no answers for them.

One night, three hours after midnight, Cyrus's mother woke up after a disturbing dream. In the dream she saw that Cyrus was going to be executed. Gunmen were pointing their guns at him. Cyrus was calm, firm and resolute. With a resonant voice he said, 'You can hang me, but you cannot put out the sparks of hope for a new world. You can execute me, but you cannot divert the trend of time. A mysterious force has moved the world.'

The leader of the squad shouted, 'Don't let him speak. Shut him up. Fire!'

His mother was terrified and woke up trembling. She sat up in the bed and sobbed bitterly, intensely disturbed by the dream. She worried that Cyrus had been executed. She decided to wake up Feri to share with her the horrible dream. But unconsciously she wanted someone to reassure her that her dream did not mean that Cyrus had been executed. She tried to turn the light on but could not. The power had gone; everything was dark.

Her hand on the wall, she slowly groped to get to Feri's bedroom to wake her up. It was difficult to find her way in the thick darkness. With a muffled voice she called, 'Feri, Feri, where are you? Please wake up.'

Feri heard her mother's voice and woke up. She became worried to find her mother groping like a blind person in the pitch black, calling her with a throat choked with tears. She rushed to her help, 'Yes, Mum, I'm coming. What has happened? Don't you feel well? Are you in pain?'

'Not my body, but my soul is in great pain.'

'Why don't you switch on the light?' asked Feri.

'My love, the whole city is plunged in darkness. It's a blackout. No light, everything is dark.' Then her mother burst into tears and started sobbing. With a husky voice, mixed with the sound of her crying, she called, 'Feri, please help me. I'm going to collapse.'

'I'm here. Mum, dear Mum, why are you crying?'

'Feri! I had a horrible dream. Could you find some candles?'

Feri helped her mother to the lounge, sat her on the sofa and went to fetch some candles. Feri lit the candles, and her mother tried to narrate the dream with a choked throat.

'Please, don't cry, Mum. This is just a dream. Don't you remember that Cyrus said several times that he wouldn't be martyred?'

'How can we trust that?'

'You know whenever Cyrus sensed something he was right. I trust his intuition. Let's pray.'

Their shadows reflecting on the wall, they closed their eyes and prayed in the dim light of the candles. Feri opened her eyes and stared at a teardrop hanging on the distressed face of her mother. The candlelight was reflected in it. Feri kissed her mother and suggested that she go back to bed.

'No, my love, I'll wait here until the day breaks.'

It was about 4:30 a.m. when Feri went to her bedroom to go to bed, but she did not fall asleep. She sat up thinking about her brother and tried to avoid thinking that Cyrus might be executed, but she could not help shedding tears. She got out of the bed and stepped into the hall to stay with her mother. Feri noticed that her mother was quietly crying. She tried to comfort her mother, 'Mum, I'm sure that before long Cyrus will knock at the door and come in.'

Her mother misheard. A ray of joy flashed in her eyes and she exclaimed, 'Really! Is Cyrus knocking at the door?'

'No, I meant they will realise that he just advocates truth and justice. It'll be proven to them that Cyrus is innocent and they'll release him soon.'

'My love! You're too innocent to realise that truth is dangerous and justice is threatening.'

They sat silent, brooding over a world where to love truth and justice was a crime.

Gradually the dawn began breaking.

As if waking up from a dream, Feri exclaimed, 'Mum! I feel in my heart that a miracle will occur and my brother's life will be saved.'

The sun peeped through, but to them the sunlight was pale. They went out and sat in armchairs on the sunlit balcony.

'The sun has risen,' murmured her mother, 'but for me there's no day. My sunshine has been locked up in a dark cell.'

'Do you want me to make tea and bring you breakfast?' asked Feri.

'Not breakfast, just bring me a cup of tea.'

Feri put the teapot on the coffee table and poured tea into a glass for her mother. The sun was reflecting in the wine-coloured tea.

The cage of a beautiful songbird hung on the wall close to the entrance of the hall. The bird started twittering but its singing brought Feri and her mother sadness, not joy. Their psychological mood was projected into the surrounding world.

The bird hopped to and fro in the cage. The songbird seemed not to like being confined with no space to fly.

Feri felt pity for the poor bird fluttering in a barred prison. So, she decided to set the bird free to fly in the limitless atmosphere, in the bush, over mountains, rivers, and lakes. She opened the door of the cage so that the bird could fly away. The bird stared at the cage door. It realised the door was open, but could not understand why. It had got used to the cage, and had never thought that it could be possible to wing its way in the fresh air. The bird came closer to the cage door to make sure that the door to freedom was really open and that it was not just an illusion. But it hopped back. It could not trust the newfound freedom. She did not believe her human captors were setting her free.

Her captors were the same as the people who had made

prisons and cages in the name of ideology, political systems and customs. Sometimes they made a prison as big as a country. Then, all forces were mobilised to keep the people in that prison, not to let them escape. Even thinking of freedom could endanger their lives. The blissful joy that one could experience in detachment was beyond their experience. They were more satisfied in bondage than in freedom.

At last the bird came to the cage door and looked around. It became quite sure that the door of the cage was really open but it could not believe it had been left open so that it could gain its freedom and fly in the open air. It thought it might be a trap in the name of freedom to get it caught in a tighter snare. The bird stood near the door and looked at the vast horizon. It gave itself the courage to fly in the open air. It stepped out and stood on the small balcony of the cage door and looked around to make sure no hand was going to stretch towards it and push it back into the cage, or catch it to cut its head off. It started to fly but was not sure of its ability after a long period of confinement. It gathered its energy and soared. Halfway in its flight the bird still could not believe that it was free. A bullet might be fired from an unknown place to bring it down.

Feri was sitting next to her mother watching the bird come out of the cage to fly away. When the bird took flight, Feri smiled. She turned to her mother and with mild enthusiasm said, 'Look, Mum. How beautiful! How uplifting it is to be free, to fly, to enjoy the bliss of liberty.'

They fixed their eyes on the flying bird.

As if talking to herself, Feri muttered 'One day Cyrus will be freed from prison. He'll wing his way through the air and fly from country to country. He'll sing his melodious song that humanity is entering a new era-- an era free from the fetters of man-made systems and superstitions.'

5.

Cyrus's family tried hard to stop the news from reaching Gloria. But word of Cyrus's arrest spread somehow. It was a sort of kidnapping by one group because various groups were involved in that political situation. Maria received the news and tried to look relaxed as if everything was normal. But Gloria sensed that something had happened without knowing anything. Several times she asked her mother if she knew why Cyrus had not returned from his homeland. Each time Maria replied, 'My love! Cyrus is okay. His Mum was sick. That's the reason he has stayed longer than he promised. He'll join us soon. Don'y worry.'

One afternoon, unexpectedly, Gloria came home early. Maria was on the phone and Gloria sensed that her mother was talking about Cyrus. She listened stealthily to the conversation. It was then that she realised Cyrus had been taken away by armed men after midnight. She burst in upon her mother's phone conversation and with trembling voice and choked with tears, she said, 'Mum, why did you hide it from me?' Maria put the phone down and rushed to Gloria, embraced her affectionately and burst into tears without saying a word. The shocking news immersed Gloria in an ocean of painful grief. Maria became worried about Gloria's mental and physical health. She phoned Sophia, Gloria's close friend, to come over and stay with them for a few nights. She did not disclose the news to Sophia, she just told her that Gloria needed her help.

On the way to Gloria's house, many thoughts passed through Sophia's mind. She rang the doorbell. Maria welcomed her in, embraced her and thanked her for coming.

'What has happened?' asked Sophia immediately.

'Gloria, Gloria, my daughter, my sweet one, may die.'

'Is she sick?'

'No, if it was only that I could take her to the doctor. Her pain cannot be treated. No doctor can cure her. No treatment can help her.'

'Where's Gloria?'

'She's imprisoned herself in her room. Most of the time she cries like a child. Oh! My child.' Maria heaved a deep sigh. 'We cannot solace her. She eats very little. She doesn't sleep properly.'

'Could you please tell me what's happened?'

'She's received news that after midnight Cyrus was arrested and taken to an unknown place. She believes they will hang him, they will execute him. There's no information of his whereabouts.' Maria's voice, charged with emotion, broke and she burst into tears.

Sophia was shocked. Her face lost colour. She tried hard to pull herself together. She kissed Maria and rushed to Gloria's room.

Wearing a blue dressing gown embroidered with gold thread, Gloria rushed to her friend and put her head on Sophia's shoulder and wept bitterly.

Sophia hugged her affectionately.

'Sophia, Sophia, my sun has set,' sobbed Gloria, 'No light. Everything's dark.'

Sophia did not say anything and just caressed Gloria's long hair.

Gloria sat up in bed, took a pillow, pressed her head on the soft pillow and cried like a child. 'It was my fault. I did it. I rang him and got him into trouble. Because of my telephone conversation, they realised Cyrus was in his homeland. I didn't take it seriously that someone's telephone could be under surveillance. We're not used to this sort of control. There are people who take it for granted that if they seize power by force they own the land, the air, the lives, the minds and even the consciences of the people.' Gloria's voice rose high. She poured out her anger, 'They think they have the right to decide who can breathe and who cannot, who can live and who should die. They cannot tolerate any thought, or belief, or ideal different from their own. They are very shortsighted. They are very selfish.'

'Sparks of truth flash when different ideas clash,' said Sophia. 'Why do they not tolerate ideals different from theirs?'

After a brief conversation, Gloria became restless again, tossed her head on the pillow and wailed. 'They will kill my Cyrus. They will hang my love.'

'I don't think so. They arrested him just to find out why Cyrus was there. When they understand that he went there just to see his sick mother they will release him.'

'Release him!' Gloria raised her head, frowned and stared into Sophia's eyes. 'You're kidding. If you knew what's going on in this advanced age of science and technology you'd go crazy. The crimes and tyranny of this century are more horrible than the events of past.'

'Some ruling groups in underdeveloped countries commit crimes which are incredible,' said Sophia with a belittling tone. 'But the mastermind is not situated there.'

'You mean the mastermind is somewhere else?' Sophia was shocked. Her eyes opened widely.

Gloria withdrew and did not reply. Silence overtook

them.

'How? I don't understand,' said Sophia.

'False politics have plagued the whole world.' Gloria stared into Sophia's eyes.

'You mean, the political plans are made somewhere else, not in the underdeveloped countries? It is situated in--' mumbled Sophia and became silent and pensive.

'That's right,' nodded Gloria, as if it was so obvious to them that there was no need to locate the inhuman, terrifying machine.

'The Roman civilisation,' Gloria added, 'ended up submerged by arrogance, hypocrisy and corruption.'

'That's history. It has nothing to do with the present time.'

'History repeats itself.'

When Sophia heard 'Roman civilisation' she remembered a song about Rome. Sophia wanted to change the mood. She suddenly got up and started singing the song she had picked up somewhere without knowing why that song was written. She began dancing to its rhythm: 'Let's dance while Rome is burning.'

She came to Gloria and took her hands, pleading. 'Gloria, come on, let's dance. Let the world take care of itself.'

Gloria's wet blue eyes flashed with a faint smile. 'My dear, I can't dance while Rome's burning. This song brings tears to my eyes, not joy to my heart.'

'Why?'

'A Roman emperor made a plot to make an excuse to chase and kill the poor Christians. He set Rome on fire through his secret agents and put the blame on Christians. The emperor and his courtiers indulged in drinking and debauchery in their dirty palaces. The innocent Christians were dragged from their humble houses and huts to be hanged group by group. My dear, you must now understand why I cannot dance while Rome is burning.'

In the days that followed, Gloria did her best to get information through any possible channel. There was a rumour that Cyrus had been taken to a small dark cell, no bigger than a grave. She heard that some prisoners had been put in solitary dark rooms and had gone blind because they had not seen sunlight for a long period. What made Gloria so worried was that Cyrus might be tortured, a common practice in that country. Some people who shared the same beliefs and ideals as Cyrus had already died under torture. The burn marks of hot irons and cigars had been noticed on the chests and legs of victims. Broken arms, legs and ribs had shocked relatives and observers. In some cases, the bereaved mothers had been forced to wash and bury the lacerated and mutilated bodies of their loved ones.

6.

After three months in prison, Cyrus woke up in horror at about one o'clock in the morning. He felt somebody was in the cell but could not see anything, as if ghosts had entered his prison room. It was terribly dark. He rubbed his eyes and said, 'Who are you?'

'We have come to tell that you'll be executed at three o'clock. You can write your last will and wish.' Three armed guards had come to him; one was in the cell and two were standing at the prison door.

Cyrus asked if he could take a shower. They agreed. Two gunmen followed him into the shower room. They stood on guard until he came out.

They brought him back to his cell, gave him pen, paper and a lantern to write his last will. They left the cell and locked the door.

Two revolutionary guards left the place, but one gunman stood outside, guarding the door.

Cyrus put on some clean soft cotton clothes which had been brought to him and sat up a while, thinking. He heaved a sigh. 'That's the end.' He was not worried about soaring into a celestial atmosphere in the higher realms. Gloria and his family were the only ties binding him to the earth.

He decided to pray to cleanse his soul from all the vanities of earthly life, to prepare himself for martyrdom. He wanted to beseech the Almighty to give strength to his dearest Gloria and his dear mother to endure the devastating grief. He believed the prayers uttered by the prophets themselves would release a tremendous power. He knew a few of the prayers by heart.

He knelt down, meditating. With great humility he approached God, beseeching him to give him strength to face his death with dignity and courage. He prayed for the entire planet to be purged from the defilement of hatred. He beseeched that ignorance would change into wisdom, blindness into vision.

He was willing to fly to heaven; his earthly life was not futile and meaningless. That gave him a feeling of delight and courage. His soul was filled with love; there was no room for hatred. He could not hate anyone; even those who wanted to execute him. He felt astonished that he wanted to pray for his opponents to be transformed. He realised that when the soul is touched with the love of God, it emanates love.

The dim light of the lantern lit the cell. He stared at his shadow reflected on the wall of the prison. His physical body appeared to him as a shadow, it had no permanence. His earthly life seemed a fleeting dream.

He picked up pen and paper to write his last words to his mother, but he hesitated. He put aside his pen and paper, closed his eyes and prayed that God might give his mother strength to sustain such a devastating blow. He knew his mother loved him dearly and his death might break her and result in her death.

It was painful but he tried to write his last words to his dearly loved mother. He had to do it without delay. His remaining earthly life was short.

He solaced himself with the thought that he believed: every human has a beginning, but no end, and lives as long as God lives. Human beings continue their lives in a celestial atmosphere when their physical bodies no longer function. 'Ere long I will see my mother in a higher realm.'

Cyrus decided to encourage his mother to submit her will to the will of God, and bring to her attention that the essence of human beings is everlasting. To assure her that they would meet each other in the spiritual realm. That gave him some relief from the agonising worry.

He picked up his pen and paper and wrote with confidence:

Dear Mum,
When I was a child you used to enthuse me to stand for truth. Your melodious voice is still ringing in my ears that one should have faith in the ultimate triumph of truth. Now you should be sure that you've achieved your desire to educate your son to defend the truth and die for it.

Dear Mum! I can see your lovely face so vividly as if you are seated in front of me. A great love shines in your eyes. My earthly life is counted in minutes. I will soon soar to a celestial realm, an atmosphere of joy, bliss and light.

Dear Mum! I kneel before you, beseeching you not to grieve for my temporary separation from you. You have always conveyed to me the belief that those who love one another will recognise each other in the next world, fly together in the rose garden of the spiritual world.

I am sure you will face this event with great courage. You will prove in deed what you always preached in theory. I expect you to stand like a mountain at this grievous time, to inspire others to be brave and courageous. I kiss your hands.

Imperishable

love

Your son, Cyrus

Cyrus finished the letter and put it in the envelope. He wrote the name of his mother at the back of the envelope. Then, he kissed the name of his mother.

Holding the envelope in his hand and looking pensive, he stared at it.

He picked up another sheet of paper to write his last farewell to his beloved Gloria. It was painful to feel that his life was a dream, a vanishing dream.

He hesitated to put pen to paper to write his last words to his love. He looked at the low ceiling of his prison cell and sighed. His belief in the immortality of spirit, his conviction of the eternal life was not sufficient to solace his sad soul.

His heart sank.

Gloria was the only tie connecting him to the world. He did not mind breaking his cord to the earthly life, but could not break his tie to Gloria-- a tie woven with the warp of tender love and the weft of his soul. He wanted to live with her forever. To break that tie meant cutting the cord of his heart.

There was not much time before his execution. Time was running out and he had to write something to solace Gloria.

He knew Gloria would lament and weep endlessly over his death, and no one would be able to comfort her.

He reluctantly picked up the paper and pen to write his last words to his love. He wrote, *Dearest Gloria.* Then he paused and gazed at the words. He bent his head and lovingly kissed the name of Gloria written on the paper. His eyes welled and a teardrop fell on the paper. It blurred the word 'Gloria'.

He thought the smudged word on the letter might give Gloria the impression that he had shed tears at the closing hour of his earthly life. That could torture her soul. He decided to tear it up and write another letter. With a heavy heart he wrote:

Dearest Gloria,

No words can express my love for you. I am filled to the brim with you. You are always with me.

They can kill my body, but they cannot kill my thoughts of a new world. They can chain me, but they cannot chain the ideals that are the spirit of the new age. They can stifle my words, but they cannot stifle a celestial voice already vibrating throughout the planet.

The world is under the impact of mysterious forces, impelling it towards a new destination. In springtime, the nasty wind may make the early flowers drop. But it cannot stop the transforming influence of the spring.

We can still communicate through prayers. The next world is in this world but we cannot see it. Between this world and the next there is no distance; there is only a veil. Some can partially remove the veil and see a glimpse of the glory and beauty of the heavenly atmosphere.

I will carry your love with me to the next world. I wil always be with you in spirit.

I want you to be a shining lamp, shedding light to lift the surrounding darkness. Never let the intense darkness frighten you.

With warmest love

Your Cyrus

He put aside the pen while his eyes remained fixed on the letter. He could not believe that was his last letter to his most loved one. Holding the letter in his hand, he gazed on the word, Gloria. His heart melted. He prayed ardently for her.

His heartfelt prayer, like a magnet, attracted a mysterious force and a tremendous energy was released within him. His whole body in the grap of intense emotion, and his face aglow, he felt that he was close to God. His love for Gloria ignited the divine love, it did not bar the love for his Divine Beloved, but it acted as a bridge.

It seemed Gloria entered his cell, standing in dim light, staring at him. He stretched his hands to touch her, to hold firmly her skirt, not to let her to leave him. His hand did not touch anything tangible. She disappeared.

He remained thoughtful a while.

He knew the bodies of people like him, executed by the revolutionary guards, would disappear. Images invaded his mind—Gloria, in the mourning black clothes, was carrying a bunch of red roses to put on his grave.

In tears, Gloria searched for his grave but could not find it. He had no grave. She gave up. She sat on a bench and sobbed bitterly, lamenting his death. His heart sank at the image. His eyes welled with tears.

He wiped his tears and opened his eyes to find himself sitting alone in a small cell. He looked like a ghost, as if he had no body. His shadow was reflected on the wall in the dim light of the lantern.

The time of his death was close. He stared at the door expecting a key to turn in the lock at any moment to take him to the field of execution.

At 3.10 a key twisted in the lock. The door was unlocked and two armed guards entered his cell.

They blindfolded him and put the end of a rope into his hand to follow them to the field of his execution.

He descended into the underground corridor. The descent conveyed to him that the excavation was at a great depth below the surface of the earth. He heard the moaning and groaning of prisoners, a sob, which turned into a long, loud and continuous scream, completely inhuman. Some were howling like animals while being whipped with wire cables. There were howls, wails and shrieks of horror everywhere. The terrifying sounds came out of the throats of the prisoners in their agony. It was a hell with all the meaning and implication of the word. It was unbearable.

Swearing and cursing, the gunmen dragged him, telling him repeatedly that he would be executed immediately and he would never see his fiancée or loved ones again.

They climbed down another set of stairs, two storeys below the ground floor, and entered a large room in the basement where many prisoners had been executed.

Still blindfolded, he was instructed to walk torwards the wall and stand with his hands on the wall.

Calm and firm, he stepped towards the spot where he was to be executed. A tremendous energy was suddenly released in his soul. He wondered where it came from. It was amazing, as if he was going somewhere full of joy and bliss.

Cyrus put his hands on the wall, waiting to be shot. He murmured in his heart, *O God! Please take care of my dearest Gloria*. 'Gloria' was the last word he uttered.

The commander of the squad shouted: 'fire!'

They shot six bullets at him. Two passed over his head, almost touching his hair. He felt the heat of the bullets. Two hit the wall close to his ears, and two bullets struck the wall near his feet.

He thought the bullets had missed their target and that they would aim at his heart or head soon. Standing with his hands on the wall, he waited for death.

Nothing happened. There was a deathly silence for a few seconds.

The commander of the squad snarled and said something. Cyrus did not hear him clearly for his ears were almost deaf from the terrible sound of the shots.

The commander of the squad shouted again, 'We have just received an instruction not to execute you tonight. You will be executed soon. Don't think you'll leave this place alive. Soon you'll be hanged or executed. Walk out and wait for the time of your execution.'

Blindfolded, Cyrus started to walk. His head hit the wall and a pain went through his body. He changed his direction, but again he hit the wall.

Without complaining, he held out his hands and walked like a blind man groping in the dark.

One of the gunmen snarled at him, 'Take the end of this wire cable and follow me.'

The torture-mongers did not achieve their purpose. The mock execution did not frighten Cyrus. On the contrary, it removed any hint of fear, if it ever existed. Feeling a great spiritual strength within himself, he became more determined to withstand the dark forces of the world. Nothing could extinguish the fire of his zest for the glorious age that awaited. They had done their worst. They could do nothing more than to execute him. He had already passed his test.

They had planned the mock execution to break his will, to force him to recant his faith in the dawning of a new era. Torture and cruelty made him more aware of the decay of the collapsing old order, and stronger in his conviction of the need for a new world order.

The gunmen took Cyrus to a courtroom for interrogation. It was about 4 a.m. when they instructed him to wait at the door of the courtroom until his trial started. Blindfolded and sleepy, he stood until 9:00 a.m.

Cyrus was exhausted to the point of collapsing when he was called into the courtroom. Although he could not see the interrogator's face, he felt four people were present, as if there were ghosts intending to harm him.

Frail in body but strong in spirit, Cyrus was determined to defend his faith in the ideals of the new era, not to bow before the false idols. He was prepared to die for truth if necessary.

Cyrus's trial started while he was standing blindfolded.

'How do you feel today?' asked a person in a harsh voice.

'I am quite all right. My body is fatigued, but my soul is fresh.'

'It seems you don't want to be released from prison to enjoy your life.'

'How can I indulge in pleasure when the majority of the people of the world live in misery?'

'Why are you worried about the others? Let them take care of themselves.'

'Apathy toward the sufferings of others has made the world vulnerable and miserable.'

'We are going to judge you for what you have done, not the others.'

'Could I ask you why you are judging me? What crime have I committed?'

'What crime have you committed!' thundered the Magistrate. He banged a book on the table, 'You still believe you have done nothing wrong?'

'Yes, that's right. I still believe I have done nothing wrong.'

'You should be executed without any trial. It's out of kindness that the new regime is showing you the right way.'

'You still have not answered my question.'

'You pretend to have done nothing. This book in front of me is a document to condemn you to death.'

'I don't think there is anything in my book that condemns me to death.'

'You think so! I will quote from your book: *The day is approaching when the present-day systems are rolled up, and a new world order spread out in its stead.*

'Yes, I have quoted that statement from a Great One. It's not mine. What's wrong with that? It indicates a glorious future is in store for humankind. It inspires a hope to those who suffer under the lashes of poverty and tyranny.'

'That's dangerous. That's threatening,' shouted the Magistrate.

'It's threatening to what? It may be threatening to outworn and obsolete systems.'

'You admit that it is a threat to the established systems. It is subversive. So it is dangerous as well.'

'It is an evolutionary process. The old static systems will be replaced by a new dynamic world order.'

'Why do the old systems have to be replaced by a so-called new world order?'

'The old systems do not meet the requirements of the time. They are based on an outworn concept of society and the world. We are enmeshed in a situation that breeds war, terrorism, poverty and conflict.'

'Individual and social life is a struggle. It requires all these things.'

'Yes, the present-day system requires war, poverty, and so on, as you said.'

'You devil! You use my words against me!' shouted the Magistrate.

'I am just explaining the nature of the present-day systems. And you are confirming it.'

'I am not confirming your misleading ideas. It is as it should be.'

'That's what I'm arguing against. It is as you say, but it should not be,' explained Cyrus. 'We are enslaved in systems that create suffering such as unemployment, poverty, insecurity and the miseries of war. But they're unnecessary.'

'People are satisfied within these systems. If they were

not, they would have searched for an alternative. As you see, they don't try to find a new social pattern, so they are happy with what they have.'

'An increasing number of people feel they are enmeshed in systems they cannot escape from. They have to function within those systems. But they are not satisfied.'

'I don't want to go any further. You have to renounce your faith in the new era, and the ideals for a new age,' ordered the Magistrate.

'Why do I have to deny what I believe to be the truth?'

'It is not the truth. It is the belief of misguided people. You have to wipe those beliefs from your mind.'

'My faith in the ideals of a new era is engraved on my soul with fiery characters. How can I erase them?'

'You have to deny your belief in the new revelation,' demanded the Magistrate.

'The new revelation is a phenomenon of modern times. It is proof in itself. It doesn't rely on my affirming or denying it.'

'We demand you to deny its existence,' ordered the Magistrate.

'When the sun rises it doesn't make any difference if I deny its existence or not. My denial doesn't change the reality of the existence of the sun, because the sun is already shining with majesty and glory in the sky.'

'We want you to renounce your faith. We believe it is a delusion,' said the Magistrate.

'This is a part of my being. I cannot cut a part of my being.'

'So we have to kill the being itself, that part must be removed as well,' shouted the Magistrate.

Suddenly, Cyrus turned into a flame of fire. His eyes

flashed with the intensity of his emotions and his face was aglow with the heat of burning faith.

He pulled open his shirt forcefully. The shirt tore and a part of his chest was exposed. With his hand on his chest, he addressed the revolutionary court in a resonant voice: 'shoot me, then! Kill me! Hang me! You cannot force me to reject the ideals that I am willing to die for. You cannot force me to renounce my faith in the New Divine Revelation. I am on fire with my love for the dawn of a new age, an age cleansed from all defilement and injustice.'

'You will be hanged,' said the Magistrate, shaking with anger. 'You have lived too long. Take him back to his solitary prison until his day of execution.'

Cyrus's body was afire with an intense emotion.

One of the guards was impressed by Cyrus's sincerity and felt sympathy for him. He escorted Cyrus to his cell and when they reached the door, cautiously and in a low voice he said, 'They'll kill you. You had better deny your faith. You have to recant your words. Then, you'll be released. You can go back home and enjoy life.'

Then, the guard got closer and whispered into Cyrus's ear, 'Think of someone you love most-- your mother, your fiancée, your love.'

The guard made Cyrus enter the cell and locked the door.

Cyrus sat on the ground, leaning against the wall. The words of the guard were still ringing in his ears: *Think of someone that you love most-- your mother, your fiancée, your love.* It brought Gloria to his mind. He heaved a deep sigh and his eyes welled with tears.

The chief magistrate ordered that Cyrus be lashed one hundred strokes every day with wire cable. From that day, one hundred lashes became his daily bread.

7.

Maria tried her best to make sure that no news of Cyrus's torture reached Gloria. She felt sure that the thought of it would almost end the life of her much-loved daughter. She asked everyone not to mention anything they might hear about Cyrus's incarceration in that dark pit.

Somehow the terrible news escaped that Cyrus's feet were lashed one hundred strokes every day as regular torture. The news soon reached Cyrus's relatives and friends who were impatiently waiting for some information.

In spite of Maria's concerted efforts, the news eventually reached Gloria and immersed her in an ocean of unspeakable sorrow. This time Gloria's eyes were dry, like a wasteland burning with aridity. She sat silent without shedding a tear. There was no release for her pent-up grief. Her soul had withered like a dead flower. She felt as if she had been abandoned in a barren and terrifying land in which only the howls of wolves could be heard-- a dead land where the shadows of the dead roamed.

Maria entered Gloria's room to solace her. 'My love, come and have some tea.'

There was no response. Gloria sat in the armchair staring at a spot on the ceiling as if her soul had departed.

Feeling an agony in her soul, Maria came closer. 'My love, come and have some tea.'

No response, no nodding, no gesture. Maria became extremely worried that Gloria might have gone mad and should be taken to hospital.

Trembling, Maria approached the chair where Gloria was sitting and stood behind it. She lovingly embraced Gloria and kissed her hair. With a voice charged with love, she said, 'My love, my child, please, don't think so much.'

Gloria stared at Maria with a blank expression as if not recognising her mother. 'Think! Think of what?' Gloria uttered in a husky voice.

'Think of nothing. Leave everything to God.'

'Leave …everything …to God,' repeated Gloria. 'There's no God. They've already killed God. They feel free to commit all sorts of tyranny and atrocities. They have no fear of the wrath of God.'

Maria listened and her heart sank. Neither spoke.

Suddenly Gloria stood up forcefully. Maria startled and stepped back. In anger, Gloria said loudly, 'The thunder of the wrath of God will strike them down. The lightning of God's anger will turn them into ashes scattered by the wind.'

Gloria sat down, looking gloomy.

Maria got closer to the chair. 'My child! We have to accept the world as it is. I think I have more experience in life than you. You young people do not realise that we cannot change the world. Many know there's exploitation. Many understand there's no fair share of wealth. Many see injustice in political systems. But they're wise enough to keep quiet, not to make troubles for themselves. They try to just manage their affairs. They don't bother about whether the world is going on the right track or the wrong track.'

Gloria put her face between her palms and said in a bitter voice, 'Yes, yes, that's right. Injustice is normal and acceptable. Justice is abnormal. Profanity is normal and spirituality is abnormal.'

'My love! These are truths, but who cares to support truths?'

With a deep sense of rebellion in her soul, Gloria suddenly rose and roared like a lioness, 'Falsehood dominates the world. You're advising me to bow down before false gods. No, I'll never kneel before corrupt idols. Never!'

'My child! We have to accept reality.'

Gloria stared at her mother, anger flaring in her eyes. But Maria did not notice the flame of rage. She embraced her daughter with tender affection and suddenly burst into tears. Sobbing, she muttered. 'My life, my love, you don't know how much I suffer when I see you sad and in torment. Please, have mercy on me. Please, have mercy on me.'

Gloria felt pity for her mother. She kissed Maria. 'Please, forgive me, Mum.'

Maria rang Sophia and explained what had happened. She asked Sophia to come to their house and stay there the weekend. Sophia immediately rushed to Gloria.

When Sophia arrived, Maria, choking back the tears, explained Gloria's mood and situation, and added, 'The older generation have got used to injustice. Their minds and hearts are tarnished with the defilement of the old order. They accept the rotting systems as normal and unchangeable. The younger generation is more idealistic. They're more detached than the old ones. They cannot tolerate injustice.'

'There are,' said Sophia, 'many young people like me who sense that the world could be much better than it is. Miseries are man-made. But we don't know how to start to build a new world.'

'The world is doomed to misery. We know it may end in a world convulsion, but we feel we can do nothing to prevent it. We dread the fateful moment of the final explosion!'

'But tell me about Gloria,' said Sophia, changing the subject.

'After hearing the terrible news of Cyrus's torture, she doesn't shed tears. Her heart and soul have turned into a burning desert. I wish she could weep.'

Sophia tapped at the door of Gloria's room, but there was no answer. She entered the room. Gloria stared at Sophia for a few seconds before recognising her. Suddenly, she got up and rushed towards Sophia and embraced her and started crying like a child. Sophia did not try to stop her. She hugged Gloria, kissed her and let her shed tears to pour out the pent-up grief.

Gloria released Sophia and sat on the edge of the bed. Then Sophia fetched a chair and sat face to face with Gloria, their knees touching.

Sophia took Gloria's hands, pleading. 'Gloria, please pull yourself together. Everything will be okay soon.'

'Do you know Cyrus has been tortured?'

'Cyrus is a strong man. Nothing can break his will.'

'That's the problem. They cannot possess his soul so they'll torture his body until the soul departs.' Gloria paused, then, choking with emotion, she continued.
'They've lashed him, they've lashed his feet and back with wire cord. After his feet were lashed he had to crawl to get back to his cell. But they forced him with lashes to walk on his lacerated and swollen feet.'

Gloria picked up the pillow and pressed it against her chest. 'I wish, I could stop the pain and treat his lacerated feet with my kisses.'

Chapter Ten

SYDNEY

1.

Gloria prayed day and night that, by some miracle, Cyrus would be released. She knew that only a miracle could save him.

One night, feeling restless, Gloria could not sleep. She tossed and turned in bed thinking of Cyrus, wondering what was happening to him. An image flashed in her mind of Cyrus, his lacerated feet in stocks, lying on a bare floor in a small dark cell, groaning with pain. Worse than that, she thought of the torturers pressing hot iron on his chest to lacerate it, a common method of torture used in that black pit. She turned aside and involuntarily sobbed. 'Oh! It's horrible to burn with hot iron a chest protecting a heart beating with the love of human beings!'

She could not bear to think of it any longer. She rolled over, threw the blanket aside, swung her legs over the edge of the bed, sprang to her feet and started to pace the room. 'O Lord! What can I do?'

She switched on the light and staggered to the wardrobe to put on her robe. She stared at a picture of Cyrus hanging on the wall, smiling at her. She pursed her lips and blew him a kiss, then stretched her hands towards the portrait. 'Come back to my arms, my love.'

She walked to and fro restlessly, stood at the window and stared at the sky. She stretched her hands upwards. 'O God, O my Lord! Where are you? Come down to help us.

Don't turn your back on us. Don't leave this planet to a dreadful doom. Please, please.' She clawed at the walls in pain and pressed her head on the pillow, but nothing could calm her. She knelt down in supplication to pray, to turn to a celestial source for assistance. Tears running down her face, she prayed like an innocent child, 'O my God! O my Lord! O good God, O gentle God save my love from the claws of wolves.   Don't let them strangle the throat that defends truth.'

She prostrated herself. Her forehead on the floor, she sobbed bitterly, pleading and praying to God ardently. She cried, 'Good God, gentle God, have mercy on me, give me back my Cyrus.' Tears running down her face, she moaned and groaned, imploring the assistance of God from the depths of her heart.

For about an hour she cried, prayed and pleaded with God for the release of Cyrus. Her forehead was still on the ground when she felt the presence of God. Kneeling before the Heavenly Father, she felt his gentle hand on her shoulder. Raising her up, He whispered to her, 'O my child, don't worry. I'm everywhere.   I'm Omniscient.   I'm Almighty.' She raised her head from the ground and stared heavenwards with wet eyes. She sat, her arms crossed on her chest. The release of a great force in her soul changed her mood amazingly. Feeling unburdened, she stopped crying. A great joy filled her soul, but it was not clear where the joy came from. It seemed her prayer was answered.

Gloria knew that only a miracle could save Cyrus from that terrible dungeon and she desperately wanted that miracle to be performed.   She wanted her dream to come true.

2.

In Cyrus's homeland, his relatives and friends had heard from a foreign radio program that an armed gang had kidnapped Cyrus after midnight. They became horrified because they knew that he would be tortured to death. Some prayed that he would be executed soon. Torture in that terrible pit was so awful that immediate hanging or execution would be a relief.

Cyrus's mother constantly thought of her adored son and of his assurance that he would not be martyred. His words brought her some solace in her agony.

After Cyrus was kidnapped, the news spread to outside his homeland. It took a while before some organisations overseas started trying to get Cyrus released from prison. They put all efforts into convincing the authorities of his homeland to release him. The Human Rights Commission and other organisations protested against his imprisonment and probable execution. They argued that Cyrus was a prisoner of conscience. Moreover, he was a citizen of Australia as well as a writer. Notwithstanding all appeals and protests, it looked as if his release was impossible because one of the political groups running the country could not tolerate a book Cyrus had written about the future of his homeland. They had searched for him everywhere; they had shot at any shadow they suspected to be his. They had wanted to find him, to torture him to death. When they finally realised that Cyrus was in his homeland they were surprised but delighted. A gang had kidnapped him after midnight immediately. Now he was in their grasp. He was at their mercy.

The overseas organisations did not give up. They wrote letters of appeal, condemnation and rebuke. But there was some need for a special spark. Gloria's sincere and wholehearted prayers brought into operation mysterious forces. The continuous efforts of the overseas organisations achieved success, and at last the authorities responded to their appeals and protests. Their response was a sudden and delightful surprise.

Two weeks after Gloria's intense prayer, Cyrus's brother and some relatives were listening to the overseas radio program when suddenly they all jumped up. There was great mirth and laughter. They threw their arms in the air, hugged one another, danced and shed tears of joy. It had been announced that Cyrus was going to be released from prison.

A female relative rushed to Cyrus's mother to tell her the exciting news in person. As soon as Feri opened the door, she hugged Feri with excitement. Tears of joy in her eyes, she said, 'Do you know that Cyrus is going to be released?' Feri's face lit up with great delight; her eyes shone through her tears. She kissed her relative affectionately and they rushed to Cyrus's mother to tell her the good news. They thought that to tell her straight out of the sudden release of Cyrus might be too exciting for his mother. After hugging and kissing her, they told her they had some good news but did not tell her exactly what it was.

Mother smiled. 'Please tell me, what's the good news?'

They stood silent, but their eyes and lips were smiling. Staring at them with enquiring eyes, mother tried to guess. Panting with excitement, she asked, 'Is it about Cyrus?' She hesitated a few seconds, then opened her mouth but no word came out. Suddenly a great light flashed in her eyes. A great joy lit up her face. 'Is Cyrus going to be released from prison?' A broad smile on their lips, Feri and her relative nodded their heads.

Tears of joy running down her face, Cyrus's mother jumped up briskly like a teenager and hugged them.

Feri wiped away her mother's tears with kisses. The three clasped one another, shedding tears of joy.

'Who brought the good news?' asked Mother.

Feri looked at her relative, pointed to her and smiled. Cyrus's mother rushed out of the room and came back, holding a precious necklace of pure white gold, decorated with an expensive ruby.

'This is very precious to me. I have kept it for decades. Now I give it to you as a reward for the good news you brought me. One strand of Cyrus's hair is more precious to me than this necklace.' She placed the necklace around the relative's neck and kissed her cheeks.

They stepped out onto the terrace. Silent and thoughtful, they stood staring at the horizon. It was early morning. The air was fresh, the sky clear, and the sun was rising high.

A flock of birds flew over them. Gazing at the birds, Feri followed their flight. They reminded her the day she had let the songbird free to soar in the limitless space. Now Cyrus had been released from the black pit. It flashed through her mind that Cyrus had experienced the horrors of the iron cage of a regime of tyranny and dictatorship, which was corrupt and corrupting. Now he could better appreciate the bliss of liberty, the bounty of freedom to express his ideals, beliefs and thoughts.

Cyrus's brother still lived in his homeland. He had been arrested, interrogated, harassed and occasionally lashed by the revolutionary guards to tell them of Cyrus's whereabouts. The revolutionary guards had searched for Cyrus everywhere for four years. They inspected every street and lane he had passed through, and any house he had visited.

They became frustrated at not finding him in his homeland. Cyrus's visit to his homeland happened more than a decade later, when they had stopped searching for him.

The prison authorities contacted Cyrus's brother to go to the prison to collect Cyrus. His brother was so excited that he took some local money with him equivalent to six hundred dollars. He threw it in the air on his way to the prison. Some passers-by noticed a car going fast with a man in the car throwing handfuls of paper money out of the window, shouting "hurrah". They were surprised and did not know what was going on. Others could not believe their eyes when they saw money raining down from the air like flower petals. Boys and girls rushed to collect the money. They grabbed the notes with great excitement. Counting and comparing their amounts, they laughed and expressed their surprise. 'How wonderful! Instead of rain and snow, money notes come down from heaven!'

On the way home, Cyrus told his brother that he would see his mother first and asked that none of his relatives and friends go to his mother's house. He would see them in the house of a relative that night. He told his brother that his release from prison was a real miracle, but that his life was still not secure. The fanatical extremists might kill or kidnap him in the street.

Standing at the door, Cyrus's mother was impatiently waiting for his arrival. When Cyrus entered the house, mother and son embraced each other for a long time without saying a word.

Tears in her eyes, she stared at Cyrus and muttered, 'My love! You look so frail. My shining lamp! May God bless you and protect you from all evil.'

Three days after Cyrus's release, Feri found a note in the front yard thrown in the previous night. She instinctively sensed danger. She stared at the note as if looking at a sleepy serpent. She hesitated to touch it. Her hand shaking, she picked it up and read it anxiously. She paled, started trembling, and decided not to disclose the contents of the note to anyone. She rushed to the kitchen, furtively tore the note into pieces, threw them into the rubbish bin and angrily uttered, 'You damned terrorists.'

Feri tried to ignore the contents of the note, pretending to be happy and joyful, but it haunted her like a ghost. Now and then her face was shadowed with fear and anxiety.

When she saw Cyrus in the morning, Feri tried to smile, but only a cold smile iced on her lips.

Cyrus climbed up to the second floor of a travel agency to see a friend. His friend was out so he sat there waiting for his return. He was thinking of his departure when he had a sudden intuition to leave the country immediately. He tried to ignore it but the intuition became more clear and demanding, as if a voice whispered into his ears: 'Leave the country immediately. They're after you to kill you.' Cyrus was a man of vision, and he trusted his intuition.

He thought it would be almost impossible to book a seat without producing his passport and paying for a ticket. He knew he also had to wait for a flight because many people were on the waiting list. He timidly approached the girl sitting at a computer. He asked if he could reserve a seat. She checked the computer and with smile said, 'A reservation has just been cancelled. You can fly in a few days' time.'

'I have no money and no passport with me.'

'Don't worry. You can pay when you collect the ticket.'

'Oh! Thank you.' He could not believe it had been so easy to reserve a seat. He was certain that mysterious forces were at work.

That night he told his family: 'Today I had a special intuition. It was like a voice whispering to me, telling me to leave the country immediately.'

'What happened?' his brother asked, his curiosity aroused.

When Cyrus told them what had happened, his mother did not seem at all surprised. She looked at Cyrus and did not say anything.

When Feri heard the story her eyes filled with tears. Cyrus moved to his sister and kissed her forehead. 'Dear Feri, don't be sad. I think it is the will of God that I leave the country immediately. Please, be happy.'

'Yes, yes, you should follow the will of God.' Feri wiped away her tears and smiled.

3.

Wearing her nightgown, Gloria stepped out onto the veranda, breathed in the fresh air of the early morning. Her eyes swept over the garden where the sunlight was kissing the fingers of the twigs. Small birds in various colours had filled the air with their sweet songs. She was thinking of Cyrus, happy that he had been released from the horrible pit, but anxious that it might take a long time, maybe months, before Cyrus would arrive in Sydney. She knew that it would be difficult to get a seat to fly out of his homeland. She prayed that God might fulfil her wish that Cyrus would return to Australia soon.

Absorbed in her thoughts, she heard the phone ringing.

She rushed into the hall. It was a call from overseas. 'Cyrus will arrive in Sydney on Sunday afternoon.' It was Feri at the other end of the phone. Gloria could not breathe for a few seconds out of excitement. 'Thank you Feri for phoning me; thank you very much. I wish you were here to kiss you and to hug you. Please, come and visit us.' Gloria kissed the receiver several times to convey her love and joy to Feri.

She rushed to her mother and jumped into her arms. Shedding tears and laughing, she told Maria the good news. Caressing Gloria's hair and pressing her to her chest, Maria affectionately wiped Gloria's tears with her fingers.

She was impatient for the time to pass. Each day seemed ages and every hour seemed an eternity.

4.

Gloria paced to and fro impatiently at the airport and could not wait for the plane carrying Cyrus to land. She looked anxiously either at her watch on her delicate wrist or the clock on the wall every minute. She feared something might happen to delay Cyrus's arrival. Joking and laughing, several relatives and friends were waiting at the airport.

Gloria convinced the airport staff that Cyrus might not be well and would need help. She was allowed to go to the exit door. She waited impatiently for Cyrus to disembark. Her heart was beating fast in expection to see Cyrus at any moment. She wondered what he would look like after his torture. Could he stand on his feet properly? Could he walk? Would he be looking ill?

Suddenly Cyrus appeared at the exit door. His body looked frail and his face pale. It was obvious that he had endured much pain and suffering. But his face was luminous. There was some special quality shining in his eyes. It was as if his soul had been polished by his trials and suffering.

Gloria rushed towards him and hugged him with great love. He embraced her tenderly. They clasped each other as one soul in two bodies.

Gloria, nestling herself in his arms, raised her head and stared at Cyrus's pale face. Her eyes filled with tears. 'My love! My adored one, welcome back, welcome back. Oh! It's a dream to see you alive. You don't know how I prayed for your safety. God heard my cries and saw my tears. Many nights I woke up and could not sleep. Staring up at the stars through the window and shedding tears, I prayed to God to save your life by a miracle.'

Cyrus pressed her in his arms passionately, kissed her cheeks and eyes and forehead, swept his fingers through her beautiful hair and whispered to her. 'My sweetheart, my adored one, your prayers saved my life. It's a real miracle that I'm still alive.'

Cyrus opened his eyes and looked around as if awakened from a sweet dream. He realised that they were blocking the way, but the smiling passengers seemed pleased to watch the expression of an intense love. They were waiting patiently and had no intention of expressing resentment.

Cyrus apologised, 'Sorry to keep you waiting.'

'That's all right, no worries.'

They walked to the hall where relatives and friends, standing in a line like soldiers ready to be inspected by their commander, were waiting to welcome Cyrus. With their arms around each other, Cyrus and Gloria stepped into the hall.

The faces of the welcomers lit up with great happiness. They clapped and cried 'Hooray'. Their cheering echoed in the hall and many passengers looked back to see who had arrived. Cyrus walked into the hall like someone coming back from the field of battle, crowned with the glory of victory. He was showered with flowers and kisses.

Nineteen cars, moving in procession, followed the car carrying Cyrus and Gloria. The caravan headed towards Gloria's house.

On the way home, Gloria played love songs. When the song, 'The Power of Love' echoed in the car, Gloria felt she was sitting on a magic carpet moving through the air. Her eyes emanating her deep love, she gazed at Cyrus. Cyrus took her hand into his, pressed it with warm affection and smiled.

She moved a bit closer and whispered, 'Do you mind if I put my head on your shoulder a while?'

'It's a pleasure.' Cyrus smiled.

Love songs played on the car radio, and when the words, 'I love you, I honestly love you' echoed in the car, Gloria felt that song was expressing her love. She was ecstatic and overjoyed. The world looked more beautiful and resplendent than ever, as if every flower was smiling, every tree was nodding its head and every bird was singing love songs, all welcoming Cyrus.

Holding Gloria's hands in his, Cyrus suddenly remembered the horrible scenes of torture in the prison. He remembered that he was detached and not afraid of being executed, and that Gloria was the only tie fastening him to the world. The memories of those days and nights had been printed in his mind and nothing could erase them. He wondered how human beings could be so cruel, so atrocious, and so corrupt. But those horrors did not darken his spirit and could not dampen his enthusiasm for a golden age.

Rather it made him more determined to dedicate his life in helping to build a new world.

Bustling about in the house, Maria was busy instructing relatives to prepare the house for a great party. It was the most significant party that had ever been held there. Whispering and shouting, gesticulating and giving orders, Maria was joyously supervising the preparation of a great feast.

The large two-storey building was immersed in an ocean of light. The big hall on the second floor, where the guests were to be entertained, was beautifully decorated.

Hand in hand like a bride and groom, Cyrus and Gloria entered the front yard. They were the first ones who stepped into the house and climbed up the stairs leading to the second floor. Holding Cyrus's arm, Gloria helped him to carry his persecuted, frail body up the stairs. Maria was standing at the top of the stairs on the second floor holding a tray full of scented roses of various colours. Cyrus and Gloria were in the middle of the stairs when Maria joyously showered the roses on them. Those following, laughing delightedly, rushed to pick up a rose each.

They crowded into the large hall and Cyrus, with great dignity, sat in an armchair. To Gloria, his head bore an invisible crown. She sat beside him like a queen.

There was a sudden hush. Cyrus sensed everybody was waiting for him to say something. He smiled and thanked them for coming to the airport. His eyes radiated the light reflecting his polished soul.

'It is a miracle that I'm still alive. Your prayers performed a miracle. Thank you for your prayers. Thank you indeed.'

He stared down at the floor, thinking. All remained silent. Then he raised his head and looked around. 'It was horrible to experience the work of dark forces. The world is plagued with prejudices, secret plans, tyranny and profanity. There's a great contrast in this century. On one side you see the flourishing of a new world where an increasing number of people of thought and goodwill are advocating high ideals. On the other side, you observe injustice and evil of the worst kind.'

Gradually Cyrus's voice rose louder: 'Collective will and effort are needed to combat this horrible giant, this soulless and godless machinery. Sacrifice is demanded; martyrdom is required to purify and cleanse the face of the earth from the defilement of the ungodly. I witnessed that some, tortured for their beliefs and ideals, welcomed death. They rushed towards the bullets in the hope that their death might help to change their world of war, tyranny, injustice and misery into a homeland of peace, justice, prosperity and love. They had faith that a Golden Age was destined to dawn. They had faith that a new sun had risen and its light would chase away the darkness. They danced on their way to the gallows.'

Everyone remained silent while Cyrus spoke. His face was luminous.

'I remember a scene when a Bahá'í, a follower of the new global Faith, danced on his way to the gallows.'

Suddenly Cyrus got up and started dancing briskly to show the dance of the martyr moments before his death.

Gloria jumped up immediately to join him.

Maria invited everyone to join Cyrus in the dance. 'Please, get up and dance. Play music.' Everybody in the large hall started dancing.

Gloria named a piece of music to be played, which she knew Cyrus liked very much.

With a pale face and frail body, Cyrus whirled and whirled ecstatically. Pretending to dance with Cyrus, Gloria stayed close to him to hold him if he should collapse. Maria's eyes filled with tears. She was encouraging everybody to dance. 'Dim the lights. Dim the lights.'

Totally oblivious of the world around him, Cyrus tried to show how the martyr danced on his way to his execution. With eyes closed, Cyrus danced briskly, not aware that Gloria was beside him. He looked like a shadow moving to and fro. It was not his body but his soul that was dancing. An amazing energy flowed through his soul, affecting all those present. From the outside, the shadows of the dancers, moving to and fro in the dim light, were reflected on the curtain. All were dancing, absorbed in their thoughts about those who had given their lives to help the world become a better place. They tried to catch a glimpse of the ecstatic mood of the martyrs on their way to the gallows.